Soul On Fire

BARBARA M. LANTZ

HOLON

PUBLISHING

* * *

You may also enjoy
The Return of Chief Joseph by Barbara M. Lantz.

Visit The Author's website:
www.BarbaraLantz.com
For more information about her works, speaking dates,
and other projects.

* * *

COVER ART BY J.D. BILLS.
DESIGN & PRODUCTION
BY THE HOLON CREATIVE TEAM.

Published by Holon Publishing & Collective Press
A Publishing Company and Digital Agency. Collective of
Authors, Artists, Businesses, Non-profits, and
Creative Professionals.

www.Holon.co

This book is dedicated to my mother,

Carolyn Marie Gerhart, who passed away

October 2015.

Without her love and dedication, this story might not

Have ever been written

Table of Contents

Chapter 1
Fame

The toast of Paris lay in her wooden coffin that had been made precisely to the actress's specifications. An adoring fan, who spent many nights in the front row of the Theatre Des Les Enfants, blowing kisses to her Highness, made the coffin from freshly-hewn rosewood that grew in the forest by his cottage. Though the outside was a stark wood, the inside was just the opposite: lush, luxurious red velvet lined the inside, and a pillow of fire engine red satin rested on top. She had decked it out with her many awards and jewelry given to her by all the European royalty that had spent time under her hypnotic spell. Madame de la Bernhardt was the most talented and celebrated French actress of her time. Theaters in Europe, Asia, and America thrilled to her brilliant stage performances.

Although she had spent many nights in her safe, warm sarcophagus, she did so for the rest and comfort of a bed. Now, her illness forced her to spend days in her beloved coffin and it would allow her the luxury of reminiscing about her life. The moments of thunderous applause were exhilarating, and she deeply loved the craft of which she bore so great a talent. With fondness, she fingered the huge diamond pendant that was shaped like a teardrop. The playwright Moliere had given her the exquisite gem the night of her opening performance of a play he had written just for her.

"Mon chérie, you have brought to my eyes tears as big as raindrops. Take this as a token of my undying adoration of your immense talent."

That was a magical evening and it made her feel so alive. The interruption of a huge coughing spell reminded her that those moments were numbered. She lay dying, and she knew this round of fighting the pneumonia would be her last. As she mused over her beloved playwright, she heard the sound of footsteps making their way down the dusty old stairs to the basement where she lay.

"Mother, is there anything I can do?" Maurice asked. Maurice's slender body stood in the shadows of a world that was now passing away.

The frail actress turned ever so slightly to the left to see the silhouette of her only son, Maurice. He was born in a heated romance only to find a life with his mother on the road, journeying by stage coach from one grand European city and theatre to the next ...and the next. Living out of a suitcase was a fair and accurate assessment of Maurice's childhood. Sarah had always wished that one day before he grew up she could give him a proper home, one that had a tree fort for him to play in with brothers to play with and sisters to tease. Ah, that wound was so deep that a searing pain pierced its way straight to her heart. She moaned lowly in the dungeon-like basement. The life of a successful French actress could not permit such lifestyle indulgences.

Her soft whispering voice beckoned her beloved Maurice to her side.

"Mother, you should see a doctor. Jacques Brieyard is a huge fan. He would be happy to give you something for the pain."

"I have my medicine," she retorted. Next to her in the coffin was a small pipe filled with opium. The good doctor had thought of her after all.

"Come close, my darling." She was gasping for breath and wished she had more strength. "I want you to know that I..." her voice began to recede in a series of coughing stints that she could not suppress no matter how hard she tried.

"Mother..." Maurice's voice trailed off as he stared into her eyes. Her eyes were still bright and shiny and he looked deep within her to hear her inner voice. No words were exchanged, but a lifelong story was shared between them in those two minutes. Tears fell slowly down his cheeks and he knew that his mother wanted to do what she had always done: be alone. It was such a profound characteristic of hers. She could not share her world with anyone, not even those that she loved the most.

Silently Maurice stole back up the stairway to let his mother pass the way she wanted to go. They never spoke much during their lives together, so there was no reason to think that her impending death could change that. He did not want to see the grisly last moment. He only had one parent and this one was breaking his heart all over again. She had an aloneness like that. That, much more than the suitcase life that he had growing up, was the wall that existed around his heart. This wall guarded anything that resembled love. He knew he was right on cue to exit back up the flight of stairs. Everything was a stage direction in his mother's life, and these were directions that he knew by heart.

At the top of the stairs he turned and made a gallant French bow and bid her adieu. The ominous silence in the dark theatre was pierced with the slow breath of Sarah. In and out. One more moment of life, in and out. Clutching to each, yet wanting to let go.

As Sarah Bernhardt lay dying, the angel of death came close.

At first she was startled by the shadowy figure. His robes of darkness brought a chill to the theatre basement which was already dank and moist. Yet as he drew near, she found herself astonished by his markedly "theatrical" appearance.

He wore a mask that showed nothing of his face but his lips. They were red... blood red. His mask had a gossamer sheen and glittered in the soft light coming through the lone basement window that always caught the street light of St. Jacques Way. His gate was lumbered, yet his mask suggested that he was a being who loved the exorbitant frivolity of the theatre. If there was an angel fitted perfectly to the life of Sarah, then this was he. The ashen robes graced the coffin and Sarah knew it was her time, but she was not prepared to go.

In her mind's eye, Sarah played the movie of her life, carefully reviewing the scenes of Maurice's childhood. Her regret poured through her whole body as she watched the birth of her only child. Her mind raced through his childhood, aching for a life for her son that had a hearth and home, a life where he could gleefully play under her gentle yet watchful eye. Sarah winced in pain. This agony was to her much more unbearable than the shooting pains in her lungs. She thought of Maurice sleeping in her luggage trunk even though his feet stuck out the side from his being too large for it. "I was a bad mother," she whispered to herself.

The angel of death moved close to Sarah and she realized that the angelic creature was about to take her breath away. The moment of death had arrived. The angel leaned forward and surprised Sarah with a last request.

"God has granted you a boon," the angel announced. "You may choose one aspect of your next life and it will manifest for you."

Sarah's eyes widened with pleasure. God was real and God was merciful. God had answered her prayers. With much difficulty, she spoke.

"Children, I want many children, and a secure and content family life for them to grow up in that would include a loving father. I want a husband that I can love and one that deeply loves me."

Her passionate request oozed from her ethereal layers. Sarah was a hot-blooded woman. Her deep love of sexual pleasures was well known amongst the European elite. Maurice's father was one who ate heartily from the depths of her carnal orchards. One to love was in fact a tall order for the part in this play. Sarah's play... Sarah's GRAND play. One that was about to stretch out into the realms of death. Her fear began to overcome her strength. It took her last ounce of strength to utter her response.

The angel peered into the depths of her soul. Beyond Sarah, beyond all the other names she had ever been called, was this essence, this place where her soul was created.

"Your acceptance of the boon has been granted," the angel whispered softly into her ear. His voice was Sarah's only connection to the material world. Her expiration was at hand.

"But, be forewarned. Your request, though true and pure of heart, will only manifest upon a rejection of a life in thirst of the stage. Your talents as Sarah Bernhardt are known throughout the world and in fact, your soul will carry these talents into your new incarnation. However, you must not seek success in the performing arts or the boon will dissipate like sand in an hourglass. You are forbidden to practice your craft."

Sarah opened her eyes one last time as the breath began to leave her body. In came her breath. Time seemed suspended. In the world of spirit there is no time.

Sarah had visited Hollywood many times and she often

wanted to expand her career by starring in the "movies." What a temptation it had been; yet, the enduring notions of artistic nobility, run rampant among the aristocrats of Europe, turned her from the lure of Hollywood. Her career as an actress was everything to her… well everything to Sarah… but Sarah was fading, never to be again. Never to be again… Never! NEVER!

"Beware of this as your soul migrates to the shores of America," whispered the dark angel.

"There in the 1950's will you be born. You will grow up in an era of abundance, part of a new generation aching for release. You could easily pursue a life of acting, but you will yearn to be a star. A rock star."

Rock star. His voice stated something that caught and toyed with a deep emotion that went straight to Sarah's heart.

"Rock star, rock star…" Sarah mumbled to herself in her inner mind.

"The era of the rock star will be born at the same time and the desire to pursue this dream will overwhelm you."

Sarah's eyes rolled to the back of her head as the angel watched her finish her very last breath.

"If you walk this path, your desire for the perfect family life will be destroyed. It will cause you excruciating mental anguish and unbearable pain if you choose the path of the artist. It will take you to places so abysmal and places so lonely that you will feel as if you are in hell. Please be aware of the tremendous gravity of a boon. All desires can become chains that hold the soul to an endless recreation of the coveted object… endless re-creations that can NEVER be achieved. Beware! Remember that it can NEVER be achieved."

Armed with this final instruction, the soul of the great French actress, la Bernhardt de Sarah, expired.

Fame, makes a man who wants to do things over
Fame, makes it very hard to swallow,
Fame, things are all so cheap and hollow….

Fame. Fame. Fame. Fame. Fame.
Sing it, David Bowie! Thank you, John Lennon.

Chapter 2
Long Live Rock!

My mother's wrist watch said precisely eight o'clock in the evening as my father drove our old '48 Buick to the hospital while she screamed at the top of her lungs, "Get this baby out of me NOW!" My father was trying to focus on the song on the radio, "Rock Around the Clock," by Bill Halley and the Comets. His foot was tapping to the beat as he enjoyed this new type of music that everyone was calling "rock and roll."

"Turn that thing off; I hate that loud and obnoxious song, what is that... rock and roll?" Mom was not very much of a music lover save for maybe Perry Como and Frank Sinatra. This new music was not enjoyable to her ears. In fact, she would state that it physically hurt her ability to hear.

Dad on the other hand, loved a beat and got excited over this new genre of music. It was different and the element of black music it borrowed from was contagious. He said when he started listening he would feel this uncontrollable feeling and it was almost addictive.

There could not be two more opposite people on the planet than my mother and my father. I could hear the song too, even though I was still floating around in mom's womb. I didn't want him to turn it off either. I liked it, what a beat! It was a shame when he dutifully turned it off after her second request.

The silence was deafening inside the womb. I wanted to hear that music again and again. I was in love with rock and roll before I was even born

Living in a small bedroom community of a steel town subdivision had its pros and cons. There was always enough food on the table and I can say that I never really did without anything. The 1950's in America was a time of peace and prosperity. The fact that the United States of America was now considered the most powerful nation on earth had not really sunk in for the average American, however most of the soldiers who came back from World War II found good paying jobs that could support a generous livelihood for a man and his family. My father was one of those soldiers, never quite forgetting the horrors of war and forever grateful that he made it through, and that he could drive the family car to church on Sunday without fear of bombs dropping or foreign troops taking over the town. Perhaps it was this contrast that made him and so many of his peers want a peaceful existence, and the 1950's lifestyle reflected the weary soldier's dream come true. It was peppered with this rebellious type of music, but my father often shared with me that he was tired of Perry Como and that Elvis Presley's music was a welcome change, but "don't tell your mother," he would add as if right on cue.

To me, that was the con of living in a bedroom community. Everything was just a little too peaceful. Why not shake things up? When I first heard Jerry Lee Lewis sing, "Whole Lotta Shakin' Going On," I felt inspired to sing it out loud. I had heard that he played it while standing at the piano and would kick over the piano bench and bring down the house when he did. The feeling it must have given to him as an artist was too exquisite to describe but I found myself longing for it.

I loved when my father would bring out his small phonograph and stack a few records for us to listen to when my mom would go to Tri Kappa meetings every other Monday night. We would set it up in the living room and when "You Ain't Nothing But a Hound Dog" would come on, I would sing along. I instinctively knew how to sing the blues and my dad would tell me what a good voice I had for such a small girl. I can still remember how proud I felt that he liked my singing. It caused me to join the girl's chorus in junior high and glee club for all but my senior year of high school. Singing did come naturally to me. So did acting. My father had a small Kodak movie camera that he would bring out for all of our important family events. Christmas, Baptisms, Holy Communion, Birthdays! At all of these occasions, I would naturally get right in front of the camera, smiling and posing, singing and dancing, hogging the attention. Many times, my mom would pull me away from the camera and tell me that other children needed to be included in my dad's filming.

"Oh, that's my little actress," she would announce to the friends and relatives at the party, as I received one swiftly placed slap on my behind. "She's such a hog for that camera," she would say apologetically. "I don't know where she gets it, honestly." The sting on my rear end was duly noted. Even as a five year old I knew that doing something that felt perfectly normal and natural could get me a punishment as a reward.

No matter how many times I was corrected, it didn't stop me from listening to my father's records again and again and again. I knew the Elvis Presley, Buddy Holly and Jerry Lee Lewis songs by heart. Dad also appreciated country music and I found myself singing along to Patsy Cline. People would say that when she sang, the hairs would stand up on the back of their necks. Sometimes I would perform them for my grandmother who was always the most appreciative fan. She would clap after I performed a song, and sometimes whistle through her teeth, and she was always encouraging me to sing. It was my grandmother who took me to church one Saturday afternoon to audition for the church choir.

We climbed the stairs into the loft where the choir sang. There in the middle of this overlook was the most magnificent organ. It had rows and rows of keys as well as black and white levers that the organist used to imitate the sounds of other instruments. Trumpets, clarinets, violins and more were at her command, and she made that organ sing. Sister Hermanita played the organ with great passion. After all, I thought, what other passion could she have besides that? She was extremely possessive of the organ and would not let anyone else touch it. I learned that the hard way when I was caught trying to play it one afternoon. I was promptly bent over the organ bench where I was introduced to Sister H's birch stick. Again, I thought it was so harsh a punishment. I just wanted to hear how well I could do, but one time was all it took for me to decide that I would not touch the organ again. I did, however, excel as her first soprano. She told me many times that I had a gift from God in my voice. She featured my voice in many of the Christmas programs that we would have at midnight Mass. I loved it! All through grade school, I would practice my songs for hours.

8

In the summertime, I would go out in my postage stamp-sized backyard and swing on my swing set. My father bought it from Sears when I was five and my nightly ritual was to go out and swing on my swing and sing songs. I loved to make up my own songs, songs about my life, but I would always gravitate to singing songs about God. Many of them were not all that great, but my volume and enthusiasm seemed to make up for it.

One summer night, my mom looked out the back porch window and told me to stop singing. I was "annoying everyone in the neighborhood!" she lamented. My father, overhearing this, came to my rescue.

"What harm is the child doing?" he asked her innocently. My mom was caught off guard a bit and relented. It was a huge victory for me. I could sing and sing and sing and not get punished as a result. It was June 26th, 1963.

I was so emboldened that I began sneaking my small Hitachi radio into bed at night with the ear plugs so that my parents could not hear. I would listen to WLS radio disc jockey Ron Riley. He would count down the top ten songs of the week on his show and I would listen to Neil Sedaka, Leslie Gore, and many other favorites. I loved listening to the radio at night, under the covers, nice and cozy, and took to doing it regularly. One cold January night in 1964, I stayed up late and heard a new group called the Beatles. My ears perked up as WLS played "I Wanna Hold Your Hand." I could not even believe my passion for this group and its music. I loved each and every song that the band released. One was never enough. I wanted more and more. Within a few days, the Top Five at Five were all Beatles tunes and all of my friends at school began to turn on their radios to listen. Even my mother, who was not a huge fan of any kind of music, came home one afternoon and announced that she heard that my favorite band, the Beatles, was going to be on next Sunday's Ed Sullivan Show.

"Oh, I can't wait, I can't wait, I can't wait!" I shouted as I jumped up and down in sheer exhilaration. "That is so great! I will tell everyone at school tomorrow."

My sixth grade friends were buzzing like bees with the news. We had all started bringing our transistor radios with ear pieces to school and listening to the radio during class. One of the few advantages to our ugly Catholic school uniforms was the pocket in the vest. It was just perfect to hide the radio in and the lines in the plaid uniform hid the wire that led up to the ear. Of course, having long hair was the clincher, so several girls in the class with short hair were just out of luck.

I became obsessed with the Beatles. The night of the Ed Sullivan Show, I pleaded with the whole family to find something else to do. Of course, they were just as curious as I was as to what they looked like. When the curtain went up, there were four men with very cute haircuts, kind of moppet looking, in stylish suits and the boots to make it all work. They were overwhelmingly mesmerizing. Three of them had guitars and the one with the big nose played drums. As they started to play, I got so excited that I could not contain myself and I jumped off our couch and started to scream. Not just scream, but scream hysterically. My brother was startled, my father asked me to sit down and my mother's jaw just hit the floor. Was this a typical response to the event in living rooms all across America? Apparently so. My friend Kathy knocked over a lamp at her house and she was pulling her hair out. Her father was so angry at her that he forbade the entire family from watching the next two shows. My friend Theresa said that all six of her sisters got up at the same time and started screaming, and her dad left the room and said he did not have the energy to shut all seven of them up. It was amazing. The second time around, the family was not as shocked to see me sobbing, but I heard my dad talking in the kitchen later with my mother about the "phenomenon" the Beatles had become. Several of his co-workers at the steel mill had stated that their daughters watched the Beatles on Sullivan's show and had gone berserk. Screaming, crying, and going crazy, it was unbelievable to watch.

Shockingly, my mom popped back, "Oh, they screamed for Elvis, too. These guys are from England so these girls think that their long hair is cute. They probably just wear it longer because it's cold over there most of the time. It keeps their ears warm."

Mom? Defending the Beatles? How quaint that she thought it was because it was too cold in England for the short American marine hair cuts. She had never even been to the United Kingdome and I learned that making up something that sounded plausible was a good way to stay in charge of things. I could hardly believe it, but

I sensed that she was moved by the band and their music too. That, itself, was a phenomenon.

Everything began to revolve around the Beatles and all of my girlfriends seemed to be wholly enthusiastic. No one wanted to be left out. The entire class of 6th grade girls spent an entire week writing the word BEATLES as many times as they could. Everyone had their Beatles paper underneath the current subject in class, ready to write an extra 30 or 40 times. WLS radio station in Chicago sponsored a contest and the winner was going to receive 2 free tickets to the Beatles' upcoming show at the Chicago International Amphitheater on September 4, 1964. It was a dream come true, and when we submitted our 89,246 names, we thought we were shoe-ins. What we didn't know was that some girls from another Catholic school had sent in 1,203,299. I was crushed!

School ended on a sour note for me in May of '64. The concert was sold out but I told my family I would find a way to go and see the Beatles. For the entire summer I racked my brain. I had almost given up when I found the golden opportunity. As I walked out of Albertsons Grocery store in August, there, on the community bulletin board a sign read: FOR SALE 2 TICKETS FOR THE BEATLES! I tore the entire notice off the board, hoping no one else had seen it as I ran down the alley back to my house.

My dad was working on paying bills at the kitchen table and I triumphantly shouted as I walked in, "I found a notice at the grocery store and they are selling two Beatles tickets!" As I dialed the phone my father chuckled, "If anyone was going to find a way to get those tickets, it would be you, Anne Marie."

The tickets were 5 dollars apiece. It took every nickel of my babysitting money, but it was worth it. My cousin, Cindy, bought the other ticket and we convinced my dad to take us up there since we didn't drive. When we got there, the arena was huge and we were on the main floor. I was ecstatic. I wanted to run up to Paul and ask him to marry me.

My dad sat in a little coffee shop across the street, waiting for us. As he sipped his cup of coffee, four young mop-topped English lads were ushered in the door to avoid the mob of teenage girls that gathered in front of the Amphitheater waiting to get a piece of them. Dad was sitting in the back, having some blueberry pie with

11

his coffee and the four men that were scurrying past him were the Beatles themselves! Dad said the one with the clear glasses turned to him and said, "Evening, Governor, enjoyin' your pie?" Before my dad had a chance to respond, they were through the back exit and gone.

"You saw the Beatles?" I later said to my father in disbelief. "John Lennon talked to you!" I was so jealous that I could hardly believe it.

My cousin and I, on the other hand, stood on top of our chairs in the 12th row trying to see them when they hit the stage. All we saw were the backs of other girls standing on their chairs, and all we heard were the screams: yelling, shrieking, and screaming of thousands of girls who wanted nothing more than to touch their beloved Beatles and tear off a piece of a shirt or trouser as a memento. The screaming went on for the whole hour-and-a-half concert and Cindy and I screamed along with everyone else. It was primordial. Sometimes I thought I could feel my voice go hoarse but then somewhere in the back of my throat was a deep groan that would surface again and again. Sometime toward the end of the concert I noticed that all I could hear was a loud whistling sound in my ears. When we got back to the car, I realized that I could not hear. I asked my cousin to cover for me as I knew this condition would greatly displease both my parents and I still couldn't believe the strange turn of events. I didn't even see or hear the Beatles, and suffered temporary deafness, and my dad who couldn't care less about them had a brief conversation with John Lennon. The irony of life!

All of my babysitting money went to buying every teen magazine that had a story about the Beatles. I would hoard them under my bed and pull out a particular issue if there was some fact about one of the Beatles that I wanted to recheck.

What a romantic notion that George was too young at 17 to go to Hamburg, Germany and his mum had signed the slip anyway so that they could play at the famous Cavern club in Hamburg. Some called that night the birth of the Beatles. Moms can do such wonderful things for their children.

And then, the tragedy that Paul's mum died of breast cancer when he was a young prepubescent boy. His saving grace was his father's knack for finding the melody that brought the joy and happiness into any occasion.

What a lucky move made by Richard Starkey, when he changed his name to Ringo Starr, replacing Pete Best as the Beatles drummer for the Hamburg gig. Had he not made that gig, his life would have turned out very differently! Life in Liverpool didn't give a bloke too many chances.

Then there was John, who embodied the strife-ridden life story of a rock and roll musician. He was born to a couple of partiers who had one bottle of whiskey too many, one Saturday night. His mother, the flirtatious Julia, found Freddie Lennon, the rip-roaring sailor, to be ripe for some sex. Not just any type of sex, like the kind I gleaned from the hundreds of magazines that carried all the John news, but rock and roll sex.

But with rock and roll sex comes rock and roll children and John was the only child of what was basically a one night stand with a whole lotta shakin' going on. Long after the orgasms had subsided, the boy born during an air raid in London became an unusually gifted artist. He began to bloom, living with Julia's sister Mimi, trying to make sense of a life devoid of the simple pleasures of family. John would escape into his art and later his music. Mimi's love for him gave him the only stability he ever had. John plunged into sketches, and at age 11 was admitted to the local school of art. Along with art, there was music. It was his first guitar and inspiration from his hero, Elvis Presley, that gave John a driving force in his life. It drove him from Mimi's cottage to the Dakota in New York City. God bless you, John, God bless you for the life that you wound up living.

Thirteen-year-old Anne Marie gazed into the window of a magical world. Instead of being a teacher or a nurse or getting a job as a car hop, I fantasized about being up on stage and singing with the band. Absolutely everyone was putting together their own garage bands in the 1960's. However, as was typical of the "British Invasion," the bands were made of boys. Four boys: three guitars and a drum kit. It was formulaic. I found myself musing on the fact that, just as with altar boys, this was another all-male club that I had difficulty penetrating.

My cousin Cindy's brother, Ron, had a band that he rehearsed with down in his basement called the Rooks. One Sunday afternoon, when my family was visiting, we all went downstairs to listen to the Rooks. I could not stop myself from asking my Aunt if I could sing a song with the band. She told my cousin Ron that the next song would be performed by me and he begrudgingly gave me a microphone. It was "Louie, Louie," which admittedly sounded a bit strange coming from a girl, but I instantly adapted the lyrics and I put my heart and soul into it. My cousin, Cindy, sang backup which gave the entire song a lot of production and all of us got into the song and gave it our all. All of my relatives applauded loudly and the feeling I got from that rousing applause was like getting bitten by a bug. I laid in bed for hours that night thinking about that applause. My grandmother whistled and my dad clapped loudly. My Aunt Jane, who enjoyed a party with a kick, hoisted a toast to the latest rock and roll band success, "Four Rooks and a Queen."

I laughed under the covers, re-hashing the event, feeling that indescribable feeling of my love for that applause. This new music gave people a passion for living and to be the voice that spoke the lyrics to the crowds was all I wanted. It was addictive!

Long Live Rock!

The Who sang it all in this brief lyric.

Chapter 3
Satisfaction

Being a teenager and sitting in a Catholic school's eighth grade catechism class was at best, an oxymoron. Transistor radios and their earplugs had long been confiscated by the invasive nuns, who prided themselves in righting every wrong. To most of the world, rock and roll was this fad that was catching on and making Englishmen in their twenties rich, and nothing more.

To me, someone who was standing in the back of the room reciting things like, "Who is God? God is the supreme being that made all things," it was a lifeline. The Rolling Stones' guitar riffs were dancing around in my head, and my inner bitch was singing, "I can't get any satisfaction." My mind jumped off the page of the booklet and down the line to Bob Markely. He was standing three persons away from me and obviously he was as disinterested in the religious class as I was. Our eyes made contact and I instinctively licked my lips, ever so slightly. Sister Theodora was mindlessly grading papers while we recited in the back of the room, so now was the time and place. I stared at the crotch of his pants and low and behold, his zipper was halfway unzipped. I licked my lips again and to my delight, he began to grow a boner. Alice Williams,, who was standing next to me, noticed the incident and we both stared in great satisfaction as my flirtations had caused Bob to get hard as a rock. My first thought was, "Wow, that's so big!" My fantasy of where this might go burst like a bubble when Sister Theo looked up because Bob was not reciting.

"Robert Markley, please recite questions 34 and 35," Sister Theo barked out. God love Bob. He was trying to recite as best he could, but his mind was elsewhere.

So was mine for the rest of that year. I had taken to writing

15

a book about John Lennon and every free moment in class was spent writing it. The last couple of years had given me so much information about the quartet that I found myself writing about them - well, John, in particular. He had recently made a statement to the press that had caused quite an uproar. Allow me to quote it exactly to avoid misrepresentation.

"Christianity will end, it will disappear. I do not have to argue about that, I am certain. Jesus was OK but his subjects were too simple, today we (the Beatles) are more famous than him."

Christian groups were burning Beatles records and everyone was denouncing what John had said. Fact was, they were more famous than Jesus. You never saw young teenage girls screaming for Jesus with tears running down their faces, but then again it was like comparing apples to oranges. Teenage kids in the South were destroying Beatles paraphernalia and it made me sad. How could they misunderstand someone as brilliant as John Lennon? Disc jockeys were organizing destruction events, and something in my about-to-graduate-eighth-grade-from-a-Catholic-school-girl mind shuddered. Years later, when the movie Easy Rider came out, I noted again that Dennis Hopper was shot and killed by some southern redneck. It made me want to reach out to what I thought was simple ignorance and help to bridge this prejudice with knowledge. Hence: the book about John. But what would make John say that Christianity would disappear? One May morning at 8 a.m. Mass, shortly before eighth grade graduation, I noted that I did feel that the archaic forms of worshipping God would fade away, and I remember not knowing where that feeling was coming from. As I looked at the priest lifting up the chalice, while the altar boys rang the bells, I realized that this did nothing for me spiritually. As hard as I tried, I did not see Jesus in anything we were doing there. The monotonous rituals of the church felt more like a senseless, meaningless drone. I longed for a deeper relationship with Jesus. I wanted him to sit down with us across the street from the church and have a picnic and talk.

John was right. The Beatles did fill a void. So did all the wonderful music coming out of England. All day long my head was filled with songs; after school, we would go home and turn on the radio and listen and listen and listen. Rock and roll was the food of the Gods to young baby boomer teenagers and we couldn't get enough. The Who gave me feelings of ecstasy and when Tommy came out I would play the whole album and look into the mirror and sing. The finale was always my favorite... I heard choruses of angels singing with me. My voice was booming; I looked like one of those saints on my holy card pictures. I could see the aura of light, my own personal halo, in the mirror.

"Anne Marie, what in God's name are you doing in here?" My mother had opened my bedroom door and had a horrified look on her face as she stared at me, in a rage.

I stood still, like a ninja that did not want to be detected. It diffused her. She calmed down rather quickly and I turned it off immediately. I could tell that it frightened her. My mother needed soothing music but then she dealt with 6 year olds every day as a first grade teacher, so it was understable.

"Is that those Beatles?" she asked.

"No, mom."

"Good, I don't want any of the neighbors knowing that I let you buy those horrible Beatles records."

"But I buy those with my own money! Besides, what's wrong with the Beatles?"

My mom did not have an answer for that, opting instead to give me the five-minute warning before supper. My father arrived promptly at 4:45 p.m. and we ate at 4:50 p.m. She had seen him pull into the driveway.

I pulled my Tommy album off the record player and put it back into its jacket sleeve. I stared at the cover until I heard my father washing his hands for dinner. I slid the album into a crate filled with my albums in the corner of my bedroom. It was my treasure chest, filled with Beatles and The Who and Herman's Hermits, Freddie and the Dreamers, Beach Boys, the Zombies, the Animals and more and I played them all as often as I could get away with it.

One of the enticements of rock and roll was getting away with it. Fight on all you rock and roll rebels, we are entering a new dimension... not of sight and sound but of mind...Welcome to the Outer Limits... 1967 is on the horizon and rock and roll is going to go cerebral. It was everything romantic about being 15.

Chapter 4
The Magical Mystery Tour

Summer came. While I sat on the beach and got a tan, The Beatles went to India and became associated with Transcendental Meditation and the Maharishi Mahesh yogi.

The summer began to explode with music and all I could do was listen and sing, not only English bands but great music from California, the Mommas and the Poppas, the Doors, Jefferson Airplane, Janis Joplin and I thought of myself as a natural backup singer for any live performance. I could sing thirds and fifths to any of the lead singers, from Jagger to Janis.

Summer slipped away like it always does and I found myself at a public high school filled with good-looking junior and senior boys. There were no Nazi nuns around to ruin what could be potentially exciting and passionate.

For the first few weeks, walking down the hallways in between classes was a staring match. I would stare at guys and they would stare right back. One pair of eyes that I found extremely delightful, those of Danny Waite, would flash in the most mischievous way, and one crisp autumn morning he shoved a note into my hands as we passed each other following first period

"Meet me at the Walgreens soda fountain at 3:30 today."

My heart skipped a beat and my mind raced to the end of the day. I had no obligations and I desperately wanted to go. My girlfriends were all twittering like birds at lunch about it.

Danny was not in the lunch room; he had a car and would drive to his job at Burger King after fourth period. Jackie Lambert, my very closest friend, told me to just go and see what happens. A freshman dating a senior was a big leap, especially for a Catholic school girl, who had no experience with such things.

18

"Are you gonna tell your mom?" Jackie asked.

"Ha, are you kidding?" I snorted, knowing that she would not allow it. "Besides, it's not a date, I am just meeting him."

Sitting on the bar stool at the drug store, I ordered my usual Green River, a classy drink for a 15 year old, I thought. In the background, the radio was playing and I asked the soda jerk to turn it up.

The prickly feeling that was running down the inside of my right thigh made my entire body quiver as Danny walked in to sit down. He wore his hair long, like the Beatles, which was difficult to do while attending high school. Other high schools in the area had banned students from wearing their hair that long. Danny had huge brown eyes peeking out from underneath his curly brown locks. He could be the fifth Beatle, I said to myself. John, Paul, George, Ringo, and Danny.

When he walked in, he nearly took my breath away. He swaggered up to the bar stool like a rock star. In his hand, he was carrying an album. It wound up being the very first demo album that the Doors recorded at Sunset Sound Studios just a month earlier in August.

"Where did you get that?" I asked with great curiosity.

"You like the Doors?" He asked with delight.

"If the Doors of perception were cleansed, everything would appear to man as it is, infinite…" we chanted at each other as though we had come from some distant planet and this coded verse was how the chosen ones recognized each other.

We talked for almost an hour. Our eyes sank into each other's like crescent moons on a lake and a strange new and sensational feeling came over me. It was hot. It was intoxicating. It grabbed your soul and took it on a wild ride. It was addicting. It was rock and roll.

When he told me he was playing in a band, I started shaking inside. Delight poured over every fiber of my being as he invited me to come to a gig that they were performing that Saturday night. Follow that with an extreme rush of disappointment that sank down to my toes.

"What time and where?" I squeaked out.

"I will come and pick you up at about seven. You will have to watch us tune up and do a sound check before the show. Do you mind?"

Mind? Are you kidding! I would love that, I thought. My mind was racing to figure out a way to make it happen as Danny asked, "Where do you live?"

"Two blocks from the high school. 1214 Arborgast." I blurted out Jackie's address knowing he could never come to my house.

"I will meet you out on the steps, ok? My dad gets drunk a lot and well…"

"You don't have to explain, Anne Marie, my dad and mom both do." An awkward silence filled the air as I looked at the clock. 4:35! Yikes, I had ten minutes to get home before my dad did. All was well in my house as long as I was home before he got home.

"Pick me up at seven, I will be waiting," I said as I picked up my school books. Then I did something I would have never expected. I leaned forward and kissed him on the lips as my perfume permeated his sweater. He was adorable, like a deer in headlights. He was startled, but yet he had a smile of satisfaction on his face as I waved goodbye and ran out the revolving door.

I could hear the opening guitar riff of Rolling Stones' "Satisfaction" pounding in my head as I got permission to spend the night at Jackie's house. My mom bought the pajama party story and as I packed up a small night case, wondering where I was going to end up by the time night turned into morning, a pang of Catholic guilt crossed my mind.

"Hey, are you listening to me or are you fading off into your own private world again?" mom was screaming in my ear. I was sticking a sweatshirt in my backpack.

"Don't forget your toothbrush and don't use too much of the Lamberts' toothpaste. Do they use anti-cavity toothpaste? Maybe you should bring your own?"

"I am good, mom," I said as I kissed her on the cheek, wiggling my way out the front door before she could get one more insane question out of her mouth.

My feet left the ground numerous times as I ran the three-and-a-half blocks down the street to Jackie's. I sat on the stump that was six steps up their walkway. A large bush that covered the left side was an easy perch to hide in and the cool October evening caused me to zip up my jacket as I waited for Danny to show up.

The back of the bush rustled as I heard Jackie crawling to where I was perched.

"What are you doing here?" I asked, just a tad vexed.

"Both my parents are passed out from whiskey in the living room. The TV's on and they won't be up for hours."

"Which means what?" I asked to get her to stop beating around the bush about what she wanted.

"I'm coming with you." Jackie was defiant in her response. Rather than argue with her, my attention turned to the oncoming headlights of Danny's car.

Chapter 5
Light My Fire

It was like being picked up in a rock star limo and Jackie and I were giggling little girls in Danny's front seat. Danny had the radio blasting the Beach Boys, and I found my opportunity to sing harmonies. I did some fancy woo hoo's and blended in nicely holding a counter melody in the background, a feat not easily achieved since the Beach Boys and Brian Wilson had a knack for complicated vocals, but I managed to find a fit.

I was entranced with my own abilities and Jackie was caught up in the entire vibe of the evening. She didn't even notice that my vocals were magical and anyone who knew music could hear that.

I turned to Danny hoping to get a little morsel of praise, but he was smoking his Marlboro cigarette and humming a Doors tune that the band was going to play. My voice trailed off as we pulled into the parking lot, feeling undervalued yet excited at the huge line forming at the ticket door. Danny saw the line and smiled as he grabbed his guitar case from the back seat.

"Looks like a full house tonight!" He was pumped and poised, like a gladiator ready to do battle. His black leather jacket and jeans cupped and cradled his muscular body, and the white sleeveless T-shirt revealed his hunky hairy chest.

He threw his cigarette on the ground.

"Step on that for me, baby, won't you?" he asked me with his sweet voice.

I instinctively recoiled from doing what he had asked me as if automatically sensing the misogyny. Taking a deep breath, I swallowed my pride and ground the cigarette into the dirt. Digging my fingers into my back pockets, I swaggered next to him like a hot little groupie, not even knowing what that meant... yet.

We slid into the side entrance where other members of his band were already waiting, smoking cigarettes one right after another. I sensed that they were all nervous. I, on the other hand, was excited, totally clueless of what to expect. We snaked through a sectioned-off security area to a small room backstage. Danny stashed Jackie and I like a couple of little rag dolls in the back while he and the other four guys got on stage to do a quick sound check. I peered from behind a black velvet curtain and saw the small wooden stage. People were starting to wander in, which promptly annoyed Danny.

"They aren't supposed to let the crowd in until after sound check. Fucking club people piss me off. No fucking respect for a band's sound check. Fuckers!"

It was during this frenzy that the main act arrived. It was a local Chicago group who had cut a hit single that landed #22 on the WLS hit list, The Sighing James'. Jackie about fainted with delight. We had followed them to the stage and were idly standing around when the lead singer, Rory James, looked in our direction.

"Are these the backup singers?" He asked matter-of-factly.

"Yes," I somehow managed to find a voice and state a rather loud affirmative.

Before Danny's band knew what had hit them, security ushered his band, The Renegades, offstage. Jackie and I stood alone out on the stage with the lights blazing as the band went through a quick rehearsal of the lighting.

Jacks tugged on my blouse and whispered, "I can't sing a note, you know that."

"Yeah, I know, but just lip sync. I can sing most of this. I can even sing like a Mongolian throat singer," I proudly exclaimed.

"A what?" Jackie was totally thrown off-guard by my random proclamation.

"Hey, I get creative with my detention time... ordered these tapes from China that were on the back of a comic book. The tapes taught me how to split my voice..." I trailed off as Rory looked in my direction.

"Hey gorgeous, why don't you and your friend sing a few notes so we can get our levels adjusted?"

That's how I want to be addressed, I thought. I snuck a peak from out of the corner of my eye at Danny, who was sulking offstage. He wouldn't even look at me. The ugly green monster of jealousy had raised its head. My heartstrings tugged at me as I wondered if this would be a problem.

No doubt about that. Danny said nothing to us as we left the club and was silent the whole way home. I made a feeble attempt to say something but the deafening silence in response left little to the imagination. The squeal of Danny's back tires as he pulled away from the curb after dropping us in front of Jackie's house was like a huge punctuation mark. As Jacks had suspected, both of her parents were snoring on their respective couch and chair when we walked in. The Star Spangled Banner was playing on the TV and even God was ready to turn out the light and go to bed. As I curled up in my Cinderella sleeping bag, a Christmas gift from several years ago, I pulled a piece of paper from my pocket. It was Rory's handwritten note that he had shoved into my hand as we left the stage.

Let's get together soon. You were an angel singing in my choir. Let me make your bells chime. Rory

Call me 988-2989

I closed my eyes and relived every moment on that stage. When the lights came up on the backup singers, I felt like I was in heaven. Everything seemed so natural and normal. The crowd loved the set, and even though I did not know the words to all of their songs, I had an uncanny ear for a melody line. I sang a third underneath Rory on the chorus of most of the tunes, and by delaying just a fraction of a second, I could hear the notes and words and could cup my voice around every utterance from Rory's mouth. Jacks did exactly as I instructed her to do and lip synced the words without even uttering a sound, I knew she was having the time of her life. I knew just exactly how the Beatles felt when they took the stage. Although the girls were not screaming for me, I knew that I was contributing to the beautiful sound that was the Sighing James'. I was ready to run away with the band. I was going to be a rock and roll gypsy and I would be on the run, from town to town, singing with the band. On and on my mind raced until I realized that it was past 3 a.m. and I needed to fall asleep.

Bright and early the next morning, I was whistling around the kitchen and my parents both commented on how nice it was that I

24

had taken out the trash and mopped the kitchen floor without being asked. My dad even slipped me fifty cents for my work. I felt a bit guilty taking it but got over that within five minutes. This was just a little assurance that my ability to go out again would not be ruined.

Monday morning was a teenage girl's fantasy come true. People who didn't even know me were coming up to me and asking to see the handwritten note I had from Rory James, lead singer and front man for the fabulous Sighing James'. All the attention was getting a bit heady and at one point, I wanted to walk out of fourth period and climb into the limousine I had imagined was waiting outside the front doors of the school. How could I get through the day? My whole focus was on getting home and calling him again. I tried all day Sunday but there was no answer so I was even more determined to get a hold of him after school.

Monday rolled into Thursday and then one week blended into a sea of malaise. I called over 100 times but there was never an answer. There was a weight bigger than a boulder was on my shoulders and I could not shake it. Rock and roll was an elusive butterfly that I seemed to miss when I reached out to grab it.

I was not only good, I was great. "I added a lot to their sound," I thought. "It was heartless of me to ditch Danny, and it was heartless of Rory to ditch me! Is this what all those heartbreak songs are about?" I took to singing "Heartbreak Hotel" in my shower every morning and somehow got through a school year so that I could wake up one morning in June of 1967 listening to a gypsy queen wail a song on my radio.

This summer offered a glimpse into another world and the music from Jefferson Airplane. Grace Slick was everything I wanted to be. She even sang in my key. I went out and bought the album and noticed that she even looked like me. Grace had dark hair, dark eyes, just a gypsy princess living an enchanted life of psychedelic wonder and awe in San Francisco. Running away to "Hippie City" was a newly-discovered fantasy for me as well as asking the Airplane if I could sing as a second backup to Grace.

I sat up in the perch of our large maple tree in the backyard, belting out the tune. I towered over the small subdivision that I lived in and my mom couldn't find me. The summer of love was alive and well in my self-made tree fort and my sanctuary afforded me the solace of singing every song on the Surrealistic Pillow album. I got it the week it came out and spent the rest of the summer singing with Grace. I became obsessed with finding a way to get out of town and go to California.

Instead, I found myself dragging my feet down the hallways of my high school, wondering why I had to do this. I began to use my babysitting money to buy all the albums I could and spent my evenings locked up in my tiny upstairs bedroom to memorize every lyric of every song that spoke of the summer of love. The hippies of California had caught my attention because they were tribal. This tribal vibration jogged an ancient memory in me. Were these the reincarnated souls of the many Indian tribes slaughtered by the US Cavalry? My sense of the migration of souls was strong and although everyone else thought my notion to be crazy, I felt strongly about it.

Chapter 6
Blowin in the Wind

My parents had been keeping a watchful eye on me because I had become such a recluse. My mom requested that I take a basket to church for her and as I handed it off to the office secretary, Father Zoller came walking in.

"Anne Marie, how are you? How is public school treating you?" His tone suggested that my parents' choice of education for me left something to be desired.

"Gonna be a sophomore next fall, Father," I squeaked out.

"You know, we have a new project that I am looking to recruit some teenagers for. What plans do you have for the summer?"

I shrugged my shoulders, thinking he wanted me to volunteer for some sand bagging project or something that required blood, sweat and tears. My eyes avoided his as I tried to slip out the door.

Father Z was on a mission, however, and side stepped directly into my exit path.

"We are having a meeting tomorrow night here in the church office, some other kids will be here from St John Bosco. Why don't you come? Bring a friend. I bet you will like it."

In life, one can step through doors without a clue as to where it will take them. The meeting I attended included college kids from St Joe College, and they were working with Father Z to create a coffeehouse. This was just such a phenomenon. Things came together so easily and quickly. The neighboring community, Highland, had an old, small abandoned church that the parish of St John Bosco had no use for anymore. Larry, Ed and Jerry were three twenty-something kids from the St Joe college that wanted to convert the basement of the old church into a coffeehouse. They were seeking the support of other area churches and Father Z volunteered our church's youth group to help with the renovation.

I had spent almost a whole year without even the tiniest bit of interest in the boys at my high school. None of them could ever compare to Danny or Rory, but these three cute, intelligent, quirky guys from St Joe's sparked me like a firefly in the summer night. I spent every summer afternoon I could spare cleaning and painting the basement. Father Savio, who was the assistant at St John's, was a cool and innovative young priest who wanted the coffeehouse to be a community gathering place to discuss important ideas that were of current interest. We got donations from many businesses in town and it afforded us a room with tables and chairs and a stage.

Oh yes, the stage was my idea. Father Savio had some speakers in mind to invite to the coffeehouse to discuss issues he found relevant. Jerry, Ed and Larry had only one issue that they found relevant, and that was the Vietnam War. All three of them had college deferments but one of their friends, Roy, did not go to school and was being drafted. Father Savio, a true young idealist, wanted to encourage public debate in his coffeehouse and thought discussing the Vietnam War could be a good starting point. Having a stage afforded each speaker a dignified platform to speak from and Father Savio thought the suggestion of occasional poetry readings from the St Joe college literary professor, John Studdard, added a touch of class.

My suggestion of the stage was a hit. We created a real theatre setting. The dark basement was lit with candles and the local hardware store had donated the lights that we used as backlighting. When I asked Father if we could have an occasional musical guest, he seemed genuinely pleased.

"You know, Anne Marie, I am a huge fan of Joan Baez," Father confessed.

"Oh yeah, me too." Boy, there was a fib I would need to tell in confession. I had never even heard of her, although I seemed to remember her name being linked to Bob Dylan's.

"Really?" His eyes widened with delight. I saw my opportunity and I took it.

"If you like, I can sing a few of her songs when we have our Grand Opening in October." My mind raced and I asked myself how that was going to happen. For starters, I could not play the guitar. I never bothered with the details. I get a Grand Plan and then run with it, knowing that God will help you if you are doing it from your heart.

"That would be great! It will be a wonderful start to a fantastic community project sponsored by St John Bosco." Father Savio was almost walking on air as he made his way back to the rectory. His vision of bringing Jesus Christ's saving grace to his hometown through intelligent, spirited dialogue and debate was about to be sorely tested by the times.

"Please sing 'Kumbaya,'" he asked as he swung open the big wide screen to the front door of the office rectory. He started to whistle as I leaned on the old wooden trellis of the old church which was just next door to Father's rectory. Father Savio had recently been transferred to our neighboring town, enjoying his new life as an anointed priest of the most holy Roman Catholic Church. His idealism was admirable and he sincerely wanted to do God's work, but our town, our church, and our country was being jettisoned from 1968 through to 1970. Dear Father S was oblivious to what the world had in store.

I, on the other hand, was on board and sailing into the hurricane with excitement and anticipation. Finding a guitar player was going to be a lot more difficult than I thought. I even begged my little brother, Rocky, who played drums, to learn guitar and accompany me. Everyone was turning me down to the point where I sat at the dinner table one evening and begged for a used guitar.

"This is August, no early Christmas gifts! Where is your babysitting money?" Mom, practical as ever, would not hear of getting me a guitar, not even for a CYO event.

I gave dad my "poor little me" look but I could see that mom had already gotten to him first.

No help there. Summer faded into a brilliant and early autumn and we worked very hard all weekend long the last weekend of September. Father S decided to test the beast before our scheduled October 6th opening and that night I was assigned to take tickets. We charged a dollar for entrance which included all the coffee you could drink and popcorn you could eat. The entire coffeehouse staff got behind putting together a program. Father S was going to make some opening remarks, and then we planned for a group of us to get up and entertain with folk songs for an hour. I found it exciting and was hoping for a big crowd.

The place was starting to fill up with young people; teens in high school and college kids crammed into all the chairs we could spare. It seemed like an outpouring of everyone who didn't make it to Haight-Ashbury for the "Summer of Love." As I continuously looked up into the face of one handsome guy after another, one blonde and one dark-haired fellow appeared at our doorway. I coyly glanced up as I stamped the hands of the couples in front of them.

Greg was the blonde. He introduced himself to me.

"Gregory Montgomery's the name. New to these Midwestern parts. From Connecticut. Dad got transferred so looks like I get to spend my senior year here in your sleepy little town. I hope this is the cool place to hang."

I took his dollar and stamped his hand all at the same time.

"Oh you won't be disappointed, I'm the entertainment tonight," I said with great pride and authority.

The shorter dark-haired man pushed his way up to the table. His penetrating blue eyes looked right into mine and I noticed that I felt my heart skip a beat. How romantic, and who is this guy? I thought.

"And you are?" I managed playfully.

"Terrence Dale Woolcott the Third," he stated with as much enthusiasm as I had proclaimed my onstage appearance.

"I play guitar." He kept talking. I watched his lips move but I could not hear another word he said. He plays guitar... my inner self kept chanting over and over again. Finally coming to my senses, I realized that Terrence was staring at me expectantly.

"Hello? Where did you float off to?" He seemed charmed rather than annoyed by the absentee look that always irked my family.

"Come on in, I am sure we have a lot to talk about..." I said as he disappeared behind the partition. I couldn't wait to get on stage.

"Welcome to our refuge for rational thought!" Father Savio was as excited as I was and he grinned like the Cheshire cat as he spoke. A few claps and a couple of laughs rang out throughout the audience. "Karolle coffeehouse was established in the spirit of brotherly love and compassion two years ago as the joint effort of St. John Bosco parish along with several other CYO groups. Through a true spirit of cooperation of many business groups here in Highland, we are able to bring you our vision for the future of our community ... Karolle coffeehouse."

To my surprise, many of the kids in the audience clapped and whistled loudly at this introduction. Father Savio was hoping for more adults than teenagers but he was pleased with the turnout, nonetheless. The fact that these kids were showing their appreciation for a place where ideas could be discussed was more than enough thanks to Father S.

"I am pleased to announce our Grand Opening on Saturday, October 6th and our featured speaker will be Ed Heidelberg from our own Cane County draft board." A few boos rose from the audience.

"No, no, let's have none of that. He is coming to explain his side and his argument for the conscription of our young men into the military. Our other speaker is Father Bill Donelly, a national activist against the Vietnam War and..." Large applause and cheering broke out amongst the college-aged men in the audience. "And..." Father continued with authority, "we will have the talents of several local artists who will perform some wonderful tunes for you."

God, Father S sounds like Lawrence Welk. Wunnerful, wunnerful. Our next tune is ... I thought to myself but as I did I was interrupted by his brief and somewhat awkward introduction of the band.

"... and now the Karolle coffeehouse band." A thunderous applause broke out and I felt the intoxication of it as we all jumped on stage.

Jerry Skittles was a wonderful singer songwriter and bounced on stage and jumped right into his opening song, "Blowin' In The Wind" by Bob Dylan.

In the background, my ooohs and aaahs were a nice counter-melody to Jerry's lead vocals and it sounded good. The basement of the old church had a resonance like none other I had ever experienced. Ed had his big bass fiddle up there and Larry played some sort of Indian percussion instrument. We sounded great and I was so happy to be on stage with these guys. It was unbelievable. Even more blissful, in the audience sat Terence the Third, watching my every move, mesmerized by my performance.

Jerry then performed two original songs, both were anti-war songs. I thought they had great melody lines and they had great lyrics, weaving a storyline about Jerry's older brother, Richard.

Richard Skittles had recently returned from duty in Vietnam in a pine box and the sorrow that the family felt was awful. At a young impressionable 17 years of age, I knew that parents should never have to bury their child, not for any reason. Jerry's song was a beautiful tribute and there was not a single dry eye in the house. My moist eyes were squarely on the guitar player in the front row. When Jerry finished, the entire coffeehouse burst into thundering applause. Wow! It gave me goose bumps. Here was meaningful art, being performed in a dingy little church basement in a small Midwestern town. The set was over but Jerry looked at me, sensing the need for an encore.

I stepped up to the microphone, trembling like a leaf. His eyes, and everyone else's in the house, were glued on me.

"God is love ... and he who abides in love, abides in God and God in him." It was my best impersonation of an angel to date. My voice was soft and lilting slightly and everyone was moved by the tremendous amount of love and compassion present in our candlelit cavern. The crowd began to chant along and I thought I saw Father Savio floating in the air at the back of the coffeehouse. He was ecstatic, like a saint I had once read about that had levitated over the altar during Mass because he felt the Holy Spirit. Everything he had hoped his coffeehouse to represent was blossoming before his eyes.

I shall never forget the applause that followed. I was intoxicated beyond words. If there was such a thing as being filled with the Holy Spirit, I was brimming over with it, then and there. The lights came up and I saw everyone's faces. Tears of joy, hearts on fire, minds that were blown flickered in front of me. The band began to pack it up but I remained transfixed at the microphone and some people were still clapping. I was mesmerized and could not move. Finally, Terrence came up to the stage and put his hands around mine as they were cupped to the mic.

"That was beautiful," he whispered in my ear. Then, he nibbled on it and I pulled him offstage to a dimly lit corner of the coffeehouse and we began to feast on each other's lips. Never in my

32

life had I felt so ecstatic. I fell in love so completely that night that it took me years to finally figure out what exactly I fell in love with.

Was it Terrence, was it singing, was it performing, was it God? Or was it all of these things tumbling over me like a waterfall of grace? I was languishing in its depth of divine experience and I spent the next few days as if in a dream world. My mother mentioned that she could not even get through to me because I had my head in the clouds again.

I couldn't wait for our Grand Opening. Mom kept encouraging me to try out for Pom Pom squad again. I had been in the squad for two years and seemed to really enjoy it. It kept me involved in high school activities and my parents were growing a bit uneasy with my constant participation with the Karolle coffeehouse.

"Why aren't you trying out for the squad?" she asked one afternoon, not long after my divine performance.

"God wants me to sing and work at the coffeehouse. I believe it is my calling, the way a man hears the call to priesthood or a woman to a nunnery."

My mother's mouth hit the floor and I almost wanted to go over and push it back up against her upper lip. Sufficed to say, I left her speechless, and I finished folding the clothes out of the dryer and took them to my room.

"God told her this?" My mother was mumbling to herself with a certain incoherency. Being a devout Catholic, she did not want to question the validity of my experience. After all, Bernadette of Lourdes had regular visits from the Virgin Mary, so perhaps her daughter did hear directions from the mouth of God.

I was impressed by the fact that this revelation had completely shut my mom up about her opinions of my life after that. It took a lot to shake that cathedral to the ground.

My entire focus began to dwell on the Grand Opening. We were going to have a famous speaker and Father S was so excited about this event, he was like a kid who just met Santa Clause.

A week after my performance, Father Savio called me aside as we worked on getting the kitchen cleaned.

"I think you really understand your religion, Anne Marie, and I want you to be in charge of all the youth CCD classes for the kids in kindergarten through the fifth grade. Work with Sister Angeline to create a program that will inspire children to understand the essence of our Catholic faith and help guide them into fruitful lives as young teenage Catholics."

I was honored, sure, but I also sensed a tremendous burden in taking on this role. Hesitating slightly, I finally spoke.

"I would be delighted ... as long as it doesn't interfere with my work here at the coffeehouse. I believe that God wants me to do this work."

"Oh, I do too, Anne Marie. I think this is a supreme achievement for all of our parishes. I am so blessed to be a part of what we are doing."

"Without you Father, this would never have happened." Father drank in these words like wine from the chalice. He was proud as a peacock of the coffeehouse and he would expect big things from it in the coming months.

"You will be fine in both roles, I know you can do it." He patted me on the shoulder in his typical patronizing manner.

"Thanks, Father," I smiled back. "I know that I can. I will help Sister H create a wonderful program."

Father had already cruised past this scenario and was busy thinking about his beloved Grand Opening. My time was dedicated to thinking about Terrence. He called me every day after school from work and we spent Saturdays at Jackie's house. I marveled at how her house could even function with her mom and dad perpetually drunk or passed out in some part of the house. I found a shelter in their basement where we would sit on the discarded sofa and love seat where Terrence would strum his guitar and I would sing. Always starting with our favorite Beatles tune of the day, we progressed into the Stones, The Who, and my most recent favorite, Jefferson Airplane.

Grace Slick had caught my imagination. I began to rehearse "White Rabbit" in the comfort of Jackie's parents' basement. Saturday afternoons were spent downstairs where Jackie was chained to the laundry area with a mountain of clothes in front of her and Terrence and I were there to serenade her and give her moral support. Jackie's folks were oblivious to us, slamming down beers in the family room and watching roller derby on television.

"I want to write a new song for the Karolle Coffeehouse's

opening. I want one that reflects the wonderful achievement in human consciousness that we are supporting."

"Ha, you mean getting people to talk to one another? I'll give you that but, Anne Marie, this is not the beginning of an era."

"How do you know that?" I snapped back. "How do you know that kids just like us all over the country aren't opening coffeehouses that support peace, love and hippies?"

"Beautiful dreamer, wake unto me, starlight and moon drops are waiting for thee," Terrence strummed his guitar on bended knee, serenading me with his sarcasm.

"Come on you big jerk, write something with me." He put down his guitar and slid on top of me, sticking his tongue down my throat to show he meant business.

"Get a room you guys," Jackie jumped in. She was stuffing as many bed sheets in the dryer as was mechanically possible.

Terrence was not in the mood to stop and was just about dry humping me when I pushed him off the couch.

"What the fuck, Anne Marie?" Terrence was pissed. He was not in the habit of controlling himself, especially when he was turned on. He surprised both of us by grabbing his guitar and exiting without so much as a goodbye.

"Do you think he'll come back?" Jacks ventured after the stillness as the abrupt departure settled.

"Ah, fuck him. He'll get over it. What did he want to do? Ball me right in front of you?"

The look on Jackie's face made me sense that, in fact, that is exactly what she wanted, with her inserted into the equation as well. My thoughts became erratic for a moment, and then I instinctively started to help Jackie with the clothes she had just pulled out of the dryer. We folded clothes in silence and then I left without saying a word.

Chapter 7
White Rabbit

A frosty autumn night was present to witness the birth of a dream. All of us in our own way, with our own agendas, had given our hopes, dreams, and desires to the coffeehouse and there had been a great deal of publicity for a small northern Indiana town. Several of the local colleges in the area had put a brief advertisement in their paper about the opening and posted a list of the guest speakers. I was disappointed to see that the billing for the band read –HOUSE BAND.

Gee, we need a name for the band, I thought as I looked over the ads in the papers Father S had brought into the kitchen. He was like a theatre owner on opening night. He kept peeking out of the kitchen door into the main room and was giggling like a schoolgirl at the way the place was filling up so quickly.

"We are going to have a packed house tonight!" he chirped. "Girls, get those popcorn baskets filled and be sure everyone gets coffee. Do we have the sugar and creams out on the table?"

He was driving me nuts. I had my own stomach jitters over the band's 9 p.m. performance. I did as he asked and sat patiently through the speaker, who was, in my opinion, unabashedly anti-Vietnam War, and the questions from the audience just kept going on and on. Father S was in heaven. I, however, was in hell and frantically paced the kitchen, looking at the clock that now glared 9:30 p.m. at me.

Just about the time I was ready to blow a fuse, I heard Father Savio announcing us to come up on stage. Jerry played to a crowd that was fired up and the applause was huge. This time, however, I brought Terrence on stage with me and when it came time for my solos, I chose the famous Joan Baez tune "Diamonds and Rust,"

36

which was met with strong applause. It was written by Joan but I could see Father Savio and many of the audience were not as familiar with this tune so I went right into, "We Shall Overcome." The applause meter went up a couple of notches, especially among the anti Vietnam protesters. Then, because I was determined to rock the place and make it mine, I broke into the Airplane's song "White Rabbit."

I watched as the coffeehouse got still; even those who were chattering lightly during the Baez song stopped, and the entire packed place was listening with great intent.

Father Savio was talking with some of the guest speaker's friends and turned to me as he put down his coffee. His mouth was open and his jaw was dropping to the floor. Had he never heard the Airplane song before? That thought crossed my mind as I began my robust finale.

My bellowing voice filled the entire coffeehouse as we bowed like the Beatles on stage after a set. For one long and eternal second, there was nothing. You could hear a pin drop in that old dank basement. Father Savio sat frozen, unable to move.

Then, to my surprise, thunderous applause came roaring out of the audience, followed by whistles and hoots and hollers, and I looked out to the fans that were in adoration of me. "Move over Grace, I have arrived and I can sing the Key of E better than anybody!" I thought.

People came up to me after we got off stage and told me how great my last song was, and that I sounded exactly like Grace Slick. Terrence seemed a bit annoyed by all the attention I was getting. He went outside in the parking lot to have a cigarette until all the "brouhaha" had subsided.

Promptly at 11 p.m., Father S had us clean up and get all the tables cleared off. He found a quiet moment and stood next to me as I washed the coffee cups.

"What was that song you sang at the end?" He seemed to be asking quite disarmingly.

"White Rabbit.' It's been on the charts for a while. The band is Jefferson Airplane and they are out of San Fran-"

Father stopped me mid-sentence with a brisk wave of his hand.

"No rock and roll, Anne Marie." He stated this with great

authority as if masquerading as supreme Lord and Master of the coffeehouse.

"What? We sang that Beatles song last week!"

"That's not rock and roll ... well. OK, it is, but it's not ... well. This is a song about drugs, Anne Marie. I cannot have you singing a song like that in this establishment again." He looked squarely at me, demanding that I get the picture.

"Are we clear?" He was in no mood for a disagreement.

"Yes, Father," I stated as dutifully as if I were in the confessional and he was giving me penance.

Karolle began to get a reputation as a cool place to hang out. One evening, two authentic Berkeley California graduate students came down to check out the reconverted basement. One, who called himself OT, had an afro that extended at least 2 feet in all directions. He boasted that he was a member of the Black Panthers. The other guy was an East Coast Massachusetts type with a long golden ponytail and a gift for gab. Both of them had heads turning and tongues wagging.

"Black people have been oppressed for too long! Martin Luther King is the first one to stand up, but what we need is radical black men with guns in their hands fightin' back. Like Malcolm X!" OT spoke with a moral gravitas that was compelling, but Father S sat in on our discussion to comment.

"Martin Luther King is a man of non-violence, a man of God."

"A man of God." OT repeated those words with the slightest hint of derision. "And those police officers who beat our young black men? Are they men of God?" OT slammed his fist on the table, an exclamation point to drive the intensity of his message home.

Father S graciously let that outburst go and began to steer the discussion back to the teachings of Jesus Christ.

"Come on brother," OT mentioned to his friend, "Let's go outside for a minute or two." He turned to me and asked, "Why don't you join us, beautiful singer?"

I was enchanted with the Berkeley radicals and walked out back into the parking lot to find out more about them.

"Here saucy momma, why don't you do the honors?"

He handed me a thinly rolled cigarette. I thought it looked homemade.

"I don't smoke cigarettes," I said shyly.

"This ain't no cigarette, bitch! This here is fine cannabis sativa," he proudly stated. He could see I did not understand the reference.

"Pot, bitch, it's pot! That's a joint I just handed you. Light it up and smoke it."

I stared at it, rolling it over and over in my fingers. Then, I sniffed it. It smelled delicious and I found the fragrance enjoyable. I took the lighter he handed me and lit up the joint and sucked in a big puff.

Aaah, I spewed as I coughed out a big ball of smoke.

Both of them just laughed.

"My oh my, we have a virgin," OT laughed. "Take a smaller puff. Now hold it for a few seconds." OT seemed pleased that I was smoking it at last.

As I let out the smoke, everything felt pleasant. Groovy! I could feel the texture of groovy. I took in another big hit and held it.

"Quit bogarting that joint!" As I handed the joint back to him, I blew the smoke back in his face.

"Check this bitch out, she has balls. She has no idea what I do to ballsy bitches. But first I need to partake of the herb." OT took a big hit and passed the jay to his friend.

Before he could take another hit, Father Savio walked out the back door of the coffeehouse and glared in our direction. Seeing him, his friend dropped the joint on the asphalt and smashed the butt deep into the pavement of the parking lot. They walked down the alley without ever looking back, but I heard them laughing.

I turned to walk back into the coffeehouse. Father began to walk with me.

"Don't let them back into the coffeehouse, Anne Marie, we don't need their kind here."

I was surprised. His attitude had always been one of tolerance and he invited differences of opinion.

"I thought you would like their West Coast perspective and progressive attitudes."

"Really, is that what you thought that was Anne Marie? They were nothing more than thugs."

I didn't really care. I felt as light as the air and my attitude was one of peace and contentment. I thoroughly enjoyed having the smoke with them and I was glad they showed up. I said nothing. I hoped to see them again.

Fast forward one week and I was enjoying the old mattress with Terrence in Jackie's basement. It was pouring down rain and we were both entangled in each other's arms, watching a small dingy basement window get cleansed by the torrential downpour outside.

I was in heaven.

"I hit every note so it could reverberate around the entire coffeehouse," I bragged to him.

"Did you hear that whining lead guitar I put on that song? I felt teleported to the Haight, picking out a cosmic lead part that was blowing everyone's socks off!"

We both bolted out laughter that resounded so loud in the basement that Jackie walked away from the washing machine she was unloading to see what was so funny.

"Hey, lovebirds, what's so amusing?"

Jacks, did you not love our cover of "White Rabbit" at last week's opening?

"Oh my God, yes!" she coughed up with no hesitation.

"Father S says we can never sing it again."

I had not told Terrence of this new rule so the information came as a huge shock to him.

"You have got to be fucking kidding me!" he screamed.

Jackie and I jumped back a notch at the ferocity of his response.

"Hey, don't kill the messenger; I am not happy about it either. I loved singing that song and so did most of the audience!" I shot back.

"Fuck Father S," Terrence stated with surprising contempt.

"He has to say that," Jackie offered. "If he didn't he would lose his assignment to this parish. The bishop would have him farmed out to God knows where."

My sympathies lied with the rationale to please Father Savio, but my passions lay with the young pirate guitar player who rivaled any hot guitar player out there. Move over Pete Townsend, Jerry Garcia and the rest of the rock and roll apocalyptic horsemen. Power guitar riffs were looking to be Terrence's specialty and he was blazing a trail. I was hitching my wagon to that train and I fell back against his chest and listened to his breath come in and out. It was so soothing and soon our focus had calmed down to just watching the rain again.

As Jacks was taking a basket of folded laundry up the stairs, she looked back at the two of us curled up like kittens on the old mattress.

"My parents are going to be waking up soon. I have to go pick up my brother from football practice so you should be forewarned. I will say no more." She giggled as she hurried back up the steps.

Terrence seized his opportunity and rolled on top of me, covering my neck in a cascade of kisses. His breath was sizzling warm and it aroused a deep all-consuming feeling in between my legs. This time, I did not want to draw the line that I had done so many times before. My need was greater than his at this moment, or so I believed. He was a knight in shining armor to me and I wanted to feel him inside of me. I wanted to experience the "oneness" that my cousin, Marcia, had often bragged about during numerous holiday visits.

My breath was labored and when he slid off my bell-bottom jeans to the floor and began licking my bare bottom, the intense feelings of pleasure were everywhere. Surely God wanted me to have experiences like this in my life. I was deeply in love and my happiness was his happiness. We were panting like dogs as crescendo after crescendo of lovemaking swept over us both. His powerful thrusts and my welcome and accepting moaning could have woken the dead.

It almost did as we had a simultaneous orgasm that blasted me two inches above the mattress. Follow that with a huge noise from upstairs as Jackie's dad fell off the couch he had been sleeping on. We heard him snorting himself awake as our hearts pounded feverishly in our chests.

Within a minute, we heard the basement door open and quick thinking Terrence opened the basement window and slid us both out onto the wet grass. I barely had time to grab my jeans as we rolled out to a loud thunderclap. Laughing deliriously, we popped back into our pants and ran for the gate before either of Jackie's parents could discover us fleeing through the yard from the basement window. I was soaking wet by the time I got out of the gate and down the alleyway.

I can remember that moment as if it was yesterday. My clothes were drenched, my hair was soaking wet, and my heart was so full of love that it was bursting into undiscovered ecstasy. My God, what could be wrong with something so right? As we exchanged tongue diving kisses in the pouring rain, I felt like my feet were not even touching the ground. Long Live Rock!

Chapter 8
We Shall Overcome

The Karolle coffeehouse thrived during the holidays as we raced through to the New Year. Music poured like a jug of water upon parched souls such as myself during these times. I couldn't get enough, nor could I get enough of Terrence. The year of 1967 had brought all these new faces into the limelight, not only in music but also in politics. Discussions were hot and heavy at Karolle. Issues concerning Vietnam, race riots, and the addition of Eugene McCarthy to the presidential race had everyone talking.

I had never seen Father S so happy. Even some of the businessmen in the town had stopped by for some coffee and conversation in the early evening hours of Saturday. This was Father's dream and it was coming true. Terrence and I became the house band and ever so slowly and carefully I was able to sneak in some contemporary rock and roll songs and weave them into our folk songs of the Vietnam War era. Staying away from drugs, sex, and rock and roll, we performed some yummy Beatles tunes and I was in heaven. Their new shift into mysticism and transcendental meditation brought songs that Father S actually liked. I found singing on that small wooden stage surrounded by tables made out of cable spools and rickety old folding chairs filled with people drinking coffee to be thoroughly enchanting.

Even more enchanting was the applause. Although Father would get the crowd whipped into a frenzy for Dylan's "Blowin' in the Wind," I brought down the house one Saturday evening in early April with my angelic performance of the Beatles, "Norwegian Wood." Terrence had found the most amazing Indian guy from his college. He played an Indian instrument called the sitar. The recent collaborations between George Harrison and Ravi Shankar had this

43

wonderful sound and we had reproduced the mystical song right there in the basement of old St. Lucy's church. Karolle had begun to get a reputation around the area for its hip atmosphere and great music.

Saturday afternoons had become the other enchanting activity that I began to participate in more and more often. Jackie had long since given up getting us to do anything else. My mind wandered as I laid in Terrence's arms, thinking of the potential impact that music was having in America. Everyone I knew bought albums as often as they could afford them and the addition of an old phonograph down in the basement gave us the opportunity to sit and listen to the Doors, the Beatles, The Who, the Rolling Stones, the Grateful Dead and Jefferson Airplane and any other hot English or West Coast bands. I marveled at its amazing impact on all of our lives. Music was everywhere and I loved to sit and listen for hours. I stacked up twelve albums once with Terrence one afternoon that broke Jackie's record player and we spent the long month of March waiting for me to have enough money to buy a new one.

Music spoke to me in a language that could not be poisoned by the outside world. The sound of an electric guitar was so pleasing to my ears, and the backbeat was as natural to my body as breathing. Rock and roll. In and out. Up and Down. Day and night.

Oh my God, rock and roll!

Summer was coming in and the heated campaigning of candidates for the Democratic nomination was in full swing. My dad would follow it on the news and found a kindred spirit in me to discuss the politics of the day.

"So why do all the kids down at your coffeehouse think that Eugene McCarthy is the new voice of the Democratic party, Anne Marie?" Dad was quizzing me one morning at the breakfast table.

"Probably because most of the staff are guys from St. Joe College and they don't want to go to Vietnam," I quipped back.

"That's not a good enough reason to become president, honey." That seemed logical to my father.

"Well, who do you like dad, Bobby Kennedy?"

My dad paused for a moment. I don't think he had quite made up his mind yet but my question seemed to cement his position.

"John Fitzgerald Kennedy was a good president. He and his brother stood down the commies in Cuba and I have always admired he and his brother's courage. You know, I voted for Bobby in the primary last month and he's looking good in the polls for California."

"I kinda figured that, dad."

"I almost voted for Humphrey but I don't think he or Johnson took this country in the right direction."

"Oh, I know that, I can still hear mom's reaction when you told us that you voted for Barry Goldwater back in '64."

We both chuckled over that. Dad was fixing pancakes for breakfast and flipped a few cakes onto my plate. As he seated himself to eat, he wanted to bring home his point.

"Those socialists gave us all social security numbers, and the government will be able to monitor every move you make. It's like the Gestapo in Germany twenty years ago ... taking the country in the wrong direction there."

"No argument there dad. Sometimes you sound like a Republican."

"Ha! I am not. That shifty-eyed used car salesman they have running on their ticket would be much worse."

Both of us blurted out a hearty laugh at that accurate analysis.

The following Thursday, I was preparing to go to the license bureau. The long-awaited day to get my driver's license had come and I couldn't wait.

"They shot Bobby Kennedy," said the man who had walked into the license branch and sat down next to me.

"Some Mideast raghead guy, shot him in the head, just like his brother. Now, ain't that something?"

I was stunned and couldn't reply. They called my name for the test and I had just enough presence of mind to get up off my seat.

"They shot Bobby Kennedy." Father Savio was staring directly into my eyes when I told him and I saw tears well up in his. I had driven straight to the rectory after passing my driving test.

He sat down on his large comfortable red chair but just teetered on the edge of it, making himself as uncomfortable as someone could be in a chair that was warm and inviting.

"Who did this?"

"I don't know his name. Why don't we turn on the television

and find out more?" I offered.

Father reached over the chair handle to his large Philco radio that sat on the very edge of his desk.

"We don't have a TV. The bishop thinks it would corrupt our minds and keep us from our prayers and duties. Hmm, I thought you knew that."

How would I know what goes on in a priest's house, I thought to myself. Father nervously searched the radio as "Revolution" by the Beatles came through the airwaves.

"What's this… a Beatles song on the radio, now, when I need news about a current event and this stupid radio station is playing rock and roll."

Father turned off the radio abruptly and shoved it to the middle of the desk. I had not seen him so agitated before and was surprised at how emotional he got over the incident.

"The harder you try to make it a better world, the worse it gets." Father pounded his fist on the desk and shook his head. I wanted nothing more than to calm him down but it seemed nothing could break the spell that had taken a hold of him.

Throughout the summer, all Father would talk about at the coffeehouse was the assassination. It was as if he needed to talk his way through the fact that bad things happen to good people. Trying to stand up and make a difference can be lethal and the impression it left on me was to be passionately involved in working for good, no matter what the consequences.

"Father S has got to stop with the Kennedy thing, it's been over two months and he isn't talking about anything else. I asked him to come up to Chicago next weekend for the Peace and Love festival they are having in Grant Park. They're having it to raise awareness during the Democratic National Convention and he told me I was wasting my time. He is getting so cynical." Jerry and I were cleaning up in the coffeehouse kitchen.

Even though I agreed, my approach was to be positive.

"Well, I want to go, can we take your car up there?"

Jerry winced a bit.

"I was hoping you could get the car from your dad and take us up, my car needs a brake job and my brother is going to help me, but it will take a few days. It's so groovy that you have your license now,

Anne Marie. Your dad's big Buick can hold all 8 of us."

"Damn," I thought to myself. "If I ask my father for the car to take my friends to the festival in Chicago, he will say no. Mmmm. I am sure I can get a good excuse going."

"Sure, that's fine. I will pick you up right after Mass on Sunday."

Of course, my devious and delightful friend, Bernie Kay, had just the excuse.

"Tell your dad we're using the car to visit my grandma. She's in that nursing home in Dyer, so we need a car to go and see her. Remember, corporal work of mercy here, visiting the sick." For being Jewish, Bernie had schooled herself in all the Catholic dogma quite well.

Visiting grandma, corporal work of mercy... "Works for me!" I said.

And it did, in fact, as my father was actually touched by our selfless act on a Sunday afternoon.

"Sure, Anne Marie," he said. "Mom and I are going to visit our friends, the Smiths, out in Indiana Dunes Shores. You can have the Chevy 2."

"Thanks so much dad," I said, knowing that dad's work vehicle was small. He and mom were taking the Buick.

My Catholic guilt was gushing out all over me and I thanked dad again as I took the keys and got ready.

Terrence drove, I sat on his lap, Jackie sat on the stick shift, and Bernie and Larry sat in the passenger seat. Ed, JP, Jerry and Riley were all piled into the back. I fretted all the way down I-94, expecting to be pulled over by a policeman.

However, as we found out when we got to the festival, all the cops in Chicago were there. Several police were on horses and a line of officers flanked the eastern edge of the park.

"Here, brother," said a tie-dyed long-haired man in bell bottoms. He handed Terrence a flower to put in his hair. Terry gave it to me as we watched several hippies approach the police line, trying to give them flowers as well.

The cops were not as appreciative and a small skirmish broke out. Several of the kids were bashed over the heads with billy clubs and dragged into paddy wagons.

"Oh my God!" I kept saying over and over again. This was no

peace and love festival. Fear began to rise in me like a thermometer detecting a fever. I quickly grabbed Jacks and Bernie and headed towards a circle where folks were chanting and singing.

"Kumbaya, my Lord, Kumbaya ..." To me the song was droning on as the tensions mounted between the police and hippies. I stood up.

"Kumbaya..." The crowd echoed back, "Kumbaya..." I sang that song with all the vibrato and punch I could muster and it seemed as if the crowd had picked up on it and the whole group was singing at full force.

Turning around I saw someone hand a flower to a police officer. I don't know if the cop thought it was an act of aggression but he shoved the guy down and several other officers had begun to club him. An entire group of hippies jumped onto the pile of people and this alerted several officers on horseback. Tear gas was thrown into the crowd.

"All you need is ..." then my voice sank to my knees as I saw that Terry was close to the skirmish.

"Terrence!" I screamed. A wall of police began to close in on his area, and I broke out of the circle with Jackie on my arm and we were closely followed by Bernie.

"Stop!" I screamed as the wall of police began clubbing everyone, moving like soldiers across a battlefield. A second wave of police began taking the wounded into custody and loading them into police vehicles.

The song had stopped mid-sentence only to be replaced by screams of terror as everyone was running for cover or trying to escape the wall of police that were coming at us. The dust of a dry, hot August afternoon made it hard to see Terrence in the din, but just as I got close, Jackie spotted him.

"Let's get out of here!" I yelled at the top of my lungs. I turned to see that a cop had grabbed Bernie's long dark hair. I grabbed her arms and pulled her away and the four of us took off in a hard run. Hearts pounding, we raced across the park toward the back streets where the car was parked.

In the sprint of a lifetime, we were back at the car. The others were already there.

"It's like a war out there!" Larry screamed. "We need to get out

48

of here while we can!"

No one disagreed with that and we piled into that little Chevy 2 in record time. Terrence had received a blow to the head and I insisted that he not drive. I raced down East Jackson Drive trying to get on Lake Shore Drive. I thought it was the easiest way back to Indiana. As I got close to Lake Shore Drive, we saw a police barricade in the road. I quickly noticed it was just one board and the police were busy in an area just south of it. Putting the pedal to the metal, I busted through and turned down Lake Shore Drive as fast as I could.

As I had suspected, the police were too busy controlling the crowd to bother with me and I sped down the highway like a banshee out of hell. We drove in silence for a while as Terrence nursed his head wound. For a distraction, he turned on the radio which was forever tuned to WLS. The Beatles were singing, "All You Need is Love," as if championing the bleeding heroes as we all drove home. The synchronicity was not lost on me. I felt part of a great moment in history.

When I pulled into the driveway at my house, I nearly collapsed. Not more than five minutes later, my parents arrived.

My dad bounded in and barked out an order to me, something he rarely did.

"Anne Marie, turn on the television," dad said. "There was a big skirmish in Chicago today."

We turned to the early news hour that had footage of the police bashing heads of young people and the blood was everywhere. Mayor Richard Daley had issued a statement calling for law and order, justifying the police action that he had ordered and stating that no disruptions to the Democratic Convention would be tolerated.

"I couldn't agree more," said my father to the entire family which was now huddled around the TV. "Bash their heads in. Those filthy hippies are troublemakers and they will ruin any chances Hubert Humphrey has at becoming president. They are helping to elect Nixon."

I did not want to add anything, yet I was shocked that my father would be so callous. I wondered if he would have softened his position if he had known that his only daughter was one of those "dirty filthy hippies." I was just grateful that I had managed to

49

get out without a scratch and even more grateful that dad's car had broken through the barricade in one piece.

Father Savio actually laughed out loud when I told him the story later that week, although he was obviously not sympathetic to Mayor Daley's position.

"Anne Marie, I want you to know that I, the church, and Karolle coffeehouse do not officially endorse you going up there. You are just a junior in high school. Leave the protesting to Larry and the rest. They are the ones who will be drafted to serve in Vietnam."

"Isn't this about the love, Father?" I asked. "We wanted to let the candidates know that we supported peace. It was a peace and love festival for heaven's sake!" I protested.

I hit a nerve in him that had been festering since Kennedy's assassination. He became quiet for a while then spoke.

"I became a priest because I believe in the love of Jesus Christ. Beyond that Anne Marie, I have no idea."

I instinctively gave him a big hug. This man had a heart of gold, but he did not know where to plug into this society to share it.

Terrence healed, but his gash to the head left a small scar. He wore it like a sailor with a new tattoo. When the colors came on my maple tree, we climbed up to a high bough that acted like a cradle and sat viewing the town from our lofty and secluded perch.

Terrence's voice was wonderful as he sang "Let's Live For Today." Rich, with a John Lennon falsetto, he carried its luxurious sound high above the treetops and they all seemed to sway to the rhythm of the song.

"You like it?" he asked.

"I love it," I said.

"Heard it yesterday on the radio. I love it, too. We should do it at the coffeehouse."

I nodded in approval. Terrence felt emboldened.

"Why don't you try some harmonies on the chorus?"

I did and we spent the afternoon making that song our own. Then, we climaxed with some sweet treetop sex and the orgasm I experienced had such a depth to it, I thought I would melt down the side of the tree like syrup running in the late winter.

My feelings of contentment stretched out over the whole universe that afternoon. I could not even imagine why people wanted war instead of peace. Peace and contentment, this is what God created us to experience, I surmised.

I did not even have the wildest notion that this was also the feeling a woman has when she conceives.

Chapter 9
Sympathy for the Devil

The cold winds of November were frosting Terrence's cheeks as he came over to my house one afternoon right after school. He always came for the precious 45 minutes from when school let out to when my mom came home from work.

"Got tickets to the Stones concert at the Amphitheater on the 16th!"

Terrence was ecstatic and fire was dancing in his eyes. He had talked about going to see them for months.

I looked at my calendar.

"The 16th is my final CCD class! I can't get out of that."

Terrence was shocked.

"You are kidding me, right? I have tickets to see the fucking Rolling Stones. Get someone to substitute!"

"No, this is my service to God. Those kids are counting on me and I said we would have a special celebration for our last class."

"Are you crazy?" Terrence was yelling at the top of his lungs. "Did you hear what I said, I said: THE ROLLING STONES ... I have tickets for the Rolling Stones!"

"I said NO!" I had never screamed that loudly before at him, or for that matter, anyone else.

"No, no, no. This is not something I can get out of."

"Father Savio can take over this time."

"No."

"Why are you being so Goddamned stubborn about this, Anne Marie?"

"It's my service to God. I can go and see the Rolling Stones the next time. I am sure they will be around again in another year or so."

"You are so full of shit, Anne Marie. You are letting your

religion get in the way of having fun… with ME!"

He didn't even wait for a response from me but stormed out of the back door, slamming it hard behind him.

I was scared and stood frozen for a couple of minutes after he left. Tears welled up inside and they spilled out over my cheeks as I saw my mom pulling in our driveway. Drying my eyes immediately, I began to set the table for dinner and when she asked me how my day was, I put on the phoniest smile in history, and told her that it was a great day and I got an A on my chemistry test.

He never called me and I heard via the coffeehouse clan that he had asked a girl from his high school, a senior just like him, to the concert. A week after the concert, I called his house. We had not performed at the coffeehouse together in five weeks. It was like he had vanished. There was never an answer. The phone would ring and ring and ring… but no one ever picked up.

I began inviting Jackie over for little afternoon strategy sessions which turned into stealing a couple of shots from my mother's brandy snifter or bottle of Jim Beam. She kept it in her dining room hutch for holidays and special occasions.

We took turns calling Terrence's house. Finally, one cold December afternoon, his mother answered.

"Yes, hello, is Terrence there?" I asked gingerly.

"Who is this please?" she asked. Her voice was authoritative even if it was small and tiny.

"Anne Marie." I offered her no last name.

"Well, Anne Marie, you should know that Terry doesn't live with us here anymore. He's moved into an apartment on Walnut Street."

I was stunned.

"Where on Walnut Street is this apartment?" My voice had trumped hers in authority.

"Right next to Bob's Used Car Lot, there's a few apartments there and he lives in C. Yes, apartment C." Her voice started to sound a bit shaky.

My quivering hand put the receiver back in its cradle. I turned to Jacks with tears in my eyes.

"He's living in the building where your aunt Audrey lives. Let's go over there, it's apartment C."

We both bundled up in scarves and mittens. The wind was blowing pretty hard and there had just been a four inch snowfall the night before. I plowed down the street and ran across the park to Walnut Street with Jackie scurrying to keep up with me.

I stood behind the red brick building that was the sales office for Bob's Car Lot, watching for his van. Several minutes later, he pulled up and got out with a blonde girl with long hair and a blue jean jacket.

It felt like someone had stuck a knife into my heart and was now ripping it out of my body. Jackie grabbed me as I sank to my knees, sobbing.

"How could he do this to me over a fucking Rolling Stones concert? Fuck him! Fuck the blonde! Fuck everything!"

Jackie put her hands over my mouth as we saw Terrence and the blonde walk back out of the apartment and drive away. Both of us quickly scrambled up the stairs to his apartment. I pulled an old class note card from my purse and penciled a message on it to leave on the door.

I have something very important to tell you. It will affect the future of your musical career. Meet me at Karolle Saturday at 9 p.m. You know who.

"Why are you saying that?" Jackie asked.

"What do you want me to say? That I am pregnant? He wouldn't care."

Jackie stared at me bug-eyed. I had not breathed a word of what I had suspected for weeks.

"Are you?"

I nodded my head up and down. We walked in silence in the snow back to my house.

Word spread to me that he read my note and was planning on coming. I rehearsed with an old piano that I had my brothers bring down from the upstairs choir loft of the church. It was a rickety old thing, out of tune and not much but I decided I had not taken eight years of piano lessons for nothing and I started rehearsing my song.

The evening started out rather tensely. Every table was overflowing with people, which was a good thing. Father S had a table of local businessmen and the popcorn and coffee were flowing. I watched from the kitchen as Terrence came in with his new girlfriend, Suzi. They sat at a table with a few new people that I did not recognize.

A local poet from St Joe College started out the evening with a poem. It was another in an endless stream of poetry that I had heard concerning the Vietnam war. Just more "blah blah blah blah... peace." Peace is when human beings start treating each other the way they would want to be treated. That certainly wasn't happening in my world.

Finally, I got up and brought both my brothers on stage. Eddie swore he had the Wyman bass part down and Billy insisted he could do some chord fills. It was a small price to pay for having them move the piano and I knew I could drown them out if I had to with my vocals. I did not even introduce the song but just jumped into it. I was pleased to hear a nice steady bass line from Ed and a few chords from Billy that were in key.

"Been around for a long long year. Stole a man's soul and faith. I was around when Jesus Christ had his moment of pain and suffering, made damn sure that Pilate walked away and sealed his fate... Pleased to meet you, hope you've guessed my name!"

Both brothers were singing backups. I was elated. The crowd was so intently following the song that you heard nothing in the basement but that song.

Father Savio was swallowing hard into his coffee cup, since he had never heard the Rolling Stones song before and I was pretty positive he would not be in approval but then, I was not seeking any approval tonight. I would submit to being part of what killed Robert Kennedy. At least tonight I would.

Who hooo. Everyone under 25 knew this song and they began to chant the "who hoo" backup vocals and the place was totally rocking. Father Savio and the two businessmen at his table looked like they were not sure if they liked it.

I jumped off the stage and stood in front of Terrence's table.

I got right up close and in Terrence's face. "...hope you can guess my game..."

I leaned in close and said to Terrence, "You're going to be a father, I'm pregnant."

Father S, who was sitting at the next table, overheard what was said and dropped his coffee all over his frock. Everyone else was singing the chant… who hoooooo, who hoo!

I walked out of the coffeehouse to thunderous applause. Everyone loved it. My two brothers who knew next to nothing about performing stood on the stage to gladly receive all the accolades the crowd could generate.

Father Savio quickly jumped on stage and grabbed the microphone I had left behind.

"Thanks to all of our performers," said Father S. Let's take this next hour to discuss some of the important issues brought up by our poet, Dr. Theo Nelson. More coffee and popcorn are available to anyone who wants it and again, let's give a warm round of applause to all of our performers."

Beads of sweat were running down Father's forehead, and he was hoping that everyone would settle back down. While he was on stage, the two businessmen politely exited the rear door. Father's face sunk as he watched them leave.

Out in the back parking lot, Terrence had bolted out after me.

"Goddammit Anne Marie, fucking stop and turn around and talk to me!"

"Oh, so now you want to talk to me?" I stopped and turned around like a gunfighter read to pull pistols and fire.

"You are such a sanctimonious Catholic, acting like God, judge and jury over everything. I'm surprised you would even sing a Stones song."

"It fit the occasion," I fired back.

Terrence was held speechless for a moment. "Look, I am sorry for the way I've handled things but …"

His voice trailed off as Suzi walked out to join the discussion. Seeing her set me off like a volcano.

"But what? You're fucking someone else?"

"You and I just don't match up… hell, I'm not even Catholic. I just came to this coffeehouse because I heard it was cool."

I was furious. He had packaged everything into a neat four squared platitude.

"This is about you and me and what goes on… on stage. Listen to that applause in there, it's for me asshole. They like me. You couldn't get that kind of applause if you PAID for it. You can't handle the fact that I am much more talented than you are."

Bullet fired! Direct hit! Button pushed. Terrence screamed at the top of his lungs, "You fucking bitch!" then took Suzi's arm and walked away.

Even though I had won the duel, I didn't feel like much of a winner. What difference did it make if I was more talented, I had just permanently lost my boyfriend, the father of my child, to some Suzi milk toast.

I turned sullenly and walked to my car. I tried to turn the key but my hand shook, then I broke down sobbing. I was so lost in my tears that I did not even hear Father S knock on my window.

"Hey, in there, can you help me clean up? Everyone just left in a hurry and the kitchen is a mess. It's not my job to clean up."

My first thought was to tell him to fuck off but I decided to bite my tongue and go inside and help him. I cleaned off all the tables and started a sink full of dishes, working in complete silence. I could tell it made it all the harder for Father to speak with me but he found a way.

"Anne Marie, I thought your performance tonight was inspired and I want you to know I am here to help."

I was moved and touched by his offer.

"How kind of you, Father," I said as a tear rolled down my cheek. I slid down onto my haunches and flopped onto the middle of floor right there in the kitchen and cried.

"I am afraid, Father. What should I do? I can't tell anyone about this."

"Well, I'm glad you didn't use the stage tonight to tell the world about it."

We both smiled at each other, acknowledging my dramatic tendencies.

"There is a group of nuns that run a home for unwed mothers down in Albany and we can get you down there," Father Savio said softly. "They have a wonderful placement agency."

My eyes burrowed down into the floor. I said nothing. Father sensed it was time to pack me off to my home. As we walked to the car, he turned to me.

"You know there's a reason that the church asks that you save your virginity for marriage." He cleared his throat. "It's for situations just like this."

"It feels so good, how come something that feels as natural as drinking water be bad for you?"

Father looked sternly at me as if he was trying to make a deep point. "You tell me, Anne Marie, you tell me. You're the one that's going to have the baby."

"That's just it, Father. Why is it that I have to deal with this, it's not just my baby, it's Terrence's too. Yet, the entire burden falls on me, why is that?"

"Well, it shouldn't but your boyfriend is a degenerate Methodist."

"Father!" I said a bit shocked, "Terrence is a degenerate but it's not because he is a Methodist."

The levity of the moment caught us both off guard and we laughed. He gave me a hug and I went back home.

When my mother found out, she would not hear of any "home" that Father Savio had recommended.

"He's done enough," she stated. "It's because of that damn coffeehouse that all this has happened. He's let all kinds of unsavory characters into that place. Obviously, you didn't talk about anything, you just wound up making babies with some loser."

Her anger went on for days and I sat silently under its daily torrential downpours. She decided that she would send me to California, to stay with my Aunt Vivian. She was a clinical psychologist who had a nice roomy home in Pomona, was on the faculty at Pomona State College and she had just lost her husband to cancer. She had two boys and a girl, all preschoolers. I would stay and be her nanny and when the time came, Aunt Vivian had a wealthy childless couple who wanted to adopt my baby.

I left for California, glad to be out of the house. I had wanted to find a way to get to California to be a rock star for years but this was not what I had in mind. I stuffed my feelings so far down my throat, I think they were in my intestines. When I arrived, to my delight, Aunt Viv had a beautiful living room with a baby grand piano, sitting in all its glory on a brilliantly polished tile floor.

"Wow," I turned to Aunt Viv.

"Do you play dear? Then by all means, play something."

Resisting the temptation to play some Beatles tune, I broke into Fur Elise by Beethoven and the room filled with the sound of music. I knew God had given me a way to contact him during this desperate time in my life.

Aunt Viv expected me to clean the house, do the laundry, take the kids to the park, arrange nap time and have dinner ready for the family when she arrived at 6:30 p.m. from the office. At first, it wasn't hard but as time wore on, it was. The melon growing inside my belly was getting huge and the total disconnect my brain had to have about that melon, well… it was hard. My feelings were seeping up from the bottoms of my feet, trying to reach higher ground. My stubborn will kept pushing them back down. The melon was just a melon.

One afternoon, I had brought the kids home from the park and they were restless and were fighting me on taking naps. I was exhausted on all fronts and was ready to lose the war.

I wandered into the living room and sat at the piano, suddenly lifted by words of wisdom, "Let it Be."

I noticed all three of them out of the corner of my eye, sitting on the couch, curled up and looking comforted. I finished my song. To my surprise, all three children broke into heartfelt applause.

"Oh, Anne Marie that was good. Play more. Play us some more!"

"Will you all promise to go to sleep if I do?" I asked, knowing the answer before the question left my mouth.

"Yes!" all three chimed in unison.

Instead of putting them to sleep, my rendition of "Yellow Submarine" made them lively; they enjoyed the dickens out of it! I was enjoying it, too. Like the leader of the band, I played and the children laughed and sang. We all shouted for joy when we finished that song. I changed pace with the next one and they cuddled back on the couch. I had succeeded in getting the last bit of energy out of them.

They were asleep and I spent the next hour singing and playing to myself. It was therapeutic. I started feeling at home there.

Songs before nap time became a ritual and the kids would do almost anything I asked if I promised to sing them songs. It became a bit of an intoxicating trip for me. A mere month of such frivolity was suddenly interrupted by my water breaking one evening after dinner.

Aunt Viv took me to the hospital where I was deposited onto a cold table, screaming in pain until the doctor finally said the magic words, "You can push now." With two giant sized pushes, the baby was out and I heard it crying. My heart broke into a million pieces when I heard that cry.

"Is it a boy or a girl?" I cried out. The nurses seemed to ignore me and instead gave me a shot while the doctor began stitching my tears. "Please, please," I begged, "let me hold my baby."

"It's best if you just let this go honey," an elderly nurse said as she wrapped the baby in a toasty little white blanket. As she walked away with the precious little bundle that was my baby, I saw the tiniest little foot make its way outside the blanket. It wiggled and it seemed as if the baby was trying to signal me.

"Bye, bye," it said to me.

"Bye. Bye."

I watched with frozen tears as the nurse carried that baby out of the room and out of my life…forever.

Chapter 10
Stayin' Alive

Back home again in Indiana!" my mother sang to me as I returned to my childhood home. She was genuinely glad to see me and had been behind the scenes, coaching me to get my GED while in California and apply to colleges in Indiana.

She waived a letter around for me to read and I could tell that it was an acceptance letter from somebody.

"You got in at IU and Indiana State. You know ISU is my alma mater and it would please me to no end if you went there."

I hadn't even unpacked. There was no let down time to process the loss of a child, which is what had happened to me. No, it had been swept underneath the carpet with a swoosh of my mother's hand.

I vowed to never attend her school, and Indiana University had a reputation for being a haven for hippies. Luckily, my mother knew nothing of that. She knew that it was highly regarded, so when I announced I would be going there in the fall, she reluctantly gave in.

The next two months dragged on and when the day finally arrived when I was leaving, I started to sing in the shower, something I hadn't done for a while.

I did look at it as a new chance in my life and was grateful to both parents for giving it to me. I told them I was going to become a doctor and since IU had one of the best schools in the country, I knew I would win parental approval.

Problem was, I had not received my approval. I was so delighted to be on my own and making new friends in a new world that I did not consider the fact that I had approved this course of action in my life without weighing in on the consequences.

I dismissed it as a necessary evil and found myself taking

classes in philosophy, horseback riding and a few science classes like anatomy, biology, and chemistry.

You can tell the exact moment when your life goes off course, but only in hindsight. After living through an insincere boyfriend, trying to be a successful physician seemed logical, rational and well thought out. Problem was that I was not following my heart, I was following my head.

The mind can be a wonderful slave and a terrible master. Following the heart is the only way to live happily in this life. Understanding how to navigate that difficult path should be the goal of every human being. As I found out many a time, mistakes will be made, mistakes can help me learn and I can forgive myself for making them.

One of these was going to college. At the time, I had seen it as a way to redeem myself. As intelligent as I was, the classes tried my soul. Nothing seemed to be falling into place.

As I endured my typical academic struggle one sunny Thursday morning, I found a friendly face in my chemistry class. His name was Craig Channing and he was handsome, with soft blondish locks and eyes that were crystal clear blue.

"You look like you could use some help," he offered as my books came crashing down on the floor in lab.

"You don't know the half of it," I managed.

He gathered them up and put them neatly on the lab table, never taking his eyes off of me.

"This is all stuff I've already learned in high school. I looked at the syllabus and it seems like everything is a repeat for me."

"Lucky you," I said a bit flippantly.

"I can help you if you want. I am studying to be a cardiologist."

"Wow," I said a bit stunned. "You already know that you want to be a cardiologist? I'm just trying to be a doctor… any kind of doctor will do."

Craig laughed infectiously.

"Well, then, let's start by being lab partners. If you want to get into the Indiana University medical school, you'd better get all A's or as close to that as is humanly possible for you."

I searched his face, looking for any indication that he was like Terrence. His smile was softer, more genuine, and he seemed to be much more intelligent. Terrence hated any and all science and math classes and preferred to be plucking on a guitar rather than studying for any test.

I found myself pondering the possibilities, but I held myself back. After what had happened to me, I had no intentions of getting screwed over again by a man.

Weeks passed and Craig began to grow on me. He took me to the opera and I was entranced by the music and the performers. I could go downtown with him, enjoy a Stromboli, and have a marvelous time. We began to kiss and lo and behold, he was even good at that as well.

By the time summer break came around, he began to sleep over regularly. I had discovered a new resource on campus: Planned Parenthood. Their office was in town in an old Victorian house that had been converted into offices, and I started to take birth control pills. It was against what the church taught but as I saw it, the church never had to go through getting pregnant and giving up your baby. Their knowledge on this subject was so dogmatic. Walk a mile in my shoes, I would often think, then legislate your morality.

The summer was agonizingly long and I found a job packing rat bait for an exterminator. I would spend hours in the warehouse, stuffing plastic baggies with a cornmeal filled with poison. To pass the time without losing my mind, I sang.

"God is love…and he who abides in love, abides in God and God in him."

The warehouse acoustics accentuated my voice, and I would dig deep in my diaphragm to give it a bluesy, soulful touch. One afternoon, I turned around to find my boss, Melvin, staring at me as I sang. Seeing him, I was startled and stopped.

"No, please, keep singing. Your voice sounded like Aretha Franklin."

That was a huge compliment that I felt I didn't deserve. However, I was delighted that he felt I was that good.

Mel kept a beat with his foot and clapped his hands as I sang "Respect." I could see that he was genuinely enjoying it.

"You're good! You can sing like a howling wolf." I really considered that a fabulous compliment since there actually was someone named Howlin' Wolf!

"What did you say you're going to college to be?"

"A doctor."

We both laughed at the absurd sound of that answer, but it was the only thing that got me through the summer.

Chapter 11
Ziggy Stardust

Well, a man shall leave his mother, and a woman leave her home. And they shall travel on to where the two shall be as one.

Sometime in the middle of the first semester, Craig got a romantic notion up his ass and at the tender age of 19.7 years of age, we wed in a fantastic Christmas wedding.

Father Savio was asked to preside over the wedding and he was grinning from ear to ear when he met us.

"Craig, I can't tell you what a wonderful girl you have in Anne Marie."

"Oh, I know sir."

"Don't call me sir, just call me Father."

Father Savio had moved into the 1970's with grace. The Bishop had ordered Father S to close down the coffeehouse in December 1969 because those two Berkeley students had returned one evening and brought in another joint to smoke after the old people left. Nevertheless, Father persevered in his quest to experience grounding in his religion.

The coffeehouse was resurrected a few times during the early 70's in a few different church basements in the area, but it was never quite the same.

I had been whisked away, first taken downstate to be a student and now to be a bride and housewife. My mother had decided that being married to a doctor trumped getting the college education.

"She's marrying a doctor...a cardiologist." She was practically gloating when she said it to friends and family.

I didn't want to go to school anyhow and Craig was a wonderful man. I felt safe. After Terrence, it was mandatory for me to feel safe with a man. He made me feel safe. Our married campus apartment was small but I made it cozy. He thrived in this environment and was easily accepted into medical school in just three years, on the Dean's List, with a perfect 4.0 GPA.

Rock and roll was still on my radar. I played the radio while I cooked, when I cleaned, in our car, still singing every tune. I used that as a life raft because as the years passed, my rock and roll got mellow. Sweet Baby James Taylor, Carole King and soft rock tunes filled my performances in the shower. I took to stretching my repertoire with some Marvin Gay, Gladys Knight and Smoky Robinson. For fun, I would perform for Craig using the wooden spoon I cooked with as a microphone.

My world expanded in Craig's second year of medical school with the birth of our son, Caleb. Craig struggled with the name at first, telling me he found it a bit "undignified."

"Caleb sounds like a hippie name," he told me.

"No, it's the name of a warrior. It's not hippie. Hippie is Zarathustra Zack Water Bearer, now that's hippie."

I had a talent to disarm Craig and get my way. Upon his graduation from medical school, I was holding my daughter, Mia, in my arms with Caleb standing by my side. Thinking his family was complete, Craig was going to get a vasectomy but work sidetracked him and the following year, our second son, Michael, was born.

This deviation from the master plan irked Craig. He also found it odd that I wanted to name him Michael.

"It's a rather common name don't you think?" he said on the night before his baptism.

"He is one of four archangels. Only four! And this one has dominion over all the angels. It is a very, very powerful name, Craig."

Not knowing much about the Catholic religion, or any other religion, put Craig at a disadvantage when he found himself in conversations about it.

"It's fine, Anne Marie," he said, kissing my head adoringly. "Michael it is."

Having three toddlers was a huge responsibility, and so was managing my life as a doctor's wife. I found myself on committees, golf outings and all the things that were important to Craig. That year for Christmas, my mom got me a subscription to "Better Homes and Gardens" magazine, a staple read for her generation. I winced when

I saw it but I put on my usual happy face.

Why couldn't it be something I would love to read? I mused. I really want a subscription to Rolling Stone Magazine.

Well, I didn't get Rolling Stone for Christmas, but I did get a visit from old college friends: Amy, JJ, and Corey, girls I had known when I first came to school and roomed with in the dorm.

We made ourselves comfortable on my back porch. Corey had asked me if it was ok to bring over some pot.

"Wow, pot," I said with some alarm. "I haven't smoked that in years, well, since I had Caleb … so that would be …" I visibly struggled to make sense of the numbers.

"Too long," Corey sighed directly into the phone. "I am bringing a little for you, you sound like you need it."

"I do?" That seemed a little disconcerting to me. I was, however, really wanting to connect with old friends. Life as a mother was rewarding to me but there was the constant "itch" for something more. The only thing that scratched that itch was to listen to rock. I started listening to some T-Rex, Moody Blues and Led Zeppelin. Craig even indulged me in tickets to the Zeppelin concert in Chicago. I was hypnotized by Robert Plant and Jimmy Page. They created magic on stage. I sat mesmerized in my seat, knowing that Plant was singing in my key. I longed to sing with him or at least sing some thirds underneath him in the chorus. I dared not even think about such a thing. Rock and roll was something I listened to and observed. It was if I was living my life about 2 inches out of my body. What has happened to me in the last 5 years? Nothing tastes sweet.

Corey was just as I remembered her. She had the same ponytail and crisp blouses look that she wore five years ago. Amy and JJ looked like they had turned into corporate cadets. It seemed odd that we wound up on my back porch rolling a big fat joint.

I inhaled deeply, enjoying the delicious taste. It was Maui Waui and it smelled great. I remembered the first time with the Berkeley students and it was just as enjoyable then as now.

"Hey, don't bogart that joint," JJ said impatiently.

"Don't bogart that joint…" We all sang the phrase from the old hit song together and then laughed.

I smoked like a little piggy, asking Corey to roll another and then another. We finally went back into the den and Amy brought out a few new albums that she wanted to play.

I shuffled through the albums before I stopped on one that completely caught me off guard. The album The Rise and Fall of Ziggy Stardust by David Bowie had been my absolute favorite when I bought it in 1973.

"Ziggy, I had almost forgotten how much I loved you," I said to myself under my breath. I had played this album a thousand times, adoring the exquisite rock star character that Mr. Bowie had designed. "You were so brilliant," I whispered under my breath.

"Still am," a voiced boomed out of nowhere. I did a double take, not sure if I had heard something or not. Mmm. I must be too high, I thought, scolding myself for losing control.

JJ grabbed a new album she had just purchased at Karma Records. It was the latest David Bowie album, Station to Station. She popped it on the record player. She smiled at me as she put her arm around Amy and their looks reassured me that my intuitions about their relationship were correct.

Huh, who would have guessed? I thought. They looked so straight in college.

The very first guitar riff sent me into the stratosphere.

My heart hammered with such intensity that I was afraid I might faint. I couldn't help but get the uncanny feeling that he was singing that song to me. My anxiousness heightened and I felt the need to get up and walk around my living room. My fidgeting had awoken my sleeping toddlers and nothing can kill a girl's party like a poopy diaper.

I finished my day folding a mountain of laundry as I sang to myself.

"TVC 15" - It was off the Bowie album. The song came bubbling up from my consciousness and it jolted me into a different awareness.

"Agh, what is it with these lyrics, I keep getting the feeling that I am being communicated to by someone…or something," I whispered to myself.

Later that evening, in bed, I recounted the day's activities to Craig. As usual, he was not even listening to me but turned on Sports Report to get the final score on the Bulls.

Tonight for some reason, although Craig had done this a thousand times before, it stung. I felt hurt and wanted his comfort. I slid up next to him, rubbing him seductively with my hands.

"Bulls 103; Celtics 101," the sportscaster announced.

"Yes!" shouted Craig.

"Hey, what's more important here, baby." I slid my hands around his cock and squeezed gently in a pulsating grip.

"Ouch, hey watch it, honey. That hurt."

It was like throwing gasoline on a fire to put it out. His insensitive response pushed a button in me. Almost as if by instinct, I grabbed the long-handled Westmoreland milk glass vase on my nightstand and hurled it at the TV.

Crash! Although I was aiming at the TV, I hit the wall, smashing the expensive vase into pieces.

"Jesus Christ, Anne Marie, what in the hell is the matter with you? What are you so goddamned pissed off about?! I'm the one who has my dick in a death grip."

I wanted to scream at him, recounting the many times any romance in our bedroom would be silenced by his snoring, his ball games, or an endless recant of everything that went wrong at St. Anthony's hospital that day. However, I had walked down that path once too often and I grabbed my pillow and my blanket and went downstairs.

Even though it was a chilly October evening, I went out on our back screened porch, cuddling up on the wicker couch with the plump overstuffed cushions and peered out at the night sky.

"You know, David Bowie," I professed to the night sky, "I am just as talented as you are. I have this cool character, too."

I sounded like a jealous little kid. "I'm as good as you are" was a dialogue both narcissistic and beneath me. I slumped back into the cushions, burying my head into the comforter, tears now flowing down my cheeks. Sobs seemed to be close by as I thought of Ziggy Stardust.

My costume was hidden in a trunk in the attic. Long black leather boots with huge spiked heels, my black fringe jacket and the lovely black French bustier, cupping my perfect, perky tits to tease and titillate. I began to be seized with a dark deep desire to be paddled by one of the nuns back at my Catholic grade school.

69

I needed the desire to be that character, my Black Jet princess, and sing her songs to be spanked out of me. I fantasized about being bent over Sister Hermanita's knees while she whacked away at my exposed white, soon to be pink fanny. Crying in pain, I watched the full moon drift over the kids' backyard swing set, trying to figure out what it was that was making me cry.

Drifting off with the faint whiff of undeniable satisfaction surrounding the comforter, I started singing another favorite song…

Masturbation overtook the pleasure-filled comforter. The moon nodded in approval as the climax filled me with such a strong shudder that I moaned softly.

"Oh my God, I am so jealous of you David. I am so jealous that I am coming all over this damned comforter and I am having a fucking cosmic, yes, cosmic orgasm. How many months have I waited to have this absolutely divine pleasure?"

The moon faded as the sun rose to greet my back porch shenanigans. In the distance, I saw the light going on in our bathroom. Craig is up. I jumped in the shower to rinse off my lust, then headed for the kids' bedroom where I heard Michael.

My little three-year-old wonder, Michael, was playing drums with some of the pails and shovels that he and Mia had collected over the summer. The joy on his face broke through all my feelings of isolation. I loved being a mother.

Chapter 12
Dazed and Confused

Craig received a huge promotion to practice medicine in Miami, Florida as the head of a very elite and prestigious cardiology group in Miami Beach.. We had movers come to our home and pack everything up and whisked it away to southern Florida. I cried for days after moving into a neighborhood in south Miami that had only one other English speaking person. I didn't seem to fit into this world at all but I kept trying to hold it all together for the sake of my husband and three beautiful children.

Days and nights passed in a blur for a few years as I carefully cared for and nurtured my three angels. I never forgot my first born, the sting of that parting still haunting me somewhere in the back of my mind. I never even knew if that baby was a girl or a boy but sometimes in my dreams, I would see that tiny little foot waving good-bye. It was so poignantly agonizing that I thought about getting involved with a local adoption agency to see if I could locate the baby. However, my three children kept me so busy and Craig was so painfully against it that I relented.

A crisp September morning in 1980 found me dressing my sweet darling Caleb in his new school outfit. He was on his way to Pinecrest Elementary kindergarten and I could not have been prouder. He held his little hand in the air as he walked into school and waved at me. Some moments are like snapshots in your mind that you can never forget. However, that day I had a camera and took the picture for his children to enjoy someday.

Mia and Michael were waving good-bye. We were going to my friend Annie's place. I watched them in the rear view mirror as we sped along the highway, one busying himself with the plastic key chain I had mounted on his car seat and the other hugging her teddy

71

bear, Andy, to her chest, showing him all the tall buildings as we drove through downtown Miami on the way to Miami Beach. As I drove past the hospital, I remembered that Craig had told me he was performing surgery today on an elderly man who he thought too frail for a triple bypass heart surgery. The family had insisted.

"Want juice, momma," Mia chanted from the back seat. My thoughts descended on the little coffee shop down the street from the hospital. I was really dragging myself and decided that we could stop for a juice and coffee break at Molly's Café. It was a bright and cheery place.

"Ok, baby, we are stopping here for drinks," I said as we pulled into the parking lot. With Michael in my arms, and Mia clinging to her Andy bear and my hand, we walked into the restaurant. There was a familiar voice at the far end of the café and we all walked towards the sound. It was Craig's voice.

I turned the corner to find Craig in the back booth, hugging and kissing a blonde nurse.

My shock was so complete that I dropped my precious Michael as I yelled out, "What in the fuck is all this?"

Michael began screaming, Mia started crying and the happy sunny café turned into a hurricane of emotional upheaval.

I picked up Michael, realizing what I had done, and Craig rushed to pick up Mia who was working herself into a terrible cry. In the chaos, the bimbo slithered out the back entrance of the café without a word.

I looked into Craig's eyes and wondered who I was looking at. His eyes tried to avert mine.

"Let's get the kids back into the car, Anne Marie," Craig stated with authority.

"Need juice," Mia shouted. "Momma, need juice."

"Sit back down in the booth, you piece of shit. Your kids and your wife are thirsty, you are going to get them juice and coffee and we are going to talk about this right now. I don't care if you have somebody in the emergency room dying of a gunshot wound, you will sit here and order drinks for your family."

The tone and gravitas were so authoritative that the kids and the husband sat down and the kids both stopped crying. It was at that opportune moment that the waitress arrived to take our order.

72

"How is everyone today?" she blurted out as if she had decided to block out all the noise and confusion coming from the back booth.

We sat in silence for the five or six minutes it took the waitress to get our order. Both kids huddled around me, instinctively feeling the tension in the air. Mia began sucking her thumb. I gave Michael his juice bottle and he leaned against my breast, sucking out all the apple juice he could get.

"Mia, quit sucking your thumb, honey," Craig said. He was obviously trying to gain some sort of control over the situation.

"I don't think it's such a bad idea considering the circumstances. I feel like sucking on my thumb right now myself."

My air of authority had never been so strong. I was furious over the situation and wasn't about to let him have a shred of dignity.

As Craig opened his mouth, ready to defend himself, his pager went off. He looked down at the pager and it said, "Policeman down, gunshot wound to chest, need you in ER immediately." He handed it to me to read because I think even he would've thought he was lying. The unlikely coincidence gave him the perfect excuse to dash and he couldn't leave fast enough.

"We'll talk about this tonight, honey," he said flippantly as if nothing had happened.

Later that evening after getting the kids to sleep, Craig came rolling up the driveway. Even though I was seething in anger, I held my temper and tried to be polite as I offered him some dinner, braised pot roast with homemade biscuits and mango salad. Finally, I needed to take some pressure off the pressure cooker.

"Why are you rolling in at 9:30 at night?"

Craig turned and glared at me.

"I have just put in ten hours to save a man's life. Do you know what that makes me, Anne Marie?"

"A hero?"

"No, Anne Marie, just tired. Very fucking tired."

Sometimes deep down inside you there is a lever you can pull that gets your life back on course. I feared pulling this lever because I instinctively knew that it would bring hardship. However, I checked my fear at the door this time because my heart was asking me to make my husband accountable for his actions earlier. A heart that was breaking.

"I don't give a shit if you had to stitch back together half of the 7th Cavalry. Why were you sitting across the street making out with some blonde bimbo nurse?"

"Because I was on break and I needed a little down time."

"Down time?!" I roared like Hagar the Horrible.

Craig pushed the mango salad so far away from him that the bowl slid off the table and broke.

"Don't you lecture me. You can stay home all day and play with your children, cooking meals, which you love to do and not worry about a dime. I have to go to that hospital every day and make decisions that affect whether people live or die. Live or die...Do you have any idea the type of stress I am under?"

"So you go play kissy face with some nurse to relieve the stress?"

"Jesus, Anne Marie, listen to you. This is the 80's not the 50's. What part of the Women's Liberation Movement left you behind?"

Craig was up on his feet, pacing the kitchen as he spoke, his voice ascending at each crescendo word. I tried to speak, but he was like a Pentecostal preacher who was just getting started.

"Your lifestyle is more like Lucy Ricardo than Peg Bundy. You have a college degree why don't you use it? Whatever happened to your career aspirations?"

"What career aspirations?" I was yelling at the top of my lungs.

"I hope you think there is more to life than raising a family." Craig was clearly jockeying for position, but I was truly surprised at this "modern" attitude he was blabbering away about.

"I want to have an open marriage, Anne Marie. Nicole and her husband have an agreement to sleep with other people if they so choose and I think it's really helped their marriage."

"Wait a minute, how did we go from career aspirations to sleeping around? And who the hell is Nicole?"

Worlds collided as I began to put two and two together about who she was and what had been going on behind my back.

"You fucking asshole!" I screamed at the top of my lungs. That note blew the top off the pressure cooker and woke Michael. His crying in the nursery ended the "discussion" in the kitchen.

I spent the next hour rocking Michael back to sleep.

"Open marriage," I repeated the phrase over and over to myself. "What the hell does he mean about the 1980's anyway?"

"He's getting all Sheena Easton and Prince on me."

When Michael dropped off, I gently placed him in his bed and walked over to the lanai on the other side of the house. Our beautiful pool shimmered in the gentle breeze of a warm Miami night. The moon had risen over the small grove of mango trees that lined the eastern edge of the property. I sat back on my favorite bamboo recliner with the overstuffed cushions. Craig had long since gone to bed and since the master bedroom was on the other side of the house, I knew he wouldn't hear the radio. I turned it on and found the joint that I had tucked under the ponytail palm plant.

"Oh, fabulous, the new David Bowie song is on," I thought as I lit up my joint.

I took a long drag of some Maui Waui that one of the women in my playdate group had given me as payment for taking her to the grocery. "Ah," I thought as I took another toke, "this is relaxing, just what I needed."

I stood up, picked a hibiscus flower, put it between my teeth, and began dancing around the pool. It was a bit intoxicating.

A cool breeze wafted through my hair and I felt goose bumps along the back of my neck. My eyes lulled shut as I continued to dance around the pool.

My eyes opened as the luscious moonlight beamed down from the heavens. I felt blinded for just a moment and when my focus came back, I was standing in front of the stage. On stage, David Bowie was performing the very song I was hearing.

"The serious moonlight."

I'd heard about this type of experience before and the term was "remote viewing." He was actually performing this song and I was standing in front of the stage. Amazing!

My body quivered at the sound of those lyrics and watching him perform at such close range was beyond intoxicating. Every fiber of my being was titillating with the pulsating backbeat of the song.

The song ended as I looked back up at the moonlight, and just as quickly as the vision had come, it left.

The sunlight and Mia simultaneously woke me in the morning, one shining brightly in my face and the other tugging on my pajama top. I felt sluggish, as if I had been heavily intoxicated the night before with some sort of magic elixir.

No time to dwell on anything but the present as Michael was crying from his crib and Caleb was busy trying to put together a peanut butter and jelly sandwich. I rescued Michael, assisted Caleb, and put Mia in her chair at the breakfast table. While I was making breakfast, Craig came in, dressed in doctor, ready for another day at the hospital.

"Good morning," he said to everyone while kissing me on the forehead. I wanted to puke, but instead I put on a good face for the kids. He took Michael off my hip and put him in his high chair, grabbing the plate of bacon that I had just finished frying. Craig was a good multi-tasker and genuinely loved his children so we sat and ate breakfast as if we were "The Cleavers."

Thoughts of last night started to appear but before I had a chance to process them, Craig got up, ready to leave, Michael needed his diaper changed and Caleb reminded me that we needed to get him to school.

Craig grabbed a briefcase and bounded out the door, calling out behind my turned back, "Open marriage, think about it."

My attitude sharpened with rage, yet I did what I always did, which was to get Mia and Michael dressed. I could always keep a lid on my emotions when I was around my kids but it was boiling around the edges.

As I dropped Caleb off at the school parking lot, he turned to me inquisitively.

"What is an open marriage, mom?"

"I have no idea, my darling," I said kissing his head. "Have a fun day at kindergarten and we will pick you up after school."

I drove off, pondering why the 1980's was deemed the no holds-barred-decade. Nothing is off limits and no rules need apply except self-gratification.

"I miss the 70's," I mused, "Seems like there was more soul searching then. Everyone was trying to find God. Now, everybody wants to fuck everybody."

I tried to take my focus and put it somewhere else.

Today's epiphany began at lunch. I would meet in Miami Springs regularly with several other moms and we would have all the kids in someone's backyard. Andrea had a huge gym set with swings and climbing bars and even a rope swing for the older kids. Patsy had a huge avocado tree and the kids built forts and kingdoms in its boughs. Sandy lived across the street from the city park and I had the big swimming pool with palm trees. Today we were at Sandy's. The four of us were buzzing up a blender full of cafe con leche. Sandy made the best espresso as she used freshly-ground beans from a gourmet coffee shop. Until motherhood, I did not even think of coffee. I always had plenty of energy. Now, I found it intoxicating.

"Buzz me up a strong one today, Sandy," I said with exuberance.

Sandy laughed and soon we were all drinking our coffee super drinks out of large A&W root beer mugs. I drank mine down like an old sailor who had just come in from a fierce storm.

"Whoa, Anne Marie, you better slow your mustang down," chortled Andrea. Her voice gave a fleeting resemblance to the old Wilson Picket song.

Patsy chimed in, and everyone started singing along and clapping their hands to keep the beat. I became overwhelmed with the urge to belt out the next line loud and clear, like I was singing lead in an old time tent revival spiritual.

Everyone howled with laughter. I had cut loose and sang it out, loud and clear, and now stood staring at the three of them, laughing and applauding.

"Who knew you were so fucking talented. Damn, where did you get that saucy voice lady?" Andrea seemed to have a hint of jealousy in her tone.

Patsy, softer and more loving, jumped up clapping and ranting on.

"You were good, you were sooooooooo good."

I stared like a deer in the headlights. Their accolades were appreciated but what made me stop and stare in fear was the ethereal looking image of David Bowie standing about ten feet behind the table.

"You should go and perform tomorrow night at the open mic. They have one tonight at The Hunter's Lounge, you know."

As Bowie spoke these words, so did Patsy. Simultaneously. It even sounded like a verse from a song, with Pats singing a third under Bowie's stellar lead.

The universe had cracked open. Beings such as Bowie had entered through some mysterious portal. Patsy, who often visited psychics on Miami Beach, seemed to be the friend with the most sympathetic vibrational pattern.

It became too disruptive, this clash of realities. I turned to shrug off the vision and mumbled something about going to the bathroom.

All the way back to Caleb's school, I questioned myself mercilessly about the validity of what I had just seen. Fearful that I was having a nervous breakdown due to Craig's indiscretions, I pulled into a local fast food drive-through to get some more coffee. I nursed my cup of coffee as I picked up my kid from school and when I finally finished making dinner, I licked my lips with the last drops. The dinner was finished and I had created another gourmet delight. Roasted lamb with small dill potatoes, acorn squash soufflé, glazed asparagus and a strawberry rhubarb pie for dessert.

"Ah, I can cook," I whispered to myself. Just then, the phone rang. It was Craig.

"Hey, I'm working late tonight, just put my dinner in the fridge." He sounded so innocent but my intuition told me he was not.

"What are you working on?" I asked innocently. He knew I was baiting him.

"What do you care, I'm making money, I'll see you later. Bye."

He hung up the phone and all I heard was a loud click.

I stared at my dinner and the three small faces of joy that were looking at me. Even though they seemed too young to appreciate it, they all ate heartily and then went to bed with not as much as a whimper.

Perhaps it was God being kind to me, because I felt so fragile that I knew one child making trouble would send me over the edge. We read the story of Pinocchio before going to sleep. I found myself singing.

"Hi-dittle-dee-dee, an actor's life for me."

As we got to the part where the fox tricks Pinocchio into

joining the circus, I mused on these words as perfectly fitting. If there was something other than a mother that I wanted to be, it was an actress. Thinking back to the many plays I starred in during my freshman and sophomore years in high school, I wondered what my life might have been like if I had taken that road.

The kids all drifted off peacefully and I took to tidying up and busying myself, trying not to think about what Craig was doing. After the dishes were done, I sat in the big easy chair and picked up the newspaper to see what might distract me from my ugly thoughts.

Skimming through the Lifetime section, I happened across a quarter-page article about the Hunter's Lounge. Tomorrow night was indeed an open mic there from 7-9 p.m.

"How in the hell did Bowie know about this?"

"Well, it was actually Patsy who knew."

"Then who was the man with piercing eyes and blonde hair?"

The conversation I was having with myself began to drive me nuts. It didn't make sense and again my thoughts of mental instability due to the rocky state of my marriage began to resurface.

"So what you're saying, Craig, is that the perfect marriage is an open marriage," I scoffed to myself.

Perfect marriage. The thought hung in the deep recesses of my living room cathedral ceiling. I thought I had the perfect marriage. My mind wandered back through my days at the university in Bloomington and the birth of our children. Craig was so wonderful. He was like superman. He spent quality time with us, breezed through his medical school when we moved to Indianapolis and was even at Michael's birth during his cardiology residency.

However, since moving to Miami and the sunny tropical paradise with year-round summers, things had changed. Working at Mt. Zion, he was asked to do long hours and long meetings, leaving no time for us. I had often felt more like a widow than a wife in the last year.

Craig crawled in at 1 a.m. and I laid there faking sleep.

In the morning, he was his charming self again, fussing over the kids and kissing me on the forehead before he left.

"Shit," I said rubbing my forehead. "What kind of a great Aunt Millie kiss was that?"

I dropped off Caleb and drove like a banshee to my mom's

playgroup.

"Do you think he is cheating on me?" I asked the girls over coffee at Andrea's big table.

"Yes," they all chimed in unison.

I was shocked. I could not believe that my rock solid seven-year marriage was on the rocks.

"Have you ever heard of the seven year itch?" Andrea always brought in the Hollywood manufactured side to life. "It was a movie with Tom Ewell and Marilyn Monroe."

"Yeah, I remember watching it one Saturday night while I was babysitting for the twins down the street from mom and dad's house."

There was a moment when all of us shared an extremely worried look.

"What about going to open mic night at the Hunter's Lounge?" Patsy was the eternal optimist and decided to shift the conversation to calmer waters.

"I don't know, I don't have a babysitter for the kids," I said, groping for excuses.

"Leave them with me tonight, Anne Marie. I am happy to watch them, Caleb and Dakota have such a great time together, and since they are both in school this year, they really haven't had too much time to play. Oh, c'mon Anne Marie," Sandy said with a certain demanding tone.

"Andrea and I will go with you," said Patsy. "You will need a fan club in the audience."

I looked at my friends and a small tear came to my eye. They were being so supportive and I knew they were trying to give me a new focus.

"Do you think I could pull it off? I mean, do you really think I have a rock and roll voice? I mean, I sang choir in church and in high school. This is a big difference."

My insecurities were beating on me and I was succumbing to it. I had performed rock at the coffeehouse. Or was it folk? Or folk rock? I couldn't tell I was so aflutter with emotion.

"No different, just do it," Patsy said with great compassion.

I gave a quick thought to letting them in on Bowie's take on things but decided that, again, I did not want to appear mentally off.

Their support was like water to a thirsty man. I was grateful for their enthusiasm.

Deep down in my soul, I felt as if something had gone back on track in my life. I was about to give myself permission to fulfill a secret dream. I was going to perform on stage. I was going to sing rock and roll to the world, well, at least the rock and roll world of the Hunter's Lounge in Miami Springs, Florida.

Chapter 13
Stairway to Heaven

I skimmed through all the clothes in my closet to find just the right outfit. I went through dresses, jackets, and just about everything else I owned and the only thing that caught my eye was an old black leather jacket of Craig's. I found a white t-shirt of mine and I tore off a sleeve and pulled the collar of the shirt down over my right shoulder. I hung the jacket to the other side and pulled out a pair of old jeans from twenty years ago. It still had a peace patch on it as well as other numerous repairs. It was a symbol of my moxie during those years that Craig was in school and I was proud of it.

I stood in front of the mirror. How James Dean I looked, almost a bit "butch," but once I undid the barrette that I usually put in my hair and let it cascade down, I was pleased. God had given me gorgeous dark hair, big brown eyes and a taut body. I felt so confident, I could hardly wait.

After dropping the kids off at Sandy's, I picked up Andrea and Patsy and we headed over to the bar. I walked up to the management and signed up for the open mic. They escorted me to the back stage area where the other musicians were hanging out.

Most of the performers were guys with guitars, and suddenly I realized that I did not have any musical accompaniment. Why is the devil in the details? I, sure as hell, didn't know.

I panicked. What was I thinking? I sat down next to a longhaired guitar player who was picking out the melody line to "Stairway to Heaven."

"Nice picking," I said, trying to ease into the conversation.

"Thanks," he said looking right into my eyes.

"Do you know 'Whole Lotta Love' too?" I asked with a begging tone in my voice.

"My name is Randy Whaley," he said, extending his hand. I shook it, confused as to where the conversation was headed. Then he plugged in his guitar to the amp he had with him, set his distortion level, and started banging out the first few riffs.

My eyes lit up like a pumpkin on Halloween. Even though he seemed like he liked me, I knew not to assume that anyone would do something for nothing. I pulled out a twenty-dollar bill from my wallet and put it in his guitar case.

"Will you accompany me on that tune"?

Maybe he was just in need of some cash, but he nodded his head and we quietly rehearsed the whole tune so we knew where the breaks were and when he was going to do his solo.

I actually got quite excited by his mastery of a Jimmy Page guitar solo. He was good. I felt relieved.

I heard the applause from the audience as the performer before me was leaving the stage.

"Next up, we have a raven-haired fox… please give a warm welcome to Anne Marie… Anne Marie Pussy."

A drunken roar came from the crowd, mostly older men who were the chronic barflies in the lounge.

As I passed the MC, I looked at him and screeched, "Anne Marie Pussy? That's not my name!"

"Sorry doll, but you didn't tell me what your last name was, so I gave you one." He gave me a little slap on the ass.

"Knock 'em dead, sweetie."

Randy rolled past him, guitar in hand, as if he had considered bashing the MC with it, but instead strutted on by and set up on stage.

I looked out into the audience, searching for Patsy and Andrea. Instead, I found Craig and Nicole, his co-worker, sitting at the bar. When she saw me, she instinctively grabbed his left arm and put it around her waist, much like a dog pissing on an area to mark their territory.

Terror struck deep in my heart as visions of the performance at the coffeehouse awakened. I struggled to make sure I was going to keep my composure this time and not make it some kind of personal vendetta.

Craig sat there with his mouth hanging down to his knees.

Rather than focus on them, I turned to Randy to signal my readiness to begin. He obliged by kicking in with a rousing opening riff. I opened my mouth and let it rip.

I was prancing around on that small wooden stage like a cat in heat. I held onto my voice like a lifeline from God. Robert Plant and I both liked the same key. I belted out my voice to the very back of the bar and I watched as I mesmerized the audience. Craig never did get his jaw off the floor. At one point, he even threw off Nicole's arm. He along with everyone else at the bar was up on their feet, dancing along with just a singer and guitar player on open mic night.

Led Zeppelin was definitely being appreciated in the small town of Miami Springs. Randy played the shit out of that Jimmy solo. For the cheap, crappy little Fender guitar he had, the song was stellar Zeppelin.

I grabbed the round cement pole toward the back of the stage. It seemed to be holding up the little add-on of the backstage area. It felt sturdy so I shimmied up while I started singing the chorus.

I slid down the pole as I reached the floor, singing softly.

"Wanna Whole Lotta Love."

The place exploded in cheers, whistles, applause and general revelry, peppered with some light debauchery, as I witnessed a man shooting a stream of pee into the air to celebrate.

I ran off the stage, my heart beating so loudly in my chest it was even drowning out the applause. My hands were wet and shaking, it was as if a huge current of electricity had been running through the entire song.

Randy began picking the opening melody for "Stairway to Heaven," and the crowd began to hush down and listen.

As he sang, I realized that Randy's voice was weak…he was massacring the song.

Then, I did the unthinkable. I came back out and grabbed a mic as I did.

Randy sang a third under, I took the Plant lead key, and the two voices gave a nice haunting delivery. I was in front of Randy's so I could not see him, but just heard him.

My high-powered voice drowned Randy out but he kept playing. Andrea and Patsy said he had a scowl on his face for the rest of the song from that point on.

Randy's voice had dropped out so I kicked it up a notch. I wondered if he was going to stop playing guitar but I heard a strong guitar threading though the vocals, holding them together.

With a swift stroke, Randy changed chords and began to play the wind down and tag our lead as if he was trying to trick me into making a mistake. I seamlessly flowed with the music.

I had the crowd right where I wanted them. My voice was so powerful that it was holding everything together at that moment, no matter what the guitarist, the husband, his girlfriend or the barflies were doing, I ruled as queen of this bar.

The roar from the crowd was deafening as I left the stage. Randy brushed by me and turned to confront me once we were back stage.

"Just who in the hell do you think you are? I didn't agree to just be your guitarist."

"Really," I said with sauce, "twenty dollars said you did."

"Not both songs, I planned on singing Stairway to Heaven."

"Oh, I'm sorry," I said with thick sarcasm, "I thought I was helping you out because you sucked at the vocals. Your guitar work was great, but if you play Zeppelin, somebody's got to step up to the plate with the vocals… so I did. You're welcome!"

"You pompous fucking bitch," Randy was now screaming at me with a hint of hostility.

"Fuck you," I said bitterly.

At that moment, the manager of the bar came back to try and break things up. Our fight was bleeding through the walls, someone else was on stage performing, and it was disruptive.

Randy stuck up his middle finger, "Fuck you, you fucking bitch."

"OK, people, take your artistic disputes outside." The manager stood between the two of us.

"No, fuck you." I held up both my middle fingers.

I decided to leave rather than continue and risk pissing off the manager of the Hunter's Lounge. I ducked out a small back exit and started walking toward Sandy's house, which was just a few blocks away.

I walked quickly in the humid evening air, lost in my thoughts, when I heard a voice.

"Well that went well."

I instantly recognized it as Bowie, but he was nowhere to be seen. I looked up at the stars in the sky and said, "I don't need your input right now so just go away."

When I got back to Sandy's, Andrea and Patsy were already there.

"We were so worried about you when we heard you left in a huff. The manager told us you got into a fight with your guitar player!" Patsy was her usual motherly self, trying to look out after my best interests.

"He's not my guitar player. He is just some stupid jerk who happens to be a talented guitar player. I paid him, but he was more interested in being the 'star' than in the success of the gig." It was obvious that I had worked myself into a real lather over this.

"Well, I hate to admit this," Andrea stated with some reserve, "but you were fabulous. You sounded great and you had all the moves. You are definitely rock star material."

"Oh my God, yes!" chimed in Patsy. "You are a rock star! You need to leave Craig and go to LA, find a band, and cut a record and be a rock star. That will serve Craig right for being such a dick to you."

I thought about that all the way home. Driving down the Palmetto freeway, the lights became like one huge white light and it was very hard to see. When I pulled into the driveway, Craig's Mercedes Benz was parked in my spot.

"How annoying, why is it that I feel like the evening has been one big pissing match."

The kids were all asleep so I just tucked them in and went into the guest room and locked the door. Sometime around 1:30am, I heard a knock at my door.

"Hey Anne Marie, c'mon sweetie, unlock the door, can't we talk?" I rolled over and covered my ears with a pillow. Craig, his open marriage, Nicole, Randy the stupid but brilliant guitar player, my crazy friends, rock and roll music… David Bowie… they could all just go away.

Morning broke on me like a sledgehammer over a piece of granite. Just because you don't want to deal with something the night before, doesn't mean it will go away. Most of the time, it multiplies.

I wandered into the kitchen to find Craig feeding the kids. Caleb's lunch was packed and a big country breakfast being served in the Florida room.

"Wow. Bacon, bagels, French toast, omelets, fresh-squeezed orange juice... did you quit your job at the hospital to become a short order cook?"

"I wanted to show my wife just how much I love her. Was I successful?"

There was lovable old Craig. I knew he might surface. He even dropped the "w" word. WIFE. He was either honestly seeking forgiveness or just looking for a new angle to use in his continual need to control our marriage.

"I don't know. Is this something that is part of the open marriage?"

Caleb, ever alert to the new buzzword in his parents' lives, popped in.

"What's an open marriage, daddy?" he asked with intention and directness.

Craig was visibly uncomfortable with the question.

"We can talk about that another time, buddy. Finish your breakfast and daddy will drive you to school."

I wanted to pounce on the moment and use it to give Craig a new asshole but I held back, knowing that my precious children were not to be harmed. As I cleared away the table, a new feeling came over me. In spite of all the craziness of my marital affairs, I felt like my life was back on track. I was a good performer. I did a great job of covering the Zeppelin tunes. My voice can command a theater, bar, or stadium. I knew what that song needed to "sell it." I didn't want to pursue a career in counseling or use my college degree. I knew in that moment that I wanted to sing. I loved to sing. I loved to perform. I wanted to write songs and design cool outfits that go along with it. I was just as good as David Bowie. Maybe better.

Ha. That was a laugh. Bowie was an incredible performer, gifted and talented far beyond anything I could do. Yet, secretly, I harbored a strong desire to go toe-to-toe with him in some sort of a "battle of the bands" contest.

"Ha!" I said out loud. "You are letting last night's applause go to your head. You would lose, lose… lose. He is an icon and you… you are a housewife in South Miami."

The heavy dizzying weight of those words caused me to sit down on my lounger out at the pool with a cup of coffee. Mia got out her little car and Michael played in his playpen with his favorite toys, busying themselves so as not to pull on an already frazzled mother.

I replayed last night's open mic gig repeatedly in my head. I wanted to find some excuse so that I could tell myself I simply would be wasting my time pursuing a dream like becoming a rock star. A deep voice kept urging me to go on with this pursuit. An uncontrollable urge was manifesting like a cold magnetic shiver down my spine. Its energy found its way to my mouth.

"I could beat Bowie in a battle of the bands," I said to myself. The sound of those words frightened me.

"This open marriage concept is starting to make me crazy. In reality, Anne Marie, you could never, ever do that. This man is a rock legend, an icon of decades of rock and roll classics. Stop thinking like this. It is driving you crazy."

I spent the day cleaning the house and pool area, calling my housekeeper and telling her she didn't need to come. I found the physical work a great tension release. I kept trying to separate myself. There was this person inside who knew instinctively that she had a career in rock music if she could just step up to the plate and claim it. Another side of her cried out that she would forever damage her family if she were to move into that world.

"Why can't I have both?" I asked with anger.

The dual conversation going on in my head had made me sit down, mop in hand, and question my sanity. Craig's "open marriage" made me sick to my stomach. Cleaning the house had done nothing to get rid of the monkey inside my head. It was about time to pick up Caleb from school. Packing Mia and Michael in the van, I headed to Miami Springs for a late afternoon powwow with my friends.

"He still loves you, honey," Andrea stated guardedly. "This other woman is just a seven year itch."

"I don't know if I have the strength to endure this," I said candidly.

"Of course you do," Sandy offered her comfort.

"Maybe you don't have to endure it. I was out shopping in South Beach and found this interesting brochure." Patsy slid over a flyer and the headline read:

THE PEACE YOU ARE LOOKING FOR IS INSIDE OF YOU

Instantly, something in me recognized that what this said was true. My problem was that I had not found that peace and now I faced the world and the hurricane it was brewing for me. Even though it was still a small tropical storm, Hurricane Craig was about ready to take a direct hit on the island of Anne Marie.

"They are having a program at the Miami Beach Convention Center next week. We should go and listen to what this group has to say... mmmm... Elan Vital. What do you think?"

It sounded like someone had just thrown me a life preserver. Well, that was better than nothing in a hurricane.

"Why not?" I felt hopeful.

"What does that have to do with a cheating husband?"

Andrea was always the negative nelly of the group, but it did give rise to doubt in my mind.

"She can't do anything about what Craig is doing but she can do something about her reaction to it," Patsy said defiantly.

"I can watch the kids for you while you go," said Sandy. Sandy was the quintessential mother. She could take care of 2 or 20. I was so grateful to have a built-in babysitter in my mother's group.

Sometimes Patsy could be profound in her approach to life and I was impressed with her suggestion. I decided to call her later that evening to finish the conversation about going to this program.

Craig came home early and it caught me off guard.

"What, no pork loin chanteuse, boiled baby potatoes and spinach soufflé?"

It took every ounce of strength not to scream at him for his insolent comment. He distracted my hateful stare by scooping up Mia and Caleb in his arms, hugging and kissing them.

I decided to keep my temper under control until after the kids were tucked in and sleeping soundly.

Craig was sitting out on the poolside in the lounger with his swimming trunks on. He had a cold beer in his hand and there was one waiting for me next to my chair. The night air hung heavy with humidity and the smell of mangoes from the backyard was in the air.

I sat down, not knowing what I was going to do next, except take a big swig of the dark ale in front of me.

"You were fantastic the other night; I never knew that you were so sexy when you sing."

I was not sure I wanted him to come on to me but the hard on sticking out of his bathing suit let me know that this was where this conversation was going.

"You've always known that I can sing. What's the big turn on ballplayer?"

The last words dripped with sarcastic flames. My inner self did not want to have anything to do with him or the conversation but my rational mind insisted I solve the problem of the "open marriage" and end his relationship with Nicole.

"You," he said with lusty swagger.

He grabbed me and tried to push me onto his lap. I shoved him back and grabbed another swig of beer as a means of physically separating us.

He seemed surprised at the obvious repulsion I had for him so he pushed again.

"You had every guy in that bar hard as a rock including me. I think there was a lesbian beating off on her chair next to me. I had no idea you had that kind of effect on people."

He caught me off guard with this sudden praise of my singing. He liked me up there on stage and I had obviously gotten his attention. My desire for him was at an all-time low but my feelings of self-worth were at an all-time high. I cautiously took yet another large gulp of the ale and commented.

"So what was Nicole's reaction to my performance?"

The insertion of Nicole into the conversation brought an abrupt discomfort to Craig's face and now it was his turn to take a swig of beer.

"Is it the Catholic in you that has to bring up shit like this? I thought we were having a moment about YOU and you have to bring up that."

"So, it's Nicole last night, and me tonight, and who knows tomorrow night, your cardiology resident? Is this how this open marriage works?"

Craig put his best face on, trying to seem innocent and right.

"What is wrong with that?" His blue eyes screamed for attention.

"Oh, I don't know. Let's start with disease and move on from there."

My disdain for his concept and behavior was obviously not to be swayed.

"I am a doctor. Don't you think disease prevention would be at the top of my list?"

"Really? Then tell me, did you wear a condom?"

The blush on his face told me that he was too ashamed to admit that he hadn't. The anger rose to a fever pitch as I realized I could no longer remain calm.

"You think she didn't know that she might get pregnant? She is counting on it, Craig, so that she can lay claim to her 'family' with you."

Craig lost his cool and got up, hurling the chaise lounge up against the palm tree.

"Nicole is not like that! She is hip, she doesn't care about commitment, she believes in open marriage."

I sat stoic in my chair, and the only move I made was to reach down and get my beer bottle.

"How is her marriage doing?" I had already heard via Andrea's gossip line that Nicole's husband had left her two weeks ago.

Craig held his temper, determined to find the high ground in this argument.

"She decided it was time to get a little breath of fresh air, so she moved in with a girlfriend who has a condo on South Beach."

"You must think I am stupid and easily flattered. I am going to trump Nicole's ace."

Craig looked bewildered as if he did not understand what I was saying.

"Move in with those bitches and their expensive condo on Miami Beach, because you certainly aren't going to stay here and give me gonorrhea."

"You fucking sanctimonious asshole!" Craig roared back. "Don't you get it? Free love... share the wealth. Why can't you just try this concept out? Nicole thinks it's going to revolutionize relationships."

"Nicole is just trying to get pregnant and start a whole new life with you, dumbass."

"Nothing could be further from the truth. You are always so narrow minded and hateful. Why do you think this way?"

"Because I am right and you are wrong."

I stood up with my beer bottle in my right hand. Craig lunged toward me, thinking to shake some sense into me, but I countered by taking my beer bottle and cracking it across his head. Beer and broken glass went down the side of his head and all over the poolside area. Both of us were barefoot and very vulnerable but I pulled the pair of sandals that I kept in the back of the palm tree and walked off to the sliding glass door that led to the master bedroom. I pulled out a suitcase, threw in some clothes, and grabbed Craig's sandals and car keys. I walked back to where he was standing, cussing and throwing all the beer bottles and breaking them.

"Goddammit Anne Marie, why are you acting like this?"

I threw the sandals at him and opened up the suitcase, throwing in the clothes I had collected.

"Here are your keys," I said. "Take this suitcase and go. Move in with Nicole and her fucking Sheena Easton friends at South Beach."

As he put on his sandals, I decided to make sure he would go.

"Remember the handgun we found when we first moved in this place, the one we thought the South American drug dealers left behind?"

"Yeah," said Craig as he put on his other sandal.

I pulled out the revolver and pointed it at Craig.

"I always thought this would come in handy someday. Now get out. NOW!"

"Right now, you have an assault charge I can file on the busted beer bottle. Put the gun down and I'll forget the whole thing. I don't think you are the kind of person who could pull the trigger."

"Oh, don't tell me what to do here you cheating bastard. Take your suitcase full of open marriage and walk out the door now, no more chit-chat or you will see that I am mad enough right now to pull this trigger."

Craig hustled out the front door with his tail between his legs as I cocked the gun. My hand was shaking as he threw his suitcase in the trunk and yelled through the large double-doored entrance.

"I still love you, Anne Marie! You are blowing this all out of proportion." He quickly jumped in and sped away as if he feared that I would indeed shoot him or his precious BMW.

I disarmed the revolver and put it back in the cabinet above the refrigerator. I decided that someone would have to think about it for at least a minute before getting that gun from that place. It seemed like the prudent thing to do.

Chapter 14
LA Woman

Morning broke like a hangover on a virgin drinker. I coped with my life with less grace than I ever had. Michael was crying, Mia was running around with her undershirt inside-out on top of her head and Caleb was chasing her, openly defying my orders to get dressed and make his bed. Although I did not practice any type of corporal punishment or physical discipline, I found myself counting to ten several times lest I spank all three of them and stick them in their bedrooms.

"Mooooommmmmy," cried Michael, and I knew his diaper was stinking of a load. I took him out of his high chair and to the nursery, where I changed him and let him know everything was ok. He looked in my eyes and he saw that I had recovered from the wicked storm that had overtaken me.

"It's ok, baby boy. Mommy's here and you are nice and clean and dry and ready to take Caleb to school."

Caleb and Mia decided to cooperate. When I opened the door from the nursery, Caleb was brushing his teeth and he had dressed himself in his cowboy outfit. There was no time to change, and I thought he looked cute in it and damn the school if they had a problem with it.

After dropping Caleb off, I drove straight to Sandy's house. After the kids were outside playing, I found myself sobbing to Sandy as Andrea walked in.

"I can't deal with my life today," I said bitterly in-between my tears. "I know that Craig told me he loved me this morning but his actions are..."

The words would not come out, just sobs. Sobs for what I had worked for washed over me like waves on the beach. I had done everything I could to build a good home, a loving family, gourmet meals… on and on and on it went in my head until it was ready to explode.

"Let's focus on the positive here," Sandy tried to redirect my anger and frustration.

"You held that crowd in the palm of your hand, Anne Marie. I had no idea how damned talented you are. Do you even realize how good you were last night? Fuck Craig, you need to be out in LA. You need to be the next Pat Benatar."

Just then Patsy strolled in with her children and, seeing my distress, ran up to me and hugged me.

"Andy's right, you were great. Who knew?"

I felt blessed that my friends were there for me. The fact of the matter was … I knew. I had always known that it was in me. Something kept me from really excelling at it, though, which was a complete mystery to me.

"You should sell all your stuff, pack what you need in your van and head to LA," Andrea said with much conviction.

"What? Are you crazy?" Even I was afraid to imagine that scenario.

"I'll go with you," Andrea said, dead serious.

"What?" All three of us shouted back at her and it took her back just a bit.

"Why do you want to just pick up and go to Los Angeles with Anne Marie?" Patsy asked with concern.

Andrea broke down and started to sob.

"Phil is bonking some waitress in Coconut Grove. It's where he has been after work for the past several weeks. He says he wants to move in with her in some studio apartment above a tiki bar out there."

"Have all the men in this country gone completely mad?" It was Patsy's turn to get furious.

"Craig wants an open marriage, Phil wants to leave his wife and kids and become the Jimmy Buffet of Miami Springs, it makes me wonder what John has been doing when he says he is working late."

The four of us sat at the breakfast nook with our mugs full of cafe con leche, staring blankly at each other as if we didn't realize what was going on. Unseen forces were lashing out at the sacred institution of marriage and our little group of mothers in Miami Springs felt caught in the crossfires.

I felt a numbness come over me. Something in me wanted to stop in my tracks and turn around. Something frozen and lifeless inside me screamed to cease and desist on any road trips to LA.

LA Lady… neglect your vows.

All the way home from the Springs, I mindlessly weaved in and out of traffic on the Palmetto Expressway. I couldn't get my bearings and I wasn't sure which direction to turn the ship. I pulled in and tucked in three very playtime weary kids.

Down the hallway in the master bedroom, Craig had some suitcases that he was filling full of his clothes.

"Moving out?" I asked with a stone face.

"I am just moving into a condo at the Beach with a few people, so I don't have to drive so far to work. I will come back here too."

He started whistling as he nervously put his favorite golf outfit in the large Samsonite.

I grabbed his suitcase and flung it out on the pool deck which was just as close as I could get it to the front door.

"Get out now and don't come back. Let me guess, one of the other people is Nicole."

"Goddammit Anne Marie, if we could just talk about this … the concept of open ma …"

I screamed at him at the top of my lungs.

"You are moving in with some whore nurse and probably a few more of her buddies. Right? Just one big fucking orgy right there on South Beach."

I went into the kitchen looking for the gun. It was right where I left it in the cabinet above the refrigerator. I turned around to see Craig clumsily picking up his clothes off the pool deck.

Pointing the gun directly at him I screamed, "Get the fuck out of here and don't you ever come back. You can talk to my lawyer."

Craig had completely lost control. In order to regain some ground, he pathetically tried some soft touches.

"Look honey, I love you, this will make our marriage better, you wait and see. This will strengthen our marriage." He inched backwards toward the living room door, keeping his eyes on me, afraid that I would try and shoot his foot or something so he could limp off in wounded pain.

As tempting as that thought was, I held the gun on him as he slipped through the door and out of sight, with no intentions of shooting him. His own guilt made him feel badly about the whole scenario. I was in the "cover my ass" mode. It was his word against mine that I threatened him at gunpoint, but a bullet through his left leg would put me in a very bad position in negotiating this divorce.

As I heard his BMW drive away, I fell back on the bed, gun in hand, and slept like a baby until morning.

Chapter 15
Truckin'

I awoke with a hollow pit in the middle of my stomach that wouldn't quit aching. Andrea's words echoed incessantly in the chambers of my mind. It would be as much of an earthquake as my family could handle. I walked through my house, ball parking what I could get for everything. $700 for the couch. $200 for the coffee table. Oh, God, that was Aunt Stella's coffee table and the marble inlay is worth at least $1000 dollars. I can't sell that.

Tears rolled down my eyes and my heart was sick. What was I thinking? I had always wanted to have a warm, wonderful family life ever since that heartbreaking morning when I had to give my baby to another world and another life. That little foot … that little foot.

This image pushed me over the edge and I started wailing like a banshee. I grabbed the large plush pillow to muffle the noise. I couldn't wail loud enough. Everything in my life was swirling around me like I was caught in a tornadic vortex with no way out.

After what seemed like hours, I fell asleep with my mouth still biting down on the pillowcase. I was awoken by Caleb's yelling in my ear.

"Mommy, the clock says it's way past nine. I am late for school, mommy. MOMMMYYYY!"

"Okay Caleb," I said, crawling off the couch and into the bathroom. Not only did I not have the energy to put myself together, I had even less for my three children.

There must be an extra hormone or enzyme in a woman's body that allows her to summon the energy to accomplish the impossible, and that chemistry began flowing around in my bloodstream, pushing me past the breaking point until my three wonderful children were fed, clothed, and in their car seats in a mere half an hour.

Most men don't understand this phenomenon. I walked in and made up some lame and pathetic excuse as to why Caleb was late, but my tears were real. I could tell the teacher herself was having a challenging day, so I sped off to Miami Springs to receive the counsel and support of my friends.

"He left me," I announced to my three astonished friends. "Of course, he did so at gunpoint."

"You didn't really point a loaded weapon at your husband, did you? I just read in the paper that a heinous crime was reported in South Beach last night. A man was dumped into a garbage can, cut in half! You mustn't resort to violence, Anne Marie." Patsy's voice was ringing with alarm.

"It wasn't loaded but in a court of law there were no witnesses, my word against his and what do you think I will say. That I was screaming and crying and begging him to stay. When he counters with 'she was pointing a gun at me,' who do you think the judge will believe? He's the one leaving me to go live with three other nurses at their love condo on South Beach. And from the sounds of it Patsy, it's a pretty scary place. Maybe the cops will find Nicole chopped in half and stuffed in the Burger King dumpster on Collins."

We all burst into a wicked giggle over that heinous, yet hilarious image.

"It's just what she deserves," Sandy offered.

"That seems a bit harsh," countered Patsy. Her pure and simple Christian attitude was most like what I had always imagined that Christ would want in his followers.

"Fuck Craig and his little bitch, Anne Marie, you have bigger fish to fry. We should have a garage sale and leave Craig choking on your dust." Andrea was much more hardcore and to the point. Her marriage had also crumbled under the weight of the 1984 morality. She seemed much more resolved to it than I was.

"What about the kids?" I choked back. "I can't just yank Caleb out of kindergarten. What about a place to live, money, and what do you think I am going to do, stand on the corner of Hollywood and Vine and sing the blues like the banshee from banal land?"

"Oh grow a sack, Anne Marie. For starters, I have an old friend who lives with her five-year-old son in Long Beach. She will take us in 'till we get our feet on the ground. And secondly, it's May. Caleb will be out of school in just a few weeks. Craig won't have even worn out the hot tub in that condo by then."

I looked around the table at the faces staring back at me. There seemed to be so much hope and compassion staring back that I felt emboldened. I was a little concerned about Andrea's unexplained drive to go to LA with me.

"Fine," I said as I grabbed Sandy's phone and put an ad in the Miami Herald for a Moving Sale. From that moment on, it was one calculated move after another. Since we were renting our fabulous pool house and the lease was in Craig's name, I knew the only thing was to drain our savings accounts, even the un-matured CD's, and have the van looked at for road worthiness.

The van was small but it did have windows and it seemed like I could pack my life and children into it until I made it big in LA.

Patsy called me the following morning because she wanted to talk privately.

"I am worried about you. This is a big life move," choking with concern Patsy continued. "I know this incredible psychic. She lives in a condo in Bal Harbor and I think you should go see her.

"Why?" I didn't believe in psychics.

"Because I think you need some guidance. I'll go with you. Please, just humor me and go. She doesn't charge anything unless you want to give her a donation."

I have always been one to grab all the free stuff in life, right or wrong so I agreed.

Bal Harbor was a pretty swanky neighborhood and when we pulled up at the condo it was right on the ocean.

We were greeted by a young, plump cherub faced woman who was maybe 25. She had a serene look on her face, dressed in a Nehru jacket and long flowing blue chiffon pants, wearing yellow daisies in her long mousey brown hair and she introduced herself as Helen. Just Helen.

We sat on a long white leather couch and I was entranced with a full view of the ocean up here on the 22nd floor. It felt incredibly peaceful as I stared out at the blue ocean on a crystal clear sunny day.

"What is it that you want to know?" she asked with a clarity I was not expecting.

I blurted out, "I am leaving to go to LA to become a rock star and I am bringing my children with me and leaving my husband behind. Any advice?

Helen laughed out loud. At first, I was offended and then realized that I sounded so naïve, like a fifteen year old making a bad life decision, that it was, in fact, laughable.

Helen smiled and closed her eyes and went into some type of a trance. I just watched and wasn't sure what to make of all of this.

She began to sway slightly as if she was possessed and a chill slithered down my spine.

"I see you in a recording studio, you are holding a cassette tape from a song that you have just recorded, and you are laughing."

That image grabbed my attention. Being in a recording studio and laying down tracks had been a dream of mine since the coffeehouse days.

"Go on, is there more?" I pressed her.

She shocked me and Patsy by opening her eyes and going to an ornate dresser that was sitting right next to the couch. She pulled out the tarot cards and spread them face down on the soft leather couch.

"Go ahead and pick one, it doesn't matter which one it is because I already know that you will choose the ten of cups."

Grabbing a card in disbelief, I held the ten of cups in my hand. Thinking that all the cards were the ten of cups, I began to turn over several more cards, realizing that the others were different and I had pulled the exact card she predicted.

The card had a picture of a family all holding hands and happy and there was a rainbow over the house that the family was standing in front of.

"You will go to LA but the bigger answer is that you will re-unite with your husband and your union will be better and stronger than it ever was."

Patsy squealed in delight with that news. My heart began to race inside my chest and my palms began to sweat.

"How do you know this?" I asked.

"I am seeing the vision right above you. It is why I knew you would pick that card."

"How long is this going to take?" I inquired with a hint of sarcasm.

"One, no two," she answered.

"Years?"

"I am only being shown one or two."

My mind was racing around its track like a Formula 1 race car. I wanted this to be true, I wanted it to be two years, I knew I could endure two years.

"What about my singing career? Am I successful?"

"You will meet someone who will help you."

Helen swooned and Patsy lunged to grab her. Helen was covered in sweat and told us that she could not do any more today.

Even though it was "free", I laid a $100 bill on her kitchen table as we left. I didn't even know why.

The Saturday morning moving sale was well attended. Fifty people showed up even before we had the cash box set up and I was selling my beautiful furnishings as if they were hot dogs at a ball park.

"Fifty dollars for your grandmother's antique lamp?" Patsy was very distressed. "You can't replace that for less than a hundred dollars, Anne Marie. Maybe you should rethink this."

As two men loaded the chocolate velvet wrap-around couch that I loved so much into their van, I winced, realizing Patsy might be right.

"Too late, honey, the arrow has left the bow." Just then, Caleb ran up to me asking me if his Millennium Falcon had to be packed with the rest of the toys.

"Where are we going mommy?" His innocent eyes were as wide as saucers and my heart sank as I told him.

"We are embarking on a magical mystery tour."

Caleb jumped up and down with delight, making sure he could hold on to the action figure of Han Solo and the Falcon.

Chapter 16
One Toke Over the Line

We woke up on Sunday morning to an empty house. The van was loaded, and I was ready to pick up Andrea and her two children, Allison and Chance. The three small suitcases seemed like very little to take but we hit the interstate and everyone fell silent.

The tank read empty so I pulled off the interstate to gas up.

"So how do you want to work splitting the gas?" I asked innocently.

"Splitting the gas? I was married to an alcoholic plumber. You were married to a cardiologist. You do the math."

I turned to her with smoldering rage. "You mean the whole trip is going to be financed by me?"

"Hey, I have a place for us to stay, this is the least you can do," Andrea snapped back. "I have no money, Anne Marie, I thought you knew that."

The intense stress of the disintegration of my family had apparently dulled my wits. I really hadn't seen it coming until it hit me like a sharp right punch to the face.. Andrea needed a ride out of town and I fit the description of the cab driver she wanted to use. The kids were all within earshot so rather than create a big scene, I finished gassing up and went to pay the bill. We drove in silence for the rest of the night.

"Aren't we stopping for a motel? I am really getting tired," groaned Andrea.

"No. I didn't realize this road trip was being paid for exclusively by me. Unless you have some cash to throw in, it's not going to happen."

"Fuck you, Anne Marie," Andrea hissed under her breath. She turned to fluff her pillow and fell asleep. The lonely highway lay ahead and I felt like I had just jumped off a cliff. On a whim and a prayer, I had left Miami without so much as telling Craig. Catholic guilt poured all over me like an unholy baptism. My anger had caused me to lash out and I knew he would be in pain when he found out that his wife and children had left town with no idea as to where they went.

"Well, you have Nicole to take comfort in," I seethed to myself. "I am sure she will be ready to get all domestic on him and try to pop one out for him."

The agony of that thought threw my emotions into hyper drive. I pulled out a small pipe I had loaded with some exquisite hash. I lit the pipe and blew the smoke out the window.

The dull hum of the road made me sleepy, so I slipped out my small pill bottle and took a big Black Beauty.

"Huh, this should get me all the way to LA."

I was buzzing through most of Texas and when dawn hit in New Mexico, the scenery was awe-inspiring, but I was feeling the fatigue of all night driving. We pulled off the interstate and cruised for a bathroom in Santa Rosa. The first promising sight was a combination gas station/laundromat.

"Why don't you fill up here and let the kids run around for a bit. I need to do a load of laundry anyways."

The request sounded reasonable, so I pulled off and we parked the van in front of the rickety little sign, "Wash Here," and let the kids run in the empty lot while we moved a load through the laundry. As the dryer buzzed that they were finished, Andrea promptly moved her carts over and filled them up. I put my one load in the very first dryer near the door.

"I'm going to get those kids," I told Andrea and walked over to see a big argument break out between Andrea's children and mine.

"Give it back!" screamed Mia. "Give it back!"

Michael was crying and Caleb and Andrea's son, Chance, were playing a tug of war using Michael's "speak and spell" toy. Caleb, who was obviously bigger, gave one huge yank and the toy was in his possession and Chance fell to the ground, crying.

"Okay everybody, it's okay." I picked Michael up and hugged him while Mia clung to my legs. Caleb walked over to the van and put the toy in his duffel bag.

104

Rather than lecture, I watched the scene play out. Chance dusted himself off and got back in the van, sitting next to his sister. Caleb walked up to me with a bit of a swagger, obviously fancying himself to be the hero.

"I don't want them to ride in our van anymore, mommy. I don't like Chance anymore. He is not my friend."

"Caleb, honey, please be patient. We are all trying to get to California and we have two more states, this one and Arizona. Then we will be in California."

Caleb started to cry.

"I wanna go home, I wanna see daddy."

I stood in the barren empty lot with nothing but an occasional tumbleweed blowing by me in the brisk morning wind. This was not going well. I felt a certain uneasiness about having brought Andrea and her children, who were now an emotional drain as well as a financial one.

After what seemed like an eternity, I got the kids to settle down and get back inside the van. I turned it around so we could load up the bags of laundry. I nearly backed into Andrea who had bagged up her laundry as well as mine and was heading out the front door.

"I got this Anne Marie," she said as she flung those bags into the van like a hobo hopping a train. She raced into the passenger seat.

"I am gonna go gas up and then I want you to drive for a while. I am dead tired."

"Let's just get on the road," said Andrea anxiously.

"No," I said emphatically. "Our gas is very low and it is your turn to drive. You need to do a little more on this trip besides provide us with a destination.

To emphasize the point, I accelerated so that the tires squealed, and drove the 20 feet to the gas pump where I stopped abruptly. I got out to pump the gas. As I lifted the nozzle, a small Mexican woman with her two boys came walking up to me, shouting at me in Spanish. I kept brushing her away telling her I did not speak Spanish. Finally, exasperated, the woman pointed to Andrea who had slid down in her seat a bit as if to avoid detection.

"Thief, thief!" she ranted as she pointed to Andrea.

I couldn't believe how the level of chaos had risen from one to one hundred and I decided to quickly put an end to it.

"No, no Señora, we did not steal your clothes," I stated as I walked to the back of the van. I opened up the sack of Andrea's clothes to prove my point. There, at the top of the bag, was a pair of small boy's jeans, about Chance's size, but there was a Santa Rosa Blue devil patch sewed methodically into the knee.

Andrea heard the commotion and hopped out of her seat, rushing to the back of the van in time to view the pair of jeans.

"These jeans, they are MY son," she shouted in broken English.

I watched Andrea's face as if watching a movie, noticing the nuances of her facial expression as she feigned surprise.

"Oh my goodness," she gushed, "how did that get in here?" Her insincere response angered me, so I continued to pull all the laundry out of the bag.

"Mine, mine, mine," she counted off the jeans as I pulled them out. My fury rose with every piece of clothing that we discovered. In all, half the bag was filled with the Mexican woman's clothing.

"I am so sorry. Sorry." I couldn't say it enough. Andrea, however, kept with her story about it being an honest mistake. She could not even admit that she had deliberately stuffed the duffel bag.

I put the gas nozzle back on the pump handle and got in the van without saying a word to Andrea. I was afraid that World War III was about to erupt.

"Oh, I can't believe that woman thought I stole her clothes, I would never do that."

I drove on in silence. I was angry at myself for putting up with this obvious freeloader. No wonder she couldn't wait to get going. God only knows what the whole story was about the husband. I had known Andrea for three months and thought she was sound of mind and level headed, but this road trip had revealed a whole different person.

Chapter 17
California Dreamin'

The long road from Miami Springs, Florida to Long Beach, California finally came to an end. We pulled into a tiny box of a house located on the main avenue coming into downtown Long Beach. My skin began to feel like I had something crawling inside of it and I longed to have a glass of white wine. When we pulled into the driveway, I was exhausted beyond my wildest expectations.

Oh dear God, whatever made me think I could drag my three small children to LA and become a rock star.

We got all of the kids bathed and put to bed, which was a huge double mattress that we had put together in Janet's son's room. The children were more than road weary and enjoyed the soft sheets and mattress and the lull of the fan that blew across all six of them.

"Let's go out on the porch and have a smoke," she said politely.

Janet was a thirty-five-year-old black woman who had been on her own with Jason, her eight-year-old son, since his birth.

I was surprised that she lit up a joint right on the front porch since she lived on a main street.

Janet sat back into the comfy cushioned porch swing and exhaled, passing the join to me.

"So what in the world are you two doing here in California?" Janet seemed guarded, but her voice gave credence to some sincerity.

"Anne Marie, here, is going to join a rock band. She is an awesome lead singer and we are going to make some hit music and lots of money." Andrea stated this as if she was reading Janet her resume.

A blurt of smoke followed by an ill-timed cough came rushing out of Janet.

"Say what? You gotta be shitting me! The entire LA area is

107

littered with wannabe rock stars and their broken dreams. Here, take another hit and rethink this day dream girls."

She handed the joint to Andrea. "And what are you going to do?"

"Be her manager," Andrea stated with confidence.

My manager! I was seething inside, thinking that the little leech had designs on yet more of my money. A sinking feeling started to take my stomach and drive it down to my toes. I was so angry at Craig that I had not thought things through.

"Well, honey, you are a long way from LA. You are here in Long Beach. In Long Beach, you can smoke your dope on your porch because the cops are busy chasing murderers, thieves, and drive-by shooters."

I sucked down such a long hit of pot that I thought my eyeballs would pop out of their sockets. As I exhaled, I felt icy waves rushing over me as a police car with his red siren flashing came careening down the boulevard. Fear and terror were starting to take hold, so I bogarted the joint and took yet another hit, hoping to just pass out and find that this was all a big dream.

In the yard by Janet's one lone tree stood Bowie.

"Get out of here, Anne Marie," he called to me.

The next time I took a hit, I passed out in the big sofa next to the swing on the porch.

Morning broke to the scream of a loud siren. I opened my eyes to see a fire truck and an ambulance roaring down the street. The noise was deafening. I got up to go to the kitchen and see if there was coffee.

Janet was getting ready for work. I overheard her talking to Andrea.

"Now look, I can let you and your kids stay here for a while but your friend has got to find another place."

A dark cloud came over me as I heard Andrea agree. The mooch had just flitted from one free meal to the next. The promise of a safe place to stay until I got my bearings was a lie.

Janet left for work and I herded the kids into the backyard to play on Jason's swing set. When they were out of ear shot, I confronted Andrea.

"You'll just have to find a place around here to rent, that won't be too hard, and I will start making some calls to find you a band. After all, you still have money."

The word MONEY set me off like a firecracker and I was spewing obscenities everywhere.

"You fucking cunt! And you think I will let you be my manager? You are nothing less than a flim-flam man in woman's clothing. You lie, you cheat, you steal, you are a leech, a mother-fucking leech!"

Andrea spewed back and then ran into the bedroom and grabbed one of my suitcases. I ran after her as she busted through the front door and threw my suitcase on the front lawn next to my parked van. Clothes began to fly everywhere. I stuffed things back in the suitcase, shut it and threw it in the back of the van. Andrea stood by laughing. I said nothing. I went back into the house and packed up the rest of my gear faster than Mr. Clean and his white tornado.

Andrea had not expected me to go so quietly. I could see her rethinking her position as I went to the backyard to collect my children.

"Come on my darlings, let's go," I called out to Caleb, Mia, and Michael.

"Where are we going?" asked Mia innocently.

"To a magical place where we will have lots of fun." I didn't have a clue where that was but I needed to put on a good front for the kids. They needed to feel like everything was normal. The problem was that everything was anything but normal. As I walked through the kitchen to get my purse, I spied a small bag of pot on the shelf above the stove. I grabbed it quickly, ran out the door, and got the kids in the van at lightning speed.

"Hey, let me know where you find a place, I really think I could help your career as a rock star," Andrea blurted out with uncharacteristic kindness.

"You've got to be fucking kidding me, you bitch!" I screamed at her as I closed the door and rolled up the window.

The tires squealed as I peeled out of the parking spot, doing a complete U-turn onto a busy highway and headed back east to the 405.

"Mommy, why did you call Andy a bitch?" said Caleb with some surprise.

"Because she is, Caleb," I said, choking back tears.

Perhaps my children were intuitive or sensitive, but they understood the gravity of the situation and amused themselves with toys as I drove silently into the heart of Los Angeles.

Panic began to ensue as I got on the 405 and headed north. The gas gauge was on empty and I was being bombarded by six lanes of traffic. I had no idea where the next exit or gas station was. My heart began to beat so fast in my chest I thought I was going to pass out. I gripped the wheel, using the best driving skills I could and found an exit with a gas station.

My saving grace was an AM/PM Mini Market. I went inside to get the kids a treat and me a cup of coffee. In the morning madness, I had failed to roll one for myself. As I paid for gas, I saw a pay telephone on the far right side of the store. I winced, thinking how this might be a good time to call Craig and negotiate a settlement, but my pride wouldn't let me. I haven't failed yet, I thought. I am just hitting a few boulders along the highway to success.

"Do you have a rest room?" I asked the attendant.

"Here is the key, it's around back," he said. I gave the kids their treats and told them I would be a minute or two in the restroom.

I walked in, sat on the covered toilet seat, and lit up a joint. My fear of getting busted was just slightly trumped by my fear of the unknown. After several puffs, I pulled out my perfume, sprayed the place, and left. As the door shut, I realized that I had left the key in the restroom.

Seeing that the clerk had a couple of people in line, I dashed back into the van and took off back on the 405 headed north. I doubted that there would be much notice of me until I was long gone.

The sea of cars on the interstate made the Palmetto Expressway look like a cake walk. Miami was big, but Los Angeles was gigantic. My disorientation turned to panic when I saw the sign that said I was heading south on the 405 instead of north.

"I am too fucking high," I thought to myself. As I looked around I saw a billboard that said to turn north on I-5 and visit Disneyland. I took a deep breath and decided that my children needed a little relief and the budget could stand a stay in the magic kingdom.

Chapter 18
Hotel California

We spent the afternoon shaking hands with Mickey Mouse, riding tea cups with the Mad Hatter, and screaming on Mr. Toad's Wild Ride. We ate a good dinner and passed out in the comfort of the hotel beds.

Before the kids awoke the next morning, I went into the bathroom and rolled several joints for the road. Ignoring caution, I tucked a towel underneath the bathroom door, turned on the fan and shower, and blew smoke into the running water. I figured that the steamy water would absorb some of the smoke, and I had given a fake address from Miami to avoid being tracked by anyone who wanted to arrest a harried mother who needed a little ganja to calm her nerves.

Taking off down the interstate, I had no clue where to go. I headed north, hoping that God would give me a little insight. I bowed my head in prayer hoping the almighty had not forsaken me.

"What adventure are we going to have today mommy?" Caleb was full of optimism about their new life. It gave me a moment to pause and be grateful for what I had and gave me the courage to keep going.

What seemed like an endless sea of traffic flowed slowly north. When I saw a sign for "Interstate 10, west to Santa Monica," a feeling tugged at my intuition. I took a big deep breath and turned onto the 10. I followed it until it turned into Pacific Coast Highway. As we saw the endless miles of beach ahead, I felt a sense of coming home. I had always wanted to move to California and now I knew why. The PCH was a wonderful highway; it felt much like Dorothy's yellow brick road and I buzzed along looking for another sign.

Malibu was an oasis right next to the big monster city of LA.

111

No wonder all the stars lived there. It felt good there but my mind began to scream at me. This place is fucking expensive. This is where rock stars live AFTER they make it big.

Noticing that my gas was low again, I pulled off to gas up at another AM/PM mini market. As I walked in to pay for the gas, I noticed a sign for help. "Wanted: day time attendant, apply within."

Within a few minutes, I was joyfully walking back to the van. I had a job. Now, I have to find a suitable place to stay, I thought. Driving down the road, I was just about ready to turn around, thinking I was too far from the Mini Market, when a sign on the right read: "Malibu Cliff Motel 100 yards on left." A tiny little sign lit up the name and I pulled into the motel parking lot.

It was a long building, and at the end of the motel there was a small area with a hot tub and grill. It overlooked Zuma Beach and the view of the ocean and downtown Los Angeles was magnificent. I decided to venture in and see what kind of cost it would be to stay there.

The small office had a bell on the counter which I rang. After a minute, when no one came, I rang it again.

"Jesus Christ, hold your horses, I'm a-comin'!" shouted a scraggly sounding male voice. "I have to get my britches on unless you came to see my peepee." The voice laughed and soon a long-haired half naked man appeared with just a pair of jeans on.

"Can I help you, missy?" he asked. I was shocked that he was commenting on his private parts when he was supposed to be the manager of a motel in upscale Malibu.

"How much are your rooms?" I ventured.

"Depends." He looked at me as if I would have to pry the information out of him.

"Depends on what?" I said with a little irritation in my voice.

"Depends on what you want," he said with a gleam in his eye.

"How about a nice room for me and my three kids," I popped back.

"You and your three kids? Oh Lord, lady are you some rich bitch from Pacific Palisades who is trying to escape from her plastic surgeon husband? I had one like you a month ago and we had a shootout in the parking lot. I run a respectable motel here and I don't want no trouble."

Wow, things were heating up and I wanted them to de-escalate.

"No, I just got a job in town and want some little place to stay until I can get a bit more established."

"Mmmm, where did you come from?"

I had no idea if Craig had put our pictures on some sort of milk carton for missing persons so I decided to invent a story that would put this cowboy at ease.

"I am from Jacksonville, Florida, and I am moving out here to start a new life. My husband died in an auto accident and I have a sister who lives in Thousand Oaks."

"Then why aren't you moving in with her?" he asked.

"I am not going to sleep on a couch," I said with indignation. "Do you want to rent me a room or interrogate me as if I were a criminal?"

"Milton T. Boner is the name, ma'am. Pleased to meet you."

He stuck out his hand for me to shake. I shook it but couldn't believe someone had a name like that.

"Yessiree, I used to be the roady for Jerry Jeff Walker. Back in the day. Now I just run this respectable hotel."

"Well, how about showing me a respectable room."

"Seems to me," he said as he pulled a key off of the wall of keys behind him, "that you might do well being in our studio apartment. Bill Mayzee usually rents that but he is on tour with the Rolling Stones at the moment and it's free. At least for the next three months."

We walked down the row to the very end room, number 12, and Milton unlocked the door. Inside was a nice living room with a kitchenette and a bedroom and bathroom in the back part of the studio apartment. It was right next to the hot tub and it was private, bright, and cheery.

"How much?" I asked with trepidation.

Milton sighed as it seemed he was making a price up in his head. "Four hundred fifty dollars a month, includes utilities and a parking space," he finally said.

I took a deep sigh, pondering how I could justify a $3.75 an hour job to pay for it. Instantly I knew I would have to dig into the ten thousand dollars that I brought with me.

"OK, I will take it as long as it's a month-to-month lease."

Milton chortled. "Huh, it's more like a hour-to-hour lease around here but sure, let's go back to the office and fill out the paper work."

Things felt right. It was a cozy little place and I unloaded all of Miami into it and my children seemed settled. As evening set in, I noticed a plump blonde woman and her chubby son standing at the bus stop on the other side of the highway.

She looked at me and I could tell she was studying me as I unpacked the van. The bus came and left and she stood across the street staring at me with a hunger.

I had purchased some groceries earlier and proceeded to make us a spaghetti dinner. As the sauce was simmering and the pasta was ready to come out, there was a knock at the door. I opened the door to see the blonde woman and her son.

"Pardon me," she said in a sweet little southern accent. "I couldn't help but see that you had moved in and well ... we were just waiting for the bus ... and well ... we are heading for the mission in the downtown area ... and well ... my boy Bobby here is hungry and they never feed him enough at the mission and well ..."

My heart broke as I looked at the two of them. I opened the door a little wider so they could come in out of the brisk, windy Malibu evening.

"My name is Charlotte and this here is my son Bobby," she announced as she breezed into the kitchen.

"Here let me help you," she said, "it's the least I can do for you allowing us the privilege of having dinner with you and your family."

Charlotte drained the pasta and put the bread in the toaster before I could catch my breath and shut the door.

"Where did you come from?" Charlotte was buttering the toast as I set the table.

"Florida," I said, trying to give away as little information as I could. Charlotte could sense my feelings but pushed ahead.

"Hey, everyone here is from someplace far away. I came from South Carolina. Milton is from Oklahoma and Bill is from Massachusetts. No locals here."

I ate my dinner without saying much. Charlotte was a chatterbox and could make a conversation for the two of us. As if a punctuation in her ongoing dialogue, she stopped and put her hand up.

"Hey, if you need someone for childcare, you know, to watch Mia and Michael, I can do that. I mean ... if you have a job." She was fishing.

"Well, I am supposed to start tomorrow as a ..." my mouth could not form the words mini-market cashier "... as a back-up singer for Tina Turner."

"Wow, I knew you were a star ever since I started watching you across the street."

Charlotte picked up the dishes and began cleaning up. I sat on the couch, plugged in the VCR, and put on Emmet Otter's Jug Band Christmas, one of my kids' favorite videos. I was feeling rather peaceful, but I wondered if letting Charlotte and Bobby stay was a good idea. I felt a little guilty letting Charlotte do all the work, but I figured if I was going to let them stay, she had to pull her weight. From the looks of both of them, there was a lot of weight to pull.

Registering Caleb for school was a trip. My Dodge Caravan was parking next to Bentleys, Mercedes Benz, and Lamborghinis of modern and vintage makes and models.

Caleb and I stood in line behind a woman who was dripping in diamonds and furs, but when Bob Dylan walked in with his small son, I couldn't help it. I was dying to walk up to him and ask for an autograph. My hand shook as I filled out the paperwork as I heard Mr. Dylan standing next to me getting his son's schedule.

"Jakob, it says here that your home room teacher is Mrs. Bryan. Let's go find your classroom, son," he said in perfect Dylanese. His voice was as unmistakable as his songs. I watched out of the corner of my eye as they walked down the main hallway. I looked at the plump, jolly woman who was processing our paperwork.

"Could Caleb request Mrs. Bryan's first grade class? We've heard she is so good with students."

The jolly disappeared from the woman's face as she retorted, "All our teachers are good. Caleb has been assigned to Mrs. Goodwin's room."

She quickly and dismissively handed me the paperwork. I let the opportunity pass to argue and made my way down the PCH to work.

The manager of the AM/PM Mini Market was a young 25-year-old man with a Duran Duran haircut and beautiful blue eyes.

"So you see it's pretty easy, you just have to press these buttons here to control the pumps. Customers want you to get them in and out fast so that's critical to get them taken care of as quickly as you can."

"Right, gotcha," I said, only half understanding. My focus was on his looks, not his voice. I quickly turned the topic away from training.

"So what do you do besides this? The night time girl, Angela, told me she was finishing up her last semester at UCLA for editing."

"Yeah, Angie loves film. Me, I love music. I am in a band, Grind. I'm their drummer. Have a nice Ludwig kit that I practice on at my studio."

"You have a studio?" I interrupted.

"Studio apartment, you didn't let me finish."

He seemed to be checking me out as well and I think he thought I was a bit of a groupie.

"You should come by some afternoon after work," he said.

"I would like that. You know, I'm a singer. Who does the lead vocals for Grind?"

He turned a deaf ear to me as he greeted a customer.

"Good morning, Mr. Blakely. What can I do for you this beautiful morning?"

Aidan Birne ran a tight ship at the Mini Market, and I felt like I would need to work up to going to his apartment. I didn't want to sleep with him, although I wouldn't mind, but I did want to see if the band was willing to at least audition me. Somehow it seemed like a bad idea to mix business with pleasure.

I drove home a bit weary that evening, but I decided that things were going well, in general. As I pulled up to the motel, I saw Milton walking toward the ice machine, grumbling under his breath.

"Hi, Milton," I said with a friendly smile that masked my tiredness.

"Oh, don't 'hi' me, missy. I thought I got rid of her but lo and behold, you let her back in."

"Let who back in?" I was puzzled and caught off guard.

"Charlotte and her little munching machine, saw her out at the hot tub with all the kids. Did you hire her on as your nanny?" His scowl showed me that he was most unhappy.

116

"Well, I needed someone to watch the kids while I am at work. It's just a temporary thing, I promise."

"Oh, if I had a nickel for all the times I've heard that one. I will say this once. If you start a commune over there in number 12, I will be forced to evict you. Got that?"

"This will be resolved in a few weeks," I reassured him.

"Oh, yeah, I've heard that one before too. No freeloaders at the motel, got it?"

"Got it," I said as I walked in my front door.

Chapter 19
Take It to the Limit

As the days passed, I realized that I was settling into a nice routine. But that was not why I was there. I was having fun flirting with Aidan, but it was time to get down to business, I needed a band.

Aidan didn't seem too aggressive, so I decided to push a little and suggested that we go over to his place after work.

"Oh, I am burnin' for you baby."

The minute we walked in the door, he jumped on me like a wild animal and began to tear my clothes off. I sank back into a big suede pillow that he had on the floor right next to his drum set. If I was gonna fuck this guy, I wanted to make sure that the drum set was within my view at all times. The kisses all over my back and neck relaxed me, and I felt like becoming a rock star was going to be a piece of cake. Aroused, I felt the need to be on top, but my strict religious upbringing kept raising its ugly nun's head. He was being so gentle, but I found myself impatient for him to get to the rough stuff. Pull my hair, bite me on my ass, take it to the limit little drummer boy, my inner thoughts began to take my focus away from the physical pleasure.

He seemed to drag along listless, like a lost little boy. I found myself ignoring my inhibitions, rolling him over, and getting on top. I was so charged with energy that I bore down on him with great intensity, ready for some serious love making.

What happened next is still a mystery to me. There was a stray thundershower off the Malibu coastline that afternoon, and a thunderbolt crackled in the air and hit the shoreline just yards away from Aidan's beach bungalow. As I bent down to kiss him, an electrical charge raced through my body to his, and he went limp. His erection vanished and when I pulled away there was a charred spot

118

on his upper left lip. His eyes widened and then he screamed.

I jumped off of him as quickly as I could and he seemed a bit dazed.

"What the fuck, what the fuck ..." he kept mumbling out loud. "What just happened?"

He stumbled into the restroom and I heard him in there, groaning. I couldn't get dressed fast enough. Rather than stay and have an awkward moment, I let myself out and raced back to the Mini Market. Safe within the van, I roared off and held a conversation with myself all the way back to the motel.

"So much for using this band, you will never be able to repair this damage."

"What happened? His dick just went limp inside me. It's like I electrocuted him."

"Whatever happened, it's a dead end. Find another band. This is the LA area, find another band."

I pulled into the Malibu Shores Motel only to find Milton and Charlotte screaming at each other in the parking lot. Milton seemed to be guarding the entrance to my apartment. Charlotte was crying and the kids were all huddled near the hot tub area, afraid. My heart bled. Things were falling apart on yet another front.

"What the fuck is going on Milton?" I screamed as I got out of the van.

"I told you she was trouble! I caught her stealing extra sheets out of our linen room. She's gotta go, Anne Marie. Now, Today."

"Is this true, Charlotte?" I was hoping she would deny it. Instead, she started to cry.

"I just wanted to make a little nicer bed for me and Bobby. I am sorry. I didn't mean to cause any trouble."

I looked at Milton and gave him a face that said, give me a minute. I put my arms around Charlotte and we walked to the hot tub area, herded the children back in the room, and closed the door.

"Is there anywhere else you can go besides the mission, Charlotte?" I asked, pleading with her. "Anywhere?"

Charlotte looked down at her feet and whispered something almost inaudible.

"Captain's house down in San Pedro."

"What captain?"

"Captain Jack Gibbs. Retired naval officer. He has a really nice place. I know he would let me and Bobby stay there…but…"

"But what, Charlotte?"

"He loves me, he wants me to move in and be his lover."

"And of course, you don't love him, right?" What a choice for this woman, I thought. The homeless shelter or a man she does not love. Somehow I made the judgment call that Captain Gibbs's house was the lesser of two evils. I convinced Milton to let her use the motel phone to call the captain under the promise that she would be leaving.

We drove in silence down to San Pedro. We pulled up the long drive to his castle in the air in San Pedro. Leaves were blowing across the street, and even in southern California there was fall.

I left Charlotte and Bobby with Captain Jack, who looked like a confirmed alcoholic.

"Feed him a good meal, give him lots of whiskey or cognac after dinner and he will pass out. You'll never have to worry about him boning you." I said that to Charlotte, hoping to calm her fears.

"Hey, thanks for everything, Anne Marie. Here is the house number. If you ever need anything, just give us a call, if we're still here."

We both smiled, knowing that our fates were precarious and so up in the air.

"Good luck with your rock and roll career." Charlotte was kind-hearted and I hated to leave her in a situation like that, but I was holding mine together by a thread.

Chapter 20
Riding that Train, High on Cocaine

It was already nine am in Miami when I placed the phone call to Craig. I was standing in the little phone booth that was just feet from the PCH and the motel. I was watching the sun rise over the Los Angeles skyline and the lump in my throat was unbearable. Directory assistance had given me a number in Miami Beach for Craig Channing.

"Hello?" Craig answered.

"Craig, it's Anne Marie." Before I could get another word in, Craig went off on a tirade.

"You fucking piece of shit cunt! Where are my kids? What the fuck happened? You think you can just take off, you bitch, you asshole, you …"

"Yeah, this is really good for our marriage," I managed to insert as sarcastically as I could in between the expletives. Then, I hung up.

"Well, that went well," I said just as sarcastically to myself. "No chance of getting any more money from him."

I wandered around the parking lot, aimlessly talking to myself, then went inside and got Caleb ready for school. I packed them all into the van and drove off to Malibu Elementary. I dropped off Caleb and pulled out of the parking space without looking. Another car right behind me slammed on its brakes, inches from my back bumper. I rolled down the window.

"Fucking asshole, watch where you're going!" I screeched like a banshee. I looked at the driver and passenger in the shiny new Mercedes Benz. Bob Dylan and his driver peered back at me, shocked that someone would be behaving as badly as I was.

The whine of my tires might have burnt rubber as I rushed down the street, embarrassed that I had called one of rock and roll's

121

icons a "fucking asshole."

Mia, Michael and I spent our day at Zuma Beach, watching surfers, chasing sea gulls and making sand castles.

"Mommy, I am so glad that you can play with us today." Mia could charm anyone with delicate sweetness.

"Mommy ... mommy ... mommy," chanted Michael. His two-year-old world had been rocked, but his happy and contented demeanor still prevailed. I had called the owner of the minimart and told him I had to quit. I had no idea what to do next but since it was Wednesday, I decided to pick up a copy of the weekly newspaper, The Malibu Times.

Scouring through the scant want ads, I came across an ad for a florist and the shop was just down the street from the motel. The woman was in her forties, and she handed me some flowers and asked me to make an arrangement. In under five minutes, I handed her an exquisite tea cup arrangement.

"You're hired," she said. "Start Monday."

I walked back to the motel feeling pretty good. I got the kids to bed that night and made a fire in the fireplace. I laid in front of it, wondering how I would be able to come up with a babysitter. Just then the phone rang. It was odd because I had not given the number out to anyone except the school and they required one. Oh my God, did Craig somehow track me down? I wondered. With some anxiety, I answered.

"Hello, sugar, how are you?" The voice sounded inebriated.

"Who is this?" I demanded with authority.

"Oh now you don't have to yell, you're hurting my ears. Its Milton T. Your neighbor, your friendly motel manager."

"Milton, what do you want?"

"Your kids asleep?"

"Yes, of course they are, why?"

"Just lock your door and tiptoe down to my apartment, I have something for you and someone I want you to meet. I feel bad about you not having a babysitter anymore and I want to make it up to you."

He generally sounded sincere but I wanted to know who it was.

"Is it Mick Jagger?" I asked, thinking that he could stop by since the horn player in his band lived here for part of the year.

I heard Milton snickering like a little kid.

"Yeah, it's Mick," he said.

Okay, this is rock and roll. This is roots rock and roll, a super star icon to get you in the door someplace as somebody's famous backup singer, Mick Jagger of the fucking world's greatest rock and roll band, the Rolling Stones. I closed the fire doors and figured it would burn out from lack of air. I grabbed some songs I had written, hoping to show them to Mick, and walked down the parking lot to Milton's suite.

"Hello," I said pushing back the big double doors that lead to his suite. I knocked on his front door and a voice said, "Come on in Anne Marie."

Milton was sitting on his bed, pillow stuffed behind to prop up his head, smoking a joint. Next to him was a guy that I vaguely recognized. He was the lead in some movie I had seen recently.

"Anne Marie Channing, meet Gary Busey." Milton's introduction was as formal and stiff as if we were in Queen Elizabeth's court.

Gary Busey, yeah, that's who this guy is. He played Buddy Holly in The Buddy Holly Story. He fidgeted something awful as he addressed me.

"Howdy ma'am, pleased to meet you. I hope you excuse me but I am just a little bit concerned with privacy right now."

He began to peep out of the corner of Milton's drapes as if he were looking for someone in the parking lot. Then he scrambled quickly into Milton's bathroom, standing on the toilet seat, looking out the back alley way.

"What's he doing?" I asked.

"The studio execs have a private dick following Gary around so he is just being extra careful to make sure nobody followed him out here."

"Why do they have a detective following him anyways?" I asked, with a little disgust. "Never mind, I don't want to know. Where's Mick?"

Milton started chuckling and snickering like he was ready to bust out into a flat-belly laugh.

"Mick's on tour in Australia," he said starting to outright laugh.

"That's not funny, Milton. I thought you were trying to make it up to me, not get me more pissed off."

Just then, Busey came back and put a large 3-by-4 foot mirror on the bed and pulled out a large clear plastic bag with what looked like laundry detergent.

"Is that a big bag of Tide that you're pouring on that mirror?"

Both Milton and Busey burst into laughter, as if I had said something humorous.

"Tide? Shit no little girl, this is grade A pure Columbian cocaine." Busey could barely get the words out of his mouth before he pulled out a crisp thousand dollar bill and rolled it up while Milton divided the coke into three long lines."

Busey snorted up a line and then snorted the second one before running into the bathroom with what appeared to be a nosebleed.

Milton handed me the rolled-up money. "Ladies, first," he said, as he started dividing a couple more lines.

"I've never done this before, Milton."

"Oh, hell, what are you a little school marm from Indiana or something? Put the bill up your nose and lay it down next to the line and snort! How hard is that?"

I can only remember the fireworks that went off in my head as I breathed in the white powder through my nose. The sensation was unique. It was exhilarating, but I felt like I was going too fast.

I sat on the side of the bed, stunned, while Milton and Busey chattered on at a record pace. I saw several joints on the night stand and decided to ask if I could have one.

"Take them all, I hate that shit, weed brings me down. I only use it when I have to come down. Haha! …and I hate coming down. I want to snort more! Haha!"

He was acting like a wild man from Borneo and I wanted no part of it. They both hurriedly poured more white powder on the mirror and snorted it up as I watched in amazement.

"C'mon, help yourself!" Busey and Milton were so out of control they didn't even object to my taking the handful of joints. I stuck them in my pockets and got up.

"Where are you going? Come on, party!" Milton was demanding and they both seemed a bit out of control and ready to make advances.

I moved toward the window as I screamed, "I see some lights outside in the parking lot, like it's some detective's car! You guys should hide."

Busey nearly levitated straight up in the air with fear. I grabbed the extreme paranoid moment that I had manifested to make my exit.

"Quick, hide in the bath tub, I will create a diversion for you."

Both men ran into the bathroom like two scared rabbits. I bolted out the door and ran back to my room. My heart was pounding so hard, it felt like it would leap out of my mouth. I needed to calm down. I went into my bathroom to see if I had some sort of over the counter sedative when I heard glass breaking.

I looked out of my window to see Busey climbing through the busted glass of Milton's bathroom window. As he jumped, he cut his clothing and God knows what else on the jagged edges and squealed.

"Aaaaah, shit get me out of here! I am getting ready to do a film in two weeks! Don't let them find me, Milton."

He ran like the mad man he was onto PCH and took off like a long distance runner sprinting to the finish. He was just fucking nuts. I had never seen anything like it.

Several hours later, I found myself watching late night television in Los Angeles, unable to go to sleep. Finally, in a desperate attempt to come down, I went into the hot tub and lit up one of the joints that I took from Busey.

Sitting in the tub and sensually taking one toke after another had a soothing effect. Soon, my mellow feelings returned. I noticed the moon in the sky. It was waning but still bright enough to illuminate my 3 a.m. Malibu sky.

In the far side of the courtyard, a frail shadowy figure appeared. As it drew nearer, I realized it was Bowie. I sighed in relief, glad to see him. He felt more like a longtime friend instead of a hallucination. The cocaine had blurred all lines for me and I just sat in the tub, puffing away.

"Are you having a hard time, little princess of rock and roll?" he said endearingly. Whatever this was, hallucination or reality, it was comforting and I responded.

"It's just all fucked up, Bowie. I can't seem to put something together. I thought that I was going to pitch some songs to Jagger and get this ball rolling. Instead, I have no nanny, had to get a new job and I am no closer to doing something in rock and roll than your ex-wife is."

We both laughed. Angie's bid for rock and roll success had fallen flat on its face and mine seemed to be heading in that direction.

"Don't give up, you're too talented. This town may be the devil's favorite vacation spot but there are opportunities for you, just keeping looking."

His words rang like golden chimes from the church of my salvation. I took another hit. The image faded and I was alone with a third quarter moon.

Chapter 21
Let it Be

I was like a zombie going through all the motions of my day. I dropped Caleb off and took the kids to Zuma Beach. Perhaps the stiff, salty breeze could revive me from the awful cocaine hangover.

As I sat on the lonely beach, I spied a man walking down the shoreline, holding his shoes and running barefoot through the surf. As he walked past us, he smiled at me.

"Hi there, pretty windy out here today, huh?"

He seemed friendly and I needed a friend. The loneliness of being in a strange town with no one to turn to had taken its toll.

"Hi, I'm Ron Slywood ... and you are?"

"Anne Marie Channing," I said graciously. He sat down right next to me as if he needed no invitation.

"So, Anne Marie Channing, what do you do?"

I found it to be a pretty straight forward question, so I snapped back.

"I am a rock and roll singer in search of a rock and roll band. So it's not so much what I do, but what I want to do."

"Really?" he said a bit skeptically. "Sing me a few bars of something."

I decided to sing one of my original tunes.

I give you all my best love, my very best love and you throw it away ... and you throw it away.

His face was stoic, with no smile or sign that he thought it was good. I was not to be discouraged, and I belted into a well-known Cream song, adding my particular bluesy spin to it.

His interest seemed mildly sparked.

"Sing me something from the Beatles," he said with enthusiasm.

I delivered "Let it Be" soulfully, with deep resounding sound

127

to give it the gravitas I wanted, but yet sweetly as if I sang second tenor in a gospel choir.

"Wow," he stopped me. "You might have something there. Funny that I should be walking down the beach just now and chanced running into you. I have just had a meeting down the street with one of my clients, Cheryl Anne, wife of the manager of Van Halen."

I lit up like a pinball machine on full tilt. Van fucking Halen. Eddie Van Halen was the hottest guitar player in the nation. The band was world famous and I had read in some magazine that they got their start at the Whiskey a Go Go that was somewhere in the Hollywood area. I thought that I had just hit a gold mine.

"Do they need any backup singers?" I asked eagerly.

"I don't work with Van Halen," he said emphatically, dripping with disdain. "However, I do think that Cheryl might need another backup singer."

"Really?" I said, my enthusiasm sliding up a notch.

"Hey, I'm not saying you have the gig but … you never know. By the way, I think we should have lunch at the Malibu Grill, maybe Cheryl can meet us there?"

I gathered up the kids and Ron and we drove over to the grill. I kept thinking this was my lucky day. Ron darted over to a pay phone to make a call as soon as we got there. I assumed he was calling Cheryl Anne.

"So these are your kids," he said, as if he had just noticed them for the first time.

"Well, two of them, my oldest one Caleb is at Malibu Elementary."

"Really?" Ron seemed more interested in that than the menu.

He finally looked at the menu and then reached into his pocket.

"Oh, heck, it looks like I forgot my wallet?" he said apologetically.

"No problem," I said. "Order anything on the menu, my treat." I wanted to treat this guy well because I was hoping he had a gig for me to plug into.

I was shocked that the guy then proceeded to order a milkshake, a sandwich, soup, a salad, and magnanimously state to us, "Let's all get an appetizer, kids! Do you guys like cheese?"

Of course Mia and Michael roared in agreement. I wound up

spending fifty bucks for lunch, and considering I only had a small salad, it seemed like more of a pricey deal than I had bargained for.

Ron gabbed away all through lunch and he ate like a man who hadn't eaten in several days.

"I need to get you into the studio to check your levels. By the way, have you ever been in a major recording studio?"

I got goose bumps up and down my spine as I heard the word, "studio."

"No," I said shyly.

Ron had a split-second look in his eyes. I thought he was sizing me up. For what, I was not sure.

"So, we should go to your house and strategize. Do you live close?"

My heart started beating furiously in my chest. I decided to risk it.

"It's just across the street at the Malibu Cliffs, I have the studio apartment. I came from Miami just a couple months ago."

"Cool."

Ron and I and the kids went to the apartment. I occupied Mia with a puzzle and Michael with his Speak and Spell. They would easily play until it was time to pick Caleb up from school.

Ron and I sat in the dining room and I pulled out all of my notebooks with finished and unfinished lyrics. I had even chorded a few, but my ability to play was limited to the tiny keyboard I brought with me.

"Hey, gotta joint?" he asked. I was shocked, assuming a man in his position would not be a smoker, but then again, this was California.

"Yeah, I do, as a matter of fact." I slipped into the bedroom and pulled open the drawer on my nightstand. In the cigarette case my father gave me when he quit smoking in 1964, his 1942 cigarette case that he bought at the air force base canteen, were the 13 joints I had taken from Busey.

"Let's go outside," I said, motioning to Ron that I had what he was looking for. I walked to the hot tub courtyard and slid behind the tall bougainvillea that sheltered the love seat that overlooked the ocean. It was not that I wanted to set a romantic mood, but I did not want Milton out there poking his nose into my business.

After inhaling a huge hit, Ron exhaled like a junkie getting his fix. He took two more tokes before he handed it to me. I took a hit as well and relaxed, thinking that I was actually getting that opportunity that Bowie and I had talked about the other night.

"This is good shit," he remarked.

"Glad you like it." I found it an odd thing to say. Perhaps it was just a California thing. I had a few moments where I doubted Ron's authenticity so I decided to test the waters while he was under the influence.

"Why don't we go in to the studio tomorrow and check my levels. I can bring my songs and maybe get something put together for Cheryl Anne?"

"Do you have money?" he demanded.

"Yes," I managed to say after some difficulty.

"How much?" he said flippantly.

His obvious intrusion into my private financial manners unnerved me and I exploded.

"How much do you have?" I snapped back.

"Whoa, slow down, sister. Girls like you arrive on the shores of Malibu and Los Angeles every day. I am doing you a favor but I ain't gonna pay for it. Got it?"

His harsh glare, coupled with the fact that my opportunity might be flying out the window, frightened me.

"Hey, I think you got something, kid. You don't get anywhere in this town without your own demo recording. It's like a business card."

"Oh, no, I understand. My apologies. It's just that I have three small children to look out for and I can't afford to fail."

I searched his face to see if this information of great significance to me, was getting through to him. His stoned expression told me that he was off in la la land. He spent another five minutes smoking the joint by himself. I was more than stoned, and I knew I had to drive to the school.

We walked back in the apartment to see Michael and Mia fighting over the Speak and Spell.

"Give it to me!" Mia demanded.

"Whaaaaa!" Michael cried like a banshee knowing I would cave in to the noise.

I grabbed two homemade chocolate chip cookies off the plate I had on top of the refrigerator.

Each received one and I took a moment to calm them down, distracting them with different toys and asking them to get along.

Ron seemed a bit annoyed with their noise but when he realized there were cookies, he snatched the plate and sat down with it at the dining table. Then, he went back to find a glass and poured himself a glass of milk to go with the cookies.

Geez, I thought, he just ate lunch an hour ago, and a big lunch at that. My attention turned to the clock on the wall. It said twenty minutes after two.

"Gotta pick up my son at school. You wanna stay here or come with me?"

He had just about finished the entire plate of cookies.

"On second thought, why don't you come with me? Maybe we will run into Dylan."

"Bob Dylan?" Ron said.

"What other Dylan is there?"

"Dylan Thomas, poet extraordinaire, of whom, Robert Zimmerman took his name, but I digress ... let's pick up Master Caleb."

We sped off down the PCH and got there just in time. The bell was ringing and the children were racing to the cars that were waiting to pick them up. I spied Jakob Dylan and realized the silver limo was Bob's. The back window was cracked just enough for me to see that he was sitting in the back seat.

"There's Jakob Dylan," I observed, knowing I was baiting the hook for Ron.

"That kid?" said Ron, pointing at Jakob as his finger followed the boy's trail back to the limo.

As Ron reached to open the door, I snapped the doors shut with the master lock.

"I won't let you out to talk to him 'till you promise me we can go to the recording studio tomorrow."

"That's Saturday."

"So?" Again, I found it odd that it would be a problem. Rock and roll studios were supposed to be open to whenever an artist could work, or at least, that was my impression.

131

For the first time since I met him, I had him where I wanted him. I could tell he was itching to get out of the van.

"Look, I will take you to my favorite little studio here in Malibu, Cahoots. It's back off of Kanan Dume Road. We can cut you a fantastic demo. Open the fucking door."

"Deal," I said, and I unlocked the doors. Unfortunately, the limo glided out of the parking lot and headed down the canyon road. Ron looked dejected and got back in the van.

"Monday, since the fish got away. Monday."

"I can't do Monday, I've just got a new job at the florist and I start Monday."

"A job?" Ron gasped for air.

"What the fuck do you need a job for?"

"Money."

"I thought you said you wanted to be a rock and roll star. You said you got money, now's the time to spend it. I have a big country star who will be there. We are putting together a project for him, hey, maybe we could get you two working on a project?"

He winked, and I found myself feeling like I was jumping off a cliff. I reasoned that I could always get a new job, but I only had so much money and I began to feel like this guy was not quite right. I couldn't put my finger on it.

"Why don't we go to your house for a while?" I asked probingly.

"Nah, we are in the creative moment. Besides, I live all the way down in San Diego, so it's just best if I stay with you, I mean, traffic alone is crazy on the weekends. Hey, it'll be great, I love your kids."

His stock nicey-nice phrases hit me in all the right places. I felt the need for the kids to have a male role model or substitute father figure in their lives. On so many levels, I felt like I was becoming Ron's friend, and I really needed a friend.

Chapter 22
You Can't Always Get What You Want

On Monday morning I was like a little kid, wide eyed and heart beating. Walking into the studio, the first thing that caught my eye was the huge master board. It was a 16-track studio with great acoustics. I lovingly caressed each microphone that I found in the isolation booth. I put the head phones on and began to sing scales. It was heavenly to hear my voice. The amplification, the effects, and the way it felt to put my lips around the mic gave me a thrilling and uncontrollable pleasure.

Ron was orchestrating a drummer and bass player being mic'd in the larger studio room. He used a track for each of his drums and percussion instruments, and then put a track for the bass guitar and another for his vocals. Ron put music stands and sheet music in front of them and walked back to the control room. He put headphones on and gave both musicians a big thumbs up.

Worried that I was being left out, I darted out of the booth and back to the control room.

"Hey, shouldn't I be in there too?" I said with haste.

"No," he said abruptly. "I am laying down tracks for the backbeat, just bass and drums. Don't worry, you'll have your opportunity to lay down vocals."

He stared a fiery red hole though me as he said, "Don't bother me. Just let me work, I think I know a thing or two about producing. These are my songs that you are singing, so let me lay down the song so you can lay your vocals on top of them."

He gave me a look that said, shut up and be a good little girl, so I did. I did not want to jeopardize this wonderful opportunity.

"Have you ever sung backup vocals?" he asked matter-of-factly.

"Yes, church choir," I chirped back.

133

"Church choir?" his tone was probing. "How about professionally? Did you ever lay down tracks in a studio in Miami?" He looked piercingly at me, as if to sense any hint of lying.

"I performed at a coffeehouse doing acoustic music and I did some back up there. WTVJ, I was an intern and I sang lead and backup vocals to tags we did for commercials." I stopped right there, knowing it was just one time and the studio was nothing like this.

Ron seemed pleased and I passed his test.

"OK, let's lay down some tracks."

The bass and drummer put a catchy backbeat on seven of the tracks. I panicked a bit wondering how many tracks I would have. In one sense, it really didn't matter. I knew that I could deliver. When the rhythm guitarist laid down his track, his Guild 12-string filled the room with a driving, lively guitar riff and he knew where to drive the sound.

I began to feel euphoric. The song was being put together and all I had to do was stand in the control booth and watch it happen. God had answered my prayers and I was back on track in my life. This was my gift. I can sing. I can make this song soar.

I nervously fingered the head phones so I could do a sound check. I sang scales for what seemed like forever as the engineer ran sound levels. Ron seemed relaxed, happy, and in control, and any doubts I had harbored about his authenticity had been banished. He clearly knew how to craft a song, although I was surprised at how "country sounding" his rock and roll was.

The sheet music and lyrics were in front of me on a music stand, but I had memorized the words while I watched them lay down the instrumentals. Time to top off the sundae with the whipped cream and cherry.

I found my key and asked Ron to transpose it to E minor. The same dark look crossed his face as he shouted from the com link, "You will sing it in A."

Again, feeling like the little girl that was about to get scolded, I withheld any further comments and sang the lead in A. The first run-through was a practice, and Ron stood like the maestro with his baton ready to conduct his concerto. I relaxed into it and gave it everything I knew how to give. Recording a song was a brand new experience, yet deep in my soul, there was a recognition, a connection to the infinite. God, if you will.

"Hey, I think we have a hit on our hands," he said as we sat back and listened to the final mix. It was catchy, but decidedly country rock.

Nevertheless, I left the studio feeling hopeful. My first experience recording a song resounded an emotional resonance within my soul. I knew that I belonged in the studio, my lips cradling a microphone.

Chapter 23
Down Bound Train

The following Saturday, I sat down with Ron and the kids at Trancas Canyon restaurant, and like usual, I needed a large cup of coffee just to wake up. The week had been a rollercoaster of agony and ecstasy. I was informed that country legend, Sonny Martin, was going to put his lead vocals on the song. As wonderful as my vocals were, Ron had insisted that Sonny had the distribution vehicle to get the song out there. He had been offered a spot on the upcoming Kenny Rogers/Dolly Parton Christmas special and he would be singing the recording, "Sometimes, I'm Always Wrong," one of the two songs that we cut at Cahoots studio for my demo.

Ron peered at me from across the table. "Look, in this industry you have to have street creds. Do you know what I mean?" He seemed like a used car salesman as he flagged the waitress down for another cup of coffee.

"Why am I paying for the entire recording session, when Sonny is going to use the song?" My eyebrows knit together in worry as I had flashbacks of angry conversations with Craig.

"This is the way you earn those street creds. So what if you're the executive producer on the song, you stand to make the most money. This song will be on an NBC television network special. You are the executive producer. This is a sweet deal for you, quit complaining."

Ron lit up a Winston and began blowing smoke in my direction.

"Stop smoking. My kids are getting secondhand smoke. Take your cancer stick outside, now!"

Ron got up without a word and slid out to the back bar area. He would prove to be a master at manipulating a situation to his advantage. Blending just the right amount of distracting stimulus with the emotional charge of the event, he would scare you into thinking he was right.

Sonny Martin had a pot belly, barely wrangled by a big Texas belt buckle, and a three-week-old beard on his face. When he sauntered into the studio, he spat into a spittoon by the door that I had never noticed before. For someone I had never heard of, he certainly made an entrance like a star. He brought an entourage, including backup singers. I sat quietly as I watched Sonny descend upon my project. I suddenly understood why Ron had insisted I sing in the key of A. It was Sonny's key. I started to feel used, after all I was paying for this.

I walked out to the waiting area to get a drink of water. The studio technician's wife was making a fresh pot of coffee. She looked at me with sad eyes.

"What are you going to do if this doesn't take off?" She asked.

"What do you mean?" I replied, alarmed.

"Has it crossed your mind that there is no record company behind this? That's why he is having you pay for this. You have kids, honey, that's why I am saying this. Do you have income? Any extra money?"

A dark wave came over me. Panic and fear overwhelmed me as I recalled my mother's voice on the phone when I called her a few weeks back to announce my newly-found fortune as a record producer.

"You only believe him because you want to believe him. What do you really know about this Ron Slywood, anyways?"

Tears welled up inside of me that, until that moment, had no outlet. I was shaking violently and she came over to give me a hug.

"You should have a backup plan, Anne Marie. You are putting all of your eggs in this basket and I don't think this is a sure thing. I have seen bands come and go in this recording studio and each band, each lead vocalist, thinks that they are the next big thing. Believe me, dreams die hard here in dream town."

I numbed out and said nothing after the studio session. As usual, Ron and I picked up the kids from an elderly lady who lived in the Pt. Dume trailer park. She had a modest place, but the view of the Pacific Ocean from Pt. Dume was magnificent. I said next to nothing as we went to the local Chinese restaurant and ate. As we drove back to my apartment at the Malibu Cliffs motel, Ron cleared his throat, hoping to stimulate some conversation.

"I thought the studio session went well, don't you?"

"I guess, as long as Sonny Martin liked it," I stated in sarcastic drippings.

"Are you copping an attitude? You should be so grateful to even have this opportunity. You haven't even paid your dues yet and here you are an executive producer on a Sonny Martin/ Ron Slywood production. Maybe I won't tell you what Sonny offered you today after the session."

"What are you talking about?" I said, obviously unable to hide my interest.

"While you were out in the lounge area getting coffee, I played Sonny your cut. He flipped over it! Loves it! Wants to offer you a breakout new artist spot on the Kenny Rogers/Dolly Parton special and you can sing 'Sweet Tears of Laughter,' what do you think?"

My ears perked up like Vulcan antennae. I would get a shot at a network television premiere. Who cared if it was country? It was huge crossover successes like Kenny and Dolly hosting the gig.

"Uh huh, see, what happened to that attitude? I told you. Play ball with me, and I will take you to places you only dreamed about."

The idea that I was going to tell him to go and find another place to stay evaporated. Instead, we read the kids some stories, got them to go to sleep, then slipped out back to smoke a joint in the hot tub. I watched the November full moon rise over the city of Los Angeles and I felt at home, like I belonged there, and that there would be no stopping me now.

My voice had the style and depth to do country and then switch back to rock and roll. My ego was so inflated that I felt like a great helium balloon floating high above the cliffs in Malibu. I knew I had what it took to make it. I blew out a huge puff of smoke into circular rings, aiming to ring some of the flowers on the bougainvillea. Life was good.

"Sonny wants to meet with you on Sunday at his place. You can see all of his gold and platinum records hanging on the walls of his house. We will firm up the deal then." Ron's eyes were twinkling, knowing that I was thrilled with everything he was telling me. "Get Mrs. McCauley to babysit. Sonny won't want you to bring your kids."

Driving into Los Angeles is usually crowded and tedious, even on a Sunday morning. The 405 was jammed up and we inched down the southbound lane heading for Orange County, where Sonny maintained his "LA bungalow."

The "bungalow" was just that. Small, unassuming, it was located in a vast neighborhood of postage stamp-sized lots with cookie-cutter houses. It struck me as odd that a big star would live there.

Sonny met us at the door and we walked into the living room. On the walls were gold and platinum records, a big picture of Sonny when he performed for New Year's Eve at the Palamino Saloon, and a huge picture of Elvis Presley. When I extended my hand to greet him, he bypassed me like a trucker on a deadline and gave me a huge hug.

"Anne Marie, darling, you are a huge talent. Ron played me your tracks and I think you would be a perfect fit in the upcoming Christmas Special. Why ... I just talked to Dolly this morning about it and she loves the idea."

I was spinning like a top into the stratospheres of orgasmic delight. I knew this was going to work out. How I would delight in shoving this back in Craig's face. His blatant non-payment of any child support had caused me to sit precariously on top of the 5000 dollars I had left in the Malibu Savings and Loan.

"See this one," he said, pointing to the gold record closest to the hallway. "That was my very first hit, 'Truck Drivin' Man.' I performed that one at the Grand Old Opry. I was a young pup upstart just like you are now, Anne Marie."

I stared at the record and pictured a wall full of my own records. I imagined all the hits I would make ... all the tours I would go on. I was starting to feel like I was tasting the good life.

A small, blonde, ponytailed woman poked her head around the corner and asked if anyone would like some coffee out on the lanai. Her name was Lainie, and it appeared from their mutual affections that she was Sonny's wife or girlfriend. I did not ask any questions. The only question in my mind was: "When is the rehearsal, and is this live or are we going to tape it?"

Halfway through polite conversation and coffee, Sonny cleared his throat and I caught the subtlest exchange of glances between Sonny and Ron.

"Sonny and I have this deal about 99% closed but we need an additional amount of cash to finish it off and sell it to the network. We knew that you would love to be an executive producer on this project as well, and we want to bring you in on the deal."

My sunny mood broke into internal thunderstorms as I realized they were going to ask me for money. I took to offense.

"I am flattered that you would consider me, gentlemen, but I simply cannot afford to be any sort of investor on this project."

Sonny looked at Ron like someone who had dropped the ball. Ron fidgeted.

Like a brazen whore, Ron boldly stated, "What about that five thousand dollars you have in your savings account?"

My mouth dropped at least a foot, maybe all the way down to the floor. I felt exposed and betrayed. I turned to Sonny, hoping I could find a sympathetic soul.

"I have three children to feed and a husband who does not contribute a dime. This is unsafe for me. Surely, you understand ..." I pleaded.

Sonny leaned in toward me like he was about to confide some sort of valuable information.

"Honey, I am giving you a shot at an NBC network television spot. Are you a player or not? This business is not for the faint-hearted."

He looked around the room for an ashtray, snorting like an old pig. Then he turned to me again, asking, "Why in the hell are you out here in tinsel town with your kids anyways? This is no place for them. Send them back to their dad."

Lainie spotted the ashtray on the far end table, overloaded with cigarette butts, and promptly dumped them in the trash, quickly handing the emptied container to Sonny. He lit up and sat back in his lazy boy, blowing smoke rings into the air.

Ron decided to intervene at that moment.

"We need to have a contract, Sonny. Our interests must be protected."

"Of course you do," Sonny chimed back. "I will have my lawyer draw one up for us. You kids go home and come back tomorrow. We can sign it and move ahead on the project."

"That sounds reasonable, Sonny." Ron was beaming as he got

my jacket. He even put it around my shoulders as he ushered me out the door. I wanted to go ballistic on both of them but it seemed that this was an easier exit.

As soon as we got to the car, I did go ballistic on Ron.

"Are you fucking crazy? I cannot and will not give him 5000 dollars to be on his country hicks TV show. I would become penniless and homeless and I have three kids to support!" I was screaming at the top of my lungs. "It's not your money, Ron, it's my money ... and oh, did I mention that I have three kids to support ... THREE KIDS!"

Instead of engaging in verbal combat, Ron silently sat in the passenger seat and lit up a cigarette. He blew smoke rings out the window onto the crowded freeway where they merged with all the other pollutants in the air. We picked up the kids in silence and went back to the Malibu Cliffs motel.

After the kids were asleep, Ron uncharacteristically cuddled up to me as if he wanted to make out. I was tired and frustrated and I hadn't had any loving at all since months before Craig's abrupt departure. I gave in to the moment. The love making was awkward and contrived.

He kept whispering in my ear, "Don't worry, everything will be alright. We will be rich and you will be famous at this same time next year. Trust me on this," he said nibbling on my ear.

Chapter 24
Rebel, Rebel

The following morning, I woke up at around 5 a.m. feeling dirty and creepy. I grabbed a cup of coffee from the motel front office, since I knew Milton would have a pot brewing in the office entryway. I made it black and it felt like a stiff drink as I walked down the parking lot to the phone booth on the edge of the PCH.

It was 8:45 a.m. in Miami and I was praying that Craig would be answering the phone.

"Hello?" Craig answered sounding a bit groggy, certainly not bright eyed and bushy tailed like a cardiologist should be.

"Hi Craig, it's Anne Marie." There was a long pause and finally he sighed loudly. "What do you want Anne Marie?" Certainly he had not changed his attitude about anything. "I need money, Craig, money to feed your children and make sure they have a roof over their heads."

"You stupid bitch," he snapped back. "Your timing couldn't be worse. I have to leave in a minute to go to the abortion clinic with Nicole. She's pregnant."

"Typical Craig," I thought. "It's not about his kids, or his wife, it's about him. He has a problem. The blonde bimbo decided to get knocked up and it didn't fly. Instead he's rushing her to the local abortion clinic."

"Wow, Craig, tell me again how this is going to be good for our marriage?" I said trying to belabor a point.

I hung up with a loud crash and busted the receiver against the phone cradle. I slipped out of the booth and ran back down the parking lot to my room and went into the bathroom. I sat on the toilet and cried, sobbing into as much toilet paper as I could hold in my hand.

I heard Ron rumbling around, making coffee. My head was spinning. What if he was right and I was standing on the precipice of my career as a singer? What if I was wrong and I had no money left, my children depended on me and only me. I had to keep our financial heads above water. I never wanted to be in the situation that Charlotte was in. Living with a man she didn't love so that California Child Protective Services wouldn't take her son away from her.

I walked out of the bathroom like a soldier going into battle. Ron slipped his arms around me and hugged me, then gave me a kiss. "It is going to be just fine, don't worry." I melted. This soldier was a peacenik from the 1960's and I did want it to work out. I wanted to succeed.

When I walked into the Malibu Savings and Loan, there was a long line for both tellers. It seemed like a sign that I shouldn't be doing this, but Ron guided me through the whole process and in thirty minutes the deed was done. Ironically, that was about how long he lasted in bed as well.

Ron had insisted that we make a money order out to Sonny Martin. At first I balked, insisting that I should read the contract first, but he kept firm pressure on the entire process. My hand shook as I took the money order from the teller.

"Are you okay, honey?" a portly middle-aged woman said to me. My mind was in a whirl and I heard music.

Lady, Rebel, your hair's a mess. Lady, Rebel, no one can guess. Hot Slut, I adore you so.

There in the lobby stood Bowie. His eyes were so penetrating, and I knew that he could only stay for a few seconds.

"Get out Anne Marie," he said with direct force. It was as if there was a wind behind his words. The invisible force blew the money order on the floor. Ron picked it up off the floor and put it in his vest pocket.

"Wow, we don't want to lose that now, do we." It was as if the devil himself had picked up the money order. I shuddered.

When we got to Sonny's it was very cut and dry. He handed us a contract that stated, in simple terms, that I would be given a spot on the TV show in exchange for the 5000 dollar investment. Ron signed it, then I signed it, and he had Lainie go to the back office room which was nothing more than a reconverted second bedroom and make a copy.

I tried to look him in the eyes and shake hands like most business investments are conducted, but he was evasive and did not want to shake my hand. When I finally did grab it, his grip was almost palsied, weak, and lifeless. He snatched the money order from Ron and didn't even have polite conversation but instead insisted he had band practice he had to go to down at the Palamino and he was already late. I was out the door and into the car before I could even catch my breath.

"That was a mistake," I said to Ron as I drove off. "He acted like a thief."

"Stop," Ron said with commanding authority. "You are on your way to becoming a star. I was going to save this for dinner tonight but I will tell you now. Next Friday, we are auditioning a song for Tina Turner's next album. We meet in her manager's office. There may be studio time as one of her backup singers."

Ron was beaming from ear-to-ear like a Cheshire cat.

"Now that's as rock and roll as you can get! Tina is red hot and her appearance at the Live Aid concert last summer has her album sales going through the roof. Her manager, Mick Whitley, thinks we may have a shot at maybe one or both songs on your demo."

The dark cloud of worry that was hanging over me lifted as I learned of an audition with Tina Turner's management. Even though being a backup singer was not my goal, I figured that it wouldn't hurt to be on stage in arenas that she would fill and get a taste of it.

Surely Tina Turner paid her female backup singers a lot of money, at least enough to pay for room and board for a single mom and her three kids.

I put Sonny Martin out of my thoughts for the time being and concentrated on rehearsing the songs. I tried to rock them out a bit more, but was confined to the tempo and rhythm that we recorded at Cahoots studio. I was troubled with reconciling the song's styles with Tina's style. This was country and Tina was rhythm and blues-infused rock and roll.

My doubts kept building, but as we drove up to the offices in North Hollywood, I was sure that we were going to meet Tina. The hair on the back of my neck stood up and my stomach began to tie itself into several knots.

As we sat in a rather ordinary looking conference room, a tall, slender, brown haired man whose hair was pulled back into a ponytail walked in.

"Hello there," he said in a very thick Australian accent. "Pleased to meet you, I'm Mick Whitley, Tina's manager. So you have some tunes you think might work for Tina's next album?"

"Yes, I do," said Ron. He handed him a cassette tape.

Mick looked at the tape and then looked at Ron, perplexed.

"You don't have this on a DVD or CD?" He looked annoyed at Ron for what I perceived as a lack of professional standards.

Ron spied an acoustic guitar in a corner of the room and motioned to it. "Can I play it for you then?"

"By all means," said Mick, annoyed but secretly hoping he could salvage a tune for Tina out of the meeting.

He started playing and I burst into the song. I did my best to belt out the song as I thought Tina would perform it, but the song did not lend itself to the targeted singer.

When I finished, we stared blankly at each other. Mick blinked and blurted out, "Okay, right, well we thank you for coming in and performing your songs, but it just isn't the right fit for Ms. Turner. Gooday!"

He promptly got up and started to leave the room when I grabbed his sleeve. Before I could get a word out, he interrupted me with his apologetic tone.

"You have a fantastic voice my dear, but this is country, not rock and roll. Good luck, though."

He left me hanging in the wind. I was so broken hearted that I couldn't speak. I sat in the car unable to drive, unable to move. Ron could tell that I was as fragile as a fine piece of china and he said nothing. We finally drove home to Malibu in silence.

Chapter 25
Paint it Black

The week dragged on and I could not understand why Sonny Martin had not called. Ron made excuses about next week being Thanksgiving and he probably had shows. However, when December began to drag into the second week, I panicked.

"When are we taping this Christmas special?" I demanded of Ron.

"OK, it does seem a little strange that Sonny has not contacted us," Ron finally admitted. "I will call him tonight."

The phone rang and rang and rang. Each time Ron got off the phone my attitude would get a little darker. It was Christmas time and even though I bought a tree and some decorations, it just didn't feel like Christmas. I had secretly begun to take from another bank account I had back in Miami. When I set that account up shortly before I left town, I never dreamt that I would be dipping into it. That was my emergency, get out of town, if-all-else-fails-and-I-need-funds-to-regroup money.

Three days before Christmas, Ron finally got a hold of Sonny Martin. He invited us over to his place and said he had news about the TV special.

"See, it's probably going to be a live network broadcast on Christmas Eve. He will probably give you a date for the dress rehearsal. This is so exciting!"

Ron was babbling like a kid who just won the football game by catching the winning pass. It struck me as odd that a supposed "big time record producer" would be acting as if this were his first major gig.

Sonny met us at the door with a scotch and water in his hand. He reeked of liquor, and he didn't seem at all like someone who was getting ready for a major television special. He handed both Ron and I a drink and sat down in his lazy boy, dangling his right leg over the side since he said it was hurting him. It looked like gout to me, but then again, I was no doctor.

"Things at the network are getting screwed up and it looks like we won't be able to get this Kenny and Dolly special to fly." He cleared his throat as if there were a huge hairball in there.

"Sorry," he said as he scratched his balls and downed the rest of his drink.

"Sorry?" I exclaimed, standing up in shock and dropping my cocktail on the floor. "Sorry isn't good enough. I need my money back!"

"We have a contract, Sonny," said Ron with a bit of alarm in his voice as well.

Sonny just scratched his head and looked at me, then at Ron, then back at me.

"I don't know what to tell you. Like I said, this business is rough. Hey, I am out money too. I had some skin in the game too, you know. We all took it on the chin on this one."

"But hey," he said as he got up, letting us know it was time for us to go by escorting us to the door, "we keep singing our songs, sometimes we win, sometimes we lose, but all the time, it just makes us stronger."

I stood at the doorway, unable to walk back to the car without a better explanation than that.

"Are you telling me that I just lost five thousand dollars and it's just my tough luck?" I started screaming, "I have kids and I gave you every last cent I had and you're telling me tough luck … tough luck!"

Sonny reached down into a large glass bowl that was filled with chocolate candies and put a huge pile into my hands.

"Here, give this to your kids and tell them I am real, real sorry but I hope they have a merry Christmas."

The chocolates were melted and all gooey, coming out of the wrappers. He put them in my hands so that he could easily close the door on us without me having a free hand to keep it open.

"Merry Christmas, folks," he said as the door banged shut. I walked back to the car like a zombie in shock. This is not happening to me, I kept repeating over and over in my head. I deserved better than this in my life, and I decided that I had not thought through my relationship with Ron Slywood.

When the door of the car closed, I unleashed a tirade of verbal abuse.

"Who the hell does that fat fuck think he is? I am not going to put up with this, we have a contract!"

Ron felt the same way. "Exactly, we have a contract. He cannot take the money. We have a contract. I will contact my lawyer in Santa Monica first thing tomorrow morning."

Amazed that Ron was handling it so professionally, I eased back in the driver's seat for the long drive back to Malibu.

Mr. Edward Humburger was a large, portly man whose stomach extended well beyond his belt. In a profile, he resembled Alfred Hitchcock, only taller. He sat down with us at his large desk. Behind him was a wonderful view of the Pacific Ocean, and it was a warm and sunny day in Santa Monica. It was hardly the type of weather for three days before Christmas but then, I was used to it, coming from Miami.

"I regret to inform you that this contract is vague." He stated this with such brevity, I felt like that was his diagnosis, and there was no more to be said.

I countered: "Vague, what do you mean, vague?"

Edward Humburger looked down over his glasses that were perched precariously on the end of his nose and drew in a deep breath.

"Vague, my dear, as in open-ended. Just because he didn't succeed in securing this television special does not give you the right to sue. It's open-ended. If he gets you one next year, or the year after that, he is still fulfilling his contractual obligations to you for your money."

I stood up, unable to hold back tears. "So, are you telling me that my five grand is gone? I can't get it back?" Waves of tears rolled down my cheeks and I felt numb and sick inside.

"Precisely. You should have consulted me before you signed this and I could have structured this so there were conditions and time limits. You will wind up spending more money than you invested trying to get your money back."

I left the office in a fury. I got into the car and drove down the

PCH unleashing my hell upon Ron.

"What kind of a damn dumbass do you think I am, Ron? You are a nobody, you haven't produced anyone and I don't even know if you have a home. This crap about remodeling your home in San Diego is nothing but a goddamn lie. You are a creep and a con man."

"Fuck you, Anne Marie!" he fired back. "YOU are the nobody and I am working with Van Halen's manager's wife."

"Fine, then go live with her!" I spewed back. We pulled into the Malibu Cliffs motel parking lot and got out and slammed the door to the car.

"Get the fuck out of here Ron and don't come back. I am out of money and it's two days before Christmas Eve. I have kids and this fat fuck gives me gooey chocolates for them."

I threw the chocolates at Ron who was screaming back at me.

"You fucking ungrateful bitch! I had you in front of Tina Turner's people last week and this is how you repay me?"

"That's right. Get out and don't come back." I was yelling at the top of my lungs and the commotion caused Milton to stick his head out of the window.

"You both better shut up or else."

"Get out, get out, get out!" I continued to scream.

"You can't just kick me out, with all I have done for you and your kids." Ron was even louder than I was.

I walked back to the room and paid my sitter, who couldn't wait to put her jacket on and catch the bus back to Santa Monica. The kids looked at me and I could see in their eyes that they wanted a better world than I was providing.

Ron burst into the room and on his heels was Milton who was screaming at him.

"Get out of here before I call the cops, you are disturbing other motel guests!" Milton was in no mood for any crap, but then again, Ron was not one to give in easily.

"Hey, we pay you money to stay here. You better treat us with a little more respect than that."

I looked at Milton with pleading eyes. The last thing I needed was to be homeless on Christmas Eve. His cold eyes were staring back with black hate.

"You and your big-mouth boyfriend need to get your things

and leave. I have other paying customers that want peace and quiet and this loud-mouthed pervert is disrupting my business."

Ron started to take a swing at him and I ran out of the door and into Milton's office and called Charlene.

"Do you think the Captain would mind if my children and I came to stay with him on Christmas Eve? Charlene, I have no place else to go."

For one very long second or two, she put her hands over the phone and asked the Captain.

"Sure, honey. Come on over. I am baking cookies."

"Oh God," I said. "How nice. Warm Christmas cookies."

By the time that I got back to the room, Ron and Milton were trading swings. I herded all three kids into the car and as I did the mailman pulled into the parking lot.

"Hey lady, are you Anne Marie Channing? I have some packages for you."

He handed me some packages that were addressed to the kids and I saw my mom's return address. I threw them in the back of the van and pulled out of the parking lot. In the rearview mirror I saw Ron running after the van, shaking his fist and cursing at me.

Evil piece of shit. I had attracted yet another bottom feeder into my life that was ready to devour me and all my money. I had to indentify this bad behavior and stop it. I never, ever wanted another parasite like Ron Slywood in my life again.

The rat ran after the car like as if his life depended on it, which it probably did.

At least, I had the satisfaction of laughing at his pathetic attempt to catch me. The mud from a recent rainstorm had dried to dust and I made a point of grinding those tires into that dirt until the cloud of dust covered every inch of Ron Slywood. I accelerated out onto the PCH and off to the Captain's house in San Pedro for what I hoped would be a peaceful Christmas.

"Thanks, mom," I said quietly to the sky. I have Christmas presents for my kids. Perhaps 1986 would end on a positive note. I certainly seemed to need to hit a high note soon. We had just enough money to fill up the gas tank in Malibu and drive to San Pedro.

Chapter 26
And So This Is Christmas

Charlene and Captain Jack had his San Pedro rooster's nest filled with Christmas cheer. Charlene made the place shine; wreaths hung everywhere and Christmas music was on when we arrived. A large tree was decorated with lights, ornaments, and bows.

I helped Charlene cook Christmas Eve dinner and it felt good. I felt normal again and my kids were enjoying their gifts from Santa's elf, the postman in Malibu. Michael received a big plush teddy bear from mom and at 4, I thought he might be too old for a stuffed toy, but no, he snuggled up with it on the huge guest room bed with the tall iron posts and the soft beige linen scarves adorning it. There were at least ten pillows and Mia and Michael snuggled against them, with Michael clutching his teddy bear and pressing it against his chest.

I kept filling Captain Jack's brandy glass as he sat in his big lazy boy recliner, knowing he would eventually pass out from his vintage Benedictine liquor. Right before he lost consciousness I asked him if I could use his phone to make a call. I handed him a ten dollar bill.

"Are you calling your husband?" he asked with slurred speech.

"Yes."

He pushed the money back into the palm of my hand.

"Talk all you want to, honey. I'm just a lonely old man but you brought Char back to me and your children are so wonderful. This has been the nicest Christmas Eve I have spent in years."

He raised his beautiful glass and asked, "Won't you just fill it up again and sing us another Christmas carol? Then you can talk all night if you wish."

That sounded wonderful, so I went to the piano and played a song that I had learned in my Catholic grade school choir.

151

O Holy Night, the Stars are brightly shining, it is the night of the dear Savior's birth

Long lay the world in sin and error blinding, till he appeared and the soul felt its worth.

Truly I did sing like an angel that night. It was such a nice barter, it felt like I was getting a gift from God. In the lookout tower which was on the south side of the dining room, an old friend stood by the railing, smiling and enjoying the performance.

When I finished, Capt. Jack was asleep and Bowie was clapping with great enthusiasm. A tear rolled down my cheek as I turned to go to the kitchen where the phone was. I blew a kiss to him as I watched his dark silhouette against the lighted full moon sky. I felt the magic. I felt my power returning to me and I realized that Ron Slywood was nothing but a con man, who, for all I knew, was homeless.

LA was much more than I ever bargained for and I began to question my sanity. My kids were starting to fade in the wear and tear of this rock and roll madness. Worse, if I couldn't conjure up any money, we would all be homeless.

It was 4am Miami time and I wasn't even sure that Craig would answer, or be home or anything. I just dialed a number that I knew by heart and sunk into the Captain's easy chair by the breakfast nook desk, the one that swiveled in a circle.

As I swirled the phone rang twice and a shaky, drunken voice answered.

"Hello?" Craig asked in a fuzzy voice.

"Hi Craig, it's Anne Marie. Merry Christmas."

There was an unbearably long pause and then he burst into a total blather.

"Anne Marie, oh God, I am so glad you called. I called that motel in Malibu and they said you left and I thought I would never see my kids again and I just can't take any more drama in my life and I work hard as a member of ..."

His sloppy drunk talk was hard to follow, even for one who had become accustomed to it.

"Oh God, Nicole got pregnant again and I had to get my friend to give her an abortion and then she got so goddamn touchy about the abortion and she told me that I was still in love with you and that I need my family and she's tired of feeling like the whore that gets the backroom abortion…"

"Okay, Craig, I am so sorry to hear all this." I swallowed my real feelings - that the bitch got what she deserved, the little home-wrecker. Being super sweet to him was the only way I would get money. And this call was about one thing and one thing only, and that was money. I needed to do or say or not do or not say, whatever it took to get the money.

"Oh, it's true Anne Marie, I miss you and I miss my Caleb bear and my little Mia bug and what about Michael. How is he?"

Craig started to cry and I inwardly sighed, wondering if he was sober enough to remember this and wire me some money the next day. I prayed to God to help and guide me through this conversation.

"Craig, we are all ok but we need money. I need some sort of financial help here. Can you wire me some money? Western Union?"

I knew there was an office just down the hill in the town of San Pedro.

"Sure I will, I will go and send you some money. Of course. I am so bad for not sending you money. I am going to go as soon as they open. Are they open on Christmas Day? I will send you money. How much do you need?"

"Ten thousand," I said, barely able to form the words. I decided to take advantage of the moment and get myself back in business.

"Ten thousand… hell, why not twenty? I know you need money."

"Ten thousand," I repeated back to him, hoping that his subconscious would retain this amount when he sobered up tomorrow afternoon.

"Send it to the Western Union on Ocean Way in San Pedro. You know what, Craig, write this down. Do you have a piece of paper and a pen close by?"

I heard a thud and realized he was in bed. I heard him open the nightstand drawer where he had kept a pad and pen for all of our married life together. He was predictable, if nothing else.

"OK, Western Union in San Diego?"

"No, San Pedro."

"OK, Western Union in San Pedro on Ocean Way."

Amazing, I thought. He remembered the street.

"Ten thousand to the Western Union in San Pedro on Ocean

way."

"Yep, I got it."

"Thanks, Craig. Merry Christmas. Good night."

"Yeah, Merry Christmas," said a wasted Craig. "Wait! Anne Marie, don't hang up. I want to talk to you. Where are you? What's your phone number?"

I found myself just a tad glib from the conversation. The whore was getting her just deserts, I just got a promise for 10 thousand dollars from Craig and I got in the stunning last words.

"Good night."

Merry Christmas Anne Marie Channing! Nice work!

I sat with my hot cocoa in the Captain's favorite room, which he had dubbed, "The Tower." It had a Victorian flavor, circular but with thermal paned glass all around so that one had a 360 degree view, just as a Captain would on his ship. He and Charlotte had long since passed out and my children were nestled in the big king size bed with the goose down comforter. Michael had the teddy bear that mom had sent him in his arms and he was holding it tightly.

I peered out over the captivating Los Angeles nightline. It was a very formidable opponent.

"Damn you, LA, you haven't won yet. I have not been defeated but you are truly a city with a treasure that isn't achieved easily," I said laughing, half-heated.

"It seems to me you should put a band together, first."

I looked up to see David Bowie sitting with legs underneath him on the sitting bench right next to the window. He looked a bit like a yogi in that position.

"You do, huh?" I said with slight sarcasm.

"There are vultures all over the world, but this city seems to be the most adept at deceiving innocent wannabe's like you. I told you not to give Ron or Sonny the check."

I sighed apologetically.

"I know you did, and I got kicked in the ass with a steel toe boot but I have learned a valuable lesson."

"I sincerely hope so. You got lucky getting that money from your husband."

A tear slid down my cheek from somewhere deep within my soul as I stared out at the ocean view. The moon was setting on the ocean and I felt like it was the Cheshire Cat laughing at me.

"Gullibility runs in my family," I whispered to Bowie.

"Insanity runs in mine," he retorted.

As I let out a blasting laugh, Charlotte tiptoed in as Bowie evaporated into the vapor from whence he came.

"I have got to get out of here, Anne Marie. I feel like I have traded in my freedom to become his.....his..."

Charlotte broke into a sob that tugged at my heart. I put my arms around her and patted her big fat behind. She was like a 180-pound little girl. Her tears felt bitter on my blue sweatshirt from Parrot Jungle.

"OK, listen, you go back to bed, let me figure something out." I felt as lost as she but I had money in my pocket again, a voice that needed a band, and the will to find one.

"You know, my mom used to spank me when I was bad. I think it helped me. Maybe you should take me across your knee? I think it would help me."

I freaked at the thought of her dragging out her psycho-melodrama all over the place, but my current housing situations was due to her playing as the object of the Captain's affections.

"OK, listen to me Charlotte, go back to bed. I will figure this out." I said it with so much authority that she did my bidding. I stared into the night sky, the inky black Pacific ocean with its white swells that kissed the shore below us.

The blues were swirling through me like a gypsy banshee and I was hoping I would not wake everyone but I felt it was the only thing in the whole universe just then that would save my soul. I needed direction and I needed it bad. I writhed through the entire song and as I reached the end I grabbed everything in sight that would even resemble a percussion instrument or drum and began banging out a drum solo finale that Keith Moon was nodding approval on from heaven.

From somewhere in the ether, I heard Bowie's voice tell me, "That's what you sing at the Troubadour, and you will get the record contract you're looking for."

I awoke the next morning to see Charlotte nervously fixing the Captain's breakfast.

"Come and have some breakfast with me, Anne Marie.

155

Charlotte's making her special: biscuits and gravy, and it's Gooood!"

"My kids would sure enjoy a home cooked Midwestern specialty like biscuits and gravy," I said with the embarrassment a beggar must feel.

"Of course! Charlotte, make up some for all of us. It's the day after Christmas and all through my house, I have guests with young children, we shall fill every mouth."

Capt. Jack laughed at his attempt to rhyme and paraphrase and I just snuck into the bedrooms and roused the kids.

After a breakfast that was starchy and filling for southern California, even in the winter, I announced my latest attempt to regroup.

"I called on a realtor this morning and she has a place that I want to go see. I want to thank you for your hospitality."

Charlotte nearly broke into tears in the kitchen when she heard what I was doing. I saw her pained face and slid into the kitchen while Capt. Jack was giving Caleb, Mia and Michael gifts from his sea collection.

"Don't leave me," she begged.

"I have to get a place first, then I can come back and get you. Let me see."

"Then why have you packed up all your things?"

"Because I want to be prepared for any and all emergencies. If there is one thing I have learned here in LA, it's that things change on a dime and you can't expect anyone to keep their word or even be honest."

"You are just upset over the Ron Slywood thing," Charlotte returned the banter.

I was not in the mood for banter, just an exit. A swift and decisive exit. The real estate woman was going to meet me in 2 hours and I would be lucky to get to Malibu in that time period.

Chapter 27
Liquid Blue Sky

I packed up and left, giving Captain Jack and Charlotte big hugs. As I hugged Charlotte, I whispered in her ear, "maybe you should get the Captain to give you that spanking?"

I chuckled to myself as I rolled away from Palos Verdes Estates and the beautiful estate of retired sea Captain Jack.

I went straight to the Western Union and found myself twenty grand richer as I pulled into Malibu. The condominiums were located just across the street from the Malibu Cliffs Motel on Kanan Dume road. I could tell she did not like having to work on the day after Christmas and I could tell she was negotiable.

"As you can see, this is a spacious two-bedroom with a pool and hot tub," she pointed out as she went for the close.

"I have owners who want this rented by the first and it would be first, last and deposit, with a 2-year lease."

"How much?" I said with deadpan.

I felt her armor chinking. She obviously needed this sale from her body language.

"Normally, this would be 1200 dollars a month, but they are willing to take a grand a month."

Ouch, that's more than we paid for our South Miami pool home, I thought to myself. I knew that this would be more expensive but even a grand would give us maybe 5 months. I was going to have to be a rock star in five months or I would be penniless. I knew that Craig was not going to continue funding this. He had threatened divorce just so I would come back to South Florida.

A huge lump formed in my throat, but I fought it back and pretended to be a Hollywood actress for the moment.

"I know southern California and the current real estate market is slowing down here as we go into 1986."

It was perfectly delivered. I could tell I had her on the ropes.

"Nine hundred. I will write you a check for 2700 dollars and you give me the key." I thought of the deodorant commercial which said, "never let them see you sweat" and I felt just like that. My fear was freezing every molecule of sweat and I stood in front of her cool as a cucumber. I just spent a big chunk of money but I promised myself it would be worth it.

The rest of the day, I tried to make things cozy for us at our new condo in Malibu. Caleb would be back in school next Monday and I was so proud of myself for surviving the Ron Slywood fiasco.

As I had promised, I rescued Charlotte from her mansion in Palos Verdes and told her she could have the living room. We found a used furniture store in Santa Monica and got a bunk bed and twin bed with a couple of chest dressers for the kids, a bed for me, and a couch, table, and chairs for the living room. I figured that I needed to use some money to make it livable. My kids loved me but I could start to see the wear and tear on them at the Captain's house.

I arranged all the toys I had packed in the van and got the kitchen functioning, too. It was amazing that I had the foresight to bring my frying pan and waffle iron when we were leaving Miami, but, in fact, the nest was cozy when I drove Caleb to school on Monday.

"Mommy, can I have some cocoa?"

Mia asked so sweetly that I saw no harm in going over to Trancas Canyon restaurant for coffee and cocoa.

"Me, too!" said Michael, who did everything that Mia did.

I sat down to someone taking my order and added some eggs and sausages. I knew that Michael would love the sausages.

Things felt better, but I didn't know what was next. I hoped that God would lead me to the next door. At that moment, I was just enjoying some time with my two young children.

When the waitress came, she didn't have any ketchup for the eggs. I spied a bottle sitting on top of the bar and decided to just hop up and grab it. The bar was deserted except for a lone biker, who was chasing Jack Daniel shots with a Budweiser.

Ugh, beer and whiskey at 9am, what kind of a hells angel was this guy? I thought.

"Hey beautiful," he slurred as he saw my blue jean skirt hike up a couple inches as I reached across the bar for the ketchup.

I looked over at him. He was dressed like a biker that would have been cast in some movie. His clothes did not have the wear and tear of someone who rides their Harley all day.

In spite of my caution, I did smile back.

"Hi," was all I could manage to say back. That was enough, however, for him to slide over and introduce himself.

"My name is Peter Fenton, what's yours?"

"Anne Marie Channing," I said without thinking.

"Mind if I sit with you for a while? It was a long night for me."

I looked him up and down: long golden hair, moustache and beard, but all nicely groomed, and he had a southern California surfer boy charm to his look. The biker gear looked totally fake, but he was good looking and after seven months of nothing, he seemed like the perfect piece of eye candy for my new 1986 lifestyle.

When Peter saw my children, his face went a bit white.

"These yours?" he asked modestly.

"Peter, this is my daughter, Mia, and my son, Michael."

Both of my children extended their hands to shake Peter's, which took him aback some.

"Wow, these kids got manners," he said like a stupid hillbilly.

God, I hope this isn't a mistake, I thought. This guy is just pretty to look at, but not to take home to daddy.

Peter made himself at home and ordered some breakfast. Since he had started out his morning with booze, it seemed like a good idea for him to eat.

As he shoveled down a Denver omelet, he managed to ask between chews, "so what brings you to Malibu?"

His question was direct and I had never thought about it until now. What was I doing in Malibu?

"I drove here from Miami to escape a very bad situation."

I did not want to give him any clues as to whom or what I was. No more Ron Slywoods.

He looked up from his feed bag to ask, "Oh, yeah, what kind of bad situation was that?"

"Husband trouble," I said.

He put down his fork and looked up.

159

"You still married to him?" he asked.

I found that to be a rather personal question, and I did not want to give out much more information. He was cute, but dumb as a box of rocks.

"Technically," I finally said. "What about you? What do you do?"

"I am a boy toy," he said frankly.

I stared at him wide-eyed. I decided to throw off my stare and act normal.

"Sounds like an interesting gig," I finally said.

"Oh, it's OK. I live with this supermodel."

"Wow, who is it?" I asked as my curiosity suddenly peaked.

"Eileen Jenkins, yeah I know you haven't heard of her but she has a gorgeous pair of legs and did hosiery ads all through the fifties and sixties. She lives up the canyon and has lots of money from all those years."

I was a bit speechless. He made being a boy toy sound as normal as waitressing at the restaurant.

"What do you do, besides being a mother?" His tone denoted that he could tell that I had judgmental vibrations going his direction. I didn't care for his attitude and I no longer felt the need to impress him. He was just one step above a prostitute.

"I'm a singer," I stated boldly.

"Really, where have you performed?" His tone had changed. He seemed very interested in finding out more about me, even though I had promised myself I would not give him a lot of information about myself.

Damn, I thought. How is it that I break promises to myself all the time?

"I did a lot of shows in Miami, had a kick-ass band, but ran away to LA to start again. I didn't like all the Latino music we had to do to get the gigs."

"Oh yeah, right," he said, "there is a huge Mexican population in Florida."

I felt a pang of Catholic guilt run through my veins at telling such a lie, but I started to believe that if I was going to survive in this city, I had better make it up as I go along.

Peter was intrigued. He obviously liked me and thought I

was cute, but even though I felt the same way about him, he was somebody's man whore and I started to imagine all the diseases he might have.

"So are you looking for a band?" he asked.

The whole world stopped when he asked that question. I felt like I needed to stop, look, and listen.

"Why, do you know of any bands looking for a female lead singer?" I hated to think I was passing up a potential situation. What if old Peter knew bands that wanted to work with a hot tamale from Miami.

"As a matter of fact, I do," he stated with some authority.

It was at that inopportune moment that a white Bentley sedan pulled into the Trancas parking lot. Peter looked out the window and there in the car was his girlfriend, Eileen Jenkins.

She sat in the car and honked the horn again. Obviously, she was used to getting her way, and I could tell that he was on a very short leash.

"I have to go," he said as he hastily gathered his leather paraphernalia.

"I have the names of two bands that might work for you. Meet me here tomorrow for breakfast again. I will bring the information with me for you."

Eileen held down the horn for one huge long blast and Peter ran out the door like a scared rabbit.

He did turn around for a moment and wink.

"Be here tomorrow, rock star princess."

I knew that I would. Maybe he did actually know someone. I was not one to doubt the power of coincidences after watching Star Wars. Obi-Wan Kenobi stated that there was no such thing, and I believed him. Look what had just manifested in front of me.

All night long I laid in my new bed, tossing back and forth. I had to believe that this was all a part of the plan.

The next morning, Mia was running a fever and I left her with Charlotte. She made me cry before I left by pulling me close and asking me, "will I ever see my daddy again? I miss him mommy. When will I see him again?"

"Soon, sweetie," I reassured her. I felt a bit sick to my stomach as I walked into the Trancas restaurant.

161

I saw Peter sitting at the bar, his ass halfway off the stool. It looked to me like he was as drunk today as he was yesterday. Perhaps I was barking up the wrong tree again.

That thought struck terror into my spine as I thought of the miserable mess I had just gone through with a swindler like Ron Slywood.

"Hey, there you are, and you got one of your babies with you." His words were just as slovenly as yesterday, and I smiled.

"I have a table over in the corner, follow me. Did you bring the information?"

I did not hear an answer, but he did follow me and Michael over to the booth on the other side of the restaurant. I did not want to be anywhere near the parking lot in case Eileen showed back up.

"So, where are the names and phone numbers?" I said, very directly. I was prepared to punch him in the face if he pulled anything funny.

"Hey, whoa, slow down, I think I need to order some coffee, sugar buns," Peter said, like a man waking from a deep sleep.

I eyed the waitress and willed her to the table.

"Two coffees, one black, one with cream, and a cup of yogurt with fresh fruit for my baby."

"Mom, not your baby. I big boy." My darling Michael had weathered the move from Miami better than anyone.

"You gotta cute kid, honey," said Peter. He seemed genuine, and no one could pass up that blond boyish charm. No wonder that Eileen had a collar and leash around his neck. I tried to relax a little bit and be more congenial.

"Okay, so what is the name of the first band?" I asked, trying to keep on task without appearing too anxious.

"Hey, babe, I did you right." He passed an 8x10 glossy photograph of a band promo shot and bio sheet across the table for me to inspect. I looked down at three Duran Duran looking guys, only they had brighter colors in their hair, like lime green and hot pink and neon blue. A waif of a girl stood in the middle with short red hair; she looked like an extra in a Charles Dickens movie.

"The chick singer split to San Francisco. They need someone to take her place. I called them about you and they want you to come over and audition. Here is a tape of the latest stuff they recorded over at Cahoots."

Peter slid over the cassette and I picked it up and put it in my purse. I looked at the bio sheet and didn't know if this was going to be a good fit. Their influences were all bands with no discernible female vocals: The Cars, The Cure, The Thompson Twins... well, okay, they did have a female to complete their threesome, but they played a quirky kind of punk rock with heavy synthesizer that I had not had any experience singing.

What about Cyndi Lauper? I thought. She had been dominating the charts with hit after hit, but again, that was not my style.

"What is the name of the band?" I asked with feigned interest.

"The Foreseen Unseen," Peter proudly announced. I squirmed in my seat and realized that I needed to listen to the cassette tape before I did anything else. They sounded very weird and I didn't want to pass judgment on them yet.

"Who's the other band?" I was having a very bad feeling about all of this.

"They have been playing in some of the smaller LA night clubs, but they have started to attract a following. Boy, you are sure direct. No time for any conversation with you."

"What's their name?" I demanded.

"Liquid Blue Sky. I don't have their promo kit, but we can go and watch their gig tomorrow night in West Hollywood."

"Are they looking for a female singer?"

"Not exactly, but I did call Brad last night. He's their manager, and they might find a spot for you if you are good."

The fact that someone was questioning my talent shot a venomous feeling throughout my body, but I did my best to squelch it. After all, I did not have any track record myself, so how could I expect rock star treatment?

Peter handed me a second cassette tape and I had to admit, neither cassette looked very professional. I took them home to play on my little boom box to see what these groups sounded like.

I waited until the kids were all in bed and asleep before I put the tape on. Charlotte was huddled around the promo kits, looking over everyone's pictures and credentials.

My finger hit the play button for the Foreseen Unseen, and what came out was a bizarre set of sounds, obviously from a synthesizer but more like something that NASA would send to outer space to communicate with aliens. When that dissipated, a strange groaning sound intermingled with an electronic beat. I could tell it was a female voice and my stomach turned.

"She sounds like a cat in heat," chuckled Charlotte.

I was not in the mood to return the laugh. This was my fate on the line, and the sound of a howling cat was not what I had in mind for my rock and roll debut.

I gave the band the courtesy of listening to the entire song before I turned to Charlotte with a sour look on my face.

"God, I hope it gets better than this!"

"Oh, maybe that's their clunker tune. Let's hear the next one." Charlotte wanted to be encouraging.

The second song had another outrageous intro with blaring synth and a chunky rhythm guitar behind it that sounded like the songwriter was high on acid. I skipped to the middle of the song and there were still no vocals.

"I would call that major guitar masturbation, but it's not even a primarily guitar sound, so it's more like keyboard diarrhea."

We both laughed at that thought. It helped, but Charlotte could tell that I needed some soothing.

"Why don't I make us a cup of tea?" she offered.

I sat in silence, hoping to get inspired. Things were just defaulting all over the place. It was almost the end of the month and I had another rent payment and I was worried that my van was getting ready to die. I went out on the balcony so that Bobby and Charlotte could go to sleep. I looked at a crescent moon that was descending into the murky waters of the Pacific. Zuma Beach was still. It was January 8th, a few days into the New year.

"Wow, it's David Bowie's birthday," I said to myself, remembering a factoid I once read in a magazine.

"I thought you would never remember," Bowie remarked. His silhouette appeared on the other side of the deck, with the moon and ocean in the background.

I wished I had a camera for this Kodak moment for rock fans everywhere. The Thin White Duke was traveling the ether in Malibu.

"Happy Birthday," I finally said after taking a long drink of my rock and roll fantasy.

"Thanks. How is your band coming?" he asked with a casual glance.

I started to cry. I could not even tell him how badly it was going. The fact that he could read my thoughts helped our communication, although my tears spoke for most of my feelings.

"Instead of taking control of your life, you are letting life control you. Think about it. Thanks for the birthday greetings," and with that, he evaporated back from whence he came.

The next day, I went to the Mayfair grocery and as I suspected, when I got back in the van, it would not start. I knew nothing about cars, so I stood there helplessly, kicking the tires and cursing.

"You motherfucking piece of shit, start, damn you!" I screamed, probably louder than I should have.

I heard a loud roar behind me and up pulled the big Harley fat boy that Peter drove.

"Hey doll, what's up with the van?"

"Beats me! It turns over, so it's not the battery."

I figured he knew what it was and would help me. To my surprise, he asked me to hop on his bike.

"Let's buzz over to my house. Eileen has a car that she never uses and I bet she will just give it to you just so you can get it off the property."

Away we sped, my hair flying in the breeze, down the PCH and up Trancas Canyon road. Eileen lived about halfway up the mountain; her place jutted out and had a magnificent view of the Pacific as well as all of Malibu, and even the LA skyline.

Peter landed in a big spin as Eileen walked out on her bedroom balcony.

"Hey, you beautiful honey of a peach, I brought somebody who is willing to take the Maui Waui off your hands."

Eileen's stern gaze melted as she saw her boy toy back in her yard. Her slight sneer at me had been replaced by relief. I had the feeling the car was a real lemon, and I was not sure that it was the answer to my dilemma.

Eileen walked down to the driveway and motioned to me to follow her around to the second three car garage. What I saw made my jaw drop to the floor. There, in the second bay, sat a 1970 Chevy Impala painted an excruciatingly ugly chartreuse. It had Colorado license plates, and on the back dashboard, a hula dancer wiggled with every move of the car. When I started it, the car roared like a truck. I revved up the engine and it sounded more like a big Mack truck than a car.

"It runs good," Peter remarked. "It's just taking up room in her garage."

"It can barrel down the PCH, and it can march over these mountains. I don't need it, you can take it." Eileen seemed genuine enough and I decided that I had a guy who told me he would buy my van. That might be a little more difficult since it wasn't running, but the price for this Chevy was perfect: absolutely nothing.

"Peter tells me you are a single mom and I want to help."

Eileen's genuine concern triggered an emotional response in me; a tear slid off my right eye as I wiped it into my hair.

"Thanks," I said, and drove away.

The van was sold for less than 400 dollars and I began to watch all my pennies. Over a third of my money from Craig was gone, and I had nothing to show for it except a nice vacation in Malibu.

The winter months in Malibu offer that same sun-soaked weather of Miami but without any thunderstorms. They were considered a rare occurrence.

January rolled into February, and I had numerous phone calls from Liquid Blue Sky, but the opportunity to do anything seemed to elude me. I even handed them a copy of my recording, hoping to show them my talent.

"It's more country or folk than what we do and I don't know if there's a fit here," commented their manager to me one afternoon.

I picked up Caleb from school and took everyone to the Zuma to fly a kite I purchased at the grocery check-out line. Everything was always at the tips of the rich and famous and at the moment, I was enjoying this lap of luxury, even if from an obtuse angle.

I laid on the blanket and peered at the billowing clouds being swept out to sea by the wind. Caleb was flying the kite with all the athletic prowess he was endowed with naturally and Mia and Michael were following him. Zuma Beach was almost deserted for an early March afternoon. The sun was warm and I felt it take away all of my stress. I baked like a lizard under its subtle rays.

The kids were down the beach, almost out of range, and I

waved at them to head back down the beach. Right behind me a loud and roaring Harley motor came to an abrupt halt in the parking lot. The driver revved the motor and I knew who it was.

"Hey, beautiful rock star, what'ya doin, sun bathing?" Peter was bare-chested and his blond hair looked beautiful draped over his bronze and muscular shoulders.

"Trying to till I got interrupted," I snapped back, hoping to get a rise from him.

Peter was a young Grecian god, there was no part of him that wasn't luscious. The idea of sleeping with someone's boy toy seemed vulgar, at best, but my focus was on succeeding, not getting laid. The last time I had tried that in Malibu, it was disastrous.

"Hey, screw Liquid Blue Sky, I found a red hot band and they are opening for a name act at the Troubadour." Peter slid next to me in the sand like someone sliding into third base. However, he had uttered the magic word: Troubadour.

"Yeah, what's their name?" I asked, looking over at him as I turned on my side.

"Poison. Cool name, huh?"

"Poison, poison, poison… poison," I muttered out loud as if I could someone decipher their level of success by repeating their name with several different intonations.

"They want to use one of my old Harleys for parts. I get to decorate the stage with all kinds of cool shit. Here, look at their promo picture."

Peter handed me a folded up black and white 8-by-10 of the band. They were a very pretty glam rock band, and their lead glam boy had an animal magnetism. It gave me a shiver up my arm and I got goose bumps.

The Troubadour - I couldn't get that name out of my mind. I had to see them, just because it was hitting a magical sweet spot in me. Bowie had told me to go to the Troubadour. I desperately wanted to be somebody's opening act at the Troubadour.

"Are they looking for another singer?" I asked. "It seems their front man is more than enough and I don't paint myself up like that."

"Quit analyzing," he said. "Bret Michaels, their lead guy, the one you've been salivating over, said he could use a backup singer for their gig and he told me to have you come to their gig next week at the Troubadour."

"Really?"

I could hardly believe what I was hearing. A way in. A back door. If only to be on stage there for a night. I was sure I could hobnob with the crowd. I assumed that the whole crowd must be filled with the best musicians in West Hollywood.

"When is it?"

"Next Saturday, they start around 9pm."

I couldn't wait to get back to the condo and tell Charlotte the good news. Finally, after what seemed to be forever, a real shot at a band, or at least, musicians.

When I walked into the condo, Charlotte was in tears.

"What's the matter?" I asked with alarm. "You kids, go to the bedroom and play with that puzzle I got you."

As if on cue, I saw Caleb herd the other two into the bedroom as if it was a regular occurrence.

I grabbed Charlotte by the shoulders so she would look me in the eye.

"Why are you crying? What's wrong?"

"They took Bobby," she sobbed back.

"Oh Charlotte," I said, giving her a big hug. "We will get him back. Who took him?"

"Child Protective Services came right after you left to go to the beach and they told me that sleeping on a couch with Bobby was not good enough of a home. He is in Santa Monica right now at the juvenile facility."

"Not to worry, Charlotte, we will figure something out. First thing tomorrow, after I drop Caleb off at school, we will go down there and get him back."

Desperately wanting to change the subject, I gave her a couple more pats on the back and then blasted her with my news.

As I told her about my good fortune and the Saturday night gig, she walked into the hall closet and got her purse. She pulled out a wooden hair brush and brought it back to me as I sat on the couch.

"Momma always paddled me with this when I was bad. I have lost my child."

"Charlotte, please stop, I will help you get your son back but giving you a spanking will not help you, ok?"

The trip to the juvenile home proved fruitless. They were not willing to release Bobby back into Charlotte's custody because they had a court order from West Virginia, where Bobby's father lived, to find the child's whereabouts.

Charlotte was a complete mess and when I was getting ready to leave to go to the show on Saturday, she sat whimpering in the corner.

"Please Charlotte, try to compose yourself. Why don't you make the kids some popcorn and you can all play Candy land until bedtime."

I sighed as I left the condo. Things seemed alright but I couldn't help but feel uneasy.

When I drove up Sunset Strip off the PCH, I felt a heaviness. I wanted to turn around and go back to the condo and pack our bags and leave to go back to Miami and snuggle up next to Craig. I shrugged it off and parked the car. I saw Peter unloading some car parts in the rear exit of the theatre.

"Grab those Harley handlebars over there, Anne Marie, and I can sneak you in as a roady," Peter laughed as he pointed to them.

I did and found myself in the backstage area. Peter used the handle bars as a finishing touch to a very elaborate stage decorated with old car and Harley parts, and behind the stage were huge boxes that were filled with confetti.

I had hoped to talk with the band before the show but everything moved quickly and they took the stage before I had a moment to relax.

The raw metal and animal type cat scratch fever began to overtake me like a heady dream. Smoke clouds filled with marijuana dotted the crowd and I lit my own up and puffed away. I could not take my eyes off of Bret Michaels. He certainly was no Bowie, but his moves made my groin groan deeply.

He bent down as he sang and he sang the song to me. I was in the first row and he was in my face.

When they finished the last song of the set, the place went wild. Cheers, applause and wild pandemonium hit as I snuck backstage with Peter to see if I had a shot at that stage, even as a backup singer.

The entire band was chugging from a bottle of whiskey and I

got a couple of huge gulps in before I stood face-to-face with the lead singer.

"This is Anne Marie Channing, Bret. Anne Marie this is Bret Michaels."

"Hi," I squeaked out. Then the liquor took over for me so I would not have to worry about being shy.

"God, you were smoking hot up there. You made me want to bend over and give you all my sweetness." I nervously laughed since I could hardly believe that I had just said that to a total stranger.

"Baby, I think I can arrange that." He grabbed my right ass cheek and squeezed it. It was perfect. It was as if my ass was an orange and he was getting all the sweet juice out of it.

He put his arm around me and handed me the bottle of whiskey and I took a long hard drink.

I couldn't quite understand why I had turned into this little slut that wanted to do anything that he said, but I did.

I vaguely remember an ugly remark from Peter and then I left the Troubadour with Bret. He drove the Maui Waui back to Malibu while I sucked his dick all the way there.

I knew the all-night sex was noisy, and I woke up the next morning to an empty bed and a pissed off nanny.

"What were you doing with that rock and roll boy last night? I couldn't sleep. I am surprised you didn't wake the kids with all your moaning and groaning." She stood in my bedroom with the door closed, holding a cup of black coffee in her hands.

"Wow, I can't remember," I said in a fuzzy tone.

"Well, the kids are eating their breakfast, ready to go to school."

Charlotte's tone was cold and filled with acid eating bite. Since I didn't have time to make sense of it, I threw on a business suit, the expensive Rodeo drive sunglasses I found at Zuma beach one afternoon, and got in the car. For some reason that morning, I felt foolish.

I gazed straight ahead in a trance, trying to put together what had happened the night before.

"Mom, wake up, I'll be late," said Caleb with a hint of anger in his voice. As the oldest, he had guided the other two through the murky waters of the separation, but his patience was wearing thin. I could read his face and it always telegraphed, "where is the payoff in all this?"

"Okay," I snapped and chugged on down the road. I pulled into Malibu Elementary and dropped him off. As I pulled away, I spotted Dylan's limo and he rolled down his window to make a comment about my car.

"Wow," he said slowly and with some difficulty.

I stepped on the gas pedal and roared away, my ability to control my emotions waning.

I went to the Trancas Inn, knowing I would run into Peter. He was sitting at the bar, as if he had been sitting there all night, which, in fact, could be the truth.

"There you are, where did you go last night?" he slurred at me. "Come sit with us."

I got some pancakes for Mia and Michael liked fresh fruit with yogurt. It always irritated Peter that I gave all my attention to their needs before talking to him. I always thought Michael had descended to me from Gopi's, he was always shining in light and eating yogurt.

"Did you go home with Bret?" Peter finally blurted out.

"He was not sleeping in my bed this morning," I retorted, knowing that I clung to a shred of truth about the incident.

"Hey, it's cool if you did. I've been thinking, we need a three-way. It would be so much fun, out on Zuma Beach, there's a full moon this Saturday and I know Bret would be into it too."

"Mommy, what's a three-way?" asked Mia.

"It's a game that you can play with a ball," I barked back. Mia retreated inside herself, knowing that she had pissed me off. I wanted to comfort her for this whole awkward situation, but then Peter said the magic words to turn my attention away from my child.

"They are going to be in the studio Saturday afternoon, they are working on an album they are gonna release this summer. That song they played last night, 'Talk Dirty to Me' is on the album."

"What studio?" I asked as I turned my gaze to Peter and away from Mia.

"Place in West Hollywood. Nice 24 track, I heard them say that Jimmy Hendrix recorded some tracks there."

"Jimmy Hendrix?" I said, my mouth watering. The word, wow, was echoing in every chamber of my mind. Over and over, I found myself wanting to go and see the studio.

"They ever say if they needed any female backup vocals for them?"

"Hey, I know where it is, we can just stop by around 2pm… as long as you are ready to do the nasty, huh?"

As handsome and Adonis-like as Peter was, the idea repulsed me. I could not justify it to Eileen, I could not even justify it to myself. I couldn't accept the boundaries it crossed for me.

"Sure," my other voice had taken over and agreed. "I have to get home, the nanny has some issues with Child Protective Services and we are going to Santa Monica today."

I bustled everyone off to the car and drove away, hating myself for agreeing. "Jimmy Hendrix," I quietly mumbled to myself as I drove down the PCH.

The day in Santa Monica proved to be aggravating, and we desperately needed a lawyer. The caseworker told Charlotte that the only way she could get Bobby back was by getting a lawyer to file a petition or provide evidence that she had proper shelter for Bobby, not someone's couch.

All the way home, she begged me to double up with my kids so that she could have the other bedroom for herself. I felt encroached upon yet, as she pointed out, she provided me an invaluable service. I could not go to the studio if she didn't watch the kids for me.

All evening long, she begged and cried and finally I relented. The following day we provided CPS the evidence that Charlotte rented a bedroom from me at the Pointe condos of Kanan Dume. Bobby returned, and I decided to go to the studio on Saturday since my babysitter had decided to forgive me of all my nasty activities.

I couldn't look anyone in the eye when I arrived with Peter. I introduced myself to the engineer and he gave me a quick tour of the studio. There was an isolation booth and I asked him if I could test out a microphone in there. The band was still fiddling around and I hoped to hear how I sounded.

I did some slight "doo wahs" that I thought would sound good under the lead vocals.

"That sounded nice," the engineer said. "Listen and I'll play it back for you in your headphones."

The rich sound of the mic did wonders for the breathy delivery I gave it. I was in heaven. I was interrupted by a tapping on the door.

"If you're good, maybe you can do that underneath my vocals, but for now, scat."Bret said. He gave my bottom a swift smack and I was banished to the control booth.

It went on, and on, and on. I was interested at first, but the constant sound tweaking and playbacks got boring and by 10pm, I wanted to go. So did Peter, but the small pint of Jack Daniels he was guzzling had put him to sleep at 7pm so he was just waking up from a nap by then.

"I'm hungry, let's go find a Jack in the crack," he said. It was a slang term for a local burger franchise.

Peter began to get up and fart and whine and yawn. He reminded me of a two-year-old. The band wanted to finish the song they were working on and it didn't look like that would happen until either 4 or 5am.

"I think we should eat and go home," I said.

"No, eat, then come back. Sessions can last all night. You ought to know that." Peter had decided on sex with Bret and I was just the token kinky. The thought sickened me.

"You can eat that horse meat, I'm going back to Malibu."

"You said you wanted to do backup vocals, I heard the engineer say that he was getting ready to lay down harmony tracks."

My ears perked up and I walked over to Bret to ask him myself.

"No, honey, I do all my own backup vocals. I never told Peter you could do backup."

"You guys sound fucking awesome," I said to Bret and gave him a peck on the cheek.

I marched out the door as Peter came walking out the bathroom door. I raced past him and jumped in my car and sped off down the highway.

"Fucking asshole!" I shouted as I slammed the door to the Maui Waui.

Peter turned around and went back into the studio. Bret was watching the whole event with a smirk on his face.

"What did you tell her that made her so mad?" Peter asked.

"That she couldn't sing backup vocals with me," Bret replied.

"Goddamn it, you messed up a nice thing on the beach later on."

"Hey, I can nail that chick whenever I want to, you're the one that can't." Bret laughed and picked up a guitar.

When I got home everyone was asleep. I took a beer out of the fridge and went to my favorite spot on the deck. The steady drone of cars that drove down the PCH had subsided a little but I found solace. Things were not going well at all. Putting together a band had proven to be more than I could accomplish.

The children were getting tired of their gypsy lifestyle and the fact that Caleb would be graduating 2nd grade in six weeks put a strain on the need for them to have some time with their father.

I hadn't talked to Craig in four months. The weather in Malibu is similar to Miami and the change from winter to spring was very insignificant. I quietly started to cry. It was like a gentle steady rain. My mind let go of everything and I cried out all the angst I had built up.

I awoke to the sound of someone banging on my door. It was a large man, with a big extended stomach, dressed up in what appeared to be a poor version of business casual. I crawled over to the door to answer it.

"Can I help you?" I asked as I cracked the door open.

"Are you Charlotte Newton?" The man's tone was gruff.

"And you are?" I tried to ask without putting an edge on it.

"Detective Matt Richardson, ma'am."

"Come on in, I will wake her up. You do know that this is Sunday morning right?"

"I do apologize for this day and time, but I have her son Bobby down at the police station right now and I have multiple counts of vandalism, curfew violation, and other assorted charges."

"Dear Lord Jesus," I said to myself as I roused Charlotte, "never a dull moment in my life."

We drove down to the police station to find out that Bobby had been sneaking out at night and running with a gang of older kids whose sole pleasure was to destroy the expensive toys of the rich people who lived in Malibu.

Charlotte tried to pretend that Bobby was still her little angel and not an angry young teenager, which he was quickly becoming.

Charlotte met with Bobby in private while I walked across the street to the Malibu Inn and ordered some breakfast for myself and the kids. As I got ready to bite into my pancakes, I saw Charlotte walking toward us, crying.

"Oh God, this can't be good," I surmised.

"They are holding him in there and told me I needed to get a lawyer. Bobby's long lost daddy, Billy Bob, is on his way out here. He told the cops he would take him back to West Virginia."

She stopped and broke down, sobbing openly in the restaurant.

"It's OK, Char," I wrapped my arms around her to comfort her while all three of my children stared wide eyed at me.

"No, it's not, if you don't help me by paying for a lawyer, they will just hold him till his dad gets here on Tuesday."

I reeled at the thought of having to pay for a lawyer and decided it was more than I could do. However, telling Charlotte right now was not good timing. It was just one more large boulder that was pulling me under. I felt like I was drowning. I looked at my three beautiful children and I knew that they had not seen their father in almost three years.

We drove back to the condo in silence. My three were so well behaved that they knew to be quiet. Charlotte went into her bedroom and cried and I pulled out the Candyland game and played with my kids.

"I don't want to play this game, mommy," Caleb remarked. "It's for babies."

"I not a baby," Michael squawked.

"Yes, you are." Caleb was picking up on the defiant male vibe.

The squabble was about to get even worse when I decided to change gears. I hustled everyone out the door and we walked down the hill and across the street to Zuma Beach. I started to run into the waves and let the cold water make me squeal. The kids found the distraction interesting enough, and I wanted to give myself a moment to consider some sort of truce with Craig.

I felt defeated. I would rather eat dirt than go back to Miami. I didn't even know where Craig might be but I resolved to make a phone call that evening after everyone settled in and went to bed. I reclined back down on my towel, hoping to let the sun soothe all the hurt that I felt.

My son was soon shadowed by the figure of Peter standing in front of me.

"I got some great news," he said gleefully.

"And that would be what?" I asked as I sat up, not exactly happy to see him.

"Hot new band needs chick singer and I told them you were the one they should talk to."

"Oh bullshit, Peter." I'd had enough of his bands and his rhetoric.

"Look at this," he said as he handed me a rather impressive looking flyer. It featured a band called the Righteous Renegades and they were the opening band for a gala event at The Troubadour. Five bands, including Poison, were on the flyer. Van Halen was the headliner. I didn't have an answer, but my heart was not in it. I felt on the verge of tears myself and finally managed to get out a, "that's nice," to Peter.

"That's nice? That's nice!? I am trying to help you and you are just acting like some sort of a prima donna. What do you expect? That a band is just going to come up to you on the beach and beg you to front their band?"

Bands, rock and roll, the bright lights - all of these things seemed meaningless at that moment to me. I began to search inside myself for the answer I needed, but all I could feel was the pain of chaos. My money was dwindling and I was no closer to my goal than I was when I first got to California. I felt that the only kinds of people that I was able to attract to myself were leeches and losers. My children, troopers that they were, had started to feel lost and adrift on a sea of mommy's bad decisions. I had a responsibility to them and I began to cry.

Peter was not used to seeing a woman cry. He handed me the flyer.

"Why don't you just think about it? I'll talk to you later when you sober up."

He walked back up the beach to whatever crack he crawled out of and I began to build a sand castle with Mia.

"Mommy, why are you crying?" Caleb and Michael came and sat down to help.

They all looked at me and I realized I needed to pull it together for them.

"I think we might be leaving Malibu after Caleb has his graduation," I said wiping the tears from my eyes.

"Yeah!" all three of them shouted.

Each one of my crew was especially excited when I tucked them into bed that night.

"Just four more weeks and we're going home," Caleb's eyes lit up as he reminded me.

"That's right," I said. I hadn't a clue what I was doing but I couldn't help but agree. I was on the verge of tears I could no longer contain.

"MMMmmm, will we see gramma?" Mia smiled at me.

"Of course," I said as I choked on each word I uttered.

"Daddy, wanna see daddy," Michael was so adorable that I just gave him a big huge hug. I turned out the light and the only thing to shine was a small Cinderella night light that was plugged in on the back wall.

I grabbed a beer and went out on the deck. A steady stream of traffic poured back into the crevices of LA. Surfers, sun worshippers and sea shell collectors drove every car imaginable out to the outer reaches of Ventura county and then back again on Sunday, ready for another day of the LA fast lane.

The drone helped to comfort me as I dialed the number to Craig's house. The worst possible scenario unfolded when Nicole answered the phone.

"Hello, is Craig there?"

"Yes, he is, whom can I say is calling?"

It took every muscle in my face to answer.

"Anne Marie."

"Anne Marie, hi, it's Nicole. How are you?" Her voice was filled with false nicety so I sensed that Craig was nearby. She continued to chatter, not giving me even a pause to say something.

"Oh, I am so thrilled to tell you that Craig and I have announced our engagement, we are going to be married in my hometown of Gainesville, Florida this summer... and I'm pregnant. Isn't that thrilling?"

Now, she gave large pause, waiting with baited breath for my response.

Things had certainly changed from my conversation with Craig four months ago. Pregnant, again? Gee, it seemed Craig could just look at her and get her pregnant.

"I hope he plans on divorcing me before he marries you because I believe that's considered a crime in the state of Florida. I think Utah might let you, though."

I heard Nicole screech at Craig like an old barn owl.

"Have you not DIVORCED her yet?"

The phone went down and I heard lots of screaming from both of them. I took a huge slug of beer, it must have been half the bottle.

"Anne Marie?" I heard an out-of-breath Craig on the other phone.

"Is this a bad time?" I asked innocently, knowing that it was.

"Why haven't you called me? I had no idea where to call you?"

I felt guilty, and I knew I should have called him way before this. Anger can do such awful things when you leave it unchecked.

"Have you ever heard of directory assistance? Never mind, I am calling to tell you that Caleb wants to invite you to his 2nd grade graduation. He was voted most likely to succeed by the staff and teachers of the school. He's getting a certificate."

"I don't even know what school that is, Anne Marie." Craig's tone was cold and brimming over with hatred.

"Malibu Elementary, which I have mentioned a total of three times, once for every time I have called you. None for the times you've called me… cause, oh shock, you've never called me."

"Anne Marie, shut up. I don't need your sarcasm."

"Wow, just one of the many reasons why I don't call you very often. Just tell me this, how is your upcoming marriage going to help our marriage? Can't wait for those divorce papers."

My patience had come to an abrupt end and I slammed the phone down. I finished the beer, then quietly got another and then another out of the fridge. Try as I might, I could not get drunk. Soon the light of dawn hit me in the eyes and I knew I had to get Caleb to school.

I came right back after dropping Caleb off, knowing that Charlotte wanted me to help her with her Bobby problem. The phone rang before I had a chance to sit down on the couch.

"Hey gorgeous, how come you left the other night? I was going to give you a track for some backup vocals."

Wow, it was Bret. I knew I had to keep my cool. I flushed all

178

my problems down a mental toilet.

"Babysitter problems, I did tell you I have kids, didn't I?"

"Hey, we were all kids once. I am gonna give this cassette to Pete, learn it and you can record a track and sing live backup at our upcoming Troubadour show on May 12th."

I started to get weak in the knees and I felt like I would have done anything he asked.

"Sure, I can do it. Tell Peter to bring it over, the sooner the better."

I hung up, unable to speak. I fell back on the couch speechless. At the other end of the phone Bret and Peter were snickering with glee.

"We let her sing on Saturday night then we take her out to Zuma before you take her back and we nail her sweet little ass."

"I wanna stick my hot cock up her ass," they both said simultaneously.

"Jinx," they both spit out.

"OK, paper, rock, scissors," said Peter.

It was an easy win for Bret. Rock crushes scissors.

"You win at everything," Peter choked out.

Friday came and went with little out of the ordinary, until a phone call at 11pm.

"I am coming over after this gig, be there around 2am." Bret spoke with such authority that I said nothing but, "OK."

Somewhere around 1:50am, I sat quietly in the living room, with the window open. There were no cars on the PCH, it was a rainy night and the drizzle made everyone want to stay in or get to their destination. My thoughts were interrupted by a light knock on the door.

In strutted Bret and another tanned, blonde and beautiful looking male.

"This is Itch," Brett introduced.

I took them out to my deck and we lit up a joint. Itch kept eyeing me like I was a fine filet mignon.

"She is so doable," he said to Brett.

"Hey darling," Brett said sexily, "get your boom box out here and let me put in this outrageously good CD by Def Leppard."

"Who are they?" I asked meekly, not sure of the band.

179

"British band, been in the studio when they recorded this song but it's not been released yet. I just knew the engineer. Love the song, they should release it."

It did rock. I instantly liked it and got into the groove as Bret began kissing me up and down my neck.

Something took over in my brain that said, this feels good, go with it.

I was going down on Itch and Bret was filling my ass with some sweet pleasure. The chorus rang out as I moaned loudly.

"Oh God, don't stop!" I screamed.

Both of them were like marathon athletes. My heart began racing and I couldn't catch my breath. I feared I would die of a heart attack, the engorgement along with the rapid breathing had the sound of my heart pounding into my brain and I felt myself going for it.

Everyone was pumping everything and I expected to explode at any minute.

Itch let out a rebel yell and I could tell he was done for. His piercing voice caused my eyes to tilt back into my head, as an orgasm as intense as a volcano gushed forth. Moments later, Bret blew his load and the force of it sent all three of us flying.

Below us, a large convertible soared down the PCH, with two studio goons on either side of Gary Busey. He looked up to see the spectacle. He was higher than helium, on cocaine, and he roared, "Goddam that's why I love Malibu. These people know how to party, whoooooooo!"

As we lay there, strewn all over the balcony like Sunday's newspaper, I spied Charlotte going to the kitchen to get a snack. She looked out at me, freaked and ran back into the bedroom.

Shortly after that, Itch and Bret put their clothes back on. I had done so immediately after seeing Charlotte and was smoking a generic Menthol cigarette I had found at the AMPM mini market where I had worked. It was something I rarely did, but the evening's festivities pushed me into the behavior.

They both gave me a peck on the lips and slid out the front door into the night like two men that had just finished an excellent steak dinner.

I sat there and smoked the cigarette to the butt. What was that?

I asked myself.

Charlotte crawled out of her bedroom with a packed suitcase, and I roused myself to inquire what was going on.

"I had a long talk with God, last night," she said. "I am going to try and work this out with Bobby's daddy. He is here in town and I am taking the bus to meet him in LA. I think you are heading in the wrong direction if last night is any indication."

"Wait, Charlotte," I begged. "I am performing tonight with Bret's band, Poison, at the Troubadour. I need you to watch the kids, please. Just one more night."

"You are dancing with the devil," she said dismissively.

An anger rose within me. After all I had done for her, letting her and her son stay at my apartment, no charge, she was walking out when I needed her the most.

"You fucking bitch, get outta here then. After all I have done for you, I am shocked that you choose today to leave."

"I am sorry you feel that way, Anne Marie, but I am a Christian woman and I have morals."

With that, she walked out the door and I watched her from the balcony as she got on the bus and sped away.

I was freaking out as Mia got up with Michael tagging behind her.

"Mommy, need hugs," said Mia sweetly.

"Not now," I said loudly with an inflection of anger.

Mia burst into tears and Michael followed just because he heard shrill and harsh tones coming from his mother.

"Stop, both of you, stop," I said, losing control even more. The brouhaha woke up Caleb who came into the kitchen to see what all the commotion was about. He saw all three of us sitting at the dining room table, crying, even bawling.

"What's going on?" he asked.

"Stop crying!"

His voice shattered like glass and we were all startled.

"I'm sorry everyone for being mad but Charlotte just left."

"Why, mom?" Caleb was confused.

"She needs to get her life back and she isn't getting it here."

It was a jibber jabber way of confusing his sharp eight-year-old mind. Before he had a chance to disseminate the information I just gave him, I pushed on.

"Mommy is getting a chance to sing tonight with a band at a very famous LA night club. You know how important this is?"

"Yes, I do, mom. Don't worry. Jason's folks next door can watch us. She always tells me I am always welcome."

"Well, honey, that's an invitation for you so that Jason has someone to play with, not all three of you."

"No, mom, you're wrong. She told me if you ever needed help to ask her." Saying that, he popped out the front door and was knocking at our neighbor's condo door before I could get my mouth off the floor.

Ellen Cataldi walked back through my door before I could even get up. My neighbor ran the local video store and several times I had taken her son Jason to Zuma Beach as a playmate for Caleb.

"I would be happy to watch your kids tonight, Anne Marie," she said. "We are leaving first thing Sunday morning from LA and we are flying to New York. The flight leaves at 8am so we will be leaving here early in the morning."

"Oh, Ellen, if you could watch my three tonight, I would be soooo grateful. I will be back way earlier than that. Should be no later than 2am, you know I am singing at the Troubadour."

"I am happy to help," she smiled. "What happened to Charlotte?"

The busy body that lives within every woman came out and I politely escorted her to the door, mentioning that I would bring the kids over around 6 or 7. Thanking her again, I closed the door.

"Thank God, thank God," I said to myself as I made pancakes, which was Michael and Mia's favorite, along with some bacon for Caleb. The kids noticed how relieved I was and we spent the morning cleaning the condo and playing SORRY! Michael did very well and could count his moves. I was so proud of all of them for supporting me.

I spent the rest of the day primping. I had a black leather biker hard-core something going on and through all the makeup and glitter, I peered at my eyes so that I could see the real me.

"Not sure if I can anymore," I said to myself as I took a night bag, sleeping bags, and Michael's teddy bear over to the Cataldi's. As I was doing that, Peter had shown up in the parking lot. Apparently,

Bret had called bragging about the night before and it sent Peter into a rage of jealousy. He drove to my condo and pulled the plug on the alternator and closed the hood as he saw me walking down the path by the hot tub and pool.

"Hi," he said innocently. "Thought I would see if you needed a ride to the club tonight. You guys are performing at 8 right?"

"Yeah, I think Bret said be there at 7:45 for mic check. I think I would prefer to drive myself, just in case. I have to be home early for the babysitter."

Peter was playing it cool.

"Suit yourself, I thought you might want a fan club to take with you."

He sat smugly while I tried in vain to get the car started. After 2 dozen tries, I was afraid I was going to be late and freaked.

"Fine, take me to the club, I thought you said I was getting a car that ran."

"It runs," he said slowly, knowing it did.

He walked over to the Maui Waui and lifted the hood.

"Try it again," he said casually.

"Okay, Peter, I don't really have time to mess with this, it's already 6:20. Let's go!"

"Whatever you say," he said, trying to hide his grin.

We roared down the PCH and ran into some traffic once we turned onto sunset Blvd.

"Can't you go any faster?"

"It's a van, it's a slow mover on turns, baby."

As we crossed the 405, Peter let his ugly green monster out of the box.

"I thought we were doing the three-way thing, then you do it with Bret and some asshole named Itch?"

"What?" I asked. This was coming out of left field, how did he know? The thought occurred to me that it was Bret and I knew that Peter was out of control. I tried to calm down the driver who was supposed to get me to the gig on time. As we pulled into the parking lot, my watch said 7:45.

"Shit, I will barely make it," I grumbled.

As I reached for the doorknob, he hit the master button and shut off the car. He stuck the keys in his pocket then went into the back of the van to make himself a drink at his little bar.

"Are you fucking nuts?" I screamed. "What the hell is this?"

Peter drank a shot of Jack Daniels and boasted, "You aren't getting out of this van till you fuck me. You wouldn't be here if it weren't for me. You are an ungrateful bitch, now suck my dick."

I stood frozen, realizing I was a captive and the clock was ticking.

"Let me out, please Peter. They will be on stage in just a few minutes. I won't even get a mic check. You have to let me out." I was candy coat begging to get out of the van but it just emboldened Peter to demand more.

"I ain't doing no such thing. Suck my dick."

As I sat frozen in the front seat, he took another drink and I decided to take a lesson from Marian in the Indiana Jones movie.

I changed faces and hopped into the back and told him to pour another drink for both of us. Peter was intrigued, thinking his overpowering words were making me cower.

As he downed his shot glass, his eyes closed for a brief second as the whisky glass was tilted back and the brown liquid ran down his throat. I took that moment to pour out my drink in my thigh high leather boot.

"C'mon, pour us another one," I said. "What are you a pussy drinker?"

The slight insult had him annoyed enough to pour another one.

"Before we drink this, I want to see you drink yours first."

Perhaps the little prick was smarter than I gave him credit for, so I downed mine and then he downed his. Although four shots would have me reeling, Peter, being an alcoholic, had a greater tolerance.

"More," I said, feigning a slur.

Peter poured another round and this time, I got mine into the other boot before he noticed.

He did seem a bit drunk and I tried for one last knockout punch.

"I am gonna fuck your brains out but first let's do a double." I was gambling on not having to drink that one and I challenged his manhood to go first. He did and was still sitting but he started to sway. I pretended to accidentally knock my double over.

"You fucking little bitch," he slurred as he grabbed for me. "I am going to blow your mind with my huge mother fucking dick."

As he leaned over to grab me., I instinctively grabbed the half empty bottle and cracked it over his head. He slumped over and I grabbed my purse and unlocked the van. As I heard him groaning, I knew he was ok.

I checked my watch and it was 8:20. My heart sank as I walked into the club because the band had started and I was SOL. There were a dozen good looking blondes swarming all over the front row of the stage and the band sounded good. I stood in the very back and ordered a beer. I thought I would puke. They finished at about 9:30 and their groupies were all over them. I fought my way to the front, hoping to talk to Bret. I finally got within earshot and he stared a hole right through me.

"That was your shot at backup for me. RULE number one, get to the gig on time. You blew it!"

His tone was harsh and cold as a big busted blond put her tits right in his face to distract him. I felt like I was falling into a million pieces.

"It wasn't my fault. Peter made me late."

My voice was drowned out by the crowd noise and the entourage that was Poison was exiting stage right as the next band got on stage. I sat there and drank until way after midnight. I figured by then Peter would sober up. I finally gathered myself up and headed to the parking lot, but the van was nowhere to be seen. Peter left me at 1am at the Troubadour. I tried to hail a cab, but when I asked what the fare was to Malibu, I was told 300, 350 and 250 by three different cab drivers. I started walking down Sunset Blvd, wondering if I could walk back to Malibu. After about fifteen blocks and dozens of cat calls from cars passing by, I ducked into an AMPM mini market. God bless the southern California AMPM mini markets!

I couldn't stop the tears so I went into the bathroom and cried. Huge tears fell for what seemed like hours before I heard a tapping on the bathroom door.

"Lady, are you alright in there?" asked someone with a thick middle-eastern accent.

I stuck my head out to see a young attendant who looked like he was from that area.

"No, I'm not. I need a ride home."

"Where do you live?" he asked me as he handed me a handkerchief.

"M-M-Malibu, and I have to get back by 5am. The family next door has to catch a flight to New York and I don't know what they would do with my children if I wasn't there."

I started sobbing. "I'm a bad mother," I said to the young man.

He gave me a warm hug and sat me down behind the counter with a cup of coffee.

"You are not a bad mother. A bad mother would be roaming the streets of West Hollywood looking for trouble. You are trying to get home to your children because you love them and do not want to burden others. You are a good mother. What is your name?"

I felt better and offered him the information he asked of me.

"Anne Marie Channing."

"Ali Reza Pishgahi, at your service." He slightly bowed with such gallant gestures that it made me feel like things would work out. "I get off work at 4am," he looked at the clock, "which is in an hour. I can drive you back to Malibu. It should not even take an hour at this time of night. How does that sound?"

My face broke into a smile and the gratefulness in my heart was pouring all over behind the counter. A large black man walked in and wanted a pack of cigarettes and it distracted me into my coffee.

He was going to take me home. I was ecstatic. Relief began pouring down my temples in droplets that I could have swore was blood. I got a warm feeling as if angels were watching over me.

As soon as he cleaned up and cashed in his drawer to his replacement, we got in his VW bug. It had a small Christmas tree air freshener hanging from the rear view mirror. He took out a small box which had rolling papers and pot and deftly rolled us a joint for the road. Once we got out of the city and closer to the PCH, he pulled it out and I told him the story of my night on Sunset strip.

He pulled into Kanan Dume road and I motioned to the parking area on the left for the condos. We pulled in on the crest of the highest spot on the parking lot which had a horizontal view of the LA skyline. The scarlet orange trails of a magnificent view of the sunrise greeted us as we parked his car.

"Happy Mother's Day, Anne Marie," said Ali Reza. "It is your holiday in America to honor mothers, right?

My mind raced through Saturday night to Sunday morning and it was as if time had caught up to the present moment. It was May, it was Sunday, and the Cataldi's were going to New York City to visit his mother for mother's day.

Tears began flowing again as I realized that I had been given such aid and comfort from a man from Iran. A man that the American media had tried to make me fear during the Jimmy Carter/ hostages crisis.

"You have been given to me like a gift from God, Ali. Let us both thank the God that we worship for his love."

187

Chapter 28
Monday, Monday

*M*onday, Monday… *Can't trust that day. Monday, Monday,*
I wish it didn't turn out that way… Oh Monday morning you
didn't give warning….how it could be

I drug myself out of bed and got Caleb to school. Things had
reached critical mass. I was running out of money fast and decided
that I would make one final call to Craig to see if he was planning on
attending Caleb's school graduation in two weeks.

My hand was shaking uncontrollably as I dialed the number.

"Craig," I said, grateful that it was he who answered the phone.

"Anne Marie, I am so glad to hear from you." I was so happy
that there was a familiar tone to his voice.

"Are you coming to California for Caleb's big day?"

"I can't Anne Marie. I have been reprimanded by the hospital
for some stupid charges and they are sending me to rehab. I wound
up making Nicole get a fourth abortion and she went ballistic on
me and trumped up all kinds of charges and the hospital bought it."

"Oh God," I cried. "I need help, I need money, or we won't
make it through the next month."

"I am so sorry for everything, Anne Marie. Everything. I can't
give you any money. Nicole drained all my bank accounts and the
hospital is sending over a taxi for me to get to rehab. The fucking
bitch even drove off in my BMW."

I had hit rock bottom with the news and I couldn't even hold
the phone in my hand as it fell to the floor.

Pulling myself together, I drove over to the travel agency and
booked a flight from Los Angeles to Chicago the day after Caleb's
graduation. LA had won. It had chewed me up and spit me out like
a wad of chewing gum. Just like that. My dreams had gone up in

smoke.

The plane ride from LA to Chicago had cost me every dime I had. We drifted through a sea of clouds as I saw all my time, effort, and money just evaporate into thin air. The children were all nodding into dreamland. They were happy we were leaving and couldn't wait to see their grandmother.

After catching a bus from O'Hare airport, the weary travelers arrived at my mother's small three-bedroom ranch in Hammond, Indiana and I had 27 cents in my pocket.

My mother greeted us at the front door singing...

"Back Home again in Indiana..."

The kids were delighted to see their grandmother and her welcoming singing felt like salt being poured into my wounds.

I sat up for most of the night, since I was sleeping on the couch anyways, and wrote myself a silly country song. "Feelin like a failure can't be as bad as losing you."

It made me laugh and I fell asleep on my old guitar after a shot of whiskey or two from mother's cabinet.

Dawn seemed to hit me square in the face and I cringed as I peered out to greet the new day. Mom suggested we take the kids to the park. It was just three blocks from her house and I wanted to relax. Sleeping had been just passing out and waking up and all those problems were still there. Perhaps walking could shred all the failure I felt.

Mia ran for the merry-go-round and Michael wanted me to push him in the baby swing. Caleb, the new man of the family, twirled the merry-go-round for her. Mom sat in the park bench behind me and we chatted about the future while I let Michael's feet touch the sky.

"What are you going to do?" she asked.

"God, mom, give me a minute to breathe." I dug deep down, hoping to uncover the part of me that I knew wasn't a failure because I was still breathing. "I was planning on going to the library while they take naps today to see what want ads I can find in the newspapers in the area."

"Mmm, good plan," she surmised. "You know I could say I told you so about your trek to Los Angeles but..."

"Then don't," I snapped back. I got Michael out of his seat

and he ran to the jungle gym that Caleb and Mia were on.

I sat back down on the bench. I hadn't really talked to her since dad had passed. I was in Miami when it happened, and I flew in and flew out for the funeral. My other siblings had taken care of her and I was the proverbial black sheep. In my defense, I knew that Craig and I were in trouble with our marriage since he insisted that work prevented him from attending. My mom never forgave Craig for that.

"I am trying to get some money from Craig, mom, but it seems he has some work problems."

"Work problems," she snapped, "he is a cardiologist, not a ditch digger. What kind of work problems could he have?"

"Alcoholism."

"What the heck does that mean? I know he drinks too much so he should just stop. How hard is that?"

I took a moment to realize that we had a whole bunch of alcoholics in our family: my aunt, my grandfather, and both of his brothers, but that's not how my mom saw it. They just drank a little too much now and then.

"The hospital has suspended him until he goes through rehab," I offered.

"Rehab, what's that?"

"Rehabilitation, mom. He is going to something similar to the Betty Ford clinic for the next two months. If he is successful, they will place him in another hospital in their system in Gainesville, Florida."

"He is a cardiologist! I have never heard of such a thing!" Mother was adamant.

I kept a watchful eye on the kids so that Caleb would not overhear this conversation. When his father failed to attend his graduation, something in him was crushed and he no longer brought up any mention of Craig.

Chapter 29
Middle of the Road

We walked back in silence. Once I got all three of them to take a nap, I walked to the library. As I scoured through the state papers, I noticed an ad in the Bloomington Herald Times. It was for a social services director and it was in Nashville, Indiana, just a mere 10 miles from Bloomington. Since Craig and I had some wonderful years there while he got his undergraduate degree, I decided it was worth a shot. The ad provided an address where I could send a resume.

A resume. The concept was like throwing battery acid all over me. Rock stars didn't have resumes... well, bio's and press kits... but not resumes. I went back to mom's and resurrected an old typewriter she had in her attic and typed up a bogus resume. I supposed it wasn't completely bogus, since I did almost have a sociology degree, but all the jobs were from my creative imagination. After all, being the mother of three gave me job experience, I just never got paid for it.

I received a call and had an interview set up with the administrator. When I got to the address, freshly dressed in a three-piece suit, I was surprised. I thought the Nashville Care Center was a medical facility, but in fact, it was a nursing home. I had never been to one before and the old people hung over and tied in their Gerry chairs was a ghastly sight.

The administrator was a perky little woman and she asked me lots of probing questions. I kept telling myself that I needed the money and without it, my children and I would be destitute.

"So are you married?" she inquired.

"Um, separated, my husband left me for another woman and I am raising my three children on my own, without his support."

191

I was vomiting out my current situation without even thinking about the bad impression I might be making on my potential employer.

Her face brightened and she smiled.

"You're hired," she beamed. "Anyone strong enough to take care of her children when a rat bastard husband strays is strong enough to work at this nursing home. My husband ran out on me and I got a job here as the social services director and now look at me, I am the administrator. This is a great place for you. Welcome aboard."

I took a step back inside as I was taken by her genuine concern for me and my children's well-being. It was a refreshing relief from the dog-eat-dog lifestyle I had come to know in LA and Malibu.

Malibu - I missed it. Zuma Beach was like coming home to something familiar when I first got there and in spite of all the madness, I loved the ocean. It was majestic.

Brown County was OK. I found a couple of old friends from college still in the area and the school system was solid. Mia would be going to kindergarten and I hired a young college girl to live in and take care of Michael.

I got used to all the things in the small town, and I even made friends with the nursing home head cook. Molly Perkins was a large big-boned woman who was jolly and loved to sing. I heard her sometimes back in the kitchen singing some Willie Nelson. I played her some of my cassettes from my LA adventures and she took a liking to me. She had her own band and played country music gigs all over the area.

The other significant person at the home for me was this young Baptist preacher named Billy Thrasher. He would bring his guitar every Friday and sing old gospel songs to the residents of the home. His key was perfect for me to sing thirds above him in harmony and he taught me songs that were never sung in my St. Mary's Catholic church.

I saw the light, I saw the light, praise the Lord, cause I saw the light! He gave me great solace. We joked and laughed and I would look forward to Friday because I set up a little stage in the dining room and the two of us would serenade the old folks as they ate lunch.

One Friday afternoon, Molly poked her head out of the kitchen and listened. She pulled me aside after we sang and let me know that she was playing at a local restaurant next Friday evening and wanted me to sing a song with her band.

"Praise God," I thought.

"Yes, I would love to sing a song, what song?"

"Do you know any Loretta Lynn or Tammy Wynette tunes?" she asked.

"No, but I would be willing to learn it if you have a tape," I countered.

"Tell you what, why don't you sing the Bob Seger tune, you know the one about old-time rock and roll. I think the crowd would go for that."

"Give me the tape, I will rock the house down," I laughed.

"You got it," she chuckled back.

I couldn't wait for the week to pass, I was so excited. My live-in babysitter, Beth Gentry, was excited for me as well and was willing to watch the kids that evening, even though Friday nights were her time off.

I was dressed in old blue jeans with holes and patches and I was trying to capture a cross-over look, country rock and roll, and this was my entry.

Molly was great. She had the crowd all primed and ready for me. She introduced me at the beginning of the second set. I hit the stage like a prima donna and was about to feel like a deer in headlights.

"I would like to introduce to you a new face and a great talent, please welcome Anne Marie Channing."

A polite round of applause brought me to the stage.

"Are you all ready to rock and roll?" I asked thunderously.

A blankly staring audience silently looked back at me as if I was from Mars.

I turned to the band and they started playing and I sang my heart out. I was in pitch, I punched it and I thought I did a good job but when I finished, the crowd gave me another polite round of applause.

I wanted to cry, but I thanked the audience and retreated backstage. Molly sang an old Patsy Cline favorite, "Crazy," and the crowd went nuts when she finished.

I had a hard time stopping the tears and I drove home gushing like a waterfall. It seemed that I didn't have what it took. I made excuses for myself saying that it was country music and I never even listened to that music before moving to Brown County.

I did not want to get into any wallowing pity party mentality. Not every gig was going to be a success and I shook it off by the time I got home. I lied to my family and told them I was a huge success.

Chapter 30

Barracuda

It was time to get out of my safe hole and venture into Bloomington. The town was a haven for great musicians and I had heard about a jam session on Monday nights at the famous Bluebird nightclub. All you had to do was sign up. It was being run by a local guitarist of some local prominence named PK Livermore. He had lightning-fast licks and I was hoping to impress him.

He had been touring with a regional band, Wild Eyes, and after a good two year run, they had disbanded. I knew he was looking for another band to put together and I was hoping and praying that I could be a part of it.

Monday night, after a very tiring day at the nursing home, finally arrived and I drove to Bloomington with great anticipation. After all, this was the bar that had changed the life of John Mellencamp and his band. He had started there. I wrote down my name and the song I wanted to sing and found my way to a table to drink a beer.

PK was everything I thought he would be. He knew all the old classics and I was hoping my voice would rock his mojo.

"Alright, we have a newcomer here at the BlueBird, she is coming all the way from Malibu California, please give it up for Miss Anne Marie Channing."

As I suspected, PK went crazy on the Jimmy Page solos and no one could nail Robert Plant's vocals like I could. When the song was finished, PK beamed at me as the house went nuts and people were whistling and cheering. You could never go wrong with a Led Zeppelin cover, not even in 1987.

"You heard her here first," PK announced to the crowd, "Anne Marie Channing everyone." The applause was like a soothing balm on my raw and tortured soul. I could barely step off the stage, I felt like I was floating and the bass player who was coming up to do his song with PK said, "god that was great," to me as we passed each other getting on and off the stage.

I flew home, my car had wings, my soul had taken off and I felt like I had survived LA and taken my game to Bloomington Indiana.

That next week, I was back, like a junkie wanting her heroin fix. This time I took a female lead vocalist's song released by a band that I thought rocked: Heart. Ann Wilson was a fabulous singer and I knew I could nail her vocals.

PK was playing it for every riff it was worth and it sounded like the walls of the place were gonna take off. People were getting up and dancing to it and I knew that PK was happy with the crowd response.

The applause was deafening, and I thought I had done what I had hoped for - to get the attention of a guitar player, namely PK.

As I got off stage, several male guitar players gathered around me to talk. I was truly the queen of the silver dollar that night and I was being told by one musician after another that they wanted to jam with me. Everyone but PK. I never did have a conversation with him.

One guitarist did stand out for me in this crowd. His name was Karl Conklin. He was at least ten years younger than I, but he had his guitar with him and we went out backstage to smoke a cigarette together. Not something I did very often but if it furthered a conversation with someone whom I could form a band with, then I would smoke.

"I love Ann Wilson, she is the greatest vocalist in rock today," Karl said as he strummed his guitar. He began picking a wonderful melody line and he was obviously as talented as PK and much more handsome. He had a certain boyish charm and an adorable smile.

"How old are you?" I asked.

"Twenty-five," he said proudly. "And you?"

My heart raced at the idea of telling him I was 37 years old, it seemed to make me ancient.

"Twenty-four," I lied.

"Thought you looked a bit younger than me," he quipped, as he continued to play one killer riff after another. I was impressed. He was also easy to be with, not like the people in LA. Maybe that's why I had landed back in the Midwest.

Although I went back for a few more of PK's jams, it was Karl whom I began working with on songs. He was a natural at following my lead and we started to write songs at his trailer on Monday nights instead of going to the jam.

Karl lived in a small trailer court on the west side of Bloomington. I thought he lived there by himself until one day when I came by, the door was opened by a red-haired woman who was grotesquely obese.

"I am looking for Karl Conklin, he does live here doesn't he?"

"Sometimes," the woman replied as she stared at me like some grand inquisitor.

"And you would be?" she asked.

"Anne Marie Channing, we are friends. And you would be?" I asked back.

"His mother," she said as she stood in the doorway like a brick shit house.

"Karl, somebody here to see you!" she yelled in the direction of the bedrooms. Even though it was cold outside, she did not let me in. After a few minutes, Karl came to the door.

He grabbed his jacket and walked out the door towards my car. I followed him, wanting to get out of there anyways, but curious as to what was happening.

"Mom lost her job at the K-Mart and she will be home at night now so we can't rehearse at my place. What do you say we go to your place?"

Karl was obviously annoyed that I had found out that he lived with his mother but it was not half as bad as me having to tell him what my family life was like.

"I live in Nashville, Karl. It would not be cool for us to practice there."

Telling him that I had three kids was not an option for me, not yet anyways.

"Well, shit, where can we play?"

We sat in silence as the car heater kept us from freezing our tails off. Finally, Karl had an idea.

"Let me get a hold of my friend, Rudy. He plays bass. I think he would be a great addition to our band. He plays with Rick, who

197

has a kick-ass drum set and he knows how to bang it out."

"Works for me," I said.

I told him to call me and I drove away asking myself what I was looking for in this band.

"Gigs," my inner voice said back to me, "just gigs as cool as PK's jam."

The following day at work wore my patience down to the nub. As I walked in the door, Greta, one of the residents who kept trying to escape, was running out the door with two nurse aids chasing her in hot pursuit.

"Greta, where are you going?" I asked her as she whizzed past me, escaping my reach.

"Home!" she shrieked. "I am going home."

I had barely taken off my coat when I saw the two aids carrying Greta back into the nursing home. One had her feet and the other had her head and they were carrying her back in like she was a two-by-four piece of lumber, all the while she was screaming her head off, "Let me go!"

I sat in my office, hoping that things would settle down, but it only got worse.

The administrator told me that she wanted to see me. Apparently, my paperwork was not up to her standards and the state regulations committee was coming next week and she handed me a stack of folders that needed to be finished by the week's end.

By Friday, I couldn't wait for Billy the preacher to show up. Several residents had gathered in my office that morning, including one lady who was new to the nursing home.

"I want to go home," she demanded of me.

"This is your home, Ella," I said as sweetly as I could.

"No, it's not, it's not my home. I want to go back to my house and I want to go now."

Ella Thomas was a small but mighty lady who was admitted to the nursing home with dementia. She seemed fine to me but it was not my job to diagnose them, just to keep them happy once they arrive.

"Ella, try and enjoy your new home here. We want you to be as comfortable here as you were in your home."

"I want to go home, I want to go home, I want to go home,"

she demanded. Her attitude was one of a six-year-old who was not getting her way. I found myself losing my temper.

"Look, Ella, there is only one way out of this nursing home, one way out, and it's not through the front doors." I looked her directly in the eyes and she knew exactly what I was talking about.

Billy walked in at that exact moment and the relief at not having to get into a pissing match with Ella was written all over my face.

"Oh Preacher Billy's here," I announced to everyone. "Let's all go down to the dining room and get ready for lunch." A nurse aid came to get Ella and tied her to a Gerry chair and wheeled her into the dining room.

"I would love to sing that old gospel tune that you taught me a few weeks ago," I asked Billy. "You know the one about ain't no grave."

"Oh yeah, that's a good one. We can start with that one."

When we walked into the dining room, I spied Ella in the back of the dining room. She was staring a hole through me as we got started.

Meet me Jesus, meet me, meet me in the middle of the air, gonna holler high hosanna and hope to meet you there.

Cause there ain't no grave gonna hold my body down.

Billy was strumming a mean rhythm guitar and we were punching it loudly. I saw Molly peek her head out of the kitchen and she was tapping her foot to the beat.

We hit a high crescendo as we went into the final chorus.

Cause there ain't no grave gonna hold my body down........no there ain't no GRAVE that can hold my body down.

In the back of the dining room, I saw Ella yell loudly and raise her hands up in the air and then she collapsed onto the plate of food in front of her.

Several nurse aids who were feeding other residents went rushing to her side and our song ended abruptly. Chaos ensued as the director of nursing came running into the dining room with her stethoscope around her neck.

I watched in horror as the DON pronounced her dead. They quickly covered her with a sheet and rolled her out of the dining room and down the hallway to a place where they took folks when they died.

It was common for them to die in the nursing home but the manner in which she passed was not common. I felt an extreme bolt of guilt run down my spine, since I was the one who told her that it was the only way she could ever leave the nursing home.

It was no surprise to me when the administrator called me into her office on Monday morning.

"Anne Marie, I have decided to cancel the Friday lunch gospel sing-a-long that you and preacher Billy have been doing. You guys are way too loud for 80 and 90-year-old people. I am not saying that you or Preacher Billy were responsible for Ella Thomas's passing but especially since the Indiana State Board is visiting us this week, I need to make sure everything is in apple pie order with no glitches. Understand?"

"Of course, I will call him and tell him."

I walked out of the office and felt the weight of the world on my shoulders. With moist eyes I called and cancelled the only bright spot in my week except for PK's jam.

"Perhaps I should go and do the jam tonight instead of meeting with Karl," I thought to myself. I hadn't heard from him and was wondering what had happened.

When I got home that night, Beth told me that Karl had called and I called him back.

"We have a band," Karl said proudly to me over the phone. "And we can practice at my friend Ruben's studio. He has an eight track studio in his basement."

"What kind of a studio is it? An eight track? That doesn't sound very professional?"

"What are you talking about? It is used by some of the Indiana University opera singers to cut demos. Come and see it before you pass judgment on it, bitch."

I was shocked that he would call me a bitch. Instead of getting into it with him, I promptly agreed, feigning excitement about "the band" and got directions from him.

Arriving promptly at 7, Karl introduced me to his friend, Ruben, and then the bass player, the drummer, and another guitar player, Stevie.

We started with the Heart tune, "Barracuda," and they were good. The drummer kept a nice steady beat and the bass player knew how to walk up and down his guitar and I left the rehearsal singing.

"This is great, they are actually a decent band and they like me and I like them and everything is right under heaven."

I walked in the door of the small rental home we had near the county golf course. Expecting all my children to be asleep, I found Caleb and Beth in a screaming match, Mia choking Michael, and he was wailing at the top of his lungs.

"Stop!" I yelled as loudly as I could to override the din of noise in our living room.

"I have had it with your bratty son. He doesn't listen to me and defiantly told me he was going to stay up and put his puzzle together."

"Is this true?" I asked Caleb, turning to look him in the eyes.

His gaze met mine and his eyes were steel cold and I could tell he had had enough. The silence in my eyes beckoned him to speak from his heart.

"I wasn't tired, mom. I thought if worked on it for awhile, I would get sleepy."

I sank down to my knees and motioned for him to come close to me and give me a hug.

"I miss dad," he whispered in my ear.

Beth threw down the dishrag that she had in her hand and scowled at me.

"He disrespected me, I have no control whatsoever with him. You have to punish him."

I found her tone annoying. She was my hired help and she would not be dictating policy in my home.

"I will not, you will not give orders like that in my home."

Beth burst into flames of anger.

"Oh, easy for you to say, you work all day, then you go and work on your music all evening, then you come home and want to have the final word. I am the one raising these kids, not you."

Her words stung like a million stinging bees and I over reacted as usual.

"Beth, I pay you to take care of my household, if you have any problems with the way I see fit to run this household, then you can pack your things and leave."

Beth's face went white with shock. She did not expect a pink slip out of this conversation. Turning to go upstairs to her room, she left in silence.

"Come on guys, you all can sleep with me tonight in my bed," I said to delighted faces.

I cuddled them all close and felt the love we all shared. I could not shake the thought of Craig that night. All of them nodded off to sleep and I stared out of my window at a half moon sailing across the heavens with white billowy clouds.

Was it time to find a truce with Craig? Definitely, Caleb needed to see his father again. It had been over three years. It had been over eight months since I had last spoken with him, so I figured he had gotten out of rehab, but I tried to call directory assistance several times trying to locate Dr. Craig Channing, but there was no listing.

The moon kept sailing in the sky, laughing at me, mocking me with its carefree modus operandi. Human lives were too complicated, there needs to be more simplicity.

In the morning, I found a note from Beth on the table. She apologized for flying off the handle but mentioned that she would be leaving at the end of May. I looked at the calendar: March 8th, winter was almost over.

As I packed everyone in the car, I got a phone call. It was Karl, he wanted to tell me about a contest.

"Call me at work, my kids are in the car and I have to get them to school." I hung up the phone and realized that I had told him something about me that he did not know.

"Too much worry," I said running to the car. "Who cares if he knows that I am pushing forty." I closed the car door with a bang. "I am pushing forty."

When I got to my office at the nursing home, the phone was ringing off the hook.

"This is Anne Marie Channing. May I help you?"

"It's Karl. Hey, Ruben thinks we should enter the Live From Bloomington contest. Your song, 'Broken Dreams,' is a shoe-in, he thinks. We would have to pay him to cut the recording for us."

"How convenient," I thought to myself. "The guy who owns the recording studio thinks we should record a song for the Indiana University Union Board album." One of last year's winners, Patty Frazier, wound up on tour with Mellencamp as his backup vocalist.

It certainly got the artist who won a whirlwind of local gigs and great exposure. The Indianapolis Rock station WFBQ played the album.

My mind wandered down a path that made me oblivious to the conversation.

"Well, what do you think?...Anne Marie? Anne Marie?"

"Sure, let's do it. Why not?"

"Cool, and you can pay for it, right?"

Oh, there it was, the reason for a why not. "How much is it?"

"I dunno, six or seven hundred, maybe eight."

Someone must have shot me with a stun gun because I dropped the phone. That was way more money than I had. In my world there were bills to pay and mouths to feed. Nothing like that existed in Karl's world where his mom's trailer and his guitar defined his.

All day long, as I worked on a huge mound of charting, I kept wondering how I would pay for it. Craig was AWOL, my mother would not part with any money - she had cashed out on any more show business loans and my credit was crap. Trying to rebuild it meant that I had to be at a job for at least two years, one with a pay stub I could show the bank. The feeling was squeezing the life out of me until my assistant walked in.

"Anne Marie, I have a wonderful cousin that I want you to meet. You should get out and date and he is such a nice guy. Single. Makes good money, no kids. He would be perfect. His name is Bill Whitley. He runs an insurance agency in Bloomington. How about I give him your number?"

"Sure, why not," I said in a zombie-like tone. The last thing I needed was to date someone. I barely had enough time in my life to do the things that were already on my plate but my assistant, Janet Hines, was such a chatty Cathy that I said yes just to shut her up.

Bill called me that evening and wanted to take me out for dinner on Friday.

"You know, Bill, I would love to have dinner with you but I am a package. I have three children and they eat dinner with me."

The ease with which Bill agreed made me feel like he might be a nice guy after all. He took us to play putt-putt golf after that and in the end, the evening was very enjoyable.

As he drove us back to Nashville, the kids dozed off and I brought up my musical career to him.

"Have you ever heard of Live From Bloomington?" I asked.

"Are you kidding? Everyone in Bloomington knows about it. A couple of bands that I know of on the album two years ago got record deals."

"Really?" My eyes were wide open and my mouth was hanging down, my tongue was ready to drop out of my mouth and start drooling.

The wheels in my head were turning and I saw an opportunity in Bill. He had the money to fund the project but what would it take to make that happen?

God, I hoped I didn't have to fuck him for it. He was nice enough but I was not physically attracted to him. The same was not true for him. It was painfully obvious to me that he was very turned on by me. The classic school boy crush.

"You know, I play a bit of guitar myself." Bill played guitar? I was surprised, he did not seem like the rock and roll type.

"Wow, you play guitar? How cool, you have to play something for me. Let's get together tomorrow and jam." My eager attitude ignited his flame.

"Or perhaps, I could just stay the night?" he hinted.

"This was a first date, Bill. What do you take me for, an EASY girl?"

The alarm in my voice prompted an immediate apology but the evening did set a tone for a solid beginning to a friendship.

In the next two weeks, I had convinced Bill to fund the Live From Bloomington project and he thought that "Broken Dreams" was the next "Stairway to Heaven."

"I am ready to go into the studio," I called Karl one afternoon with the news.

"Wow, I thought this was dead in the water."

"Hey, it took me a while to get someone to fund it. What's the big deal?"

"The deadline is next week, April 1st. Let me call Ruben and see if we can still do it."

I freaked and spent the next five minutes sweating drops of blood. The phone rang and I picked it up with shaking hands.

"OK, we can come in tonight and lay down bass and drums, then you and I can lay down guitar parts and vocals."

"We have to let Bill lay down a guitar track, Karl."

"Who the hell is Bill?" Karl cracked back.

"The guy who is paying for us to record this song, that's who." I said it with deep authority.

"Oh gee Anne Marie, what does this guy sound like?"

"Karl, it absolutely doesn't matter. He is going to lay down a track or else this isn't going to happen."

"Whatever," he said with resignation.

Ruben knew his stuff and he did a nice job of getting the drum and bass parts. Karl and I were satisfied with what we heard. The next evening, Bill met us at the studio, with his guitar case in hand.

Karl was very aloof, preferring to stay in the engineering booth with Ruben. When we set up the mics for Bill, we could all tell that he had never played professionally. The first run-through was a nightmare. He made mistakes and we took several passes at his part.

I turned to Ruben in the control booth as it reached midnight.

"This is the last pass. Whatever we lay down is gonna be the keeper."

Bill muddled through with only three mistakes that I could hear. I came into the iso booth to congratulate him on a job well done.

Ruben was quick to get a payment from Bill which included two hours of mix down time tomorrow.

"Oh, thanks so much for letting me be a part of the band. It was a lot of fun. Who knows, maybe we'll even win?"

Bill was like a kid who made the winning touchdown for the school championship game. He was glowing. The fact that he stunk was not even obvious to him. Karl avoided looking him in the eyes the entire session and when Bill extended his hand to Karl for a goodbye shake, Karl shook it weakly.

I shot Karl a look that could kill and left with Bill. As soon as I got back to my house, the phone rang.

"You have got to be fucking kidding me, Anne Marie. The guy stunk, his track was horseshit and if you leave that on the mix, we will never ever ever win the contest."

"You think you are telling me something that I don't know? What do you want me to do, Karl? He is paying for it."

His answer was to hang up. My situation was getting to a crisis level on the home front, too. As I took Caleb to school, I turned to him and said, "We will get a hold of your father, he has been going through a rough time but he told me to tell you how much he loves you."

"Did you tell him that I love him back?" His little eyes were filled with tears.

"Of course, and he said he was coming here to Brown County to see you real soon."

"He did?" I had opened up Pandora's box by promising something I had no idea how to deliver.

"Yes, and he asked that you try and get along with Beth and be real good till gets here."

"When is he coming? When is he coming?" Caleb was just ecstatic.

"Very soon, honey, now go to class and mommy will pick you up after school."

I had a sick feeling in my stomach. I tried to dismiss it as I headed to Bloomington. I had called off sick this morning from work so that I could go to the studio and mix the tape. It had to be in the office of the Union Board by 5pm and it was already after 9am.

Arriving at the studio, I found Karl and Ruben listening to all the tracks. Karl started telling Ruben where he wanted the sound up, and where it needed more effects. He even insisted on going back into the iso booth to add an extra tasty lick to his guitar solo.

I was pleased that Karl was so dedicated and I listened to the playback of it and it added something, but as I looked at the clock it was pushing 2pm.

"We need to start mixing," I argued. "We are running out of time."

I went into the other room and called my neighbor and asked her to pick up Caleb and Mia from school. I knew I didn't want to leave until I had the tape delivered to the Union Board office.

Ruben, Karl, and I all had our hands on different control buttons as we continued to go over the mix.

Karl kept pulling up the guitar and turning down the drums.

"You are losing the backbeat of the song, Karl, quit grandstanding."

"What are you talking about, you have your vocals way out in front of the music, turn it back down."

"Both of you need to quit and think about what sounds best for the piece to keep its integrity." Ruben started to get annoyed with both of us. It felt like the blind leading the blind, as in fact, no one was a record producer in the group.

I looked at the clock, it was 4:15pm. I knew that we had to decide on the mix with this next pass.

"Okay, this is it, mix it down and put it on the cassette, I think we have it," I said to the other two.

I live in a world that's filled with broken dreams,
Too much, too fast, too little too late, I can't even see
Love is all I asked for and yet I hear the screams of the children of a generation of broken dreams.

The guitar riff that led us into the turn-around was raw metal, and I felt that the hook of the song was the downwardly progressive chord passage dressed in fat metal sounds and raw energy.

Karl was smiling at me. I had done the unthinkable at 1:45pm. I erased Bill's guitar track so that Karl could add one last highlight with a killer acoustic accent track. It made the angst of the song stand up and bite you in the ass.

"You had to do it, Anne Marie. This is our shot at stardom. We only had eight tracks, we had to erase it."

"That doesn't help ease the guilt I feel about it. After all, he paid for it."

The lump in my throat wouldn't go away. Karl grabbed the cassette and labeled it and we jumped in the car, driving to the IU campus.

We parked in a lot that we did not have a sticker for but it was a race to get to the third floor before 5pm.

When we got there, completely out of breath, they were just closing.

"Wait, there is one more entry," I said.

A young attractive woman took the cassette from me and smiled.

"You just made it. Now, are you sure that you have it rewound so that all the judges have to do is press play?"

I looked at Karl, and he nodded. He was the one who ran off a copy for the contest.

"It's queued up and ready to rock. We are the band to hear in 1987. Live from Bloomington needs to have the band, Fire Dogs, on this year's CD."

The woman smiled and put it in an envelope.

"Good luck, I hope that you do win."

As we walked out the door, I turned to Karl.

"Fire Dogs, is that what you named the band?"

"We never came up with a name. Sorry, it's the best I could do. Did you have a better name?"

"I was thinking the Anne Marie Channing Band."

"Oh listen to you, who's the hot dog in this band anyways."

"Who cares, let's just win."

I pulled up to his trailer and dropped him off and headed home. I was praying for a small miracle and I looked up at a planet I thought might be Venus. It shone in the eastern horizon as the sun started to set.

"Please God," I whispered. "I need a miracle."

I waited with anticipation for the mailman to arrive at the nursing home the following morning. The winners were to be announced in the lifestyle section of the newspaper. I had great hopes.

Jim Moore, the local mailman, hobbled in and handed it right to me.

"Is this what you were waiting for?" he smiled.

"Oh my God, he has probably already read it and knows that I won," I thought.

I nearly ripped the paper in two trying to get at Section C. My eyes scanned each column and headline like a heat seeking missile, looking for the winners. In the top left hand corner of page 3 of the Lifestyle section were the twelve songs and artists that were to be on the Live From Bloomington '87.

My heart pounded as I read and re-read all the names because Fire Dogs or Broken Dreams were not to be found. Racing to the back file closet, I closed the door and starting kicking and screaming like a first grader having a tantrum.

Finally tears cooled the broken dream and I realized that we had lost. Why? It was a good tune and Ruben, who had PhD in recital piano from IU, had done a good job of producing it. He succeeded in getting Karl's guitar on the right level and just enough reverb on my voice to make it juicy.

Picking up the kids from school, I told them I would get them a "happy meal" at the Bloomington McDonalds if they went with me to pick up my tape.

"Did you win, mom?" asked Caleb innocently.

"Naw," I said hoarsely.

"I'm sorry. You will win next time."

I hugged him and held him close as we headed over to the Student Union. I got there just as the girl was getting ready to lock up and I asked for my cassette. She was obviously annoyed as she dug through the tapes of the losers.

"Here it is, it got discarded cause I guess there was no recording on it," she said as she handed the tape to me. "Better luck next year," she said, delighting in my wince of pain.

"No recording," I grumbled as I made my way back to my car. As the kids and I walked to the car, we saw an IU parking cop putting a yellow ticket on my windshield. It was an insult to injury moment.

I got in the car and popped the tape back into the player. She was right, there was nothing. Then I tried to rewind it. I heard the tape whizz back and I knew what had happened. True to their word, the committee did not rewind the tape. When it got back to the beginning, it kicked around and out came Karl's lead guitar blazing across the heavens.

"Dumbass! You are a no good, high school dropout dumb ass!" I shrieked at Karl when I called him from my home later on that evening.

"We lost?" Karl's voice was cracking with disappointment.

"We didn't even get in the game, they never even heard the song because someone didn't rewind the tape like they should have."

There was silence on the other end and finally, with a slamming of the phone receiver, I hung up.

April 1st had become my personal April Fool's Day. Even though the trees had blossoms of spring's beauty, I was stuck with a cold ugly feeling in my heart.

Chapter 31
Nashville Skyline

The next day at work, no one could even get a smile from me. The only thing to smile about was that it was Friday. Rev. Billy Thrasher walked up to my desk with a big smile on his face and it broke my concentration.

"Are we going to sing some gospel?"

"No, I am sorry to say that I have been told by the administrator that we can't do that anymore. She told me you could read some Bible passages instead. No singing."

"Well, now that is a shame," he said. "However, I welcome the opportunity to preach the gospel of our Lord Jesus Christ to the people."

I handed him the in-house Bible and he was thumbing through looking for a good passage. He looked up at me, recalling what he wanted to tell me before hearing of the change in the schedule.

"I told my friend, Charlie Markham about you and what a great singer you are. I didn't know this but he has started to run the soundboard for the Lil Nashville Opry. He said he could set up an audition for you with the Washington's, Jethro and Patsy. They have a house band, The Lil Nashville Opry Express band and they have local and regional acts on Friday and the best ones get to open for their Saturday night headliners."

"Huh," I said, still lost in the mire of my disappointment in rock and roll.

"I know you are a single mother, Anne Marie, so it might interest you to know that they pay good money to their singers."

My ears perked up. I had been living in poverty for the past ten months. Without any help from Craig, we lived from paycheck-to-paycheck, and then just barely.

The Rev. Billy found just the passage he wanted to read and he bookmarked it with the Easter card that I had sitting on the table that read, "He has risen."

"Call him, Anne Marie. It can't hurt. Sing some of the gospel tunes that I have taught you. Add some Emmylou Harris. He told me the Washington's love her stuff and she has been on their Saturday night headliners list for years.

"Huh," I said again, as I took the piece of paper with the information on it from him.

"Thanks, preacher. Now you go out there and tell them the good news."

Over the weekend, I went into Bloomington and bought myself an album of Emmylou Harris's, Pieces of the Sky. Several of the tunes had shades of Dylan in them and I had no trouble learning a few of them, including my favorite, "Queen of the Silver Dollar."

Jethro Washington answered his phone with the smooth-as-silk radio announcer's voice. When I introduced myself, he knew who I was and was delighted to hear I wanted to audition to sing at the Opry.

"Patsy and I will be at the Opry, Thursday, around noon. Would you like to stop by then on your lunch hour and sing us a tune or two?"

"Sure would," I said with my sauciest Southern accent. "I thought I would sing you a couple of Emmylou's tunes."

"Oh, tell me you are going to sing me, 'Queen of the Silver Dollar.' I love that tune."

"Well, as a matter of fact, I do, too, Jethro." The southern accent almost sounded real to me, which I attributed to my ability to act. "Fake it 'till you make it," I chanted to myself. Although I never lived in an area that had that dialect and the only Jethro I ever knew was Jed Clampitt's nephew, it was something I was picking up naturally, living in Nashville.

I astounded my boss at the nursing home by asking to take my lunch hour outside the facility.

"We don't normally encourage that, we want the staff to be on duty in case there is an emergency," she frowned at me.

"Just this one time, Mrs. Anderson. I am going to audition for the Lil Opry."

211

"What?" Her whole demeanor changed and her sunny disposition shone through.

"Yeah, they asked me to audition so that's where I am going. It won't take long."

The drive from the nursing home to the Lil Nashville Opry was less than two miles and when I walked in the first thing to catch my eye was the stage. It was huge and there were at least five thousand seats in the place. The acoustics looked challenging, but then that was Jethro's problem.

As I walked onto the stage, the hairs on the back of my neck stood up. For a brief second, a frozen panic set in at being in front of so many people but something came and grabbed a hold of me and told me I could do this in my sleep. Even if it was country. After all, music is music. It's a universal language and it's a language that I love.

My confidence was not where it should be though. My first encounter with a country gig left me high and dry. I had never bombed so badly in all my musical career. Half of the crowd didn't even applaud and the other half that did so half heartedly.

When I finished both Jethro and Patsy were clapping loudly and cheering. I knew I had the gig. We walked into Patsy Washington's lush office set up on the backside of the stage area.

"I like to sign a contract with everyone who works here. I need you once every three weeks and I will need you to sing a minimum of four songs, if you get picked up as an opener for one of our national acts, you need six. I will pay you $400 for the Friday night gigs and you will get $650 to sing with the big stars."

This was like a gift from God for me. I would be making in one night of singing what I made in 2 weeks of eight hour shifts at the nursing home. I was ready to twang my little pea picking heart out. God bless country. To hell with rock and roll.

Karl tried calling me every day and took to leaving these sad messages, playing the song, "Broken Dreams," over and over again. I thought about responding but I didn't really know what to say.

I was cruising into the warm days of summer with money in my pockets and a new-found appreciation for country music. I especially thrilled the kids by having enough money to buy them the Nintendo video game player they had all been asking for, especially

Caleb. He had been having a hard time; it had been almost two months since he asked about his dad. He silently sulked most of the time, but the arrival of the video player brightened him into a glowing ball of light.

One Sunday morning, as the kids were huddled around the TV playing the Mario Brothers video game, the phone rang and I begrudgingly got out of bed to answer it.

"Hi Anne Marie, it's Craig."

Before I even had a chance to think, I quickly called Caleb to the phone.

"Daddy," his voice had an indescribable sound to it. At long last, his father's voice was there.

Mia and Michael both ran to the phone to mark the first and only time they ever voluntarily left a video game in progress.

My kids were floating on a cloud, and the joy that I saw on their faces was priceless.

When the phone came back to me, Craig was crying.

"I miss you, I miss my children, I am so sorry for everything I have done."

His contrition seemed genuine, and I wanted to believe things would be better but a deep gnawing in my stomach warned me to be cautious.

"What ever happened to the rehab?" I asked.

"Oh, I went to the treatment center, spent two months there, and then was right back at all my addictions as soon as I got out. Luckily, I got myself right back in and this time I seem to be alright."

"That's great news. How long have you been out of treatment?"

"Six weeks," Craig announced proudly.

"Wow," was all I could say. The small amount of time seemed ripe for relapse. As if Craig had read my mind, he continued with his news.

"My therapist says I should seek the support of my family and you are my family, Anne Marie. You're my life."

"Uh huh," I drawled. "What type of support are you talking about?"

"They gave me a good job at the main hospital here in Alachua county, and I found a nice house in a neighborhood that is walking distance to the elementary school."

213

"And Alachua county is in Gainesville?"

"Yes sireee," he yipped. "Gainesville is home to the Gators, they have one of the best football programs in the country."

"Caleb would like that. He loves football. He tosses the football all the time with his neighborhood friends, Charlie and Cooter."

"I miss you soooo much," he blubbered on. "I love you soooo much."

I could not say that I felt the same way, but as I looked at those adorable faces staring wide-eyed at me, I lied through my teeth and said that I missed and loved him, too.

Craig promised to call again tomorrow and since it was Beth's last day as our nanny, it couldn't have come at a better time.

I had practically begged my mother to come down and stay with us. Now, I could add the reconciliation factor to sweeten the pot.

I tossed and turned in bed all night, thinking about the Opry, thinking about Karl, thinking about rock and roll, and thinking about Craig and Gainesville. It felt like the weight of the world was on my shoulders so I went outside and smoked a joint.

I sucked it down, taking huge puffs and holding it until the stars in the sky twinkled and swirled around me. Things felt unclear. Even my favorite herb did nothing to clear the confusion in my head. I hadn't even had a visit from my favorite ethereal rock icon in months and I felt abandoned.

I woke up to a sparkler in my face; it was Memorial Day. Beth had promised to take the kids to the park for a goodbye picnic and mom was supposed to be arriving later that afternoon.

"Who lit that sparkler, Mia?" I asked.

"Caleb did," Mia proudly announced.

I walked upstairs and found Caleb in possession of a lighter.

"I don't want sparklers being lit inside the house Caleb," I commanded gently. "It's a fire hazard, sweetie."

"Is Daddy coming today?" Caleb was celebrating "Daddy coming back day" and not Memorial Day and I had to tread lightly when discussing the day's festivities.

"He is going to call us, honey. It takes a long time to drive from Florida, so it might not be today when he comes, but your gramma is coming."

"Yeah!" I heard Mia and Michael in chorus behind us.

I play-wrestled on the bed for a few minutes with all of them and then rushed off to work. I had the day off if I wanted, but chose to go in and be paid double time. It had come down to that in my life. Every penny counted even with the new country music money.

It was like all the hornets were swirling, getting ready to sting. Craig was coming, mother would be there, Beth was leaving, and I decided to turn on the radio before getting to the nursing home, or what I called "purgatory."

"Love is all we asked for and yet I hear the screams, of the children in a generation of Broken Dreams…"

"And that was the Fire Dogs, one of the bands that competed in this year's Live from Bloomington album and the song was, 'Broken Dreams.' And speaking of the album, I have an updated list of where this year's winners will be performing."

Click - I turned it off. While I did want to hear about the winners, however, I was more concerned that one of the losers, namely Me, got their song played. I walked into the house and clicked my heels, then headed to the office to called Karl.

"Oh now you want to talk to me. Is it because you heard our song being played on the 'Over Easy' morning drive with Lisa Morrison?"

"OK, Karl, I admit I was angry, but how did you know the song was on WTTS this morning?"

"My older brother dates her sister, so I slipped it to her at the Bluebird two weeks ago. She said she would play it when she had to plug the venues for the winners."

"Good job, Karl," I said with a certain shock in my voice.

"Oh, I've got more where that came from, we need to start rehearsing, I want to gig this summer, don't you?"

"You think Lisa Morrison will play more of our tunes?"

"As long as my brother keeps doing a good job banging her sister."

We both laughed about that and it felt good to talk with him. I desperately wanted to gig, although I did not want it to interfere with my Lil' Nashville Opry gig. Karl didn't need to hear about that though.

Suddenly, our cook, Molly, came barreling through my office

door.

"State Board just walked in the door!" she yelled.

"I gotta go," I said, and slammed down the receiver.

The entire day was spent in the laborious process of dealing with the state board and their surprise visit on a holiday. To say they caught us with our pants down would be accurate. My huge pile of folders had not been finished and my administrator was very peeved at all the marks against my department for not having timely paperwork.

"I don't care if you stay 'till midnight, you will finish and I am not paying you any overtime."

With the authority of a German Nazi, my administrator practically chained me to my chair. I got a call from mom that she had arrived, and I was relieved to know that she would be there since Beth and I had said our goodbyes the night before and she had moved everything out of the room.

It seemed as if everything had a yin and yang in my life. As I sat with a peanut butter sandwich in my mouth around 6pm, the phone rang again. It was Craig.

"Hi, I am at the Brown County Inn," he said with all the perkiness of a high school cheerleader.

"Let me give you directions to the house, mom is there and all the kids. I am stuck at work 'till who knows when. Mom knows you are coming."

With that I sat in my office until after 9pm. Every folder was on her desk, signed, sealed and delivered. I knew that I had saved up exactly two sick days and tomorrow I was going to use one.

My home was warm and happy. Craig bought a grill and some lawn furniture and they had built a fire pit and I felt like I was walking into a warm, happy place. Mia was nestled in Craig's arms and there was no getting her to move. Michael and Caleb were playing with their sparklers in the warm May evening. For the first time all day, it felt like a holiday.

I went to the cupboard, pulled out marshmallows, Hershey's chocolate bars, and a box of graham crackers. We sat by the fire and made s'mores until the kids all nodded off into what must have been a sugar coma dreamland.

Right as he drifted off, Michael turned to Craig and asked,

"You're not going to be gone in the morning, are you daddy?"

"No," said a teary-eyed Craig. "I will be here and we will go on a hike in the state park."

Michael was so groggy that I wasn't even sure he knew what that was, but he smiled and nodded off before his head hit the pillow.

Craig walked into my bedroom and took off his shirt and pants and lay in his boxers on my bed. I was not ready to go there with someone who had been an absentee father and husband for the last three years.

I sat in the dining area and lit up a cigarette, something I rarely did except when I was extremely nervous and confused.

"If you want to talk to me, meet me on the back porch. Otherwise, there's a blanket and sheet in my closet, use that for your bed on the couch."

The words reverberated in the air, buzzing like bees of hate and venom. He responded by putting on his shirt and coming out on the porch, pouting.

I held my ground, knowing that if I didn't hold it then, I would never hold it at all. Craig had the male personality of a bulldozer. He wanted what he wanted and he would do whatever it took to get it.

It wasn't a bad thing. His drive had made him succeed in school and become a good doctor, always willing to take on one more committee or honorary board position, which would result in endless meetings and time away from his family. In the end, I really think he didn't see it all coming but he did see what happened as a result and he was trying to bring it back around.

I caged my cigarette and decided to open myself up and be vulnerable again. The look on Caleb's face when he and Craig were throwing the football back-and-forth was staring at me as if there was no doubt about the positive impact it would have on all the kids, but especially Caleb.

"I can't tell you how sorry I am," he turned to me with moist eyes and a sincere gaze.

I knew he wanted some Hollywood moment where we ran into each other's arms with kisses and forgiveness, but I wasn't feeling it.

What I felt was a rip. I was being torn into two pieces. It was like someone was ripping my skin, bones, and whole body into two. Half of me wanted to go have my Clark Gable/Jean Harlow

217

moment. The other half cried out to let her go and join the band. Both bands, country and rock and roll. I wanted to sing, and after serious loads of complete bullshit and deception in LA, I had a band, and a country band had me.

How could he ask me to leave that behind?

Instead, I caved inside and put on a mask. It was a dutiful wife mask, a devoted mother mask. I embraced Craig in a tender hug and that was all it took. Like a house of cards, I tumbled into bed, knowing I did not feel a thing.

I frightened myself with the cold and calculated sexual moves I made to drive Craig into quite the frenzy. Bret had taught me so many moves, it was easy. I never really realized how inexperienced Craig was. He must have thought, since the sex was so good, that he was being forgiven. I felt like a cat toying with a mouse. It was fun, but I knew I had no emotional skin in the game.

After leaving a polite message on the administrator's voicemail, I crept back into a bed that already had Caleb and Michael up and ready for action. Before I slid under the covers, I heard Mia's little feet pitter pattering down the stairs as she dove into a pile of Craig's laughter.

Mom helped me whip up a great breakfast with eggs, sausages, and pancakes with blueberries on top and local maple syrup.

"You remembered that I love blueberries, didn't you honey," Craig said as he snatched a kiss on the cheek.

The burn of the kiss annoyed me since he hadn't shaved yet. I felt like ice inside and yet to my family, I was happy, laughing, and we were all having a good time like families should. Too bad I was AWOL.

Mom was smiling across the table as if everything had closed with a storybook, Leave It To Beaver kind of ending. I wanted to take off the mask and scream at all of them but I couldn't.

The face that shone like the sun, the one that melted my heart the most was Michael. He was so happy and content, he acted like someone that had survived a war and was now going home to live in peace. For him, for that dear soul who was so close to me, I would have done anything, including walking into the gates of hell, if need be.

After an active day at the Brown County State Park, we all

stopped for hamburgers at a local restaurant.

"So, I think you should move to my big house in Gainesville, Florida," he announced at dinner. "The park is right down the street and it has a big swimming pool."

"Yeah!" said all three kids.

"I think that's a wonderful idea," my mother chimed in.

"Anne Marie, what do you think?"

I couldn't think. My mind was blinded by anger at feeling ambushed.

"I have a contract with the Lil Nashville Opry," I said. "I just got offered the opportunity to be John Schneider's opening act on July 4th."

"Fine," said Craig. "I can stay for a couple of weeks, then I will help you pack up and move down. I would love to see you perform, it's a family place, right? We can bring the kids?"

"Yeah," all three kids chimed in. "We want to see mommy sing." They began jumping up and down like three little chimpanzees.

I gave them a pleasant smile but it hid all the despair I was feeling.

Somehow it seemed all wrong. I found myself feeling very violated by his orchestration of my life.

Mia leaned her head against Craig's chest and I melted like a snowman in July.

"Why don't you take the kids tomorrow to get their diploma from school. Mia would love for you to be at her kindergarten graduation, right honey?"

Mia got up from her chair and jumped up and down. They all started jumping up and down.

"Then you should go and take them to visit your mom and dad," I stated, trying to put together an agenda that got everyone out of the house for a day or two. I needed to take a moment and think, or be sad, or both.

"Time for me to head back north, there's some mail that's in need of my attention." My mother had an entire subplot going on over her mail. Old people would have holes in their lives if there was no mail. I vowed, then, that I would never be an old person.

Getting the family out the door the next morning was surprisingly easy. Walking in the door of the nursing home was not.

"Can I see you a minute?" the administrator asked as she stood at her office door.

As I sat down I began to make my litany of apologies.

"All the files are now current, I apologize for not getting them done before State Board but everything is now in apple pie order."

"I saw you yesterday at Charlie's Grill with your family. Is that your estranged husband?"

Suspecting that this was a setup for getting fired, I took the middle road.

"He wants me to move back to Florida with him."

Her face registered alarm, and I knew she wanted me to stay there so she could follow my career at the Opry. She was a huge country fan, the radio in her office was always on the Big Country WGDC.

"Are you?" she asked with slight trepidation.

"I want to sing, you know that. I don't know what I am doing."

Just then we heard the slamming of the front door; it was State Board. I was off the emotional hook and on the financial hook.

After work, I avoided everyone at work who by now had heard about my soap opera, and headed over to the Brown County Inn bar. The barkeep, Dusty, would let me use the bar phone if it wasn't busy.

"What are you doing?" I asked when Karl answered the phone.

"Oh, it's the long lost rock star, I could ask you the same thing. Why haven't you called me?"

"My husband came back to get the family back together, so that's kind of put a kink in my 'get the band back together' plans. I will pick you up in half an hour."

When I pulled into the trailer park and rolled up to his lot, Karl came out the door and put up his right index finger to indicate that he needed one minute. It was a common gesture of his, indicating that there was some sort of family squabble.

As I sat with the windows rolled down, I heard cursing and screaming, but I was not prepared to see Karl's mom, who weighed well over 350 pounds, being flung over the deck and landing in the kiddie pool below. Numerous items, including a small lamp that shattered against the small shed they had behind the trailer, came flying after her out the front door and onto the lawn.

Karl's mom tried to get up but kept slipping and falling back into the pool. Her enormous size was probably the biggest reason she couldn't get out of the pool. I found myself laughing. How ridiculous it all looked until I saw Karl running toward the car with his hand bandaged, blood dripping in a little trail behind him.

I started the engine and looked up to see Karl's father brandishing a small pistol in his hand. Karl hadn't even had time to close the door when I pulled away from the curb, the door dangling in the breeze then slamming shut as I made a hard left out of the exit lane.

"Jesus, what's going on, Karl?"

"Oh, dad's home and he doesn't like it that some little twenty-two-year-old peckerwood is sleeping in his bed with mom."

Karl's life was such a disaster, but my concern was the blood dripping all over the front seat of my car. I drove to the hospital emergency room and spent the next several hours there. Twenty-two stitches later, we headed to the pharmacy to get him pain meds.

Seeing no other alternative, I took him to my house where he turned into a ball of prescription mush on my couch.

"Gigs, we need to do gigs," he mumbled over and over again.

"I don't see how that's going to happen for awhile with your hand."

"Oh come and fuck me." He stumbled off the couch and I let him lean on me as we made our way to bed. I dropped him like a sack of potatoes on the bed and lit some candles. I had a headboard with several shelves, and on one shelf sat a marble angel that my father had brought me from Rome, Italy the year before he died.

Karl grabbed me and started to kiss me. I found myself more open than I was admitting and stuck my tongue down his throat for some serious mouth-to-mouth. He laid back, wanting me to get on top of him. He swung his arm around, knocking the large votive candle into the bed sheet.

As I mounted him, finishing another long, luscious kiss, I turned to see the sheets were on fire.

I screamed and shot straight up, then ran to the kitchen to fill a pitcher with water. As I rushed back, I found Karl lying in the middle of a circle of fire. I stood over him and doused the flaming mess with water. He was nearly unconscious and would not have known what was going on.

221

The bed was soaking wet, Karl was asleep, and the beautiful angels that my father bought me were blackened with the flames. I grabbed them and took them into the bathroom, filling the tub and soaking them, crying as I scrubbed the residue from their wings.

I left for work the next morning, knowing that Karl would eventually wake up. I left a note asking him to find his way back to his trailer since my family would be home that evening. Since State Board was finished, I figured that I had a little time to call around and find someone who would pick up Karl, knowing that he was incapable of managing that himself. He was an incredible lead guitar player and could come up with fantastic riffs and hooks for songs, but as a functioning adult, he was on par with an eleven-year-old.

Luckily, our bass player, Snubs, was willing to extricate him from my house. I spent the rest of the day hoping I knew what to say when my family came back. I got a call from Craig right before I left work, telling me they wanted to spend a few more days at the Channing farm.

Craig's mom and dad had a small cattle and corn farm on the eastside of Indianapolis. Both of them were strong and stout, but as they reached their seventies, they did less and less. Still, it was an idyllic place; it was where Craig grew up and there was no better time than early June to enjoy all the sights, sounds, and smells of an Indiana farm.

I came home to a house that was stinking of smoke; the bed linens were a charcoal mess and wet towels were strewn about everywhere. Cleaning it up on such a perfect evening seemed like penance to a person who already worked in purgatory.

Friday finally arrived, and I wore an outfit to the Lil Nashville Opry that was country and western and even a little rock and roll. Mrs. Washington stopped into the backstage dressing room to chat.

"I always have a big celebration on the fourth and I am pleased that you will be the opening act. I love the Dukes of Hazzard and he is so cute, that Johnny Schneider."

"I am planning on doing 'Boulder to Birmingham,' by Emmylou," I said, knowing that she loved that song. "I wrote an original to do after that called 'Brown County Evenings,' and wanted to know if the band would learn the tune."

"Of course," she said. "I will give them the tape myself."

True to form since the days of LA, I handed her a cassette of the tune that I had recorded with just my guitar and voice. I knew she would make the band learn the tune and I was excited since most of the time, guest singers had to sing standards and classics that Mrs. Washington likes.

At the intermission, I was delighted to find several people standing in line to get a black and white glossy autographed by me. I couldn't believe all the kudos they were throwing my way. I signed 23 pictures, and as the last of the crowd milled out the door, I felt a contentment greater than any other I had ever felt in my life. This was better than sex.

I slept in on Saturday. My life had become exhausting and every chance I got to sleep, I took it. I heard a car door bang, and I realized the family was back from Craig's parents' house.

Craig wanted his way again and it seemed that nothing was going to stop him. The sex became a tedious display of my acting abilities. I hated it, while Craig thought we were having a second honeymoon. Craig found the fact that I would play Def Leppard's "Animal" to be kinky and hot was enough to confirm his marital bliss. If only he knew, I would laugh to myself.

After being with other men, the size of a penis became of major concern to me. I had a theory that Craig had cheated due to the "Little Dick" complex. There was a time when size didn't matter, but only when there was an emotional connection. I had cut that off when I left Florida, and it didn't seem like it was necessary to revive it.

Finally, I convinced him to leave and take the kids with him. I decided it was his turn to worry about the child care.

"Why don't you just quit your job and come with us?"

"I have to give the nursing home three weeks' notice. I want to leave there on good terms. The entire staff has been so good to me and I want them to find a good replacement for me.If I do that tomorrow, then I will be ready to leave right after the Opry gig. Besides, next Sunday is Father's Day, don't you want the kids with you?"

"Who's going to watch them while I'm at the hospital?" He sounded like a teenage kid who had never learned responsibility.

"Oh, well, welcome to my world, Craig, figure it out!" My tone was so acidic that even Craig knew not to mess with me and relented.

We spent the rest of the day packing things up and bright and early Monday morning, my family pulled out of the driveway heading for Gainesville, Florida. I assumed it would be easy, but the thought of my little William going off with Craig was frightening. With tears flowing from both of our eyes, I put him in his car seat.

"You will be in Florida soon, right mommy?"

"Very soon, be good and I will be there shortly."

I could not sleep that night and decided that I had made a huge mistake. Every day at work, I seemed distant, like I was not even trying to do a good job. I had given my administrator my three weeks' notice and I was there only in the flesh, not in the spirit.

After work, I spent the remainder of my evenings at the Brown County Inn Bar. A couple of nights left me with a hangover that was so severe that I called off sick and spent the day in bed. Life felt awful: no flow, no charm.

One evening, I sat next to a gentleman who had seen me perform at the Lil Nashville Opry.

"My name is William Bennet, I'm an attorney and I am a huge fan of country music," he said, handing me his card, "and you were great the other night. Do you have a manager?"

"Manager?" I asked, with stars returning to my eyes. The thought of someone managing me and helping my career was intoxicating, but I tried to feign disinterest.

"I have thought about it." Then, a light bulb went off in my head. I had been working on a song that was a perfect duet song, "Best of Friends." What if I got this guy to pitch it to John Schneider? Getting a recording out with an established artist like John would boost my career and I knew it.

"I might be interested in doing something with you but I couldn't pay you."

"It would be on a commission basis, only if I cut a deal for you, and then I would take twenty-five percent."

"Whoa! Twenty-five percent is really high, most managers get ten percent."

"You are an unknown and it will take a lot of work to get you to a place where it pays off for me."

"God," I said to myself, "shades of Ron Slywood. This seems

like a con again."

After pausing for a moment to take another swig of my cranberry and vodka, I turned to Michael.

"I have a song that I wrote that would be a perfect duet for me and John Schneider. I am his opening act at the Opry in 2 weeks. If you can score us a deal for him to record the song with me and release it on his next album, or single would even be better, then I will give you fifteen percent of that deal."

I could tell the wheels of his mind were churning and he came back with a counter.

"Twenty percent."

I smiled and gathered my purse and was preparing to leave the bar since it was after 8:30pm.

"Okay fifteen," he finally said, "I can tell when I am dealing with a tough cookie."

I lay in bed that night, proud of myself that I had taken control of one of those insane male-dominated conversations. "Who knows," I said, "the sky's the limit."

The next two weeks were the two most lonely, awful weeks of my life. I called the kids every day and Craig had assured me that things were going well. I asked him who was watching the kids, and he told me that he had enrolled all three into a daycare center, Kute Kids Daycare Center.

"Do you like the daycare place, Michael?" I asked.

"No," he said with great honesty.

"Just four more days and I will be there," I told him reassuringly.

I had answered my own question. I was going to leave. My only hope was that John Schneider was going to give me a leg up.

That evening, I received a call from an extremely distraught mother.

"Your grandmother collapsed, she is in the hospital, you have to come up."

"I have my last day of work tomorrow, mom, and then I perform the next evening at the Lil Nashville Opry. I promise you, I will come after that."

"It's always about you, isn't it, Anne Marie? I am the only child and I need you to help me. They have her on life support and the doctor is scheduled to do a brain scan. If she is brain dead, you will have to pull the plug, I cannot do it."

"I will pull the plug, God knows you want me to put it on my soul and I will. However, I will not be there until after the show on Friday night. If she dies before then, well, then nobody is to blame."

I knew that it was not going to be easy but I announced that I was hanging up the phone and I did.

Work was excruciating that day, and I thought they would throw me a little party like everyone else, but they didn't.

"We are sorry to see you go," she said. "Good luck." It was cold and uncaring and I knew she was angry that I was going. I didn't care. Certainly, leaving purgatory was a relief for anyone. Of course, the hope is that you are going to heaven, not hell.

I met William about an hour before I went to the Opry to do the show.

"John has agreed to do a meeting with us," he beamed. "Give me the cassette tape and we will give it to him. You're sure it's a good song?"

"It will rock the country out of that Duke boy," I said, all smiles.

When he walked into the room, John Schneider filled it up. He was very tall, at least 6 foot 2 inches, maybe more.

"Howdy, ma'am," he said with that drawl of his. "Nice to meet you." He shook my hand and he shook William's.

William proceeded to explain our proposal to John and then he handed him the cassette. Imagine my face when John handed it back to William.

"I am getting married to this sweet little Cajun girl, not a good time for me to be doing a duet with anyone but her. You understand, don't you sweetheart?"

He looked into my eyes with great sincerity. I thought I was going to swallow my tongue.

"Take the tape, anyway, Mr. Schneider, perhaps this may be something that you could consider down the road in your career."

John looked squarely at both of us.

"It probably isn't a career move that I will make unless you gain some celebrity status. It does my career no good to do a duet with an unknown and it will do my marriage even less good. I wish you a lot of luck, honey, I know you have it in you to become a star. You sure

226

are pretty enough to be one."

With that announcement, he walked out of the room and it felt like he took all the air with him. I hurried to the bathroom down the hall and brought out a paper bag that I was blowing into. This was no time to be having an anxiety attack. I heard the stage manager calling my name.

I wiped away my tears and ran up to the backstage area. I was there just in time to hear Lincoln Washington announce me.

"It is with great Hoosier pride that I introduce to you our own homespun Nashville cutey, give a warm welcome to Miss Anne Marie Lee."

The crowd roared as I got on stage; there were several cat calls and whistles but

I smiled and started right in.

Crazy, I'm crazy for feelin so lonely... crazy, crazy for feelin so blue... I know you'd love me as long as you wanted...

Mrs. Washington was sitting in the first row. It wasn't Boulder to Birmingham, but I had done this song a month or so back and the band remembered my key. The applause was thunderous and I smiled. I looked at the very back few rows which were dappled with people. Sitting on the end of the very last row, I saw my grandmother. She looked pale, and for a minute, I thought it was a ghost.

I quickly took my attention to the new song I was going to sing.

"Thanks, ladies and gentlemen, for that warm welcome. I would like to perform a tune I wrote just for all of you, and it celebrates this wonderful town and everything I love about country music."

The roar of the applause was almost deafening and again, I saw my gramma's ghost smiling.

Sweet summer evening, the whippoorwills cry, tell me you love me but don't tell me why,

Hold me and squeeze me, thrill me with your kiss, take me to be your wife in sweet wedded bliss... in a Brown County evening, I will tell you that I love you and I know you love me toooo... in a Brown County evening... whippoorwills cry... and I know that I will love you, baby, till the day I die.

It was a polite and appreciative applause but it wasn't like I had hoped, except for my grandmother who was hootin' and hollerin' and whistling through her teeth. It was hard to get people to applaud something they weren't familiar with, and as William pointed out later, they could have booed me.

We shared a drink, me a cup of coffee and him, a whiskey sour. William said he was going to continue working for me, that I was a talent, and I headed out down the highway to grab Interstate 65 up to my mother's.

When I got there, she had tears in her eyes.

"Your grandmother passed away at about 9:35pm." Her voice waivered and was full of emotion.

"Huh," I thought. "9:35pm was when I was on stage. Maybe it was her ghost there in the audience, clapping for me before she went through the pearly gates." The thought sent a shudder down my spine. My wonderful, loving gramma had made it to my performance after all. Who knew that a Polish lady from East Chicago, Indiana could like country!

I called Craig the following morning to let him know what had transpired. He offered to fly up to Chicago and catch a bus but I told him to sit tight. I would bury my grandmother and there were plenty of relatives and friends to honor her.

I find funerals to be a necessary ritual for those that are left behind. My mother was beside herself, losing her mother just a few years after losing her father and her husband. I took care of all the details. It helped me to jump in and stay busy.

Losing the pitch to John Schneider stung more than I thought it would. I had wound up pinning all my hopes and dreams on that little gig. I had avoided Karl's calls for the past week, thinking somehow, I had a spot in WGDC's Top Ten at Ten.

I buried myself in Polish hot air for the next few days, getting through the funeral and burial. Mom seemed to recover after a while and I think she started to realize that I wanted to get on with my life and back to Brown County.

"I think this will be a good thing, even though I don't relish the idea of you being so far away in Florida."

My silence annoyed her. She prodded at me until I finally spoke.

"I am doing this for my children, mom. I don't love Craig anymore and I probably never will again. Some things you can't take back once they've been said."

"Then your marriage will fail," she said emphatically. "You need to forgive him and you need to forgive yourself."

"Myself?" I questioned. "Why should I forgive myself?"

"Forgive yourself for failing at a music career, work on your career as a wife and mother."

I stuffed the immense anger I was feeling toward my mother for her thoughtless and thoroughly wrong comment. "I have not failed, I just haven't succeeded yet," I told myself.

When I finally left Lake County, Indiana to head back to Brown County to pack, a wave of fear overtook me.

I had all of our furniture and belongings packed up and sent to Craig's address, and the house was empty except for a few suitcases with clothes and personal belongings for myself.

I sat in the empty living room and strummed my guitar. The acoustics were ideal and I sang one of my favorite sad songs, "I'm So Lonely I Could Cry."

Sometimes I enjoyed changing lyrics just a bit to craft the song to exactly what I needed to express.

I loved songs, they were the poetry of the gods, a language of love that humans were given so that they could elevate their consciousness and communicate meaningfully with one another.

I called Karl as I left the house. I got an answering machine, which was unusual for them. I left a message that said, "I sold my soul to rock and roll, I am leaving for Florida, rock on my brother!"

I got in my VW Rabbit and headed out for the long drive down to Gainesville. I put the cassette into the car stereo and listened to my song. I rewound it and played it over and over and over again.

Love is all we asked for and yet I hear the screams of the children of a generation of broken dreams…

Chapter 32
Into the Great Wide Open

There was always something about the warm, tropical humidity that I found draining. I was thinking that going to the swamp in Central Florida for July was right up there with reserving a front row seat in hell.

I smoked several joints on the way down and had to stop in Dalton, Georgia at a Holiday Inn so that I could sleep it off. When I got up, I put on my bathing suit and took a long leisurely swim in the pool. As much as I had talked myself into it, the reality of going back to Florida to live with a man that I did not trust was almost frightening to me.

It wasn't until I pulled off the second exit in Gainesville and looked at the map that I realized it was a done deal. As I saw my children running out to meet me, I knew I was committed and there was no turning back. God help the poor souls of the church of rock and roll.

I passed the rest of the summer taking the kids to the local Gainesville pool. Mia found a new found interest: diving. She got quite good and asked Craig to come and watch. The world was small in Gainesville and it seemed like Craig had turned a new leaf in his life.

Caleb was entering the fifth grade and wanted to join the pee-wee football league. Mia was going to enter the second grade and Michael was going to kindergarten.

Somehow, the Channing family had entered a period of stability. Craig took time off of his always busy schedule to go to Gator football games with Caleb. I could tell it was the missing thing in his life and with that piece now in place, he excelled at everything. His grades improved, and he was even voted president of his fifth grade class. At home, Caleb took on a variety of chores which Craig paid him for, and it almost gave me nothing to do.

Mia also excelled in academics, and she found a group of girlfriends. My favorite activity with her was to invite her friends over and we would throw a tea party. I taught her friends, Dakota, Rachael, and Anna, how to make luscious tea cakes. The girls got very creative with the decorations and the Cabbage Patch dolls always joined us for tea in the lanai.

Michael spent more time with me. I taught him how to play the guitar. He told me he liked how they all sounded together. He liked those simple country riffs and played them well for a six-year-old. For Christmas, I got him a keyboard and he really got creative with his music. Many an evening, while we were waiting for Craig to come home from work, he would ask me to accompany him on keyboards with my guitar.

Playing music with Michael became my solace. I felt isolated in Gainesville since I knew no one, and shunned social events at the hospital as Dr. Craig's wife.

To keep my sanity, I took a job at the local florist shop, which was just a few blocks from the house. In fact, everything was within a mile: school, hospital and grocery/florist. I would go and clean the flowers and get them prepped for the morning. I never tired of the intoxicating fragrance all the deliveries gave off as we unpacked them.

Every once in awhile, I would put together an arrangement and by the time Halloween rolled around, I was helping them with some of the smaller centerpieces that people were ordering.

Floral Fantasy served most of the north side of Gainesville and the delivery driver, Calvin Khouri, had been working there for just a few months more than me.

One morning, he caught me sitting in my car before work, putting on makeup and listening to, "Broken Dreams."

"Who's that singing?" he asked curiously.

"That would be me," I said.

"You… in a band?" His voice denoted great enthusiasm and I could tell he was excited.

"I was, back in Bloomington, Indiana. This song got some radio airplay on WTTS."

"You got airplay? What label were you with?" Calvin was all ears, literally.

"Yeah and none." I got out of the car, grabbed my purse and headed toward the shop. Calvin was following me like a little puppy.

"You know I play guitar," he said like a fisherman baiting a hook.

"Do me a favor," I asked. "Please say nothing about this in the shop. If you want, bring in a tape tomorrow of your work and I will listen to it."

"Listen to me," I said to myself. "Sounding like a big shot. Ha!"

Something in me left the shop that afternoon, heading for the school to pick up the kids, itching, scratching, clawing and looking for the light of day. I stopped off at the house after work and rolled and smoked a joint on the lanai before getting the kids.

"Hi, mom," they all said as they piled into the car. "They are happy," I thought. "This is worth its weight in gold."

When we got back to the house, Caleb and Mia went straight to their homework, but Michael got out the guitar and wanted to go sit on the lanai.

"Here, mom, play something," he asked. Being stoned always got me in the mood to play. I strummed and found a chord pattern I had never played before. It was haunting.

"I like that," said Michael. I did too and I played it again and again. I felt a presence behind me and I looked back to see Bowie seated on my favorite wicker rocker.

For a brief moment, I panicked, wondering what Michael would think of David. He seemed oblivious to anything except working out a chord harmony on his keyboard.

"So when are you getting your band back together?" Bowie asked.

"Never, David. Never. I am over this obsession. I am not a rock star like you are. It's important to accept one's failures with grace and dignity."

"Oh hogwash," said Bowie. "You are talented, you have the music in you, don't give up. I would have expected a bit more endurance from someone of your stature."

"My stature?" I exaggerated the second word. "You jest, monsieur."

"No, I jest not," he said in his impeccable British accent.

"What band?" I finally asked.

"I will let you answer your own question." Bowie faded into the humid mists of a Florida swamp afternoon.

"Mom, mom, mom," Michael was tugging on my sleeve trying to get my attention.

"What?" I said a little impatiently.

"Who were you talking to?" he asked innocently.

"Myself, honey."

"You said you wanted to get a band together mom, do you mean that?"

I stuttered just a little, hesitating to say what I knew would come through.

"Yes, I would ,but not if it tears apart our family."

"Good," he stated. "I don't ever want to leave daddy again."

The following morning, Calvin brought his tape in and handed it to me before we walked into the flower shop.

"Thanks, I will listen to it tonight." As I turned to grab a bucket of flowers to take to the water basin, the image of Bowie popped into my head. I looked up to see him walking through the door of the flower shop.

I shook my head in disbelief and then realized that it was a customer who had similar features to Bowie. I found myself just a bit freaked out and worked at cleaning and prepping the flowers to distract myself.

Saturday afternoon came and Craig was taking all three kids to the game. He desperately wanted me to come.

"Come on, let's make this a family event," he begged.

"I don't like football, don't care about the Florida Gators and I would prefer to stay at home. I am tired, I am on my feet a lot and I want to put them up and read my book."

Craig persisted. "Oh come on, we can tailgate."

Instead of having an ongoing tug of war, I barked out one final no and closed the door to the master bedroom.

I heard the car pull out of the driveway and I knew that they were gone.

I grabbed the tape and put it on my boom box. I turned up the volume and hoped for the best.

I was pleasantly surprised. He had a nice steady rhythm to his playing and I wondered who was playing bass and drums. As a threesome, they were tight, and even though they were jamming, I could tell that all they needed was someone to write songs for them to play.

The wheels in my head began to turn like a precision instrument.

I looked around the bedroom and expected Bowie to materialize and confirm my suspicion.

"Is this the band?" I asked the question to myself over and over and over again. It felt like something was missing.

That night I fell asleep without much trouble. Craig had wanted a brief rumble in the hay and I obliged, but I found the sex to be much more of a nuisance than inspiring.

As I drifted off to sleep, I had a dream. I was pulling up at Karl's trailer court and as I did, his mother was being tossed out again on her keester. This time, though, it was winter and she fell on a patch of ice. I laughed as she tried to get up as it seemed comical again, even in another season. Then I saw Karl at the door. This time he had his guitar in his hand and he was running. There was no blood on his hands this time, and I pulled the car onto the grass and he jumped in and we peeled out of the trailer court as fast as I could drive.

I woke up in a sweat. I hadn't thought about Karl for months. The message I left on his answering machine was the last interaction I had with him.

My Sunday was mechanical. I got up and made a great breakfast for everyone and cleaned up. The day wore on as if someone had pressed a button that put everything in slow motion. I felt a sense of suffocation. I had to take a walk in the middle of the afternoon and the humidity was still in the air. I wondered if it ever left.

I brought my Walkman on my jog through the neighborhood and decided to listen to the sounds of radio in Gainesville. They had two popular stations, WGGG and WFLG. I was hoping to find an "Over Easy" equivalent here in Gator land.

What I heard was lots of metal music on WFLG. Poison, Twisted Sister and Motley Crew graced their air waves. It made it easy to jog to, and when the DJ came on, I was winded enough to slow down and walk.

"Better than a battle of the bands, break into rock and roll with WFLG's Florida Fresh Tracks Search for the next break through sound in rock and roll.", the announcer's voice blasted in my ear.

The announcer's voice boomed in my ear, yet I turned up the volume to maximum.

"Submit your winning song to the WFLG Signature Band contest. First prize is a recording contract with Capitol Records and an evening of the band performing LIVE at DUBS right here in Gainesville."

I nearly pissed in my pants. This was the opportunity I was looking for since the idea of getting a band together needed a goal. What better goal than a recording contract, something I had coveted and wanted so badly for most of my life. Capitol Records was the label that signed the Beatles when they first came to America in the 60's. It had special significance to me.

I jumped into the air and could hardly contain myself. I wanted to tell my whole family about my new found opportunity, but I cautioned myself to say nothing as I walked back into the nice air conditioned house.

I could not wait to drop the kids off at school and go over to the flower shop. I was hoping that Calvin would get their early so that we could talk in the parking lot.

"Did you hear about the contest that WFLG is sponsoring?" I asked Calvin.

He lit up like the night sky on the Fourth of July. He was actually jumping up and down like a six-year-old as he spoke.

"Yes, I did, and I think we should put a band together and enter the contest. You are such a great songwriter. I am sure that we could win. We could even do a remix of your song, 'Broken Dreams.'"

He jibber jabbered at such a fast pace, I thought he was going to run out of breath before he finished.

I put my hand up to his mouth and try to sush him.

"No, not 'Broken Dreams,' I have another song that's even better."

"'Soul on Fire.'" I spoke the title with a booming gravitas. It was the perfect song to enter in a world of metal. It was better than anything I had heard coming from the metal bands currently on the airwaves.

I had written it a few weeks before. It was actually my way of coping with the disturbing discovery that Craig had been stopping off at a local bar on the way home from the hospital and having a drink.

I confronted Craig, and he had assured me it was just an occasional drink to relieve stress and that he was fine.

It didn't seem right. I thought that alcoholics should never take a drink. Not knowing that much about alcoholism, I found myself dismissing it. After all, he went to work, he took the kids to the football games, he paid the bills, and to my knowledge he was not cheating on me, so what harm could an occasional drink have on him?

Still, the feelings that were rising up in me were so dreadful that I could hardly contain the dark, black stranglehold they had on me.

To cope, as I so often did in my life, I turned to music. I wrote the tune, "Soul on Fire," over the course of two nights of complete sleeplessness. The lanai offered me the solace of playing in a room that was sound proof from the rest of the air-conditioned house.

It was a song that could fill up a hall like Dubs Place. DUBS had gained notoriety in the 1970's for being the rock and roll birthplace of Tom Petty. Petty played there before heading out to Los Angeles and Michael Dubs, the current owner, used that information to pilot all of his promotions for the club.

Strangely, this time there was no mention of that but then again, times had changed. It was the late 80's and it was all about metal. I knew that every band that was going to enter the contest was going to try and become the next Guns N' Roses.

I still had a question as to who I should get to play lead. Calvin was good, but he was not a lead player, his job was to fill. He was actually a very tasty rhythm guitarist. Karl was all the way back in Indiana and it seemed very improbable to have him.

One afternoon, I let Michael play the Guild. I knew it was going to be too hard for him but he kept insisting. In his frustration, he plucked at the string with too much force and it popped.

"Sorry mom," he offered.

"It's OK, it's too much for you to learn on the 12 string," I said.

Looking up the only music store in Gainesville, I found it on Main Street and after dropping the kids off at school, I went over to get new strings.

A very tall, lanky man was watching me sift through the guitar strings and sauntered up to me.

"Can I help you find the right strings?" He smiled at me with an adoring look.

"Wow," I said to myself. His presence shocked me.

"Need some strings for my Guild 12 string," I said a bit shyly, with somewhat flirty overshadowing.

"Right here, best I have."

"Perfect," I said as I fondled the guitar strings in their package.

His eyes never left mine as I walked to the cash register. Sitting next to the register was a poster for the radio contest.

"I am entering that contest; got a kick-ass song we're recording at the studio here in town."

"Do you play heavy metal?" he asked with an inquisitor's glance.

"Oh, not really, but I can kick it up there if the gig needs it."

My eyelashes fluttered downward like a wounded bird searching for a safe cliff. I felt like I would do anything I could to get music out there, but just like the bird, it had never found its sanctuary.

"Ever heard of a band called, Blackfoot?" he said, trying to hide a charming smugness.

"No, should I?"

I deflated his balloon a bit but he walked me over to the album section and there was a section titled, "Blackfoot." I thumbed through the albums then picked up the one with the snake cover.

"Wow, I have been living in LA too long, I am so sorry I did not recognize you. Yes, 'Train, Train.' That's such a great song, who hasn't heard that on the radio?"

He was very sweet as I heaped on the praise, and then he did something that made my heart leap straight up into the air and sing with joy.

"If you want me to lay down a guitar track for you in the studio, I'd be happy too. Don't know metal but I play a mean blues and I bet you can sing some down-and-out blues, can't you? If this

237

song is a soul on fire, then it could use a burning lead that has roots."

"Wow… wow. Uh… wow… wow that would be great. Fantastic, even!"

A dark cloud crossed my face when I thought of his studio fee. Clearing my throat, I did what I knew was professional.

"How much is your studio fee?" I asked with trepidation.

Charlie laughed out loud.

"Ha, you have lived in LA too long! I can just sit in your session. Maybe all you will want me to do are some fills? Can't tell, but let's not talk about cost. We'll work something out."

"Thanks so much for giving an up-and-comer a break." I had a tear in my eye and I paid for the strings, without emotion.

"Come by tomorrow night, we will be recording from 8pm till God knows when," I finally managed to squeak out as I was leaving.

I worked at a record pace cleaning flowers at the shop the next day and when Calvin came in to pick up the deliveries, I pushed him into the cooler to get some roses.

"Charlie Hargret of Blackfoot is gonna play on our song for the contest. 'Soul on Fire' is gonna blaze to the winner's circle and kick ass at Dubs." We both started jumping up and down like two kids talking about the recording studio and the song.

Craig and I had a long and drawn out discussion about me going into the studio.

"Is this gonna be a good thing for our family?" he asked.

"I can't see what hurt it would be, all I am doing is recording a song to enter into a contest.

"What if you win?"

"Let's cross that bridge when we come to it. I made a promise to Michael that my music should never be an impediment to this family's happiness again"

"But what if you win?" he pressed back.

My head began to explode, large waves in it were crashing onto the shore. If I win, I would be so incredibly happy. The band would record an album, the band would tour. The album would go multi-platinum, I would accept a grammy for new artist of the year.

The mind can be like a runaway train. You let it one thought and it leads to another and another and you are way down the road even though nothing at all has happened yet.

"Let me enter this contest and I won't say anything to you about your stopping off for a drink after work."

Craig froze in his conversation. He had thought that I didn't know about his visits to the local bar down the street from the hospital.

"Okay," he finally blurted out.

We all make deals with the devil, we just don't realize that it's the devil. Otherwise, we would never have made the deal in the first place.

Craig had promised me that he would watch the kids that night so that I could go to the studio. He had a meeting at 5pm and then he would be home. I cooked and helped everyone with homework, watching the clock like a hawk. 6, 6:15 7, 7:15pm. I began to panic, calling his office, calling the hospital.

Caleb noticed my anxiety.

"Mom, don't worry, dad will be here. You just focus on how good your song will be."

He was so unbelievably wise for an eight-year-old. Like a little Buddha sent to me from God to keep me from going off the track.

At 7:37, Craig walked through the door. He grabbed all the kids who went running up to hug him but when he got to his hug from me, I shrugged back. He stunk of alcohol and I wanted to deck him.

I weighed for all of a minute all the pros and cons to leaving the kids with a drunken daddy so that I could go and cut my hit record at the studio.

"Okay, see you later," I announced to all. I blew kisses at all four of them. Caleb winked back.

"You go get 'em mom. You are gonna win the contest, mom. You're gonna win!"

Tears filled my eyes as I pulled out of the driveway.

"Oh God, please don't think I am a bad mother. I am sure Craig could function in an emergency."

"That is, of course, if he doesn't drink more."

My evil twin had to throw her pitch fork at me.

"I'm a bad mother," I said to myself as I pulled into the studio parking lot. Calvin pulled in right behind me and as we walked into the control booth, my guilt melted like butter on hot corn on the cob.

Mickey, the drummer, got there next and we spent the next half hour setting up mics on his double bass kit. Kerry, the bass player, came in and when we told him about Charlie's presence, he was impressed.

I found Kerry and Mickey in a bar one night with a band called, Satan's Soul. I thought they were very tight and told them about the song, the contest, and the studio musician fees I would pay them. I could tell they both liked the song, but I knew they were just doing it for the money. Mickey had a kid on the way and Kerry had a daughter and a pregnant wife. Every dime counted to both of them so I wanted to get my money's worth.

I went out in the main studio to lay down a scratch vocal so they could follow the song while Calvin played a guitar part so we could follow the melody line of the song.

It was a soulful melody. I made them cut the original beat in half so that it would be a slow moving cooker. I knew Charlie's lead would work best with that sort of song style and it didn't matter to me if it was a metal tune or not.

"This ain't metal," Kerry remarked with defiance after playing the slow tempo run-through.

"It's me and no it's not, but it's hard and growlin, sort of more, oh I don't know, Joan Jett!" I said it with authority. After all, I paid the bill and I was never going to take it up the ass like I did at the Cahoots Studio fiasco.

"Joan Jett, yeah, that's cool, I like that," said Mickey, and we did a final run through before we got the backbeat of the song recorded. As we finished, Charlie walked in and we were all in awe. The room felt magical to me; I was creating a song and it made my blood feel like nectar running through my veins.

Charlie sat and listened to a few playbacks of the scratch song, then went into the iso booth and cranked out a soulful lead. Then on another pass, he added some tasty fills, including one turn around that was absolutely electric. The song sizzled and it started to come alive.

We didn't even notice the time. I was enchanted and it was fun. Everyone sat and listened to the takes until we found a mix that made the song so soulful in a metal kind of way that I felt like we had covered all the genres with an eclectic symphony.

Studio euphoria is a wonderful experience. I was cruising on it when I went into to the iso booth to sing the lead.

I shuffle my feet, to a tune with no beat,
I work every day, just to feel like a slave….
And I feel….yeah I feeeeelll like I'm living in hell
Dollars come in…but it's living in sin
How much is your soul worth to the man
A dime a dozen now do it again
And I feeeeeeeeel like I'm living in hell.
My soul is on fire, my soul is on fire, my soul is on fire
And it feeeeeels like I'm living in hell.
Life's joys can get real cheap, spending time at the bottom of the heap,
The chains that bind you are in your head,
Break them now, or you're dead
And I feel, yeah I feeeeel, like I'm living in hell.
My soul is on fire, my soul is on fire,
My soul is on fire……and it feels like I'm living in hell

It feels like I'm living in hell…..like I'm living in hell….in hell…in hell………in hell

I floated back into my house at almost 3am. To my great relief, it had not burned down, and I was glad to see all three children safely tucked in their beds. I was not happy to see Craig passed out on the kitchen table next to an empty bottle of Jameson whiskey sitting next to a glass with no ice left.

The following morning, I took the kids to school, after dragging Craig's sorry ass to bed. I knew it was his day off, so I thought a conversation about relapse was in order.

Chapter 33

Knock, Knock, Knocking on Heaven's Door

As I walked back in the house the next morning, Craig was negotiating a cup of coffee from the kettle I had on the stovetop.

"What's going on?" I asked in earnest.

"I had a rough day at work and I needed to unwind with some friends, so I went over to Aw Shucks." Aw Shucks was an oyster bar in the strip mall next to the hospital. I knew that he went there before, but he always insisted that he just had a coke.

"So when did it change from coke to whiskey?"

"Oh hell, Anne Marie, why can't you understand how hard it is to be me? Pressure, Anne Marie, I deal with constant pressure. While you go out and run around with your rock and roll band, I pay the bills."

"Fuck you, I work at the florist."

"Fuck you, that pays for your gasoline each month. What about all these bills? Who do you think is dealing with those things? Me! How about if I go out and try and be a rock star? Don't we all just want to be rock stars, with adoring fans? How come it's all about you?"

Rage set in like a plague.

"All about me, all about me? Your alcoholism is destroying this family. I refuse to put up with this anymore. It wouldn't surprise me if you had another girlfriend."

"Well, I am fucking a couple of girls at the restaurant," Craig spattered all over me like hot grease off a kitchen stove.

I screamed at the top of my lungs and grabbed the glass coffee pot and threw it on the floor. I knew that he was standing in his bare feet and I knew he would not be going anywhere.

"You pig, you alcoholic pig! I want you to know that I don't care. Sleep in the spare bedroom. Lose your job, I don't care. My songs are rockin' good. I am going to win this fucking contest and then I will shit out hundred dollar bills and stick them in your mouth, you fucking bastard!"

The energy was so negative and awful, and as much as I wanted to throw him out and never have anything to do with him again, I knew that I needed him to sober up and watch the kids tomorrow because we were going to mix it down and get it ready to give to the radio station.

Instead, I slammed the kitchen door, got into the car, and drove away, afraid that anything I would say would ruin the best chance I had ever had at getting a career going.

I got out of the Gainesville city limits and lit up a joint. It was the only thing I knew that would calm the red violent rage within my body. One puff and then another and at the third puff, a familiar voice interrupted my smoking frenzy.

"'Soul on Fire' has chart potential." The English accent was unmistakable and I saw Bowie sitting across the car, lighting a cigarette.

"It is good, I like it, has some metal aspects but is such unrelenting blues, that's what you do best. You don't screech like Sammy Hagar, thank God."

We laughed and it lightened me up. I knew that I was on the verge of something, I could just feel it. The hairs on the back of my head stood up when he mentioned "chart potential."

"You're right, it is good. All I want is the opportunity to play at Dubs. Just put me in coach, I'm ready to play," I said with a laugh. A laugh riddled with uncertainty that life might not give me that chance. That the world was in fact a cold, cruel place that delighted in breaking all your dreams into tiny pieces sent fluttered down to hell, like ashes from a burnt corpse.

"By the way, I saw you went backstage at the Joan Jett concert last month. That would be you IN THE FLESH. When am I going to visit with you in the flesh?" My eyes were searching his for an acknowledgement.

"Joan Jett was fabulous, and you will be too when you play at Dubs. How odd that they picked April 1st. Isn't that your April Fool's Day?"

"Yeah, you think we are going to make the cut?"

"I already know that you did. They just announced the winners. You made the cut."

I screamed with pure ecstasy. I floated off my ass and my feet didn't touch the pedals of the gas. I pulled over to take in what he had just said.

"You better show up in the fucking flesh," I boasted. "I got all of the Joan Jett moves and a whole helluva lot more."

I raced home and called the radio station. Sure enough, they had just announced the finalists on the radio. We were one of seven bands. The winner would receive a recording contract with Capitol records. I was orbiting to the moon.

The gig was a little over two weeks away. This was Saturday night that I had only dreamed about in LA. If I could just figure out a way to keep Craig from crashing into himself and just be my babysitter for the next three weeks, I was certain that my life would change.

The radio sent me an entire package of what they wanted for the performance. Two songs, one original and one cover, and then the nominated song as a finale. They sent me the set list and I was coming on dead last at 1 am. I was worried that it was either going to be the best spot or the worst. Rather than worrying about it I called everyone to schedule a rehearsal.

Charlie called me back shortly after I left a message on his voicemail.

"No sense in me rehearsing with you, Anne Marie, I am playing a benefit concert with Dickie Betts. I am so happy that you are one of the finalists but you're going to have to play the gig without me. You can do it. Calvin is quick, he can get that lead part down by the first of April. Sorry."

I was in the kitchen and didn't take the call. I heard the voicemail go off and listened to Charlie's message.

"Shit, just another obstacle."

When I went into the flower shop and presented the idea to Calvin, he panicked.

"I can't play the lead, Anne Marie."

"Yes, you can." I barked back at him thinking I could bully him into the role.

244

"What about the guy, Karl, who was in your band in Bloomington?"

"What about him?" I was coming unhinged.

Let him play Charlie's part. I will play the fills."

"No, no, no," I stated over and over like a round in a song.

Calvin walked into the cooler so none of the other employees at the shop could hear us arguing.

I followed him in, not willing to lose the argument.

"Look, if he was he here in Gainesville that would be different, but he is all the way back in Indiana."

I will drive us up there tonight after work. If we drive all night and turn around and come right back, we can make it."

"You are assuming that Karl is even still up there and alive."

"Call him." Calvin would not relent.

I had no idea if the phone number was still working, if he still lived at his mom's trailer, if he would pick up or anything.

I trudged out to the pay phone and dialed the number.

Beads of sweat poured off my forehead and my heart was pounding in my chest.

"Hello?"

It was Karl, I could hardly believe he answered. Perhaps the universe was conspiring to give me one last chance. My clock was ticking. Rock and roll was partial to youth and I was now 39 years old. It was now or never for me.

"I am in Gainesville, Florida and I have a band that needs a lead guitar player. We are one of seven finalists for a Battle of the Band contest. We play at Dubs nightclub and the winner will receive a recording contract with Capitol Records."

There was silence on the other end of the phone.

Finally, Karl spoke.

"So are you coming up here to get me?"

"Yes," I said, relieved to hear he would come. "We are leaving in a few hours and will probably be at your mom's trailer around 4am tomorrow morning."

"I don't have a guitar, busted mine on stage a couple of months ago. I got angry at our lead singer. He sucked."

Of course, that was just par for the course with Karl. Wild, out of control, no thought of consequences when performing an action.

245

"I will go over to the music shop and see if Charlie Hargret will let me borrow a guitar for you when we get back."

"Charlie Hargret, from Blackfoot?" Karl gasped.

"Yes he put the lead on the demo we cut at the studio. Do you think you can match him lick for lick."

"Okay, if you want me in the band, don't insult me. I would hope that you realize I am the world's best metal guitarist ever."

God, aren't we all just legends in our own minds. I did think that Karl could cover the tune and I thought his metal riffs might give it the edge the rest of the band members thought was lacking.

"It's really a blues tune but add that metal edge to it that I know you can and we should easily win.

"I will be ready and waiting for you at 4am." Karl was delighted.

"Are you still at your mom's trailer?

"Is the bear Catholic? Does the Pope shit in the woods?"

Same old Karl, same bat time, same bat station.

I grabbed Millie, the girl who comes in to the flower shop to prep and asked her if she could babysit my family for the next 24 hours.

"Your whole family?" she quizzed me.

"Yes, my husband, and three kids, get them to and from school, feed them three meals and try to make sure my husband stays sober and gets to work."

"Isn't your husband a doctor Mrs. Channing?

Please, just no questions, I will pay you $100 for your help.

As always, the money talks and the bullshit walks.

I called Craig's office and was relieved to be able to leave the message with his secretary. If we had to fight about this, it would be after I had brought back my lead guitar player.

I felt like I was fulfilling my responsibilities as a mom and apparently also, the head of the household.

We jumped into Calvin's car and barreled on down the interstate. The night sky was brilliant and star studded but there was no moon out. I always liked to see some slice of it but it was a new moon. That's an excellent phase for new beginnings, I whispered to myself.

"Karl has to stay with you, I cannot put him up at my place. That's the deal. Right?"

246

"He is welcome to stay on my couch. I called my Aunt Mary, since it is her house, and she said anything for the band's success."

"That's probably a step up for Karl," I laughed.

When will pulled into the trailer court, there was a light dusting of snow on the ground and I was freezing as I only had on a light jacket.

Karl jumped into the car and threw his duffel bag in the back seat.

"God, I missed you," he grabbed me and planted a big kiss on my mouth.

"Drive on, Calvin."

I jumped in the back seat and Karl and I made out in the back seat of Calvin's car like two teenagers at a drive in movie.

When I came up for air, we were in Tennessee and heading in to Chattanooga. The snow storm seemed to have followed us and there was an inch or so of snow on Interstate 24. The plows hadn't gotten to the interstate yet and it was slick.

"Calvin, maybe you should slow down."

"You guys sure haven't been slowing down at all."

I detected a slight tinge of jealousy in his tone but I sure as hell didn't have time for that kind of shit. I needed to get back to my house and I really shouldn't have been kissing Karl.

As we headed down the other side of the mountain towards Atlanta, I heard a large bang.

"What in the hell is that?" I shrieked.

Before Calvin could answer, the car began to shimmy back and forth.

"Our back right tire just blew and I can't pull over because there is no shoulder."

"So what's the plan?"

Karl and I were clutching each other for dear life and I thought for a minute, this was it.

The car slid down the interstate and found a resting place in the runaway truck ramp.

All of us got out of the car to survey the damage. The only thing that seemed to be amiss was the blown tire that was just in shreds.

Calvin looked at us like a man who had just looked death in the face and laughed.

"I cannot believe we made it down that mountain with that tire shredded like that.

The snow started to come down a little heavier and Calvin and Karl worked feverishly to get the spare tire on the car.

When we all got back in the car, the collective sigh of relief permeated the air.

I offered to drive because I knew Calvin was wasted and he eagerly agreed and went into the back seat and curled up like a kitten and slept all the way to the Florida state line.

We pulled into Gainesville around noon and I was so famished that I insisted we stop at Shoneys restaurant and eat.

Karl put his arm around me and I took it off.

"None of that," I said.

Karl just grunted.

"Calvin, can you and Karl rehearse the song and the two other songs this afternoon?"

I needed to get back to my house and make sure that everything was still in order and there were no children crying and/or drunken rages by my husband.

To my great relief, Millie was there and making dinner and the kids were in school and Craig was at the office.

Praise me to God.

Now if I could just hold this band together over the course of the next few days.

Chapter 34
Runnin Down a Dream

My attitude was positive, and the finalists got one rehearsal at Dubs as well as a dress rehearsal. Our rehearsal was scheduled for next Tuesday.

I found myself feeling like a juggler, saying just the right things to everyone: the kids, Craig, and the people at the flower shop. I told everyone whatever they wanted to hear.

All I wanted was to win the contest, just burn the house down and get the prize.

I pulled out a suitcase I had drug through LA, Nashville, and now down to Gainesville. Some women have hope chests; I had a suitcase with my rock and roll outfits.

The boots had been custom made. I found them at a mall in Thousand Oaks. The boots were thigh-high black leather boots and I had a shoemaker in Ventura County add a golden spike for the heel. They were boots with spiked heels that could bring authority and gravitas to any stomping I did on stage. I had a black leather bra that I found on Melrose Ave in Hollywood. It stacked up my boobs and served them up in delicious form. The black leather fringe jacket made me look like a wild gypsy banshee, and I found a sword of Caleb's that I had given him once that I figured might be fun to use as a prop on stage.

I spent the next two days smoking joint after joint as I oiled up all my leather clothing items. I was like a fighter in training and I rehearsed my songs until I could recite them in my sleep.

I avoided Craig who somehow, against all reason, had managed to keep his position at the Alachua County Hospital. I did not even speak to him. I knew he needed more counseling, or more rehab or something that God knows, I couldn't give him.

The kids were at school on the day of our first rehearsal at Dubs. I walked into the backstage area. It was impressive and just as I hoped it would look. The boys started to plug in their guitars and Mickey started banging on his drums, ready for some jamming.

As we walked in, I saw a figure on the right side of the stage. I couldn't tell until I got closer, but it was Tom Petty.

He was strumming on a guitar, sitting on what appeared to be a barstool. He was talking with Mr. Dubs in low tones and I put down my bag and was fidgeting to find the microphones I brought to rehearsal.

"Say, would anybody here have doobage to give an old man?" Petty was looking up and addressing the entire band.

"I have some yummy Humboldt county gold," I said as I handed Mr. Petty the joint.

"Yummy?" he asked as he peered up at me through his straight blond hair that practically covered his eyes.

He snickered as I pulled out my lighter to light it for him.

His gaze met mine for just a brief second, and I saw a sincere "thank you" in his smile. I could have levitated at that moment. I knew that I was going to win; I had just gotten the blessing from the Prince of Dubs himself. Mr. Petty continued to talk to Dubs as I walked back to the center stage. Petty and Dubs went out to stand in the back of the bleachers at the back of the club.

All I could see were rings of pot smoke circling Petty's head. He was like the Cheshire cat and it was hard to take my eyes off of him. Mr. Dubs signaled us to begin and I chose a Janis Joplin/Kris Kristofferson classic tune, "Me And Bobby McGee," for my cover.

It was edgy, blues, southern rock style. I figured that I needed to appeal to the local masses and they liked southern rock, so when in Dixieland, sing a little Dixie.

Apparently Tom liked it because he got up out of his seat, got on stage with his guitar, and sang back up to the ending chorus.

Stage hands, Mr. Dubs, and a few people who were milling around that I had no idea who they were, and anyone else who heard the ending, gave it a huge applause.

Tom nodded to me as he backed off the stage, almost Dylanesque, and I knew he wanted to hear my original song. Oh, how I had wished that Charlie Hargret was there to play lead, but we went with what we knew.

Karl had learned the song and seeing Tom Petty made him give it his very best effort. Who knew that Karl had that much in him to give?

Calvin started the intro and was giving it all the chunka chunka he had. Mr. Petty's assistant snuck up behind him with a phone call. At first Tom shoved the phone back at the assistant but she forcefully put the receiver in his hands and he walked down the back stage stairs so he could hear.

Tom Petty swirled in a mystical world, graced with the pungent odor of sativa, he moved in an otherworldly tai chi. I understood him. On the way back after the rehearsal, I turned on the radio, just in time to catch "Mary Jane's Last Dance."

"This is it! This time I've got what I need, right Bowie? Bowie?"

I was yelling at the top of my lungs, confident that this contest was mine for the having, and where was David? I wanted to rejoice with him about the upcoming victory. I drove along the quiet little neighborhood street with loud music and ranting in the car. "Overture, dim the lights, this is it, we'll hit the heights, no more rehearsing and nursing our parts, we know every part by heart.... and oh what heights we'll hit, on with the show this is it. This is it, this is it," I said to myself, "all my hard work has paid off." I had to wade through a sea of scum, vomit, and floating turds from Miami to LA, but way down here in the swamp lands of Gainesville, I felt a moment of redemption.

As I walked through my front door, I felt like I was kicked out of heaven and thrown into hell, as I witnessed the scene in front of me.

Craig was passed out on the couch. Mia and Michael were crying, trying to wake him up. The evidence of an empty bottle of Jameson told the story. Caleb came running out of his bedroom with the phone in hand.

"Mommy, I just called 911, daddy's not waking up."

I threw down my purse and went over to the couch to see if I could find a pulse. It was faint but it was there. I started to give Craig mouth-to-mouth, thinking if I pumped enough oxygen into him, it would keep his heart beating.

It seemed like hours, but it was only 12 minutes later when the paramedics arrived. We all followed behind in the car on the way to the hospital.

"Mommy is daddy gonna die?" Mia's eyes had tears in them.

"No, sweetie, he's gonna be fine. He just needs some medicine at the hospital."

We spent the night in the waiting room, all three of my kids and I curled up into a ball, keeping each other warm and comforted. I opened one eye as I saw a trickle of morning sunlight streaming through a clear window. Below, a young doctor came out to let me know how Craig was doing.

"Mrs. Channing? I'm Dr. Walters. Dr. Channing is doing just fine and wants to see you."

I hurriedly followed him down the hall, with my three little kittens following their mother cat. Walking into the room, I saw an alert Craig who lit up when he saw his family walk through the door.

"Oh, God, Anne Marie, I'm so glad you are here," he said like a man who had seen the light.

"What happened?" I sat on the bed, trying to be sympathetic even though on a much deeper level, I was angry.

The kids all jumped on the bed and then cuddled around Craig. Craig looked deep into my eyes.

"Mom called last night while you were at rehearsal. Dad died." The last two words caught in his throat and he began to sob.

"It's okay, daddy. I know you are sad about grandpa. It's okay to cry."

Michael's comforting words were so wise I found myself again thinking how advanced and deep he was.

We all hugged, a family moment, and I kept taking deep breaths and telling myself the ship was still holding together.

Later that morning, they released Craig and we drove home. I could not say a word.

Caleb prattled on about the football game on Friday, Mia played with her doll, and Michael clung to me as if he sensed the passing crisis that had landed on his front door.

When we got back to the house, Craig pulled me aside.

"Pack things for us and the kids, I am booking a flight for us to fly back to Indiana. Mom said that the wake is tonight and we will be lucky to get there in time for it."

I sensed that this funeral, this passing of his father, had affected him deeply. In spite of his lack of control with alcohol, he seemed to be very much in charge and needing to attend all the hoopla and ceremony that surrounds the death of someone.

I stood in the boys' room packing underwear and socks.

"I am going to miss the football game tomorrow, I am missing school now, mom can't we work it out? I can't miss the game."

"Dad is calling the coach; I think coach will understand, it's your grandpa's funeral."

"What's a funeral?" Mia asked.

"The body of the dead person is put in a coffin, like a little box with pillows and covers and everyone can come and pay their last respects... they say good-bye. Then we take him to the cemetery and they put the box in the ground and cover it with dirt."

All three of my kids looked at me in horror at the description of the event.

"Hey, when I go, you won't have to bother with any of that, I am going to go out in a blaze of glory." I stated that as if I was proud of how I foresaw my own demise.

"Mom, don't ever die," they all said in unison.

"Everyone dies someday, which is why you need to make each day count. Be happy, love God, and treat others with kindness."

"Amen," they all said loudly. It was a little game that we played. When I said something that was truer than truth, they were to all say "amen" loudly. Like a choir that sings in church, they became good at it and it made us all feel better.

Craig came in. I handed him his suitcase and told him I would take them to the airport.

"You're not coming?"

"I can't. If the funeral is Sunday morning and then the reception dinner, I would miss the show at Dubs. I can't do that Craig. I can't miss this. I know we are going to win and it means a recording contract."

"It's your father-in-law's funeral," Craig said, angered at this new twist.

"You weren't there for my father's funeral," I fired back.

"I was working, what's your excuse? You have to go try and be a rock star! You just try and try and try and it never seems to work but you won't give up."

His words burned into my soul. The pain was oozing through my body but I would not give him the satisfaction of knowing how much it hurt. However, he continued.

"Perhaps if you were more focused on being a good wife and mother, I wouldn't be drinking and chasing women."

That was a direct hit.

"Don't blame me for your addiction problems. Own it, Dr. Channing!"

"What do you think is going to happen if you win? More time away from your family, no football games with Caleb, no dance recitals for Mia, no more guitar time with Michael. Is that what you want?"

I said nothing, and we drove to the Gainesville Municipal Airport in silence. The kids didn't know until the last minute that I was not coming to the funeral.

Caleb protested, wanting to stay too, but I kissed them all and told them I would hold Grandpa Johnnie's spirit in my heart and wish him a bon voyage to the afterlife.

Craig gave me a slight peck on the cheek. He was visibly restraining his anger, but he took his children on the plane like a loving and caring father, and he was going to his father's funeral as a loving and caring son.

Chapter 35
Highway to Hell

If there was a word to describe my feelings on Saturday morning before the gig, I would have added it to the latest edition of the Webster Dictionary.

I had planned the most exciting show I could imagine. The entire band was dressed in black leather, and I had on the thigh high boots with the 5-inch spike heel and the black leather fringed jacket and my large medieval sword that I was going to wave into the air.

I had lain in bed for over an hour, arranging how the album cover would look. The loud ring of the telephone woke me out of my daydream.

"I got those big bins you asked for." Calvin woke me with the theme of the day.

"Great, bring them over and let's see if this works," I shouted as I shot up straight out of the covers and into what I was hoping would be the best day of my life.

Calvin brought five large black cauldron looking kettles out on the lanai. We filled them with several bags of charcoal.

"Let's pour gasoline on them and then see what kind of flame we can get going and how long it will sustain. I would like to make sure they stay up and burning for at least the five minutes surrounding the performance of 'Soul on Fire.'"

I grabbed a gas can out of the garage that Craig used for the lawn mower. I saw a can of lighter fluid that we had used earlier in the year to do a BBQ and I knew there was at least half a can left.

"Be careful with how much you pour on, it's not going to take that much," Calvin admonished me as I started to pour copiously on the charcoal bricks.

"Ok, so we have these cauldrons at the front of the stage and

I bring out my sword to light it."

I showed Calvin the beautiful medieval sword that I had and I swirled it around as if it was magic. I swirled around each cauldron and had mounted a small filament that would hold a flame and it would light each cauldron.

And I feel, yeah, I feeeeeel, like I'm living in hell.

Calvin's shit-eating grin told me that he liked what he saw. The kettles burst with fire that held a six foot flame for under 5 minutes, but it was an impressive 5 minutes.

"We're gonna win," he said confidently. "This is better than anybody else. Totally."

Mickey and Kerry and Karl showed up at about the same time that Calvin and I arrived and we all lugged in cauldrons, swords, black boots, and fuel for the fire. I had stopped by a local Quickie Mart to pick up lighter fluid and decided to bring 10 more gallons of gas.

I made sure Mickey brought the fuel in and stashed it in our dressing room. I put my clothes over the containers and started getting dressed and putting on my makeup.

I looked in the mirror and saw a beautiful woman with sparks and fireworks within her, and I wanted to entertain the packed venue like they had never been entertained before.

When the show started, I had just finished dressing and I wanted to watch the opening act, Scorcher. The band was tight, lick for lick they were doing everything well and their lead singer had the Sammy Hagar voice down. He nailed the vocals on "Highway to Hell" and I was happy to see that the opening band had picked out my theme and set the stage. As they walked off stage to a thunderous applause, my confidence began to wane. My guitar player should be Charlie but I was hoping Karl could fill his shoes. I hadn't even had time to hear what he did with Charlie's lead solo but the drama at my house didn't allow for that luxury.

"Excuse me, ma'am," a voice from behind me caught my attention and I turned around to see a short, red-headed man with curly hair and a handlebar moustache, kinda like Yosemite Sam.

"I have been told that your band has big pots that you plan to light on fire," he said in a very thick southern accent.

"Yes, sir," I said with school girl charm. He looked up and

down at the thigh high leather boots and spiked heels.

"Uh, huh," his tone was pessimistic.

"I need to look at these pots, how many are there, five, I hear?"

"Yes, only five." I was trying to minimize everything as I zipped my jacket to prevent bustier exposure.

"What do you have them sitting on to prevent them from burning the stage?"

I knew I had to think of something quick because telling him the truth, that I had nothing for them to sit on, would be suicide, and with Scorcher's performance being kick-ass, I needed this to work.

"Well, what would you recommend they sit on?" I asked sincerely.

He looked at me with a piercing, stabbing gaze.

"Somethin' that ain't gonna burn the stage. That's a wooden stage out there, missy. You can't just light them up and burn them if you don't have something to protect it."

"We have fire proof grates that should contain the heat," I said, wondering where I was going to conjure them up from since the band was due on stage in approximately one hour.

"Lemme see 'em," he asked with conviction.

"Calvin has them and he's out back, let me get him." I raced out back to the small backdoor patio where the musicians hung out smoking cigarettes and pot. I busted through the door to see Calvin smoking a doobie.

"Help me find something fireproof that we can set the cauldrons on, the fire marshal is here."

Calvin dropped the joint and used the toe of his boot to crush it. He looked like a didn't have a clue as to what that would be.

"Like what?" he asked sheepishly.

"Didn't you tell me that the carpeting you laid for your aunt last week was flame retardant?"

"Yeah and I have enough left that we could cut five squares out of it."

Like precision craftsman, we had them cut and brought them inside to show the fire marshal. We put the squares under each cauldron and brought the fire marshal back into the dressing room.

"Flame retardant carpeting?" He stood and looked at it for a moment and then turned to me with a definitive look.

257

"No, I am not approving them; leave your witch's cauldrons in here."

He marched out with an authoritative stomp and I looked at Calvin.

"Hey, the song is good enough without the fire. It's kinda gimmicky anyways."

I wanted to scream at Calvin and the fire marshal, but instead I decided to work within the framework of what it was.

Calvin went back outside to smoke one more before we got on stage and I grabbed a young scruffy kid, who didn't even look 21, and made him an offer he couldn't refuse.

"Here's a hundred bucks, make sure that you get the attention of the little redheaded man with the plaid shirt by smoking a cigarette in front of him, and make sure he takes you outside to deal with the issue. Make him stay out there for at least five minutes. "

"What and miss your number?" the kid said.

I was genuinely touched by his fan like response.

"Ok, look, there's another hundred once we're done with the set. As long as he walks back in after my band is offstage."

"Two hundred before and after and you guarantee he will not be back in the building till the winners are announced. "

I was being blackmailed again, but after living in LA, it didn't even shake me.

"Four hundred, fine," I said as I pulled ten twenties out of my wallet.

That was my entire money for the week and I had no idea how I was going to pay him the other two hundred. It didn't matter. I could loot Craig's account if I had to. Didn't matter. This was it, the night that I would make it and get whisked into the world of rock and roll, tours, recording sessions, limos, and big money.

"This is it," I said to myself as I heard the MC announce us.

"Let's give it up for the last band of the evening, …Heat!"

I did not like the name for the band but we had to put something on our application and everyone vetoed the Shri Annie Band. They said it didn't have the heavy feel like Heat.

Mickey and I pushed the cauldrons on stage as I saw the kid walk out the back entrance with the fire marshal.

We tore right into "Bobby McGee," and received an enthusiastic welcome but it was not quite where I thought it needed to be to win. "Broken Dreams" got them going since it had more of a metal flavor and whining guitar. Karl played his heart and soul out on that song and the crowd was into it.

As I started the chorus tag out to "Broken Dreams," I went to the back of the stage and took a huge gallon jug of the gasoline and poured it in the black pots, getting the crowd into it. I went back and got the lighter fluid and the crowd cheered as I squirted the fluid all over and then threw the empty can to the back of the stage. I brought out my sword and started lighting the cauldrons.

The crowd was roaring. The sound man had to crank up the volume to overcome the huge crowd roar.

"Here is the song you've been waiting for people, this is the song that will win this contest. SOUL ON FIRE!!!!

I nodded to Karl. This is it, you better play this tune like your life depended upon it.

I shuffle my feet to a tune with no beat
I work every day, just to feel like a slave and I feeeeeel, I feeeeeel
Like I'm Living in hell.

The crowd was electric and full of an energy of its own. I felt drunk with power; we all felt the music, we all danced around the black cauldrons, oblivious to anything but the fire and the song.

I belted out the tune; I don't think I ever gave a tune as much energy as I gave it that night. This was it! I was crossing over to the world of my dreams.

My soul is on fire, my soul is on fire, my soul is on Fire,
And I feeeeeel like I'm living in hell.

I stomped down on the stage with my spike heel and it knocked one of the pots around a little. The flames for all the pots were at least six feet in the air and when the pot wiggled from the knock, gas that was still inside leaked out and was followed by a line of fire.

The fire of another pot got higher, more like eight feet, and caught the curtains on the side of the stage. Lines of fire danced from one flammable substance to another in seconds.

People started screaming and ran for the doors, loud blood curdling yells and shrieks of fear. Smoke from the burning drapery began to fill the stage and we stopped the song and then dropped to the floor to avoid the thick smoke.

It was pandemonium. I crawled on my belly like a snake off the back of the stage and when the smoke cleared, I ran for the backstage door as fast as I could. I could hear other people behind me.

The sweet smell of the clear night air gave me an adrenalin rush as I bolted for the car.

There was no other way but to run for my car, jump in, and drive off. My heart was pounding as I started the car's ignition. I slammed it into reverse and pulled out of Dubs through a gravel road on the backside.

I drove about 2 miles and then hit the state highway. Before I got to the highway, I stopped and took off the costume, putting on a black hat and a large grey overcoat, as well as sun glasses.

I flew down the state highway to the interstate and headed north, wondering if I was going to get stopped by a policeman.

When I hit the Georgia line, I felt a small sense of relief. I had no idea what kind of catastrophe I had left behind. I was scared, frightened out of my mind, and wishing like hell that I had never decided to go against a fire marshal.

Pulling into a gas station around dawn, I overheard two truckers at the coffee bar.

"Did you hear about the big fire at Dubs place in Gainesville, Florida? The place burnt to the ground when some devil rock band lit a fire on stage."

"Rock and roll," said the other man, "or is it demon music?"

"Well, good news is that miraculously, no one was killed. God must've had his eye on the place and decided to save the souls inside."

I ran back to my car as fast as my legs would carry me. I was relieved to hear that there was no loss of life, but I was sure that they were going to charge me with some kind of crime. Arson! God, they'd send me to prison!

I was sobbing as I drove down Interstate 75. I had done all of this for rock and roll? Was I insane? My mind was weaving all over the highway but I kept the car rolling down the interstate. I was racing back to the Ohio River and the land to the north of it. I had a funeral to catch or at least some part of it. I was wrong not to go to my father in law's funeral and this tit for tat with Craig had to stop. I prayed the only funeral was for Grandpa Johnny and I hoped it would not be my own.

I watched the rear view mirror of the car, looking for anyone in any direction. It was twilight and I felt relieved to get into Tennessee and switch to I-24. It was usually pretty desolate at night coming out of Chattanooga.

I grabbed the brown leather purse that I kept all of my paraphernalia in and found my pipe and put a pinch of the good stuff in it. I watched both sides of the interstate, and as I barreled down a lonely stretch just southeast of Nashville, I lit the pipe and inhaled salvation. I turned on the radio to find every station playing country music. I found peace in hearing an old Emylou Harris classic. My solace was to sing harmonies to Emylou's stellar vocals.

I felt like part of the 3am angel's country choir. Tears rolled down my face and I prayed to God to be merciful to me and allow me to get to Greenfield, safe and sound.

My mind did not want to let go of the chaos and I ran through so many scenarios of how I could have won without the fire pots. Finally, three pipefulls later, I found a peaceful place. Nothing mattered, and I was headed to my father-in-law's funeral after all. I didn't have any clothes since I was afraid that the cops would have followed me back to the house. All I had on were jeans and a T-shirt that read, "I SOLD MY SOUL TO ROCK AND ROLL."

The road took on the monotony that night driving brings, and I pulled over to an all-night fast food stop and grabbed gas and coffee. That was all I needed, that and a pipe full, and before I knew it, the sun was coming up and I was crossing the Ohio River and back in Indiana.

Back home again in Indiana…

I got to my in-laws' farm just outside of Greenfield, the county seat for Hancock County, as everyone was getting dressed to go to church. My relatives stared at me as I got out of the car as if I was somebody from Mars.

"Oh, God, you're alright," Craig came running up to greet me with all three kids running behind.

"Mommy," they all cried out together.

Amazingly, my mother-in-law, Betty, had several black dresses that fit me, so I picked the plainest one and showered and was ready to go to the funeral. I kept looking at my face in the mirror when I was putting on my makeup, thinking I had just landed into a parallel universe where I was alright and in no trouble.

Funerals are tough on everyone but the dead person. Betty had been married to Johnny for 53 years, marrying him when she was just a teenager of 17. I couldn't even imagine her grief.

We sat in church and watched the minister bless the casket and they covered it with an American flag because Johnny was a veteran of WWII. I was crying as hard as Betty and Craig, but not because of Johnny's death. I was crying for myself. Relief that, as of yet, no one had come to put the cuffs on me, and most of all because my dream had died. It was an ugly death.

Walking to the gravesite, Craig pulled me close.

"So did you win the contest?" I started sobbing out loud and could not manage to tell him what had happened.

We stood at the gravesite. I watched them lower the casket into the ground and I felt like it was me. When the service was over, I got back into the car with my sister-in-law and her husband.

"There, there," Anna said soothingly. "We all loved daddy so much and I am so glad you could make it. Why didn't you come with Craig?"

"Long story, I will tell you later," I said. I looked in the rear view mirror and saw a state police officer's car pull alongside Anna and Jack's big Lincoln Towncar. I sank downward, feigning a fainting spell so that the policemen would not notice me.

Craig popped into the front seat and stared right at me.

"Tell me what happened." He used his no-nonsense voice to indicate his lack of patience on the issue.

Out of the corner of my eye, I watched the policeman drive past. Slowly, as if he was looking for someone.

The drive back to my in-laws' farm for the reception was a big stare down. Craig stared at me, thinking he would stare the information out of me. I looked off in the distance with no intention of talking. Words couldn't describe how heartbroken I was. Anna was never much of a sister-in-law and her insincere affection with her arm around me made me that much more resolute to never utter a peep.

Finally, she came to my defense.

"Can't you see how upset she is over your dad's death? Don't be asking her about some silly contest, what was it dear, a singing contest?" Her tone was so painfully condescending that I nearly took my big purse and wiped her face with it.

Instead I broke down in tears and found a penitent Craig, helping me into the guest bedroom to dry tears and be rescued from the dour Anna.

Craig wiped my eyes and gave me a daddy bear-hug and sat down next to me. Off in the dining room, several neighbors had come by to set up casseroles on the dining room table. The din of voices tried to reach its way down the hallway, but Craig shut it out when he closed the door to the guest room.

"So what happened? How did your performance go?"

At that precise moment, before I could speak, the bedroom phone rang. Craig grabbed for it and I fell out of his arms and onto the pillows lying across the bed. I crawled into fetal position.

"Hello? Yes, this is Dr. Craig Channing? Yes, my wife is Anne Marie Channing? Yes, Yes…" A series of "yes's" followed to answer unknown questions.

After what seemed like an eternity, Craig hung up and turned to me.

"Mr. Dubs is dropping all charges. That was the Alachua County Sheriff's Department."

"Dropping the charges?" I shot straight up off the bed, out of a fetal position, and began dancing around the guest bed.

"Hooray, whoooo hooo!" I said, jumping with joy. I twisted and turned in orgasmic gratitude.

"It seems you lit tubs of gasoline on fire and burnt the place down." He was staring at me with an incredulous look, as if he did not recognize me and could not understand why I would do such a thing.

After the initial shot of ecstasy, my feet landed on the ground. I began to question my sanity. Did I just hear Craig correctly? All charges dropped?

"The officer said Mr. Dubs told him that Tom Petty gave him an outrageous sum of money to let it go. Said it was a thank-you gesture from Mr. Petty for a gift you gave him before the concert."

"Wow," was the only word that came out of my mouth. I was free; no one would take me to jail.

"God bless Tom Petty," I said over and over again until Anna stuck her head in to stick her nose back into my business.

"Craig, Pastor Smith is here to offer his condolences," Anna offered with grace and decorum. "I will stay here and comfort Anne Marie."

Try as she might, Anna could not penetrate the bubble of bliss I had surrounded myself with. The sun was setting in the western window of the house, and I remembered how cold it is in Indiana; the old willow tree behind the house had no light green leaves blowing in the evening breeze.

I sat mesmerized and charmed by God's great mercy in my life. After endless chatter from Anna, I suggested we go into the kitchen and get things cleaned up. It was well past midnight before all the company left, and Anna left to join her husband in the second bedroom, dejected that she couldn't get a word out of me about what was really happening.

What happened was a tragedy. I sat out along the back fence and smoked a bowlful and thought about it for several hours. I knew that things were going to change again in my life and I surrendered to it.

Craig stayed on at the farm house and got situated with a large specialty group who just happened to be looking for a cardiologist. He never picked up another glass of beer or whiskey again. His father's passing seemed to rid him of a demon that had haunted him for years.

I began to learn more about alcoholism and realized that without the alcohol, Craig was a pretty mellow guy who loved his family. It made him feel good that we were there to take care of Betty. She grew weaker and weaker over the next two years. When she died, we sold the farm and moved back to Bloomington.

Chapter 36
The Long and Winding Road

My children thrived in the world that Craig and I built for them. I had vowed to Craig on my honor as a human being to never, ever do another rock and roll gig again. I watched and listened to rock music, but I found myself watching an era in rock and rock that I call the "let down period."

As talented as Nirvana was, I could see such pain in the eyes of Kurt Cobain and I found myself feeling sad for him. His eyes screamed suicide. I know, because I contemplated this idea in my own head. The spice and zest had gone out of my life, too. His lyrics searched for meaning in a world that had become meaningless. The excesses of the 1980's had taken its toll on rock and roll. The chords and the riffs had a muted sound of being tired of the era of materialism and too much of everything. It begged for something, yet got lost in the despair of not knowing what that was.

Pearl Jam was another great band that I enjoyed listening to and it defined the 90's too. Their lyrics told me tales of how poor little Jeremy had gotten the short end of the stick in his family, which seemed like an anthem for many of the young ones that had survived the 80's and the pillaging of family values. Certainly, I was one of the grown-ups that had taken my children through the roller coaster ride of 80's insanity. It's not like we meant to do it, but exploration can sometimes lead you to a dead end.

Back in Indiana, things in the 1990's were much calmer. Caleb became a star quarterback at Bloomington High School. He took his team to the state championship in 1997 in their division.

Craig was so proud and so supportive. His days of working 70-hour work weeks and serving on too many committees and boards were over. He spent many weekends playing basketball and football

265

with Caleb and Michael, and both boys thrived and grew into well-adjusted teenagers.

The summer before the greatest football season in Channing family history, Caleb coached a Little League team. I was fond of coming to watch.

Several of the boys on his team, the Racers, wore their pants down way past their hips.

"Caleb, you should tell them to wear belts and pull up their pants," I remarked one afternoon.

"Ha," he laughed. "I just want them to hit the ball, mom."

"They are all bringing these boom boxes with them and they are listening to some new kind of music that I haven't heard before. What is it?"

"It's rap music, mom."

"Rap?"

I was surprised that I hadn't heard of it before so I took to researching it a bit.

Almost all of the artists were black, and although I had listened to R&B music through the years, this music was decidedly different. There was no discernible melody line, and the lyrics were very explicit. I could understand how these artists chose this type of expression, but what puzzled me was how 8-year-old kids, whose mothers drove them to baseball practice in Mercedes Benz sedans, liked it. Perhaps this was yet another phase of rejecting the excesses of the previous decade.

Some part of me could not let go of music, and I found a solace and comfort in listening to the songs that were driving the culture.

Mia found a love of dance and studies. She consistently made all A's in school, was on the National Honor Society, and made the Pom Pom squad at school. The old hippie in me laughed at the type of daughter I found sitting in my living room one evening announcing that she had been nominated for Prom Queen. She didn't seem to care too much for any type of music except classical, sometimes jazz. It was only as a background for her to dance.

"That's okay," I thought. I was nothing like my mother either.

Two weeks later, a handsome young man knocked at our front door and Craig answered it.

"Come in," said Craig. "Mia will be ready shortly."

"Good evening Dr. Channing. I am Elliot Canfield, Mia's date for this evening's prom."

"Nice to meet you, Elliott," I said as I escorted Mia into the living room.

She was breathtaking to behold, she definitely looked like the prom queen to me.

"Have her home by 1am, Elliott," Craig ordered.

"Oh daddy, the after prom won't even be over by then."

Mia was forever daddy's girl, so Craig relented.

"OK, well, certainly by 2, then."

I watched them leave in Elliot's brand new 1999 Mustang. It was a cherry red convertible and the crab apple tree in the front yard was filled with blossoms, a few of which fell on Mia's hair as she passed underneath it. Spring was always so beautiful in Indiana.

Craig retired to his lazy boy in the den to watch the NBA playoffs and I wandered down to our soundproof basement where Michael and his friend, Jaden, were working on some music. Craig insisted it be sound proofed so that he could enjoy peace and quiet in his home.

Jaden had an interesting guitar riff going and I picked up one of the guitars and started playing a counter melody to it.

"Mia leave for the prom yet?" Michael asked.

"Yes, she looked so lovely," I boasted with pride.

"That's just such a stupid thing, a big dance, getting to be crowned 'queen,' having to rent a tuxedo," Michael's tone was dripping with sarcasm.

"We all follow our own road, Michael. Not everyone was born to be a rock star like you."

"Rock star? What is that really, Mrs. C? I think of myself as an artist," Jaden professed to both of us.

"It's an archaic term anymore, Jaden, I agree."

With that, I broke into a counter melody to Jaden's and Michael picked up his bass guitar and the three of us jammed happily for several hours.

Sometime after midnight, I heard the front door slam, and thought I heard Mia crying. I went into the living room to find her weeping on the sofa.

"What's the matter, sweetheart?" I asked as I sat down beside her.

"I lost. I lost by one damn vote, too. Rachael Himsel won."

With that announcement, she burst into full-fledged sobbing as I tried to console her.

"It was just an honor to be nominated, honey. Try to think of it in that light."

"No, I won't think of it that way. As I see it, I lost. I don't want to be a loser like you, you forever wanna be rock star."

With that, she ran down the hall and into her bedroom, slammed the door, and left me sitting on the couch with my jaw hanging down to the floor.

I knew we were different and that she wanted to be successful like her father, but I never saw her show such resentment towards what was the most painful failure of my life.

When I shared the story with Craig over coffee the following morning, he gave me a big hug.

"You will always be my rock star, honey," he said with great affection.

I did appreciate his sentiment, and it did make me feel somewhat better, but it did not take away the pain that her words brought up in me.

"You make fabulous lasagna too," he added, thinking that would lift my spirits.

Sometimes you just have to move on and let go. I kept trying to console myself the next few days while I tried to process what she had said by going down into the basement and writing a song or two, but found myself singing "Long and Winding Road."

I put the guitar down as I found I could not stop singing that classic Beatles tune. Paul wrote that song while on a farm in Scotland to ease the tensions that had arisen between the band members, and it became their last number one hit.

Everything comes to an end, even an icon like the Beatles.

Chapter 37
Smells Like Teen Spirit

Michael burst through the back kitchen door while I was busy making preparations for Mia's high school graduation party. In spite of losing her bid for prom queen, she roared back to her strongest suit, which was academics, by being named valedictorian of her class. I had promised her that her graduation party would be an occasion to remember; even Caleb was flying in from Gainesville, Florida, where he was a sophomore success as the back-up quarterback for the Gators.

"Mom, I need the car this weekend," Michael demanded. "We are entering a 'Battle of the Bands' contest in Louisville and I have to get this application to them before midnight tomorrow."

"Hey slow down," I asked. "Can't you just fax them the application?"

"There is a $25 entry fee. How are we going to fax that?" He was jumping around the table where I was busy making a centerpiece for the party like a jackrabbit on steroids.

"Gee Michael, this is the 21st Century. I am pretty sure we can fax the application and give them my credit card number for the fee. Better that than missing your sister's graduation tomorrow."

"Oh, yeah," he said as he began to settle down. "Thanks, mom. That's a great idea."

The family had a wonderful time at the graduation and Michael was there to support his sister.

The Battle of the Bands wasn't until September, so the Beings had all summer to rehearse. Caleb went back to Florida for his junior year and Mia had been accepted with a full scholarship to Stanford University, so I found myself hanging in the basement a lot listening to the band practice.

They were good, the sound was different and unique but I kept feeling like rock and roll was no more. The sound had lost its rebel yell. It seemed to be much more introspective. Even rap was introspection with beat, I thought.

Yes, there were the White Stripes, the Killers, a new band, but every band that made it to the national level did not have gravitas to command a generation. Truth be told, I felt like rock and roll had morphed into hip-hop and rap and a myriad of other music genres. Pure rock and roll seemed to be dead. These genres seemed to have an influence on the up and coming generation. The other force disrupting the rebellious magnetism of rock and roll was American Idol.

I began to watch the show because I thought it was going to give rock a new face lift, but instead, it became a hokey popularity contest. I even suggested that the voting was rigged, but I had no way to prove it. It seemed to be more than ironic that the first few winners were cross over country, and I surmised it was because there was a helluva lot more money in country and pop music.

I started to listen to Nirvana just so I could bang my head on a frying pan. I found that to be far more comforting than the show. Craig caught me one Saturday and suggested I was taking head banger music to a whole new level but in his opinion, not a healthy one.

Sadly, I found the depression-laden music a comfort, and it was addicting. Listening to the Beings, I was worried that their music had no place in modern day American culture.

The new age sounds were lovely, heavenly and ethereal, and the backbeat held the song to a different drummer. I even offered some inspirational lyrics to the band one evening when they were rehearsing.

After the band rehearsed, Michael pulled me aside.

"Mom, I appreciate all your support and enthusiasm for the band but I don't want you to interfere anymore, okay?"

I was in shock. It was the one crumb I was holding on to in a world that was decaying all around me.

"Sure, I understand," I mustered. "You do want me to come and see you when we you guys perform in Louisville, don't you?"

"Please don't take this the wrong way mom, but no, we don't

want you to come. This is our gig. I think we can handle it. Why don't you and dad go see a movie together or something?"

Like a knife through my heart, it seemed there was nothing I could hold onto that was rock and roll.

I spent days and days preparing for Mia's wedding. After graduating magna cum laude from Stanford University, she shocked everyone with her announcement of her June wedding to a wealthy San Francisco businessman, John Liebowitz.

"Why is she marrying this rich Jew, Anne Marie? Tell me this," Craig asked over a Sunday morning cup of coffee.

"Maybe, it's the safety net she never had as a kid," I fired back with fiery eyes.

Craig banged his coffee mug on the breakfast bar.

"She's trying to get back at us for everything that happened to her as a kid. How are a Catholic and a Jew going to raise their children? Will my grandchildren be baptized?"

"Let's just get them married this weekend. Besides, lots of Jews and Catholics get married. It's been going on for a long time. What year is it again, Craig?"

My patience had worn thin. I dismissed him and left for a day of shopping for my mother-of-the-bride dress. Mia was unhappy with me that I chose to go by myself and buy it alone.

"Why can't I come with?" she asked. "Why did you wait till the very last minute to buy your dress?"

In the same style I had exhibited my whole life, I left the room with Mia's jaw dangling in the wind.

Caleb and his new wife, Jill, had arrived from Florida for the dress rehearsal dinner and I picked them up at the airport. Caleb's job as assistant coach for the men's football program at Florida State was very demanding, and it was so wonderful to see him. Although the team didn't make it to the rankings they had hoped for, Caleb had been approached by some Big Ten school for a head coaching job. He was an outstanding assistant.

"Where's Michael?" Caleb asked as he loaded their luggage into the car.

"Rehearsing for his gig on Saturday night."

"Saturday night," Jill chimed in." But that's the wedding

271

reception."

"Don't worry, I know that he will leave a bit early but he will still be there for the toast and garter throw."

"Mom, this is Mia's wedding day. He should be at the wedding… for the whole time. You are just encouraging him with all this rock and roll performing. He's been out of high school for a year now and what's he doing? Playing flea ridden little night clubs in the Midwest and doing some modeling."

"I am encouraging him, backing him, and throwing whatever support I can toss his way," I barked back. My tone was stern and I shot the arrow right at Caleb and hit my mark.

Again, true to pattern, he floated his attention right out the window and we didn't say a word until we all got to the restaurant.

Mia's wedding rehearsal dinner went flawlessly, and Michael and Caleb seemed to iron out the wrinkles with a couple of beers.

I zealously guarded Michael's rock and roll dreams. He was a talented drummer, great guitarist and he did awesome backup vocals, and his booming bass voice worked as a lead vocalist at times.

Michael had been in four different bands during high school and his latest band, Beings of Light, had done fairly well on the regional tour circuits.

Any extra cash that I had available went to pay for the recording of their first album, Living in Bliss. The sounds were innovative and had much Indian musical influence. The sitar player that they found for their song, "Be Here Now" literally blew my mind with his licks.

This latest incarnation of his bands was uniquely different. It was rap music but it wasn't about the hard street life with "bitches and ho's," it was about the consciousness of bliss and what this universe inside oneself looked like. I was delighted to hear that the band's gigs were selling out and there was an email list of over 500 names who wanted to know when the album would be finished so they could purchase a copy.

Much had been said about Michael's career from his father and siblings but I remained his strongest supporter.

"After all," I thought, "this is all that I have left of my broken dreams, my broken rock and roll dreams."

Mia was a beautiful bride and she left with her husband right after the reception for a place that was unknown to everyone, including me. Craig insisted he knew it was going to be an exotic place in the South Seas.

I was just happy for her. Her life was normal and secure. Caleb's was as well. Everyone else disagreed with me, but I knew that the path Michael's life was following would be magical. Normal and secure had an entirely different feel to it for him. He was blessed with wisdom for his age and he and his band were making music that they hoped would raise the consciousness of man and help the entire human race. I found it deeply inspiring as a performer.

Chapter 38
Changes

Right after our annual Fourth of July picnic, Michael popped in to see me and found me buried in my basement studio.

"Mom, guess what?" His face had a smile that held a secret. He walked over to me as

I sat in front of my keyboards trying to pick out a melody line that kept on rolling around in my head.

"What?" I asked, not even looking up. He shoved a piece of paper in front of me as it landed on the keyboard.

As I picked it up and read it, my eyes lit up like sparklers.

"Oh my God, you are opening for Oasis on their European tour this fall. Oh Michael, this is wonderful!"

I jumped out of my chair and hugged him. We danced around hopping and hugging each other.

"This is a huge break for you, honey." As happy as I was for him, a small feeling of resentment began to trickle into my mind. Why did he get the breaks and not me?

I was so disgusted with myself for this minor attack of jealousy that I shook my head to get the thought out of there.

"Mom, this could be it, with the album ready, we might attract the attention of a record label. Next thing you know, we will be the act that everyone is wanting to see."

"Headliners," I said.

The word resonated in my studio as if the room itself longed to hear the word. We savored it.

"You are going to be a star honey," I said with a tear in my eye.

"Mom, come and see us on our opening night. It's going to be at the Theatre des les Enfants in Paris, France."

I sat back down in my chair. It was the big time. Michael and his band had made it to the place I had always longed to go. On the brink of success in rock and roll. My baby had achieved what I could not.

The mixture of feelings stayed with me for days as I told Craig about it and my desire to attend the following evening after dinner.

"Please come with me," I asked.

"I can't, it's on Tuesday Oct 4th, and you of all people should know that the first weekend in October is the annual hospital charity ball, and this year I am grand marshal. You can't leave; you have to attend the charity ball with me."

"Take your receptionist," I said with hateful undertones. "I have faithfully attended that boring function for the past ten years and I am not going this year. My son is more important than your fucking job."

I smashed a dinner plate on the floor. I grabbed the keys and drove off before Craig had any response to my tirade.

I drove to Macy's department store and proceeded to put together an outfit that would be fitting for the great event. Opening for the band, Oasis, and in a town I had always longed to visit: Paris.

Michael was ecstatic that I would be attending the concert. I had my outfit, bought my ticket, and never even exchanged another word with Craig about it. He just knew that I was going.

The band was booked in September for a regional tour of England's club scene. People were standing all the way to the door to hear, The Beings of Light. I would get calls from the English countryside as the tour bus headed to the next gig.

"Wow, there was standing room only at the Cavern in Liverpool," he told me.

"Mmm, just like the Beatles," I mused.

Michael was higher than a kite with his robust enthusiasm.

"We are sold out for the rest of this tour and then we open for Oasis. It's like a dream come true."

Somewhere in Michael's stratospheric ecstasy, the thought hit him that this had been my lifelong dream, one that I had never achieved.

"You know, maybe the guys would be ok with you singing a little backup vocals on a couple of songs? Would you like that?"

The words stung deeply. I knew that he was just trying to

be nice, but I could not turn away from the harsh reality that my deepest longing to be out front, wowing the crowd, having them hang on my every word, my every move, could not be achieved. I felt like someone diving off a very tall cliff and into waters unknown.

"This is your night, sweetie. You have taken the journey and now the crowds are yours. I think it's because your message is pure and there are so many thirsty souls out there that need to hear the songs your band plays."

I heard a tear drop. It was the precious sound of a mother and her son sharing an unbearably beautiful moment. A moment that defined who we were.

As much as I detest flying, the flight to Paris was calm. No storm clouds in the city tonight. As the cab whisked me away to the Hotel Regina, I found myself remembering certain street corners and the lamppost that shed an eerie light on a street named St. Jacques Way; it woke a sleeping giant somewhere within me.

"Why does this all look so familiar?" I asked myself over and over as I checked into the hotel and walked out on the balcony to view the city. Heavy and unconscious thoughts and feelings rolled over me like waves coming off of a stormy sea.

Michael insisted on escorting me to the concert. He knocked on the door precisely at 7pm. He wanted to take me backstage and introduce me to the band members of Oasis.

"Mother, you look stunning," Michael beamed with pride.

I gave myself a sideways glance in the long hall mirror and I sighed. I was trying to pull my consciousness away from this unbearable sadness and focus on the gig.

I was thrilled to see all the Beings, Babaji, Suchitra, Jaden and of course, Michael, who spearheaded them through the long days of putting it all together.

"Thanks for coming, Mrs. Channing," they all told me.

"This is the beginning. From here, you can get a record label and a manager and all the paparazzi that goes along with being a rock star. You've all worked hard for this moment and this music that you are creating will change the planet."

Everyone was beaming with light. I didn't think that any of them could be any happier than they were at that moment. My eyes fixed on my darling little Michael. Without really noticing it, I put the fire underneath my son that lit up his rock and roll dreams. Words couldn't begin to describe my feelings.

"We have some time, Mrs. Channing, would you like to see the older part of this theatre? It's amazing how well preserved these dressing rooms are, you know they were used in the 17th and 18th Century by all the actors and actresses in Europe."

"Yes, let's see the history here," I chimed.

We went down a small passageway that looked like it was a catacomb in Rome during the Christian persecutions.

"You do know your way around here don't you, Baba," I asked with some concern.

"Good enough, look at it as an adventure, Momma Channing." I poked Jaden.

"Psst, do you have a joint on you?"

Jaden, chronic that he is, had one and passed it to me.

"Got a lighter?"

He handed me a small one; I could feel it in my hand, but the dimly lit area made it difficult to see much. I pulled back from the rest of the group that was snaking around a corridor and found a little tiny cubicle, some type of a meditative spot. I lit the joint and sucked in the smoke and held it for a long time. The group was way in front of me now. I heard a voice.

"Mom, don't get lost," said Michael.

"I am right behind you."

I sucked in a few more hits and threw the rest of the joint to the ground and I stepped on it to extinguish the flame.

Hurriedly, I darted around a corner and saw the band half way up an old rickety wooden staircase.

"Come on, mom, don't lag behind. You can get lost in these old hallways."

We ascended the old staircase and reached a small room at the top. I did my best to fight off the feeling that I had been there before.

"Isn't this the coolest place you ever saw?" Jaden was entranced, as were the other members of the band. Gazing at the history, Michael's appreciation was disrupted.

"I smell smoke," he said.

"It's just your imagination," I said.

We could see a small mirror and dressing table to the back of the room. A small window lit the room with the street light from outside. We all looked like shadows discovering an antique world.

Then, I smelled the smoke myself. I saw a slight bit of smoke coming up the stairway and turned to look down the stairs. A large cloud of smoke smacked me back into the room. I saw that there were flames leaping around the base of the stairs.

"Jesus, you motherfucking addict," I said to myself. "You didn't cage that joint well enough, it's caught the stairway on fire."

"I smell smoke," he said a second time. Michael opened the door to see that the stairs were on fire and the smoke was so bad it knocked us all to our knees. I heard them all coughing, and I took my fist and busted through the small window so the smoke would not suffocate us.

I leaned over the shattered glass and called to a passerby who was walking on the street below.

"HELP!" I screamed.

The man looked up to see the smoke coming out of the shattered glass and even though he did not understand English, he could see me. Our eyes met and he saw the look of terror in my eyes.

"LE FEU!" I screamed the words that I knew from somewhere deep within me. "Le feu, aidier, s'il vous plaît!"

The man understood that there was a fire and we needed help. I saw him pull out his cell phone to call for help.

I turned around to see the smoke still thick in the room and Michael and the rest of the band had passed out. I punched out the rest of the glass to get as much oxygen into the room and soon heard the sound of a fire engine.

"Hurry, dear God, help us!" I screamed.

What seemed like hours, were actually only minutes before the firemen arrived. They brought out a net.

"Saut, saut!" they yelled. I saw the net and pushed Jaden and Babba and Suchitra out the window. I watched in terror as their bodies hit the net and rescue workers grabbed them. They were OK, but bleeding from the scratches from the window's broken glass.

I turned to get Michael when I saw a dark figure floating over the top of the stairs. It was the angel of death.

"I know you," I yelled at it.

278

"Of course you do," it said.

"The akashic records state that there will be a death tonight." He pointed his finger at a groggy Michael. "He is coming with me."

"Noooooooo!" I screamed as loudly as my lungs would allow. I grabbed Michael, dragging him to the window.

"I know you, you wicked thing, you promised me rock and roll stardom." From somewhere deep in my consciousness, recognition of a bargain struck began to emerge.

"You were the one who started to have sex," the eerie creature admonished.

"Sex and rock and roll go together like peanut butter and jelly!" I screeched back.

"Ha ha, don't I know that," it laughed. "You are just a foolish human wanting to have the fame and glory that only gods can have."

I looked down on the street, where the firefighters were ready with their net. Michael came around and grabbed my jacket.

"You are going first mom," he gasped. I looked around; the fire would consume us in just brief seconds. There was no time.

Just then, the fire ate up the bottom of the stairwell and the top of the stairs came crashing down.

In the debris, Bowie stood, staring at me with a long face.

Tears glistened in my eyes as I looked back. Why my life was the way it was became crystal clear, and why my heart ached. His face was like reading the novel of my life.

The fire started to burn toward Michael, and I knew what I had to do.

"Michael, help me push you out the window, there's a net waiting below." Down on the street, passers-by had stopped and everyone was shouting for us to jump.

"Mom, you go first, the net can't hold both of our weights together." Michael was pushing back at me and we both leaned over. I looked back at the demon of death and knew that a soul had to pass over that evening. I could not stop that type of energy.

"No, jump," I said, with the force of a hurricane, and pushed him out the window, scratching his forearms on the jagged glass. I watched as he landed on the net and was quickly whisked away by the French paramedics.

The fire had started to catch the bottom of my pant leg on fire and the rest of the floor beneath me burst into flames.

I fell as the landing and stairs plummeted to the bottom of the tower. The back of my shirt caught on something and I felt the huge opera curtain fall over me, covering me like a death shroud.

"I am sorry that it ended this way for you," Bowie said with a stoic and pensive gaze. A tear formed in his eye.

"I know that face that sheds that tear, I know you," I said to him.

"And I know you," he said back.

Michael had been given some oxygen and when he regained his footing he began to insist the firemen go inside the building.

"My mother is still in there!" he screamed. "Save her, please, don't let her die."

He and the firefighter looked up to see the entire tower engulfed in flames. It lit up the sky. The firefighters had begun to direct the water hoses on the theatre area but they had given up on the tower. In minutes, it would be just cinders and ashes.

"I don't think we can save her now," he said with a thick French accent. "It's too late, son. Je suis tres mal, monsieur."

Michael raised a fist to the sky, "Damn it mother, do not die in this sanctimonious 'blaze of glory' you insist on proclaiming as your death."

I shrieked at the demon angel. "You who tried to steal my soul with your cheap psychic tricks, you who prey upon the weakness of human emotions, I spit in your face. It is I who will satisfy the balance of all things. I have foiled you."

The angel of death stared at me and I stared right back.

"I have done what I had to do. I saved my son".

"I am a good mother," I whispered quietly to myself. I meant that, too. For the first time in my life I felt like I knew that I was an excellent mother and I always had been. Through it all, the entire pantheon and theatre of my rock and roll heavens and hells, I had been a devoted mother to my three children. The one that I lost, well, I had to chalk that one up to my present circumstances.

The entity before me was simply a manifestation of my deepest fears. Therefore, I had the power to dispel it, make it vanish before my eyes because I would embrace the truth and utter out loud the damning proof.

"I lived my life as only I could. The things I did were part of who I am, what talents I have bled through, no matter what kind of promises I was supposed to keep. You cannot manipulate human beings by preying on their frailties and weaknesses. The human spirit is the most magnificent creation God ever thought of and it has not failed me in my final moments. I am grateful for my life, my Lord and God, and now, I commend my soul to you, God, because I have lived my life being true to myself."

I raised my eyes to the ceiling where stone statues of cherubs still hung on in the midst of the inferno and smiled. "I love you, God."

With a look of disgust, the demonic angel of death closed his dank, black cape around himself and vanished.

As my laughter turned to screams of pain, I yelled to Bowie.

"I am your biggest fan."

Chapter 39
All You Need Is Love

The huge theatre stood like a smoldering skeleton as Inspector Claude de Pardeu and his assistant, Monsieur de la Fountaine entered the ruins. Walking through what was left of the great, historic building gave pause to the Inspector.

"Do you realize, Jean, that this famous theatre was once home to some of the great actors and playwrights of France?"

"Oui, monsieur, I do. I understand that once the great Madame Sarah performed a play written by Moliere here upon this very stage."

His grey gloved hand caressed the charred remains of the center stage. He glanced to the west to see the full moon setting as it floated above a set of limestone pillars that had escaped the blaze.

"What a pity that it should burn like this."

They strolled through, pretending not to notice how sad each one of them were. A French monument to art had been taken from them

Both men noticed the charred pillars and the long curtain that was hanging between them.

"That is the fireproof drapery that the theatre manager, Monsieur Du Pris, had insisted on getting for the 100th anniversary of this place. It is the sole survivor of this inferno last night."

The smoke and stench made them both cough as they walked closer to the area. The bright red curtain was only slightly stained from the fire as the Inspector began to reach for it. His gaze was interrupted by a stone statue toward the very back of the pillars. The morning sunlight was just peeking through and lit the otherwise

282

dark ruins.

Monsieur de la Fountaine blinked and then blinked again. The mist of the morning was wrapping itself around anything still standing in the theatre and the statue's lips seemed to be moving.

"That cannot be," he mumbled to himself, but pushed through the debris to the very back, moving past a seemingly shocked Inspector.

"Are my eyes deceiving me, Inspector, or are those lips of the statue moving?"

The figure in question was not a statue, but Anne Marie, nearly buried in soot and ash, the great curtain draping around her like a mantle of protection. The spectacle of the scene was grand. She looked like a Madonna, like a work of art, a sculpture that captured an otherworldly essence that had both men staring in awe.

The men stood silently as they heard a faint whisper. It was barely audible, but the Inspector and Monsieur de la Fountaine knew that the statue was singing the old Beatles song, "All You Need Is Love." Her voice carried the tune to their ears with the clearest yet faintest melody. It was unmistakable.

"All you need is love…"

Turning to his assistant the Inspector gasped, "Sacrebleu! We have found the young American rock star's mother. She is alive."

Chapter 40
Like A Dead Man Walking

My eyes tried desperately to focus as I felt like my body was still on fire. I looked around me to see that I was in the burn ward of a French hospital, my body wrapped and full of needles, needles that fed me intravenous nutrients and relieving me of my bodily wastes. I wanted to move but I felt trapped in the cumbersome trappings of bandages.

A young French nurse came to check on me and gave me a simple glass of water, holding the straw to my mouth. The water trickled down the back of my throat and I could not have been more grateful. Even though I was in complete pain, I was so happy to be alive. Somehow, by the grace of God, I had survived the fire.

I searched around the room and saw three men walking in to see me. It was the band and Michael. When our eyes met, tears began to stream down both of our faces simultaneously and I thanked God for the sight I beheld.

"Mom, how are you?" Michael quizzed me as he looked up and down my bandaged body.

"I've been better," I laughed. All their faces smiled back at me as if my miraculous salvation was almost beyond anyone's belief.

"Dad is on his way and Mia and Caleb are with him. You know dad, he's going to start ordering all the nurses around to make sure you are getting top notch care.

For once, I was glad to hear that. It was a bit difficult to communicate with everyone in the burn ward because everyone spoke French except for one orderly.

"I am so sorry, I have ruined your gig and I hope that it won't affect your tour schedule. You guys shouldn't be penalized because of me."

"Don't worry about anything mom. The band is fine, we are leaving for London in a few minutes and we wanted to come and see how you are doing before we left."

I carefully looked at their faces and I saw only gratitude for my being alive. I, too, could not even believe my good fortune. I was alive. Against all odds, I was alive.

"That theatre burnt to the ground and it is a very old, historic place and the reason it did was because of my carelessness. I am so ashamed."

"What are you talking about Mrs. C?" Jaden looked me in the eyes. "That place burnt because I didn't cage my cigarette. You had nothing to do with it."

I knew that Jaden was covering for me and I didn't have the will or energy to correct him. I was just grateful that they were all there, forgiving me, and it would help me to absolve myself of my sin.

The nurse came up just then and with a thick accent let the boys know it was time for me to have my treatment and the clock on the wall said it was time to go. The band promised me they would dedicate one of their songs, "Be Here Now" to me when they took the stage in London.

I was sorry they were leaving because the nurse was providing me with an excruciatingly painful treatment. I had burns on almost 60% of my body and she had to scrub and clean every inch of it.

I needed to turn my attention to something else to try and forget the pain I was feeling and looked up at a large television set that was mounted on the wall above my hospital bed.

The image that came on the screen was much more painful than any treatment the nurse was giving me. There on the news channel that had English titles was a news crawler that read:

MUSIC LEGEND DAVID BOWIE DIED EARLY THIS MORNING AT THE AGE OF 69. HE WAS SURROUNDED BY FAMILY AND DIED PEACEFULLY.

"Nooooooo, no, no," I screamed at the top of my lungs.

Several nurses came to help restrain me as I tried to get out of bed.

"This can't be," I continued to scream as one of the nurse gave me a large shot of something that immediately made me groggy and seemed to silence me.

The world stopped. The pain on the outside of my body was nowhere near the empty sick feeling I felt at hearing this news. Bowie, dead? No this can't be true.

It was like being in suspended animation as the television station cut to the breaking news. It was true, David Bowie had died, and I couldn't stop crying. Didn't matter what meds they shot in me, nothing could dull or kill the pain of this news.

My God, I thought, did that demon take his soul instead? Did he offer up his life in exchange for mine? No one on the face of this earth could answer that question for me. After all, he was in a bed at his home last night surrounded by his family, not talking with me and the angel of death in a burning French theatre, right?

There were no answers to these questions, just a sick and empty feeling that one of my closest friends had passed away. A friend that I never actually met, yet felt very close to and supported by through the years. My agony was unbearable. I kept saying to myself that this couldn't be but as the loop of the half hour news feed played the breaking news over and over, the miserable news sunk into my soul.

David Bowie had died and I was still alive. This was the death of a rock star. Something I had wanted for myself, to be as good as he was. As I lay in that hospital bed writhing in pain, I realized how full of shit I had been all these years. That clawing, itching feeling of needing to be the center of attention, the one everyone applauded and cheered for had reached its zenith and the unbearable pain of his death was slaying this feeling and shredding it into pieces of nothingness.

The ego fights to be the Lord and Commander of my life and in the end, the loss of my friend, took me to a place where I knew I needed none of this. If I wanted to sing, I could sing in my shower in my bathroom. Oddly, I was content with that. The rock star in me had finally died, but the cost of knowing it, the death of my beloved friend was a price I did not want to pay. Yet, the pieces of silver were on the table and there would be no turning back from it now.

Craig brought me back to Indiana and I had round the clock

care until I was able to get up and move around. It took months and when the bandages were finally removed there was significant scarring. My face, my neck and arms, I looked rather like a monster, something out of a horror story.

Craig told me how beautiful I was and he gave me all the support and love that any human being could want.

I looked at life differently from that day forward. As many times as I had hoped I would hear from the rock and roll icon, it never came. He was gone and there were no more conversations to have with him.

It made me think of Ash Wednesday at church when the priest would put ashes on my forehead and say, "remember man that thou art dust and to dust you shall return."

We are on this earth for a very short time. During this time, we should realize that our destiny is service. Serving that love, serving that light in whatever capacity is needed. When I think upon that, a peace unlike any other peace, descends upon me. I know that it beats being anything else, even being a rock star.

I had only been to New York City once before in 1964 to the Worlds' Fair. My parents took us there on vacation. I can remember how big it was. Big skyscrapers that towered and dwarfed the individual had haunted me ever since that experience. I found it to be too filled with these monolithic structures that glorified something that I couldn't understand. Yet here I was. Patsy had invited me to a program in New York City

What you are looking for is inside of you.

I took my seat in the audience next to Patsy. She was living in Frederick, Maryland now but came into New York City to see her grandchildren from time to time and she was the one who got the tickets.

The speaker was Mr. Prem Rawat and the subject of his presentation was inner peace. For the first time in my life, I sincerely wanted inner peace and not the fame and fortune I had searched for as a rock and roll singer.

"It's been over 20 years since I first invited you to listen to Mr. Rawat. Remember that time in Miami, before you left for LA with Andrea?"

"I should have gone to the program instead of the Hunters Lounge."

We both laughed at that and settled in to listen to the speaker.

Prem Rawat spoke with such eloquence. "We go out in this world and we search for fortune and glory, looking everywhere but where it actually is. Inside the human being."

"We want to be successful in this world but we don't realize that we already are successful. We were successful the day we took our first breath."

His discourse lifted me to such an inspired place. After it was over, we walked out of the theatre and down the street to a little coffee shop.

"You know, for the first time in my life I feel successful and it's not because of any particular reason.

Patsy was nodding her head in agreement as I continued.

"I feel successful because I just took a breath and I feel grateful that I can take another. It is just that simple…just that simple.

Amazing grace how sweet the sound that saved a wretch like me, I once was lost but now I am found

I was blind but now I see…….

Epilogue

Rock and roll is an art form and therefore it is timeless. It defined the cultural period of the late 20th century and if historians ever want to understand what made the world the way it was during this time period, all they need to do is listen to rock and roll.

Is Rock and Roll dead? Has it morphed into hip hop and rap as the ultimate indicator of the societal level of angst? I leave that discussion to the philosophers of the 21st century. Listening to this exhilarating music, being at an arena concert, having a backstage pass to meet the bands, watching a music video, playing a video game about your favorite rock band. All of it defines this art form as multi-sensual in ways that could never be reached by other art forms.

I own it. I love it. Does it speak for a generation anymore? Does it matter? It spoke to me.

Jimi Hendrix, Amy Winehouse, Janis Joplin, Kurt Cobain and many other rock stars died tragically young. Ringo Starr, Mick Jagger, Bob Dylan, Neil Young and many others are all knocking on the door of their 80's. Still rocking! Still rocking!!

Rock and roll will never die but the rock stars who sing and play it will. As much as we all want to be immortal and be on that stage forever, it only lasts so long and one day we all take that final breath and when we do, we all want to be thankful for whatever part we play....not in our own tiny play, but in the Creator's grand play.

www.ingramcontent.com/pod-product-compliance
Lightning Source LLC
Chambersburg PA
CBHW021328250626
47155CB00002B/639